"DON'T FIGHT M[E]
DON'T FIGHT Y[OU]

Paul's words were like [...]
"Such a beautiful body. Your instructor was
wrong—there _is_ passion in you when you
dance. It is only when the music stops that you
deny it."

Color rose in Karin's cheeks, and she steeled
herself against the insidious warmth that was
weakening her will. "Were none of your other
women available tonight?" she asked coldly.

"Karin! Your accusations sting me! Are you always
so sure of everything?"

She knew he was mocking her, as usual. "I just
wanted you to know that I know you for what
you are, and I'm not attracted to you."

His half smile was cynical. "No?" he whispered
as his mouth approached hers....

Super

AND NOW...

SUPERROMANCES

Worldwide Library is proud to present a
sensational new series of modern love stories —
SUPERROMANCES

Written by masters of the genre, these longer,
sensuous and dramatic novels are truly in keeping
with today's changing life-styles. Full of intriguing
conflicts, the heartaches and delights of true love,
SUPERROMANCES are absorbing stories —
satisfying and sophisticated reading that lovers
of romance fiction have long been waiting for.

SUPERROMANCES
Contemporary love stories for the woman of today!

ROSALIND CARSON

THIS DARK ENCHANTMENT

A SUPERROMANCE FROM
WORLDWIDE
TORONTO · LONDON · NEW YORK · SYDNEY

For Evelyn Grippo
With affection,
admiration, and gratitude

Published, April 1982

First printing December 1981

ISBN 0-373-70016-4

An extract of this novel appeared in the November, 1981
issue of **Good Housekeeping.**

CHAPTER ONE

THERE WAS A FEELING OF EXCITEMENT, of celebration, in the late-afternoon air of Quebec City. Karin noticed it the moment the taxi passed under the arched stone gate of the ancient town's outer wall. The narrow old streets were crowded with young people who appeared very festive in spite of the heat. They were all hurrying in one direction. Their excitement infected Karin, bringing her forward in the passenger seat as the cab inched forward in bumper-to-bumper traffic.

As she watched curiously through the open window, some of the young people waved at her, smiling warmly, and a couple of very young men looked at her with candid admiration, inviting her in French to join them. Karin shook her head, but she could not suppress an answering smile in response to their own friendliness. For the first time in weeks she felt her spirits rising.

"Merde!" the taxi driver exclaimed, slamming on his brakes.

Startled, Karin looked beyond him and saw that the street ahead was barricaded with sawhorses. She had to shout over the sound of the car horns that had begun blaring as soon as traffic piled up behind them. "What's going on? Is Quebec always this crowded?"

The driver's answering shrug was typically Gallic. He didn't seem disturbed by the delay, perhaps because the meter was ticking merrily, counting not only miles, but minutes. "Everyone is going to the Jardin des Gouverneurs," he said, pointing to a small park some distance away.

"The Governors' Garden?"

"Oui, mademoiselle." He began talking to a policeman who had appeared beside his open window. There was a lot of gesticulation going on, and Karin had never heard French spoken so rapidly. Her rusty high-school French wasn't going to be much use here.

She leaned back in her seat, looking down ruefully at the creases in the skirt of her beige linen suit. The suit had looked smart when she boarded the plane in Seattle many hours ago. Now she felt sticky with perspiration, and her dark hair lay heavy against her back. Strands of it had escaped the Indian print scarf she'd used to tie it back and were clinging damply to her hot face.

Abruptly the policeman stepped away from the cab just as a tremendous blast of sound assailed Karin's ears. The sound was so incredibly loud it was a second before she recognized it as hard-rock music, amplified beyond the limits of human endurance.

"Le rock," the driver shouted unnecessarily over his shoulder. "There is a rock concert on Dufferin Terrace beyond the Governors' Garden."

A rock concert in this picturesque city was about the last thing Karin would have expected. "Does this happen often?" she asked, both hands pressed to her ears.

The taxi driver shrugged again. "Summer festival," he explained. "But we shall move on now."

At a signal from the policeman, he swung the cab in a tight U-turn that scattered laughing pedestrians in all directions. Then, to Karin's delight he drove past the massive green-turreted Château Frontenac, which she had already admired from a distance. The hotel looked like a fairy-tale castle—Sleeping Beauty's perhaps.

Accelerating madly, the driver turned a corner and then jammed on his brakes again. Stalled traffic stretched ahead.

Karin leaned back and moved her long legs into a less cramped position. If she was fated to ride up and down Quebec's steep streets all day, she might as well relax and enjoy it. At least the sound of *le rock* was fainter here. She smiled. If Lissa had met her at the airport earlier as promised, she might have missed all this excitement. She wasn't really surprised by Lissa's failure to appear. Lissa Vincent had never been on time for anything, even when they were in college together.

The taxi inched forward past a restaurant and some small boutiques, and stopped again. To her right, between two tall buildings, Karin saw a narrow cobbled alley that might have been lifted straight out of medieval France. The alley was crowded with tourists looking at hundreds of unframed paintings and prints hanging on the walls. Scattered among them, dressed in bohemian fashion, several young artists were pointing out features of their work or perhaps haggling over prices.

Karin leaned forward. Now there was something she would want to investigate. She had always been deeply interested in art, even though she had no artistic talent herself—at least not in painting. Dancing was more her métier. She looked up at the street sign on the alley wall. Rue du Trésor. She must remember that. She suddenly felt a surge of enthusiasm for this trip, coupled with a sense of déjà vu. She felt as though she belonged here, as though she had come home. She smiled, dismissing the foolish notion. But still, she thought, this would be a marvelous city in which to make a fresh start, to forget all the heartaches of the past few months.

Idly looking around, she noticed two men standing in a doorway near the entrance to the alley, engaged in a conversation or perhaps an argument that was apparently heated enough to make them oblivious to their surroundings. Karin's gaze was caught and held by the contrast between the two. One was a very tall dark-haired man who might have stepped from the pages of a sophisticated men's magazine. He was dressed in a short-sleeved formfitting black shirt with buttoned shoulder tabs and matching pants that followed the contours of his lean hips as though they'd been designed for him. There was something arrogant about his erect posture and the angle of his head, Karin thought. He was not a man who would lose an argument too easily. His lean face held a rather disdainful expression; his well-shaped mouth was stern, unsmiling. A handsome man, probably French, aristocratic, certainly the most interesting-looking man Karin had seen in a long time. Arms folded, he was looking with barely concealed exasperation at his companion, a shabbily dressed slight young man whose brown hair and bushy beard hadn't seen comb or scissors in weeks. The bearded man, not much more than a boy really, was talking rapidly, gazing up at the taller man with a pleading expression, his hands gesticulating. There was something of the supplicant in his stance and gestures. Was he a beggar, Karin wondered.

Abruptly the dark man put his hand on the younger man's shoulder, turned him away from the street and held out something white—an envelope—toward him.

At first the young man pushed the envelope away. Then he grabbed it, stuffed it into his ragged jeans pocket. Immediately he swung around and started across the street, a mutinous expression on his bearded face. He looked at Karin without seeing her as he crossed in front of the cab, and she was astonished to see there were tears in his eyes.

Whatever had passed between the two had not pleased either of them, she thought. The dark-haired man was standing motionless in the doorway, his gaze following the other man across the street. His face was set in intolerant lines as though his patience had been tried beyond its limits. Why had he been so unkind to the younger man?

Suddenly, as though he felt her disapproving gaze on him, the man looked directly at Karin, and she saw for the first time that his eyes were a brilliant blue, a startling contrast to his Indian-black hair. As her gaze met his, she felt a shock of pleasure that ran from her spine clear up into her hair and brought her bolt upright in her seat.

Her astonished admiration must have shown on her face. The grimness disappeared from the man's face, and he inclined his head, smiling with an effortless charm that was devastating when combined with the blue shine of his eyes. As she still stared, literally unable to look away, his smile became more intimate, and his dark slanting eyebrows quirked upward in a knowing, impertinent way that brought a rush of hot blood to Karin's face.

At that moment the traffic cleared. The taxi shot off down the street and around a corner, flinging Karin off balance against the door.

She pulled herself up straight, heart thudding. What had happened back there? She'd never, never felt anything like that before. Such an instant *physical* response, as though the man had touched her—intimately. She was trembling, she realized, had begun trembling the moment the man looked at her. Not trembling from head to toe as the old cliché would have it, but with a growing tremulous heat that had begun deep in her body and was now radiating through every vein.

How could she possibly have such a strong reaction to a complete stranger? And the way he had stared at her, those blue eyes so bold, so amused, as though he knew she'd found him attractive and was not surprised.

"Mademoiselle?" the taxi driver said, startling her. The taxi had stopped. *Le rock* was louder again; they must have traveled in a circle. The driver was looking at her, his gaze curious. "Rue des Fleurs," he said.

She reached into her purse, paid him the exorbitant number of dollars that showed on the meter, plus a tip, and climbed out of the cab.

"Are you staying in Quebec long, *mademoiselle?*"

the driver asked as he piled her luggage on the sidewalk.

"Eight or nine months, possibly," she answered and wondered why she had qualified the statement. Lissa's invitation had specified that her help would be needed for at least that long. Lissa's husband, Charles, was working on an architectural history of Quebec City, and Karin had agreed to collate his notes, assist with research and type the results. She was looking forward to the work, hoping there would be enough of it to occupy her mind so that she wouldn't have time to think about herself, to remember....

Tires screeched as the taxi took off down the street. Karin came to herself with a start and looked around. The driver had deposited her luggage at the foot of a flight of stone steps leading up to a fairly large white house.

Half expecting the door at the top of the steps to be flung open in greeting, she hoisted the strap of her tote bag to her shoulder and picked up her heavy suitcases. But the door didn't open, and she stood for a moment, looking upward, checking that the house number was correct.

It was a pretty house, fresh and clean in its coat of white paint. The green roof with its dormer windows gave it an old-world look, and several window boxes blazed with bright summer flowers. A graceful wrought-iron fence, painted green, surrounded the drop-off to the basement and edged the stone steps that led up to the front door. Lissa had written that parts of the house were more than three hundred years old, Karin remembered, and it had been restored to its original French-Norman design by Charles Vincent's Uncle Maurice. According to Lissa, Maurice Vincent had died at a very convenient time, leaving the house to Charles just when he'd decided to spend his sabbatical leave from Montreal University in Quebec City, working on his book.

Karin hoped devoutly as she bumped her suitcases up the steps that Lissa was at home, but there was no response to the doorbell. The door was locked. And the house *felt* empty, silent and abandoned. Putting down the heavy cases, Karin looked helplessly along the street. There were large houses on each side. No sign of movement. No crowds here. No cars moving. Even the sound of *le rock* had stopped for the moment. Beyond the corner of the street she could see a grassy slope slanting up toward a sturdy stone wall. There were some fortresslike buildings beyond the wall, and a flag flying. The Citadel. She'd read about it in the brochures Lissa had sent her. Where *was* Lissa?

Turning at the sound of an automobile engine, she saw that a car had just entered the street at the other end—a small black Renault driven by a red-haired woman. The woman was waving. Karin hurried down the steps, feeling light-headed with relief.

Her first thought as Lissa emerged from the car and flung herself enthusiastically at her was that she looked exactly the same as she had three years ago when she and Karin graduated from college. Karin immediately felt as awkward as an overgrown colt. Lissa had always had that effect on her. She was so feminine, like a Renoir girl, petite, but lushly curved in all the right places. She looked vibrantly lovely in a full-skirted green dress that matched her knowing green eyes and set off her long tightly curled mass of red hair. Karin knew it was naturally red and naturally curly—she'd shared a college-sorority room with Lissa for four years, and they'd had few secrets.

Lissa was as talkative as ever. She began rattling away in her charming English-Canadian voice about the traffic and the concert and how crowded the stores had been before Karin could say a word.

"Would you believe this weather?" she exclaimed. "You must be boiling. I'm so pleased you've come. It's going to be super fun, the two of us together again. Has it really been three years? It seems like only yesterday we were going off to some party or other, you and Ray Covington, and me and who-ever." Her green eyes were suddenly solemn. "I'm sorry about Ray, Karin. That must have been a dreadful experience. You'll have to tell me all about it. What a beast he turned out to be. I expect you feel you're well rid of him, eh?"

Before Karin could respond to that or recover from the twist of her stomach caused by the sound of Ray's name, Lissa was off again. "You look gorgeous," she exclaimed. "With your height and those cheekbones, you should be a fashion model. I've always said so."

Karin laughed, but as she began to answer Lissa, she was distracted by the sight of a boy climbing out of the Renault. He was staring up at her with a questioning expression on his plump face. He could be a nice-looking boy if he weren't so fat. About ten years old, Karin thought, though it was hard to be sure through all that excess flesh. The poor child must be suffocating in the heat—his face was red and sweaty, and his light brown hair was plastered in tight curls against his forehead. "Oh, you haven't met Etienne," Lissa exclaimed in a strained voice. "This is Miss Hayward, Etienne, dear."

The boy's pale eyes sent Lissa a look of such utter dislike that Karin was taken aback. "Etienne is Charles's son by his first marriage," Lissa explained. "I'm sure I told you...?"

No, you didn't, Karin thought, but didn't say so in front of the child. She was conscious of a sinking sensation. The boy certainly didn't look as though he'd be a joy to live with, though his manners were polite enough, perhaps *too* polite, she thought as he bowed courteously and shook her hand. There was a sullen look about his mouth. And all that weight. He obviously had problems of some kind.

"Oh!" In the act of fumbling through her handbag for her key, Lissa suddenly stared at Karin. "I wasn't expecting you until tomorrow, June 24. What happened?"

Karin laughed. "Now I remember why we called you scatterbrain in school. *Today* is the twenty-fourth, Lissa."

The green eyes widened comically. "How awful. You must be furious with me for not meeting you."

"I got here," Karin said. "That's all that matters."

"Well, come on in. The house is air-conditioned, thank God." She led the way up the steps, pausing at the top to instruct Etienne to carry in Karin's bags.

"They're much too heavy for him," Karin protested, but the boy shot her a baleful look and manfully lifted both cases as Lissa unlocked the door.

The pretty vestibule and gracefully curving staircase was lighted by beautiful crystal chandeliers. "How lovely!" Karin exclaimed.

For the first time Etienne smiled. "You like my house, Mademoiselle Hayward?" He looked much more attractive when he smiled, and he seemed pleased by her reaction. *Poor child,* Karin thought. *I wonder if I can do anything to help him.* As though he'd seen the sudden pity in her eyes, the boy's face closed against her, and he turned abruptly away and clumped up the stairs.

She must be more careful, Karin thought. Even a ten-year-old had his pride, she knew that from her work as a children's librarian. She must not forget again.

"Drat the boy!" Lissa said, and Karin looked at her questioningly. Under the brilliant light of the chandeliers Lissa's face looked pinched and drawn. The past three years had taken some kind of toll on her after all. There were lines at the corners of her mouth that spoke of discontent and shadows beneath the green eyes. Her hands were trembling as she put her key away.

"Are you all right?" Karin asked.

Lissa shook her head, then shrugged. "I'm not the world's best stepmother, Karin. I had to take Etienne shopping for new shirts today, and he refused to like anything I picked out. I'm feeling a bit frazzled. But don't mind me—nobody else does."

There was a desperate note in her voice. Karin frowned but decided to wait a while before questioning her friend further.

Lissa began indicating each paneled door in the wide hall beyond the vestibule. "Living room, dining room, kitchen and a bathroom over there. The bedrooms are upstairs, of course."

Karin looked around, liking what she saw. The vestibule and hall floors and the curving stairs were covered with Persian carpeting in a muted blue design that contrasted pleasantly with the antique white of the walls. The effect was peaceful and clean and welcoming. The vestibule smelled fresh, like pine needles after a summer rain, and there was an additional odor coming from the back regions—a stew of some kind, perhaps, redolent with herbs.

Lissa was smiling now. "I think you'll like your room," she said. "It looks out onto the backyard, and you can see the back end of the Citadel if you crane your neck. There's not much of a yard, but the Governors' Garden is close by, so Etienne plays there. It's not really a garden, it used to be the garden of the Château Saint-Louis, which isn't around now. It's like a minipark, fronts onto Dufferin Terrace. That's a boardwalk that stretches a long way and joins up with the Promenade des Gouverneurs, which leads to the Plains of Abraham. It has a spectacular view of the St. Lawrence River. You can hike there if you want to—I take it you still walk all the time? Are you still involved in ballet? Is that how you stay so slim?"

Karin laughed and raised her hands helplessly to show she couldn't possibly absorb all the mingled questions and information. "Yes, I do try to walk every day," she said when Lissa paused. "And I still practice ballet to keep in shape. I gave up performing, though. I didn't have the necessary dedication. Where does that lead to?" She was pointing at a door at the far end of the hall, tucked behind the staircase.

"Basement," Lissa said. "We use it as a sort of recreation room—music, TV and so on. Charles's Uncle Maurice used to have parties down there. I can't imagine him having parties. He seemed rather stuffy to me, but then I only met him once a year and a half ago, when Charles and I were first married."

"Where *is* Charles?" Karin asked. "I'm dying to meet him."

Lissa stepped forward to straighten a picture on one white wall. It was a pen-and-ink drawing of a church, Karin saw. It reminded her of the paintings she'd glimpsed in the alley—rue du Trésor. The memory brought back an image of uncompromisingly straight black hair and a lean patrician face with startling blue eyes. To her chagrin, she felt her face becoming hot again, but she managed to smile as Lissa finally turned to answer her question.

"I expect Charles is at the library," Lissa said vaguely. She had a wistful expression in her eyes. She seemed about to say something more, but then she shrugged. "We have a housekeeper, Madame Durocher, but she must be out doing some last-minute marketing. We'd better get you settled before she comes back and serves dinner."

For a while both young women were busy hauling Karin's bags upstairs and unpacking them in the guest bedroom. The room was charming—wallpapered and curtained in a fresh-looking blue and white. It even had a canopied bed. For a moment Karin looked at the bed longingly, wishing she could lie down for a while. But Lissa apparently expected her to have dinner first and suggested she freshen up and change her clothes.

ONCE SHE HAD SHOWERED and brushed her dark hair loose, and dressed in a slim shot-silk dress whose dark blue color made her eyes look like black velvet, she felt much better. Lissa returned wearing a frothy print dress, her red gold curls gleaming. She showed Karin that her bedroom connected with a small study containing a drafting table and desk—perfect for working. The study's side window offered a magnificent view of the Château Frontenac's green turreted roofs, and again Karin thought how much the old building resembled an illustration from a book of fairy tales. Definitely an enchanted castle.

"The big mess is through here," Lissa said, opening a door in the back of the study. Karin stepped past her and stopped short. The only furniture in the small high-ceilinged room was a desk and chair and floor-to-ceiling shelves against one wall, but in spite of that it was impossible to move around. Books and boxes and papers were strewn haphazardly all around. More papers climbed in a teetering pile up one wall.

"Charles does need you, you see," Lissa said cheerfully. "Paul is always after him to tidy up, but he insists he's incapable of putting things in order."

Stunned by the chaos, Karin couldn't speak for a moment. Then she laughed. "It may take me six months just to get the files organized." She glanced at Lissa curiously. "Who's Paul?"

Lissa's eyes avoided her. "Paul Dufresne," she

said. Her voice was matter-of-fact, but there was sudden color in her cheeks. "Dufresnes have lived in Quebec City since Champlain's time. Paul has the most marvelous old house—Château Dufresne. He took us to see it last week. His ancestors were of noble birth and left records in the form of diaries and letters about some of the original construction. Paul has put them at Charles's disposal, and he's also helping Charles with his research. You'll be working with Paul off and on, lucky you. He's a terribly attractive man." Her gaze focused on Karin's face. "Why are you looking at me like that?"

Karin felt uncomfortable. "You surely aren't *interested* in this man, are you? I mean, when you were married, you wrote me that you and Charles were very happy and...." She broke off as Lissa's face crumpled, horrified to see that there were tears in her eyes.

"Lissa," she said softly. "Is something wrong?"

In response to the sympathy in her voice Lissa's tears increased. Karin hastily put an arm around her shoulders and ushered her back to the bedroom. Lissa sank onto the edge of the bed, and Karin sat beside her, fishing a paper tissue out of a box on the night table and pressing it into Lissa's trembling hand.

"I'm sorry," Lissa blurted out. "This is an awful thing to do to you on your first day here, but Etienne was impossible today, and it was so hot and... Charles is busy *all* the time! He's so taken with this book he hardly notices me anymore, and I hate it here. All my friends are in Montreal, and we used to go out a lot and have fun, but now Charles doesn't want to leave the house except to interview some architect or other, or to go to the library. Oh, Karin,'' she continued on a sob, "I'm so lonely, and I don't know what to do about Etienne. He doesn't like anything about me. I'm English Canadian, and his mother was French Canadian. I'm a redhead, and his mother was a brunette—a beautiful brunette, all soft and exotic and serene, you know the type. How can I compete with that? Etienne keeps asking me when I'm going to leave. Can you imagine how that makes me feel? I'm at my wit's end.''

She paused for breath, looking so miserable that Karin's heart went out to her. She patted Lissa's shoulder encouragingly. "I'm here now. We'll do things together and have fun. I'm sure Charles doesn't mean to neglect you. . . .''

"Yes, he does,'' Lissa said flatly, her eyes dry now. "All he thinks about is his precious book. But I'll show him. I'm going to *make* him sit up and take notice.''

Karin felt uneasy. "You surely aren't, well, *involved* with this Paul Dufresne, are you?''

Lissa smiled demurely, her depression apparently forgotten. "I'm a married lady, Karin. Of course I'm not involved.''

But even as Karin let out her breath in relief, Lissa's green eyes widened, and a dimple flickered mischievously in her cheek. "But that doesn't mean I'll *stay* uninvolved.'' She grinned at Karin. "You'd better not get any romantic notions about Paul yourself, even though he is a bachelor. He's a real lady killer. He's broken more hearts in this town than the gossips can keep up with.''

Karin laughed shortly, feeling distaste for the unknown Paul Dufresne. "You don't have to warn me away from anyone," she said wearily. "At the moment I don't care if I ever *see* another man."

Lissa nodded understanding. "I guess you would feel a bit wary after Ray. You really loved him, didn't you?"

"We became engaged right after college. We were going to marry as soon as Ray got established as a lawyer."

"And you had no idea he was seeing someone else?"

Karin sighed. "Until Ray informed he was going to marry Barbara Travis, I thought he was waiting for our wedding as eagerly as I was."

"It must have been a terrible shock."

Karin nodded. She hated even thinking about Ray and all her dashed expectations, but she supposed she owed Lissa more than the brief explanation she'd written her. After all, Lissa had rescued her. If Lissa hadn't invited her here, she'd still be in Seattle, watching her parents being very careful around her— so determinedly *normal*, and trying to act normally herself when her friends sympathized, or she ran into Ray and Barbara at some social function or other.

"I just want to forget Ray," she said slowly. "I can't really tell you what I felt at the time. I was numb, I guess. Ray was offered a partnership by Barbara's father. We were both delighted at first, but then when he was thrown a lot into Barbara's company, he fell in love with her. At least, I try to believe that because any other explanation would mean Ray was just an opportunist, and I'd hate to think I could be so wrong about someone.''

"Well, it's all over now," Lissa said softly.

"Yes. And I'm grateful to you and Charles for giving me a chance to get away for a while.''

"You don't have to be grateful. You're doing Charles a favor, and it will be super having you here." Lissa smiled impishly. "Anyway, I don't really have to worry about you and Paul. You're dark haired and dark eyed, and I've noticed he prefers blondes and redheads.''

Drained by the discussion about Ray, Karin had no desire to hear any more about the frivolous-sounding Paul Dufresne. She certainly didn't look forward to meeting him and hoped she could somehow avoid working with him. She was glad when Lissa changed the subject by suggesting they return to the lower floor.

They were halfway down the stairs when the front door opened, and a man entered—a tall man with shaggy brown hair and an intelligent-looking face. He was rangy, almost gangling, with the slightly stooped shoulders and pensive expression of the dedicated scholar. He hesitated inside the door as though he wasn't sure he was in the right house. He didn't look too tidy. His light brown shirt was straggling half in and half out of the waistband of his blue Levi's, and the shirt itself looked as though the buttons didn't quite match up with the buttonholes.

"There you are, Charles," Lissa said with some asperity.

Charles Vincent's gray eyes glanced nervously at Lissa's face as though he were trying to determine her mood. Then he saw Karin. He smiled engagingly, looking abruptly younger than his thirty-five years. He was a grown-up replica of his son, Karin thought, though without any of Etienne's excess flesh and sullenness.

She liked him on sight, though she did wonder for a brief moment what Lissa had seen in him. He didn't seem her type at all. He looked the epitome of the absentminded professor, and Lissa had always preferred a more dynamic, sophisticated type of man.

Nevertheless, as she descended the stairs toward him, and his welcoming smile warmed his face, she had the feeling that she had found a new friend. And that was a very nice feeling, she thought as she gave him smile for smile and extended her hand to his. His hand was firm and dry, though slightly warm. "This is a real pleasure, Karin," he said. "I'm delighted you've come to help us out."

Before Karin could reply, a slightly accented male voice spoke mildly from beyond the half-open door. "Am I allowed to come in?"

Charles laughed and called out an apology as he moved aside so the door could open all the way. "Look who I ran into on Buade Street," he said. "He gave me a ride home."

"Paul," Lissa exclaimed, hurrying forward with a brilliant smile to greet the newcomer and draw him into the house. "You're just in time for dinner. You'll stay, won't you?"

Karin had no warning, no sudden premonition, to prepare her. Afterward, she felt she must have looked like a gauche schoolgirl standing there, staring, struck dumb, totally taken aback by the sight of the tall dark man she had last seen at the entrance to the alley. His self-confident presence seemed to fill the small vestibule. His smile was as sardonic as before.

So this was Paul Dufresne, the man who was supposedly helping Charles with his research, the man Lissa had characterized as a "lady killer." She might have known. She had recognized at first glance that he was the type guaranteed to set female hearts to fluttering. For a moment or two he had even affected her own. She felt her mouth tightening and made no attempt to conceal her disapproval.

Paul Dufresne didn't look at all surprised to see her. He was not, she thought, the type who would be disconcerted by anything. He was too sure of his own charm. He took her hand in both of his as Charles introduced her, boldly studying her face with those incredibly blue eyes. With typical French gallantry he raised her hand to his lips, murmuring, *"Enchanté, mademoiselle."* His voice was low, with an almost caressing note in it. There was something too intimate about that tone of voice, she thought, and she didn't care for the amused curve of his mouth as he straightened and looked at her. Her hand tingled where his lips had touched it. She rubbed it against the skirt of her dress and saw his eyes note the childish gesture. Her face felt hot and cold at the same time. Judging by the lift of his dark eyebrows, he sensed her nervousness, or whatever it was, and was amused by it.

He switched easily to English. "Do you believe in fate?" he murmured too quietly for the others to hear.

"Not at all," she said coolly.

His eyes were intent on hers, and she felt a quickening of her pulse that didn't abate even when he turned away.

It was a good thing she wasn't the type to be seriously affected by surface attributes, she thought. With his extraordinarily virile good looks and his practiced charm, Paul Dufresne was a man who could be dangerous to a more impressionable woman's peace of mind.

Yes. Very dangerous.

CHAPTER TWO

SOME TIME LATER Karin sat uncomfortably at the dining table, her gaze fixed on the silver and china in front of her. She was becoming very disturbed by the sight of Etienne stuffing himself—there was no other word for it. At first she had thought the boy well mannered; when they entered the pretty blue and gold dining room, he held her chair for her as Charles did for Lissa. Etienne looked quite attractive in his neat gray trousers and white shirt, even though they were straining at the seams. His brown hair was parted on one side and brushed smoothly across his forehead. But as the meal progressed, his greed became apparent. His gaze didn't leave his plate for a second as he wolfed his food, and he kept his left arm folded around it as though afraid someone would snatch it from him.

Lissa watched him nervously, barely eating herself, her long white fingers drumming a tattoo on the damask tablecloth. "Etienne!" she exclaimed at last. "Don't eat like a little pig!"

Etienne immediately took his arms from the table and began eating with exaggerated, almost mincing delicacy, his gray eyes fixed on Lissa's now flushed face with a challenging expression.

Lissa held his gaze for a moment, then she gave a

brittle-sounding laugh and transferred her attention to Paul. Paul, Karin noticed, had barely glanced at Etienne when Lissa corrected him. Probably the child was beneath his notice.

No, Karin had to acknowledge, that wasn't quite fair. Paul had addressed several friendly remarks to the boy earlier, and Etienne had answered him warmly, with much more respect than he showed to his stepmother. He even called him Uncle Paul, which indicated a certain closeness. She was letting her antagonism toward this man get out of hand. But how could she not feel hostile after Lissa's far from subtle hints about him? He had certainly done nothing to change her earlier opinion of him. She could feel herself bristling every time he looked her way; his glance was much too intimate for such a short acquaintance. He had a way of looking at her as though he could see straight into her thoughts and read them easily. To add to her discomfort, there was a vague undercurrent of some kind in his voice when he spoke directly to her. He had obviously set himself out to charm her, entertaining her throughout the meal with stories about Quebec City's history.

She had to admit, though, that without him the last half hour would have been even more uncomfortable, for Charles had little to say. Most of the time he seemed to be off in a world of his own, an abstracted expression on his scholarly face. During the brief exchange between Etienne and Lissa he had looked helplessly on without comment. So far his only real conversation had been with Madame Durocher as she bustled competently about, serving the delicious goulash.

The housekeeper was a stout woman squeezed into an unrelieved black dress that might have struck a somber note except for the fact that *madame* was a determinedly cheerful woman, her round face shining with well-scrubbed cleanliness and good humor. She had greeted Karin warmly, approvingly. "It will be better for Madame Vincent to have you here," she had said—a rather ambiguous statement, Karin thought.

"Etienne," Lissa hissed through her teeth.

Karin came to herself with a start to see that Madame Durocher had served each of them *crème brûlée* and Etienne was spooning his up rapidly, holding the shallow gold-rimmed dish right under his mouth in a deliberate display of bad manners.

The boy lowered his dish slowly, looking as though he were going to defy his stepmother, but as she continued to gaze pleadingly at him, he finally set it down and shrugged. He looked at Lissa with wide, innocent eyes. "Are you going to beat me?" he asked.

"Etienne!" Lissa exclaimed. "I have never laid a hand on you. Never." Her pretty face had paled, and she seemed close to tears.

"You may be excused, Etienne," Charles said grimly, finally asserting himself. "But first you must apologize to Lissa and our guests."

The boy stood up and made a slightly mocking bow. "I am sorry, *madame*, *mademoiselle*, Uncle Paul," he said to each of them in turn. He seemed unrepentant, but Karin thought that she had never seen such sad eyes in the face of a child. He needed help, she thought. Couldn't the others see that?

"I swear that child is trying to drive me out of my mind," Lissa groaned as soon as Etienne had left the room. Her hands were clenched into fists on the table, and Paul reached over to cover one of them lightly. "Relax, my friend. The boy was simply trying to provoke you. I think he is testing you, to see how far he can go, perhaps."

Lissa flashed him a grateful glance from under her red gold eyelashes, and Karin looked quickly at Charles. Charles was smiling benignly at his wife and friend, which annoyed Karin. Didn't he see how dangerous this man could be to someone as impressionable as Lissa?

"Tell me about the Château Frontenac, Paul," Karin said abruptly, then flushed. She hadn't meant the request to sound like an order. She really couldn't blame him for looking startled and tried to soften her tone. "I admired the château on my way here. It looks like a fairy-tale castle. Is it very old?"

Paul removed his hand from Lissa's and settled his intense blue gaze on Karin's face in a quizzical way as though he were perfectly aware she had spoken so sharply to distract his attention from Lissa. But his reply was gravely courteous. "It was built in 1892 on the site of the former Château Haldimand, Mademoiselle Karin. It is impressive, is it not? But it is not one of my favorite buildings. I am not an admirer of pseudo-Gothic architecture, though I agree it could seem to be—enchanted."

Enchanted, Karin's mind echoed. His voice had hesitated, then picked on the word she herself had associated with the castle. Had he read her mind? His gaze was holding hers for too long a time again, compelling her to look at him. Why did he persist in doing that? And what was causing that vibration in the air between them, that nerve-racking tension that seemed to be affecting her breathing? She was suddenly sure that he was remembering the way she'd stared at him from the taxi.

Enchanted. The word wouldn't leave her mind, even when Charles added a comment about the château and the millions of dollars that had been spent on its restoration.

Lissa joined in the conversation, sounding much happier now, fluttering her eyelashes at Paul, leaning toward him, drawing his attention away from Karin—for which Karin was grateful. Lissa was soon talking at her usual breakneck speed, both hands drawing charming pictures in the air for Paul's benefit. She had always loved to flirt, but she had never meant anything serious by it. Paul didn't seem to understand that or perhaps didn't want to. He was watching her now, smiling, looking at her as though he were—enchanted.

Karin let her mind slide away from the discussion. She was beginning to feel tired. The flight today had been a long one, complicated by a delay in Montreal because of a malfunction of one of the plane's engines. Etienne's rude behavior hadn't helped her to feel better, nor had Lissa's earlier outburst. Yes, she was really very tired. That was why she felt so strange whenever Paul Dufresne looked at her. She would like nothing better than to go to bed in the charming blue and white bedroom upstairs. But she could hardly walk out on everyone right after the meal. And at least the tension caused by Etienne's behavior had dissipated.

AFTER DINNER they sat in the living room, a lovely light room, carpeted as richly as the rest of the house and furnished with French Provincial antiques, ivory damask draperies and upholstery.

Charles served drinks from a glass-shelved cart the housekeeper had wheeled into the room. It seemed impossible to refuse the cognac when everyone else was drinking, but Karin was determined to barely sip at hers. Her head felt woolly enough without adding alcohol. She could hear Madame Durocher ponderously clearing dishes from the dining room, but the sounds seemed muted as though she were hearing them through a fog.

She caught herself staring at Paul's hands. He was sitting in the easy chair opposite hers, holding a brandy snifter. Nice hands, she thought vaguely, strong yet sensitive, with long finely shaped fingers. She remembered how they had felt holding hers.

Suddenly she realized someone had spoken to her and was waiting for an answer. She looked up, startled to find Paul's blue gaze regarding her enigmatically. "I asked, Mademoiselle Karin," he said with what seemed to be exaggerated patience, "if you have had experience with historical research on architecture?"

She felt herself flush with annoyance. Her tired mind had wandered, certainly, but he had no right to speak to her as though she were an inattentive child. "Not specifically," she said tersely. "But of course, I have been trained to seek out references on all subjects. I am a librarian, after all. I don't foresee any difficulty in assisting *Charles*."

A small smile tugged at the corner of his well-shaped mouth when she emphasized Charles's name, but he made no comment. "Book research can be dull, though, don't you think?" he said. "Living history is much more vital. It would be well, perhaps, for you to acquaint yourself with the various important buildings of the city so that your reading will have more meaning for you."

"That's a good idea," Charles said, suddenly coming to life now that his work was being discussed. "Karin could take a week or two to get to know the city. There are many fine buildings and monuments to see, Karin—several churches, the National Assembly buildings, the Quebec Seminary and Place Royale in the Lower Town. Marvelous old church down there. To walk in Quebec City is to step back centuries, you will find. We also have a good wax museum, which will give you the highlights of the city's history, and you should visit the Citadel. I'm sure Lissa will be delighted to guide you."

"Of course," Lissa said, and she did *try* to sound delighted, though Karin could see that the prospect of studying old buildings didn't really thrill her.

"I can go by myself, Lissa," Karin said hastily. "Paul's suggestion is a good one, but there's no need for you to get involved. I can concentrate more on what I'm seeing if I'm alone. You and I can go shopping or take in a movie between my excursions."

"I wouldn't dream of allowing you to go alone," Paul interrupted. "Alone you would see only the surface that all tourists see. It will be my pleasure to escort you and interpret our architectural history for you."

"Good," Charles said. "Paul knows every building in this city inside out, Karin. You couldn't have a more informed guide."

"I don't think it's necessary for me to have a guide," Karin said weakly. "It would be too much trouble."

"Karin's right, Paul," Lissa said. "How can you possibly take the time from your practice?"

"Practice?" Karin echoed. "Practice of what?"

Paul Dufresne gave her the benefit of his sardonic smile. "I am a professional man, *mademoiselle*—a doctor of medicine, a general practitioner, in fact— one of a rare breed in today's world of specialists."

"Nobody told me—Lissa didn't mention you were a doctor," Karin stammered, feeling foolish. "I wouldn't have guessed...."

"You hadn't noticed my bedside manner?"

"No," she said shortly, taking refuge in rudeness.

"I have been remiss. You must allow me to make amends." As he spoke, his eyes again held hers. Karin was suddenly aware of her own heartbeat, half-afraid he could hear its loud drumming. She forced herself to meet his gaze as naturally as possible, though she wanted desperately to look away, to break the invisible, almost palpable thread of tension that stretched between them.

After an endless moment Paul smiled almost gently. "I really must stop teasing you. It is just that I find you so irresistible, you see."

Before Karin could respond to that, even if she'd been capable of a response, he glanced at Lissa.

"You must not worry about my patients," he said cheerfully. "Even a dedicated doctor like myself must take a vacation occasionally. It is simple enough for me to arrange for a colleague to fill in for me."

"Then that's settled," Charles said with satisfaction.

And the whole thing, Karin thought, had been arranged without anyone paying attention to her protests. She was to be shepherded around the city by this overbearing, domineering man whether she liked the arrangement or not. Well, he would soon find out that she was no Lissa, to have her head turned because a good-looking man deigned to give her attention. What kind of doctor deserted his patients at a moment's notice, anyway? She was certainly not going to be dictated to by him, no matter how charming he thought himself.

Considering this decision, it was strange that she made no further protest, but she rationalized that she couldn't be rude in front of Charles and Lissa. She would wait until she was alone with Paul Dufresne. She fought off the shiver of—anticipation, nervousness—by gulping some of her brandy with thoughtless abandon, an act that brought an immediate fiery glow to her whole body.

Lissa was smiling at Karin. "You mustn't be deceived by Paul's description of himself as a general practitioner. He's hardly the type to trudge around, black bag in hand, making house calls at all hours of the day and night. His clinic is in Ste. Foy near Laval University, on the thirtieth floor of a high rise—terribly opulent, and his patients are all disgustingly wealthy."

Paul saluted her with his glass. "Touché, my friend. Though I would not have expected you to apply the adjective 'disgusting' to wealth."

"A figure of speech," Lissa said carelessly. "As you know very well, Paul, I have nothing against money. We are alike in that, you and I, as we are in so many ways."

Paul's eyebrows rose, for which Karin couldn't blame him. Lissa's statement had sounded intimate, almost challenging.

Charles laughed, blissfully unaware. "Now, you two, stop picking on each other. You're making Karin uncomfortable. More brandy, Karin?"

"No thank you. I've more than I need here. I'm almost out on my feet as it is."

"Karin's not much of a drinker, Charles," Lissa said. "But you mustn't think she's a prude. She liked parties as much as I did when we were in school. I remember many times in our senior year when she didn't turn up for bed until almost dawn. Especially after she met Ray Covington. Remember how I used to tease you about staying out all night with Ray, Karin?"

As always when Ray's name was mentioned, the pain was immediate. Karin flinched but managed to smile. The smile felt stiff on her face. It was true that she and Ray had often come in late—he'd made a practice of waiting for her after ballet classes or performances. But Lissa's exaggerated references to dawn had probably given the wrong impression.

"Ah, the joys of impulsive youth," Paul commented.

Karin refused to look at him. Let him interpret

Lissa's remark any way he wished. She didn't have to explain to *him*. But she couldn't resist responding tartly to Lissa. "As I recall, you were the one who stayed in bed until noon. At least I managed to get up in time for classes."

Lissa made a face at her. "Touché, as Paul would say."

And then, to Karin's dismay, with a thoughtful glance at Paul, Lissa suggested Charles take Karin down to the basement to see the recreation room. "I didn't have a chance to show it to her yet," she explained, and added, "I'll stay here and entertain Paul."

I'll bet, Karin thought, then chided herself. Lissa was her friend. Just because Lissa's teasing had taken a personal turn was no reason to suspect everything she said. Charles didn't seem disturbed about leaving his wife alone with Paul.

About to plead fatigue, Karin changed her mind when Paul said, "Perhaps I should escort Mademoiselle Karin?" He was already rising from his chair, so sure was he of her agreement.

She turned her back on him. "I'd love to have you show me the recreation room, Charles," she said.

Behind her, Paul laughed softly, but she didn't look around.

The basement room was striking. It was large, with a stone-slab floor, carpeted at intervals with white bearskin rugs. Arched pillars supported the vaulted ceiling, and the windows were draped in vivid crimson silk. The lighting was dim and recessed, spotlighting framed sketches on the walls. Two long couches, flanking the beautifully tiled fireplace, were upholstered in crimson velvet, and several deep arm-chairs, covered with white velvet, added to the look of luxurious comfort.

The rest of the room was furnished with fine antiques, except for an ornate bar and a television and stereo set, housed in low walnut cabinets, which were more modern touches but blended well with the rest.

The bar had a rail at the front of it, Karin noted. She might be able to use that as support when she practiced her ballet exercises.

"This is a lovely house, Charles," she said. "Your uncle had superb taste."

Charles grunted noncommittally, and she turned to look at him. He was staring at the bearskin rug at his feet, looking defenseless and sad. "Is anything wrong?" she asked.

He attempted a smile but didn't succeed. "I'm worried about Lissa."

He suspects Lissa is attracted to Paul Dufresne, Karin thought, and her heart went out to him. But his next words showed her she had jumped to the wrong conclusion. "You must have seen that she's very nervous around Etienne. And not, well, not happy. I noticed her eyes were puffy when I came home. She'd been crying again, hadn't she?"

"I expect it's hard for her to get used to being a stepmother," Karin said gently.

He nodded. "It's been especially difficult the three months we've been here. Etienne likes it here, but he misses our friends in Montreal, and I suppose, well, he still misses his mother. She died when he was only six—they were very close. You see, I am French Canadian, but I was raised to be more English than

French. Louise, my wife, was French to the bone. Etienne looks like me, but he is his mother's son." He laughed shortly. "You have heard of the separatist question?"

Karin nodded.

"Many people want the province of Quebec to secede from Canada, to become a separate French-speaking territory. Others feel our solution lies in staying a part of Canada while preserving our French culture and language." He laughed again, ruefully. "I think in some ways I have a separatist problem in my own household. Etienne doesn't seem to like Lissa at all. He is always so rude to her." He sighed deeply. "I love Lissa dearly, but sometimes I don't think she *tries* to make Etienne like her. I don't know what to do about it."

About to suggest he might administer a little more discipline and perhaps try to spend more time with Etienne and Lissa, Karin changed her mind. She felt too sorry for Charles at the moment to point out that the situation might be his fault. He looked too vulnerable. She took a step toward him, put her hands on his arms. "Lissa and I were very close in school," she said. "And I usually relate well to children. Perhaps I can help Lissa and Etienne to get along better."

"That's not the only problem," he said, and again she thought he was going to mention Paul Dufresne. But again she was mistaken.

"I'm such a dull person," he went on. "And Lissa's so bright and lovely and full of life. It's boring for her to be shut up here. At least in Montreal she had friends, outside interests. Here she knows no one but Paul. He tries to help, takes her out sometimes when I'm too busy, but I can't expect him to fill in for me all the time.''

The poor innocent, Karin thought, all her sympathy engaged now. *He has no idea anything might develop there. He thinks of Paul Dufresne as his friend.* "I'll be able to keep Lissa company now," she said carefully.

"I'm really glad you came," Charles said. He paused, smiling at her rather sadly. "You must think I'm awful to neglect Lissa so. Things seem to get away from me, you see. I try to pay attention to my family, but there is so much work to be done and so little time. But that's no excuse. Lissa has needs, too. And Etienne. He's drawn away even from me since his mother died. And he was dreadful toward the housekeepers I hired before Lissa and I were married. His behavior drove them all away. I don't know how to reach him. You've probably noticed he's a little overweight?''

Karin managed not to wince at the understatement.

"I had hoped he and Lissa would perhaps, well. . . ." Charles's voice trailed away.

Karin patted his arms ineffectually. To be truthful, she wasn't feeling far from despair herself. She had come to Quebec City hoping to find solace for her own grieving, to make a fresh start. She hadn't expected to be plunged into other people's problems. Though perhaps, in helping Lissa and Etienne, she might be able to forget the pain she'd suffered. She felt dizzy suddenly. Fatigue, she decided. Too much had happened to her in one day. She shook her head to clear it and smiled encouragingly at Charles.

He was remarkably like a small boy himself, she thought, unable to cope with anything outside his own scholarly world. "We'll work it all out, you'll see," she said.

His face brightened with tentative hope, making him look so sweet and boyish that she couldn't resist hugging him affectionately as she might have hugged a brother if she'd had one. Charles returned the hug just as naturally.

"Excuse me," a cool voice said from behind her. She whirled to see Paul Dufresne standing halfway down the stairs, leaning nonchalantly against the stair rail, one hand resting on the banister. There was an expression of sardonic amusement on his face as he glanced at Karin.

"Lissa is requesting your presence," he said to Charles. "I think perhaps she is bored with my company, impossible as that seems."

Charles moved at once toward the staircase, turning at the foot to say thank-you to Karin. "Karin has promised to help Lissa with Etienne," he told Paul as he passed him on the stairs.

"How kind." Paul's smile at Karin seemed friendly enough, and Charles didn't seem to hear the mocking note in his voice, but Karin did. She started immediately up the stairs, but Paul blocked her way with an outstretched hand against the wall. "Why have you taken such a dislike to me, Mademoiselle Karin?" he asked softly.

Karin glared at him. "How could I not? You take too much on yourself, Dr. Dufresne. I don't care for people who think they can decide what others should do. You didn't even *ask* me if I wanted you to escort me around the city.''

"Ah, I have been remiss again. May I show my city to you?''

"No.''

He grinned at her. "There, you see, that is why I didn't ask you. Is there any other way in which I have annoyed you?''

"Well, I certainly don't approve...." She hesitated. After the scene he'd just witnessed, she could hardly accuse him of showing too much interest in Lissa. But his smile was still provoking her. At least she could set him straight about herself and Charles. "I was just trying to comfort Charles,'' she said abruptly.

"And succeeding admirably, I'm sure.''

"I...felt sorry for him. And I do want to help with Etienne. It wasn't what you thought....''

His slanted eyebrows indicated pained surprise. "How can you possibly know what I thought?''

Karin took a deep breath and let it out explosively, suddenly impatient with his verbal fencing. "If you'll step aside, Dr. Dufresne, I'll go on up, if you don't mind.''

"But I do mind. I am a guest here. Someone has to look after me.''

"I'm sure you are capable of looking after yourself.'' When he didn't move, she tried to push his arm aside. But his arm held like a bar of iron, and he was clearly amused by her efforts to dislodge it. "Are you going to wrestle with me, Mademoiselle Karin?'' he asked. "I assure you I have no objection.''

She took her hand away from his arm as though the contact had burned her, and he laughed, his gaze sweeping the length of her body in an admiring way that aroused her to fury.

"You are quite lovely, you know," he murmured. "Sylphlike. You move like a dancer. *Are* you a dancer?"

"I have studied ballet, yes," she said stiffly.

"I thought so. I can imagine you in one of those little skirts, what are they called?"

"Tutus."

"Of course. Yes, you would look good on the stage. Such long, long legs. Very lovely." Again his eyes appraised her. "Your cheekbones are very fine, also. Almost Slavic. Are you Russian, perhaps?"

"Nothing so exotic, I'm afraid," she said briskly. Why on earth was she standing here on the stairway, indulging in this idiotic conversation? There was certainly no reason for the suffocating sensation that was beginning to leave her breathless. It was time to call a halt to this nonsense. But he was still blocking the stairway, his whole manner daring her to try to pass. "Not Russian? But European, surely? Such dark, dark eyes."

"Irish. My ancestors were Irish. Now will you please...."

"Ah, that explains the sudden flashes of temper."

Unwilling to dispense with dignity and duck under his arm, she turned on her heel and stalked back down the stairs. "Let me know when you are tired of your game," she said flatly.

"I never tire of games," he said, following her down the stairs. "Also, I think Charles should be allowed a few moments alone with his wife. She is a very troubled woman, our Lissa.''

"And you know all about troubled women, of course?''

He smiled. "Such a prickly young lady. Dare I hope you are jealous of my affection for Lissa, *chérie*?''

"Of course I'm not jealous. And don't call me *chérie*. Or that ridiculous Mademoiselle Karin. It makes me sound like a . . . like a . . . .''

"Librarian?''

He was impossible. She turned away from him and began studying a sketch on the wall, but to her annoyance, she was still acutely aware of his presence behind her.

There was a small silence, then he said, "I think I am beginning to know you, Mademoiselle Karin. You shy away from compliments, and you distrust the people who offer them. I think, too, that you are attracted to me. But you are afraid of the attraction so you are trying to convince yourself you dislike me. That way you are safe. You like safety, don't you?''

She didn't answer. What could she possibly say to such absurd statements?

He didn't wait for an answer, anyway. "I am curious about something,'' he continued. "When Lissa mentioned a man named Ray Covington, your face became very sad. Who is this man?''

She was glad her back was turned to him so that he couldn't see her face. "That's none of your business,'' she said when she could speak.

He didn't respond, and the silence became intolerable. "He was someone I used to know,'' she

said at last. "We were engaged. He. . .married someone else."

"You loved him?"

"Yes."

"You would agree with my use of the past tense?"

"Yes. No. Er. . . ."

"Ah, there is some doubt? It will be a while, then,
before I know where I stand."

She had no idea what he meant by that and
thought it prudent not to ask.

He sighed. "I have the idea you do not admire me
as much as I first thought. I am desolated. I was sure
when I saw you in the taxi that you were quite enchanted by my person."

Enchanted. There was that word again. How conceited he was! She swung around and stared at him
with exasperation. "You were mistaken, Dr.
Dufresne. I was merely amazed that you should be so
brutally unkind to that young man. He was almost in
tears."

"'Brutally unkind,'" he repeated slowly. "I am to
be judged guilty of brutality without benefit of trial
or explanations?"

"I'm not in the least interested in your explanations."

"That is fortunate. If I am to be condemned on the
basis of such fragile evidence, I will certainly not explain."

"Fragile evidence!" Karin exclaimed. "You were
obviously berating that poor young man and—" She
stopped, incensed by the amused slant of those
wicked dark eyebrows. He was taunting her for the
sheer enjoyment of it. And she had allowed herself to

be tormented into behaving like a shrew when, in any case, the situation was none of her concern.

"I'm sorry," she said tersely. "I had no right to shout at you like that. I'm extremely tired. Please forgive me."

"But of course."

"I'm not usually so . . . ."

"So brutally unkind?"

She looked at him helplessly. "Is it impossible for us to act in a civilized way?"

"Absolutely."

Before she could recover from the shock of that, he added very softly, "There is strong chemistry between us. I felt it at once. We are destined to be enemies or lovers, *chérie*—definitely not civilized friends."

His gaze was steady on hers, and she found she could not look away. There was a long breathless moment in which she had the uncalled-for feeling that she had been waiting a long time for this man to come into her life. But how could that be? He was a stranger to her—a complete stranger. She didn't even like him, and she was so tired, so very tired. Her body seemed to have taken on a great weight, as though she were moving through sluggish water or thick heavy air, even though, in reality, she wasn't moving at all. On top of her fatigue the brandy she had drunk so rapidly was beginning to affect her mind and body. She had no reserves left to meet and fight the challenge in Paul Dufresne's blue eyes. Why was he so determined to torment her?

She closed her eyes and sighed, hoping he would go away and leave her alone. But the act of closing her eyes disturbed her sense of balance, and she felt herself sway. There was only a step between them, and he took it. His hands closed on her shoulders, supporting her. At the contact she felt an almost electric shock, but before she could react, his hands drew her close against him. His mouth touched her cheek as he murmured tenderly, "But you are exhausted, my poor girl."

The warmth of his hands seemed to pour through the silky stuff of her dress, chasing tension away, drowning her in lassitude, so that she couldn't seem to prevent herself from leaning against him just for a moment. She heard the swift intake of his breath, and then his lips moved across her face to her mouth. At once her bones seemed to melt, and she was suddenly pressed close to him, her own hands moving up his arms to his shoulders, to his neck, her fingers tangling in his crisp dark hair.

This couldn't be happening, she thought in a single startled moment of sanity, but the thought spun away into nothingness as Paul's hands moved over her, and her body moved to match the rhythm of his urgency, her pulses pounding in her ears. Hungrily she clung to him as his tongue invaded her mouth, sending involuntary shivers along her spine. She was trembling again, and the trembling grew uncontrollable as his mouth became fierce against hers, demanding more and more from her.

It had been such a long time since a man held her in his arms—such a long time since Ray held her and kissed her and told her he would love her forever. *Ray*. Had she whispered his name? This wasn't Ray.

Ray's kisses were gentle and pleasant, not demanding, not threatening. . . .

Somehow she wrenched herself free of Paul's grip, staring at him in confusion.

He held her at arm's length, his eyes grave, unsmiling. *"Mon Dieu,"* he said huskily. "You are full of surprises, Mademoiselle Karin."

The words were like a splash of cold water on her face. There was a moment more when she felt disoriented, bewildered, and then she recoiled from him and would have run to the stairway if he hadn't caught her by the wrist and stopped her.

"I apologize," he said in a serious voice. "My mother tells me I behave impossibly at times, and she is right. I should not have taken advantage of your fatigue, even though I have been wanting to kiss you for at least two hours."

She stared at him uncertainly. Was he making fun of her? She didn't think so. The arrogance was gone from his face, and no mockery showed in his eyes. Tiredly she pushed her hair back from her forehead. "It's all right, I guess," she said dully. "I don't know why I—" She broke off. "I didn't sleep much last night, and the trip today. . . ." Her voice trailed away as he released her wrist. For a moment he continued to gaze at her, then he smiled with a total return of confidence. "We will begin again tomorrow. And we will not be enemies, after all. Don't you agree?"

"I don't know," she said weakly.

She averted her eyes, but his hand reached for her chin and tilted it so that she was forced to meet his gaze. Gently his thumb traced the outline of her lips, awakening sensations in her body she had never felt before. "I have behaved abominably," he said softly. "But you must know that something has begun between us. It is very strong and cannot be denied. So you must not fight against it, *chérie*. It would be a waste of time and energy."

He studied her face, smiling. "You will not admit agreement at the moment, I see, but you will eventually. And do not worry yourself. At our next confrontation I will be more restrained. I shall give you a little time to free yourself from the ghosts of the past—from this man Ray you cannot bring yourself to forget."

She *had* said Ray's name aloud.

"Please. . . ." She had to try to sound more assertive. With an effort she pulled herself free of his hand and stared at him defiantly. "There won't be any confrontations. I don't particularly want to see you again."

"But you *will* see me, Karin. Apart from anything else, you will be working some of the time at my home. I refuse to risk my precious documents among Charles's chaos. And then there is our tour of the city. I shall call for you at one o'clock tomorrow afternoon. That should give you time to rest yourself."

"No," Karin said, but he ignored her as though she hadn't spoken. He brushed her cheek tenderly with the back of one hand. "Like satin," he murmured, "or perhaps more like the surface of rose petals—hothouse roses raised specially to speak the language of love." His eyes looked into hers. "You are very lovely, my Karin, but I think unawakened.

It will be my mission to awaken you, to teach you."

His voice was low, hypnotic, and it was beyond her power to move. After a moment he smiled confidently and turned toward the stairway. "Tomorrow at one o'clock," he repeated, and before she could break free of her paralysis, he went up the stairs, moving lightly with an animal grace that she couldn't help admiring.

Unawakened, she thought. What had he meant by that? His mission, indeed! How conceited he was. It would be a pleasure to show him that not all women were susceptible to his charm.

She smiled wryly to herself. She had certainly not offered him proof of that so far.

CHAPTER THREE

S<small>HE AWOKE THE NEXT MORNING</small> to the faint strains of martial music—a brass band and drums—playing nearby. What on earth was going on, she wondered. Was there a parade in town?

Disoriented, she sat up, staring at the blue and white window curtains billowing above the air-conditioning unit. Of course. She was in Lissa's house. This wasn't Seattle. It was Quebec City.

But why was a band playing at this time of the day? Was this more of the summer festival? What time was it, anyway? Her inner clock was unreliable, confused by the change of time zones, and a glance at her watch on the bedside table showed her she'd forgotten to wind it, it had stopped at three.

As she blinked sleep from her eyes, she remembered the travel brochures Lissa had sent her before she left Seattle. The music must be coming from the Citadel. The Changing of the Guard took place every morning at ten.

Ten o'clock! Paul Dufresne was coming for her at one, and her last thought the previous night had been that she would make some excuse to go out and then not return until midafternoon. That would be very rude, but after all, she hadn't *agreed* to go with him. And she was not going to allow him to dictate to her or to bewitch her again with his practiced compliments: "You are very lovely, my Karin, but I think unawakened." How dare he!

Apart from anything else, she was not *his* Karin and never would be. Ray had never spoken so possessively. He had never made her feel he owned her or wanted to own her.

On the other hand, she *had* expected him to always be there. She had not expected him to cast her aside for someone else. But at least she had learned a lesson from Ray. She had learned that the only person she could rely on was herself. And she was not now going to fall into the trap of being flattered because a very different kind of man wanted to prove his masculinity by *dominating* her. And the best way to assert her independence was to be gone when Paul Dufresne arrived.

She swung her legs over the side of the bed as she realized the music from the Citadel had stopped. The ceremony was evidently over. She must hurry.

Hastily she showered, made her bed, then dressed comfortably in blue jeans, a mulberry silk shirt and a denim vest. Aware that the weather was probably hot outside, she pulled her hair back into a single long braid and tied it with a narrow mulberry ribbon. Studying the severe effect in the mirror, she decided to add to it by not wearing makeup. But she changed her mind as she realized how stupid it was to deliberately try to make herself unattractive. Was she really so afraid of Paul Dufresne? She wasn't going to see him, anyway, was she?

Annoyed by her vacillation, she applied makeup

with more care than usual, then hurried down the stairs.

Lissa was in the kitchen, sitting at the white Parsons table, sipping tea, morosely eyeing Etienne's plump face as he spooned cornflakes into his mouth. She greeted Karin with a tight smile, then rolled her eyes at her stepson. "You're just in time to join Etienne at his second breakfast," she said in a flat voice.

Karin sat down at the table, feeling uncomfortable. "I'm sorry I'm late," she said quietly. "I guess I'm still on Seattle time."

Lissa smiled more naturally. Standing up, she busied herself at the stove. "Don't worry about it. I never get up early. That way I don't have so many hours to fill."

Karin stared at Lissa's back, feeling a spasm of irritation. Lissa looked so pretty standing there in a white shirt knotted at the waist above yellow slacks, her red curls bouncing as she broke eggs into a bowl and whisked them into froth. She was young and pretty and smart, and she was letting life pass her by. Not so many hours to fill indeed! She must have some interests, some hobbies. She'd always liked drawing in school—what had happened to that?

Sighing inaudibly, Karin turned her head and found Etienne's gaze on her, his gray eyes examining her without expression. When he didn't respond to her smile, she looked down and noticed that his bowl was piled so high with soggy cornflakes that they were spilling over the edges of the dish. Why on earth did Lissa let him eat so much?

As though Lissa had read her mind, she turned

from the stove, glanced at Etienne, then at Karin. "Paul says we should let him eat what he wants," she said.

"Oh," Karin said. Presumably the lordly Dr. Dufresne knew what he was doing. All the same. . . .

With an effort she smiled at the boy again as Lissa set a plate of scrambled eggs in front of her. "What are your plans for the day, Etienne?" she asked in as cheerful a voice as she could manage.

The boy shrugged wordlessly and returned his attention avidly to his food.

Lissa made a face. "Etienne does what I do; he sits around and gets bored." She grinned at Karin. "Don't mind me; I'm not at my best in the mornings, never have been, as you may remember. And Madame Durocher is off today, so I'm stuck with domesticity."

"We could all do something together," Karin suggested.

"Paul is coming for you. Surely you didn't forget?" Bringing another cup of tea to the table and coffee for Karin, Lissa sat down and raised her red gold eyebrows, her gaze on Karin's face. "What do you think of Paul?"

"He's very. . . unusual," Karin said, conscious that Etienne was studying her from beneath lowered eyelids.

Lissa chuckled. "Isn't he, though? I do believe he was quite taken with you. I must say I was surprised. He hardly took his eyes off you all evening. I'll have to look out, won't I, or all my plans for Paul will go astray."

Abruptly Karin put down her fork and stood up,

leaving half her eggs and toast uneaten. She forced a smile. "I think I'll go out for a walk, if you don't mind. Perhaps you'd like to come with me? We could walk along—what did you call it—Dufferin Terrace? Some fresh air would do us both good."

Lissa was regarding her with an expression of curiosity. "Did I touch on a nerve? Sorry. I didn't mean to be rotten. It's just that I'm upset with Charles. He's already shut himself up in his study and informed me he's not to be disturbed." She sighed. "No, I don't feel up to walking for the sake of walking, thank you. Besides, I thought I'd make a quiche. Paul might like to have lunch before you two take off. He's very fond of quiche Lorraine." Her smile returned, mischievous as a kitten's. "Do you think it's too much of a cliché to approach a man's heart through his stomach?"

Karin swallowed the sharp retort that came to her lips. No wonder Etienne didn't like Lissa, if he knew of his stepmother's disloyalty to Charles! If Lissa was determined to initiate a relationship with Paul Dufresne, there wasn't much Kårin could do about it, but she wasn't going to stand there while Lissa further alienated Etienne. Nor would she join in any discussion of the man's culinary tastes. "Perhaps Etienne would like to come with me, then," she suggested, not expecting for a minute that the boy would agree. But to her surprise, he pushed the last of the damp cornflakes into his mouth, swallowed hastily and stood up. "All right, *mademoiselle*," he said ungraciously. "I'll come with you."

Lissa looked surprised, then pleased. "Are you sure, Karin?"

"Of course," Karin said heartily to cover up her dismay. What on earth would she find to say to the boy? He was standing expectantly in the doorway now, waiting for her, though his expression was anything but enthused. Why had he taken her up on her halfhearted invitation? Boredom perhaps? Remembering the bright happy children who had invaded her library every day, so boisterous she'd had to constantly remind them that silence was the rule, she felt a rush of sympathy for this somber overweight child. But this time she remembered to keep the pity from showing on her face. "Okay, then, let's go," she said in a bright voice that she felt sure wouldn't fool anybody.

"Don't go far. Remember you have to be back by one o'clock," Lissa called after them as they descended the front steps.

Karin smiled over her shoulder and waved in apparent agreement, but she didn't commit herself with words. She had deliberately left her watch in her bedroom. If she was late, she could hardly be called to account. And possibly, she thought sourly, Paul and Lissa wouldn't even notice her absence; they'd be too engrossed in their quiche Lorraine.

She and Etienne crossed the Governors' Garden at a brisk pace, not talking. Men were cleaning up the litter left by the previous night's rock-concert audience. There seemed to be an incredible amount of it. "It always annoys me to see that," Karin commented for the sake of something to say. "I wish people wouldn't litter public places. It's the same in Seattle. People wouldn't throw cans and paper plates and wrappers in their own backyards, so why do they spoil the countryside with them?"

Etienne didn't reply, but she thought she heard him sigh. His head was bent, his eyes evidently studying his own feet as he trundled along beside her. Probably he thought she was *lecturing* him, she thought despondently. What was the matter with her—she'd never had trouble talking to a child before.

Her spirits rose as they passed the towering Château Frontenac and reached the boardwalk beyond the park. Some distance to the left she noticed a horde of young people gathered near a large kiosk with a round green-and-white top. In front of them in the street were several horse-and-buggy rigs of various colors. The scene looked festive and picturesque, and she paused to stare. "They are calèches," Etienne explained. "They are hired by tourists who want to see the city." His voice had a hopeful note.

For a moment Karin was tempted, but then she remembered she hadn't changed any of her traveler's checks yet. "Another time, maybe," she said to Etienne.

The boy shrugged. A shrug seemed to be his answer to most things. But at least he had addressed two whole sentences to her. That was encouraging, wasn't it?

Turning right, she began to walk along beside a wrought-iron railing. Etienne fell into step beside her. The boardwalk felt springy beneath her feet, comfortable for walking. Out of habit, she stepped out fairly briskly, even as she admired the view.

From this vantage point she could look down on the docks below and the wide St. Lawrence River.

On the opposite shore she could see buildings of all kinds and sizes among the trees. "What is that place?" she asked.

Etienne glanced up, shrugged. "Lévis." Immediately he went back to studying his shoes.

So much for that conversational gambit, Karin thought. Ahead of them a wooden staircase led up in front of the Citadel to another promenade that wound around the upper edge of the cliff. "Is that the Governors' Promenade?" she asked, trying again.

"Oui."

They climbed the steps in silence. Then Etienne added, "Promenade des Gouverneurs."

He was quite right, Karin thought, chastened. This was a French city. The streets and alleys and buildings had French names. She should use them correctly. "Promenade des Gouverneurs," she echoed and was rewarded by a small smile. Progress at last.

She paused at the top of the steps, leaning on the green railing to admire the darting glittering play of sunlight on the choppy water of the river. A small ferryboat was chugging away from the shore below, and an excursion boat loaded with cheerful-looking tourists headed downriver toward the Ile d'Orléans. There were no tourists on the boardwalk, she noticed as she resumed walking—only some young mothers pushing babies in strollers, sometimes with another child or two toddling alongside, chattering in piping French. A few older couples walked slowly arm in arm, faces upturned toward the sun. The city sounds were muted here—a muffled hum of traffic and the occasional impatient toot of a car horn. To Karin's right, Canada's maple-leaf flag snapped briskly above the now silent Citadel. The sun felt hot on her head, and the breeze teased tendrils of hair free to blow around her cheeks and forehead. Such a lovely day to be alive, she thought.

She glanced down at the tousled brown hair of the silent boy beside her. There must be a way to reach him. She could at least try. "Do you miss Montreal?" she asked.

"No, *mademoiselle.*"

"You like Quebec City better?"

"Oui."

"Why?"

No answer. Karin checked a sigh. And then she noticed for the first time the sound of Etienne's labored breathing. The boy was not speaking tersely out of rudeness or shyness, but because he was totally out of breath. After their brisk walk, during which he'd manfully kept up with her long stride, the steep climb up the steps had been too much for him. She slanted a look at his face. It was bright red with exertion. Yet he had not complained once.

Belatedly tactful, she suggested she needed to rest a while. With obvious relief he guided her to a slatted green bench. They sat in silence for a few minutes, and then Karin repeated her earlier question. "Why do you prefer Quebec City, Etienne?"

For a moment he studied his hands in his lap, then he shrugged. "I do not know." Suddenly he blurted out, "Perhaps because there is no school just now."

"You don't like school?"

"I like the lessons, but the others...." There was

a long painful pause, then he said, "The other children tease me."

"Oh."

She heard him take a deep breath. When he spoke again, his voice was low. "Because I am fat, you see."

Such a simple statement. So much pain.

What could she say? There must be something to say. "Well," she said at last, "you don't *have* to be fat, you know."

No answer.

I've lost him, she thought, looking at the hunched shoulders, the bent head, the downcast eyes. "Tell you what," she said in a voice of false cheer. "Why don't we walk slowly back to the city and, well, go look at something?"

"At what, *mademoiselle*?" Such a polite voice.

"I don't know. Maybe the Château Frontenac or else...." Inspiration struck. "How about the alley of the artists? Rue du Trésor?"

A spark of interest lit the boy's eyes. "If you wish."

"And Etienne...."

"Mademoiselle?"

"How about if we sometimes talk in French, you and I? I really need to improve. If you would be patient with me?"

His rare smile, his father's engaging smile, lit up his plump face as he stood up and faced her directly for the first time that day. "*Certainement*, Mademoiselle Karin," he said, nodding.

His method of address reminded her of Paul Dufresne, but she managed not to flinch as she stood up and put her hand on his shoulder. "*Alors, allons*—then come along." It wasn't much of a play on words, but it brought another smile from Etienne. Did he ever laugh, she wondered. Sometime she would make him laugh.

During the walk back to the city, which she kept purposely slow, he offered several sentences in French, which she got the gist of as long as he spoke slowly. "You will learn," he assured her earnestly.

Karin smiled. On a certain level, at least, she and Etienne were communicating.

Rue du Trésor wasn't as crowded with sightseers as it had been when Karin saw it from the taxi. But there were several artists there, squatting on stools they'd placed against the walls beneath their wares, chatting to one another in rapid French. Slowly Karin walked along the alley, critically eyeing the various works, Etienne beside her, silent now, as engrossed as she was.

The Château Frontenac predominated, she saw, just as it dominated the town. It appeared in almost every sketch and lithograph and watercolor, pictured with varying degrees of skill. There were some excellent watercolors and several oils that were definitely worth studying. As always Karin wished she had some artistic talent but comforted herself with the thought that at least she was able to enjoy the works of others.

One painting in particular caught her eye—a painting of a narrow Quebec street edged with three-storied buildings with a church in the background. The whole painting had been done in several shades of brown, ranging from lightest beige to almost black. Above the painted street, threatening-looking clouds boiled across the sky, giving a somber, almost angry mood. She was impressed by the artist's perspective; her gaze was inescapably drawn into the painted street. She couldn't recognize the medium though, and without thinking, she reached out and touched the shiny surface.

"You wish to buy the painting, *mademoiselle*?" a male voice said over her left shoulder.

She jumped, startled and guilty, and turned apologetically to the man behind her. "I'm sorry, I wondered what medium—I didn't think...."

"Oil paint sprayed with a fixative," he said tersely, but Karin hardly heard him, she was so astonished to see the young man who had been arguing with Paul Dufresne outside this very alley yesterday.

He looked no neater today, though Karin noticed he seemed clean, at least. His brown hair and beard hadn't been combed, and his clothes looked as scruffy as before. His jeans and shirt were almost bleached with much washing.

There was something wrong with his eyes, she thought. Such sad-looking eyes, too old for his face—and red rimmed as though he didn't sleep well or often.

She was aware that she was staring, but all her earlier curiosity had returned. Yet she could hardly question him. For one thing, his facial expression was not encouraging. His brows were drawn together, and the lips she could glimpse between the heavy mustache and beard were set in a thin line. Well, she couldn't blame him for being annoyed. "I'm sorry," she said again. "I shouldn't have touched your painting. I would like to buy it, but I haven't changed my money yet." She hesitated. "That is, if I can afford—"

"Anyone can afford my paintings, *mademoiselle*."

"Oh, well, in that case...." At a loss, Karin turned to look at the painting again, trying to decipher the scrawled signature on the canvas. André something. "André Moreau?" she hazarded.

"Oui, mademoiselle." He gave an almost mocking bow. She thought she saw a glint of friendliness in his tired-looking eyes now, but she wasn't sure.

"Do you have other paintings?" she asked awkwardly.

Silently he pointed to several others on the wall, mostly of the château. She examined them carefully, searching for something to say that would breach the barrier between them. "These are all very good," she said, and was afraid she sounded unconvincing and condescending. "I mean, I like your work...." That wasn't any better. Finally, after several more minutes of awkward silence she plunged in with both feet. "I think we have a mutual acquaintance—Paul Dufresne."

Her voice trailed away as the young man's eyes narrowed. He was suddenly looking at her as though he suspected her of some ghastly crime. She averted her gaze, feeling embarrassed, though why the mere mention of Paul's name should bring such a reaction she had no idea. Her gaze fell on Etienne standing attentively beside her, staring at André Moreau. She'd forgotten Etienne completely. "Oh, Etienne," she said gratefully. "Isn't this a fine painting?"

But Etienne was frowning up at the young man. He said something in French. "Do you not know me, Monsieur Moreau?" Karin translated to herself.

The young man frowned in turn, then his face cleared. "Vincent?" he queried, and at Etienne's nod he spoke volubly and rapidly. Karin caught a reference to Paul and to Charles. Then the artist spoke to her in a kinder voice. "You are staying with the Vincents?"

"Yes. You know them?"

"No, but I have heard Dr. Dufresne speak of them, and I met young Etienne once in the doctor's company."

"Then you *do* know Paul?"

For some reason the young man suddenly looked quite agitated. His eyes darted from side to side as though he were checking for eavesdroppers. "We have met, yes," he admitted at last.

"I see," Karin said, though she didn't see at all.

"I think we should go home now," Etienne said. "It is long after one o'clock, *mademoiselle*. We will miss lunch."

"Oh." Karin hesitated. Etienne was offering her a graceful exit, but she was still curious, and besides, she didn't want to see Paul. . . .

"I can go alone," Etienne offered as though divining her dilemma. "I can manage perfectly well. I will tell Madame Lissa that you are delayed."

"Would you mind? I'd really like to talk to Monsieur Moreau some more. Are you sure?"

Etienne was already turning away. "Lunch, *mademoiselle*," he repeated gravely. He didn't seem to mind going home by himself; he looked relieved.

Was lunch so important to him? Did his whole life center around food? Perhaps she shouldn't let him go alone, but the house was only a few blocks away, and he was hardly an infant. He gave her a little wave from the end of the alley. Good, he wasn't offended. She didn't want to lose the advantage of the tentative friendship they had begun to form.

She turned back to the young artist, who was now regarding her with curiosity. "I really would like to buy the painting, Monsieur Moreau," she said awkwardly. "If you could keep it for me, perhaps, and tell me what—how much...."

"Ten dollars, *mademoiselle*."

"But that's much too cheap. I would expect to—"

"It is merely tourist junk."

"It's not junk at all," she protested, but he waved her protest aside. "This one is perhaps not so bad, but it is not my real work. It is junk. I do these things very quickly for the tourists. It is sometimes necessary to eat, you see."

There was a sardonic expression on his face now, which annoyed her, and his tone had been distinctly rude. She surely hadn't sounded *that* condescending, had she?

"Whatever you say, Monsieur Moreau," she said stiffly. "But I do like this painting, and I want to buy it."

"As you wish. I will hold it for you." He reached around her to take the painting from the wall and put it behind a large leather portfolio that was propped against a bench. His hand hesitated as he replaced the portfolio, and to her surprise, his face smoothed out, and he glanced at her almost shyly. "Would you care to see some of my better work?" he asked.

"Very much," she said promptly, recognizing an olive branch when she saw one.

He opened the portfolio so that it lay flat on the bench and silently presented its contents for her inspection.

She caught her breath. Now she was truly impressed. One of the paintings was an abstract seascape—a lyric of bright watercolor, featuring rich expressionist waves and rocks, and dashing whitecaps that pulsed with spirit and danger. So much vitality, Karin thought. If she had seen this painting hanging in a gallery, she would have expected the artist to be a giant of a man, not the slight young man at her side.

The other painting showed a dramatic shift in style. It was a pastel portrait of an enchantingly lovely young woman with a mane of curling blond hair and mermaid blue green eyes. This work had a gentler turn and was much more direct in presentation. Genius was obvious in the fine overtones of complex expression on the delicate face of the sitter. There was sadness there and pain, but a promise of laughter over all—and mischief, with just a hint of wistfulness. The artist's use of light and shade, his subtle handling of textures, conveyed a mood of heartbreaking tenderness. This was a young girl trembling on the very brink of life, afraid perhaps to step forward, but bold enough not to step back. She was undoubtedly French, though Karin could not have said how she knew that.

Reluctantly she straightened. "Oh, yes," she said

softly, and was amazed to find there were tears in her eyes. The young man regarded her in silence for a while, and then he smiled, showing remarkably even white teeth. "Thank you," he said.

For a moment neither of them moved, but the quality of the air between them seemed to alter subtly, almost as though they had touched. Karin cleared her throat. "You work full-time as an artist?" she asked.

Moreau's smile turned down at the corners. "Unfortunately no." He moved away a little, carefully replacing the canvases in the portfolio. "You still wish to purchase the other painting?" There was a glimmer of humor in his eyes.

"I do," Karin said, and they both laughed at the defensiveness of her tone.

"I am a student at Laval University," Moreau offered, and she recognized that he was trying to make up for his earlier rudeness.

"Majoring in art?"

"No. Business administration."

Her surprise must have shown on her face. André Moreau laughed again, but there was an edge of bitterness in the sound this time. "It is my father's idea. I'm afraid I play—what is the English word—'hooky'? I play hooky very often so that I can paint."

"Your father doesn't approve of your painting?"

His face was bleak. "My father is a manufacturer of shoes in Montreal. He wishes that I also make shoes. Do you think I should make shoes, *mademoiselle*?"

"Certainly not."

"Thank you."

Karin hesitated. "The girl in the painting—she is a close friend?"

The bleak look left his face to be replaced by a look of yearning. And then his expression hardened, and he seemed to withdraw into himself, away from her. "She is just a girl named Céleste," he said rudely, then turned and began straightening the paintings on the wall.

"What a lovely name," Karin exclaimed. His shoulders stiffened, but he didn't speak. Obviously he didn't want to discuss this girl named Céleste. Was he in love with her, she wondered. Could he have painted her so tenderly if he wasn't?

None of your business, Karin, she told herself. But Paul Dufresne was. "Have you known Dr. Dufresne long?" she asked hesitantly. "I met him only yesterday. I don't quite know what to make of him. He's a bit—overpowering, isn't he?"

André turned around and looked at her, frowning, hesitating, as though he wanted to tell her something but didn't know where to begin.

"I'm going to be working with him on Charles Vincent's book," Karin explained, hoping this would provide an opening. When he didn't comment, she decided to be frank. "I'd like to know more about him. Can you tell me. . . ." Her voice faded as anger appeared in the artist's face once more. Evidently she wasn't the only one Paul Dufresne aroused to hostility.

"Paul Dufresne is a meddler in other people's business," André blurted out. "He tries to take over people's lives. And he makes people. . . ."

"Yes?" Karin encouraged as the flow of words seemed about to dry up.

"He makes people too...dependent upon him," he finished.

Before Karin could comment or even ponder this strange statement, the artist's expression changed again, became guarded. "Here he is now, *mademoiselle*," he said. "I think he is looking for you."

At once he became immensely busy, moving the bench, flicking imaginary dust from his paintings, setting his portfolio down against the wall and putting the painting Karin had admired in front of it.

At first she didn't see Paul. More people had entered the alley while she was talking to André and were milling all around. Then she caught sight of him looming above a group of elderly ladies in Japanese kimonos, his dark head bent courteously as he evidently murmured apologies while maneuvering around them.

And then he was in front of her, looking down at her with amused vexation. "Karin, Karin," he chided, his French accent giving her name a caressing sound. "Why do you treat me so badly?"

She stared back at him defiantly, trying to disguise how much his sudden appearance had disturbed her. All breath had left her body the moment she saw him, leaving her dazed, almost paralyzed. Why did his presence affect her so strongly—so disproportionately? All right, he was an attractive man, and he looked even more attractive today, casually dressed in narrow dark pants and a short-sleeved knit shirt whose pristine whiteness emphasized the darkness of his hair. But she had known attractive men before.

Was she suffering embarrassment because the sight of him had triggered an immediate mental picture of her body moving against his, her hands rising to tangle in that thick black hair? Yes. That's all it was. Embarrassment.

"Why were you avoiding me?" he demanded.

She hesitated, about to make some excuse, then wondered why she should. "I don't like high-handedness, Dr. Dufresne. I told you that yesterday."

"So you thought you'd teach me a lesson by making me wait?"

"No. I didn't intend to turn up at all."

She'd forgotten about those wickedly slanting dark brows, that sardonic twist of his mouth. "How refreshingly honest you are," he said in a voice whose lightness failed to disguise its sarcasm.

"I try to be. I value honesty very highly."

"Do you indeed?"

He was looking suggestively at her mouth now, and she was having difficulty with her breathing. She looked away from him and saw André Moreau regarding them both with curiosity. "I've been admiring Monsieur Moreau's paintings," she said awkwardly.

The distraction worked. Paul turned to the younger man. "André. How goes it?"

"Okay," André replied flatly.

Paul's mouth tightened, but he didn't comment on André's curtness. Turning back to Karin, he took hold of her arm just above the elbow, sending a flash of electricity through the thin silk of her shirt. Ignoring her instinctive recoil, he drew her close to his side, 'turning her away from André, his other hand indicating the end of the alley that gave way to Place d'Armes, a grassy square with a fountain at its center.

A small light blue calèche with a folding top was waiting at the curb. Beside the horse's head stood a young frizzy-haired girl in a white peasant blouse and jeans covered with embroidered flowers. "I've hired Maggie to drive us," Paul said.

"Maggie?"

"She's a student at Laval University—from Nova Scotia originally. She supports herself by acting as a guide in her spare time. She is a good businesswoman. She has already started charging us, and at twenty dollars an hour we must not keep her waiting."

"Twenty dollars an hour!" André exploded. "Perhaps I should give up painting and drive a calèche."

"You'll do nothing of the sort." Paul's tone was as dictatorial as though he were speaking to a child.

André flushed and muttered something in French. Paul replied swiftly and emphatically, then paused and said something else more slowly.

Karin understood, "Have you...?" But the rest of the sentence eluded her. She puzzled over it as Paul continued to question André. Then she heard her own name and saw that Paul was looking at her quizzically. "André tells me you were asking questions about me," he said.

"I was just...making conversation," she said lamely.

The black brows rose. "Your questions did not indicate a personal interest?"

"Not at all."

"How disappointing." For a moment he held her gaze, then he turned back to André. Evidently André was disagreeing with something Paul had suggested, and his bearded face was becoming more and more surly.

Both men were speaking so rapidly that Karin could not follow their discussion, and she went back to pondering the words that had eluded her before, hardly noticing when Paul began easing her along the alley toward the waiting calèche.

Suddenly she had the rest of the sentence: "Have you done what I told you to do?" And André had answered no and looked extremely uncomfortable. What on earth had Paul wanted him to do? What gave him the right to order André around?

She risked a glance at Paul's face and saw that his jaw was clenched, his mouth set in a straight line. "Why are you angry with André?" she asked.

"I'm not angry with André," he said tightly, without slowing his pace.

"You *look* as though you are."

"Looks are deceiving."

Exasperated, Karin gave up, then realized that Paul hadn't even given her a chance to say goodbye to André or to make arrangements to pick up her painting. She stopped abruptly, causing a young woman with a baby in her arms to bump into her from behind.

After apologizing to the girl, she glared at Paul. "Just where do you think you are taking me?" she demanded.

His expression was all innocent surprise now, but

his hand had not loosened its hold on her arm. "Forgive me," he said in a soothing tone she didn't trust for a second. "I forgot to explain. I have made an appointment for us at the house of friends."

"But I'm not dressed for visiting," she protested.

His gaze examined her braided hair, then traveled thoughtfully and lingeringly over her silk shirt, denim vest and jeans—an act that did nothing for her equilibrium. "You look enchanting," he pronounced. "Like the heroine in a Western movie—the one who falls in love with the handsome hero."

"Who loves only his horse," she countered.

His humorous expression gave way to a somber slumberous look that perfectly mimicked the villain in a movie such as he had just described. "Not all heroes are alike," he said softly. Then he shrugged and smiled. "You will like my friends, I'm sure. Marcel Savard is French, and his wife, Sara, is Ethiopian—a charming lady. They have very lovingly restored their home to its original seventeenth-century design. It is in the purest style of architecture of that era, and Charles is very interested in it. Seeing it will give you a feeling for his work, I am sure. It will at least be a good place to start."

With a sinking feeling, Karin realized she was trapped. It was impossible for her to refuse to see the house. After all, she was in Quebec to assist Charles, and if Paul had made an appointment with the Savards, she would have to go. But this would be the last time she would give in, she determined as Paul handed her up into the buggy, and she settled down on the leather-upholstered seat. She was no André to be treated like a child. She was not going to let Paul Dufresne take over *her* life.

She became aware that Paul was still standing in the street, looking at her with an amused frown. "I was attempting to introduce you to Maggie," he said dryly.

Hastily she leaned down to take the girl's upraised hand. "I'm sorry, I was miles away, I'm afraid."

Maggie laughed. She was a pretty, healthy-looking girl with a fresh complexion and pink cheeks. "Don't give it a thought," she said. "Dr. Paul affects me the same way."

Paul laughed and hugged the girl's shoulders in an intimate way that obscurely annoyed Karin. Then he assisted Maggie up to the high front seat and climbed in beside Karin.

At once she realized that the buggy seat was very narrow. The two of them barely fitted into it, and it was impossible for their bodies to avoid touching from shoulders to knees. Paul apologized profusely for the lack of space, remarking that it was fortunate they were both slender. "But it is very cozy, don't you think?" he asked with a gleam in his blue eyes that made her uneasy.

"Cramped is the word that came to my mind," she said.

The dark eyebrows rose. "Cramped? How singularly unromantic."

"Isn't it?"

Maggie had turned around to look at them. Her lively face had a mischievous expression. "Do you wish me to proceed, Dr. Paul?" she asked.

"Just as soon as I make Mademoiselle Karin more

comfortable.'' Carefully he raised one arm and placed it around Karin's shoulders. "There. Is that not much better?''

Maggie chose that moment to make a clucking sound to the horse, and the buggy started off with such a lurch that Karin was saved from having to reply.

However, that same lurch forced her back against Paul's arm. His hand immediately tightened around her upper arm. Incredibly, she shuddered. She could hardly believe that she could be so disturbed by a mere touch. Yet there it was. His touch had found a nerve that sent a shiver through her whole body. It was only by a supreme effort of will that she was able to hold still. She had to say something, anything, to distract herself.

Stupidly she blurted out the first thing that came to mind. "Did you enjoy your quiche?''

Paul laughed. "Of course. Lissa is a good cook. And a hostess par excellence.''

"I'm sure.'' She had not meant to sound so sarcastic. Paul responded as she might have expected.

"Jealous again, Mademoiselle Karin?''

She didn't bother to reply. She sat as stiffly as she could, staring straight ahead as the calèche rattled over the cobbles of rue Ste. Anne. But then, when the horse trotted around the corner at the end of the street, the swaying of the carriage forced her even more tightly against Paul's side.

She felt his warm breath tingling against her cheek as palpably as though he'd touched her there. Unthinkingly she turned her face, moistening her lips against their sudden dryness, a movement he took as an invitation. Before she could retreat, his mouth touched hers, his lips barely exerting any pressure. Maddeningly his restraint affected her more strongly than if he'd forced her lips apart. She felt that light touch of his mouth all the way down to her toes. Alarmed, she put up a hand to push him away, but his free hand trapped her fingers, and he smiled at her lazily, triumphantly, then moved their joined hands to brush against her neck, just above her collarbone, in the vulnerable spot where her silk shirt lay open at her throat. "But how nervous you are," he murmured. "See how your pulse throbs. Does riding in a calèche frighten you so much?"

"Not...not at all."

She was aware all at once of the hard strength of the fingers that were holding hers, aware, too, of the smell of him—a clean male smell compounded of shaving soap and laundry starch, and a slight lingering odor of antiseptic that reminded her he was a doctor.

"You promised not to..." she stammered.

At once he released her hand. "So I did. How unkind of you to remind me." His long-suffering tone mocked her.

She swallowed. "How long is the drive?" she asked in as calm a tone as she could manage.

"The house is outside the old city. It will take us just over an hour." There was satisfaction in his voice.

Maggie leaned back to say something, and he turned his head to answer her. For a moment Karin could relax. But only for a moment. Her body tensed again as she realized what he'd said. *Over an hour.*

How on earth could she endure such proximity to him for so long without revealing. . . .

She caught her thoughts in mid-flight. Without revealing *what*? That he excited her? That if he decided he wanted to kiss her again, she might not be able to refuse him? How weak she was to be so physically aroused by a man she disliked simply because he was attractive and masculine and sexually aggressive.

Desperately she reached for composure as he leaned back in his seat and turned to her again, smiling, the clear blue of his eyes startlingly vivid in the sunlight. He was studying her knowingly now, reading her mind, reading her body, his mouth curving at the corners.

Over an hour, her mind echoed relentlessly. Over an hour in this rocking, swaying carriage that kept them pressed together as intimately as lovers. His hand and bare forearm were burning through the silk of her blouse so that she would not be surprised to find a red brand marking her shoulder when he finally released her. *If* he released her.

But of course he would have to let her go eventually, she thought with relief. He could hardly enter his friends' house with her clamped to his side as though they were joined at the hip.

Yes, eventually she would escape this enforced proximity. But how could she ever explain to herself her own intense reactions to this man?

CHAPTER FOUR

"THERE, *MADEMOISELLE*, just a few more stitches, and we shall be complete."

Standing as still as possible, Karin smiled uncertainly at Madame Savard's maid as Thérèse again inserted her sewing needle at the waistline of the long white dress Karin was wearing.

She felt, she decided, like Cinderella, getting ready for the ball—though the slight young maid with her rosy-apple cheeks and urchin haircut was an unlikely candidate for Fairy Godmother.

She glanced in the wall mirror beside her, admiring the hairstyle Thérèse had designed for her. The girl had parted her hair in the center, then folded it up and over itself into a sophisticated style that did wonders for Karin's cheekbones and made her eyes look even darker than usual. Or perhaps, she thought, her eyes were dark with bewilderment. She was still not quite sure how she came to be in Madame Savard's guest bedroom with its satin-striped wall covering, charming French furnishings and ornate gold-framed mirrors. The decision to stay had not been hers. Once again Paul Dufresne had arranged things to suit himself.

"Will there be many guests at the party?" she asked Thérèse as the girl skillfully bit off an end of thread and straightened to look at the finished effect of her work.

"About twenty, I think."

"All Ethiopian?"

"Four or five only besides *madame*. But the party will be traditionally Ethiopian because of *madame*'s niece, of course."

"Of course," Karin murmured, remembering that her dress belonged to *madame*'s niece. What was her name? Medhin. Medhin was close to Karin's size, so the dress had required little alteration—only a few tucks at the waistline.

"You wish help with your cosmetics, *mademoiselle*?" Thérèse asked.

"I can manage, thank you."

"Then I will leave now." The girl's hazel eyes sparkled. "You look very pretty," she added.

Karin managed a smile, though she still felt dazed by the surprising turn events had taken. After the maid closed the door quietly behind her, she stood unmoving for a minute, regarding herself in the mirror.

The dress was very becoming—long and full skirted, made of handwoven cotton that was so fine it clung to Karin's upper body, emphasizing her high firm breasts and slender shoulders. The short sleeves were edged with a woven band of rose and blue, yellow and green—a precise geometrical design that was repeated in the wide border at the bottom of the gown. An elaborate Coptic cross was embroidered on the bodice, and more embroidery decorated the full skirt.

At last, Karin moved to the dressing table and sat

down on the velvet-covered stool. With careful fingers she touched the crystal jars and bottles and bowls that ornamented the polished walnut surface, thinking ruefully of the plain pink glass powder bowls that embellished her modest dressing table at home.

What on earth was she, Karin Hayward, children's librarian, doing in a place like this?

Smiling at the thought, she began to apply her makeup, using the small pouch of cosmetics she'd taken from her handbag rather than disturb the elegant arrangement in front of her.

As she worked, she tried to sort out in her mind the sequence of events that had led her here.

The calèche ride had not been as difficult as she'd feared. Once she'd reminded Paul of his promise, he had become most circumspect, though he had not removed his arm from around her shoulders, and he had not been above making an innuendo or two. When he pointed out the Ursuline Convent, for example, he had remarked innocently that she would find it most interesting and would probably feel quite at home there—a double entendre she had let pass. But after they passed under the stone arch of the St. Louis Gate, he assumed the role of tour guide, insisting Maggie pull in to the imposing National Assembly buildings, which he told Karin were designed by Eugène Taché in the French Renaissance style. He described every one of the larger-than-life statues that stood in niches in the building's facade— governors, soldiers, adventurers and missionaries. He had then indicated the more modern parliamentary buildings that he felt were an architectural faux pas. When they resumed their journey, he discoursed at interminable length on the Roman and Greek influence on architecture, tossing out references to scale, proportion, space and geometrical form, until by the time they arrived at the Savard house, Karin was thoroughly dazed.

"You see how well I can keep my mind on business," he said cheerfully as he helped Karin down into the Savards' courtyard.

She didn't comment but turned away and pretended an interest in the exterior of the house. While she was admiring the huge oak door, she heard Paul speak to the calèche driver. "It is Thursday tomorrow," he said. "Will I be seeing you?"

From her high seat the girl gazed at him adoringly. "Of course," she said softly.

For a moment Karin had felt extremely irritated. Maggie couldn't be more than eighteen. Was every female fair game for this man? But then she had put the incident out of her mind.

Now she frowned at herself in the mirror, her mascara wand poised in midair. Maggie had said something about Paul later. What was it? Karin had lingered to say goodbye to the girl as Paul crossed the courtyard to the front door. "You'd better watch out for Dr. Paul," Maggie had said, her face alight with mischief. "He's irresistible, isn't he?"

"You know him well?" Karin asked.

"Know him?" Maggie laughed. "I couldn't get along without him."

An ambiguous remark, Karin thought as she applied the mascara sparingly to her eyelashes. What kind of man was this Paul Dufresne? On the one hand, he seemed to be something of a spoiled-playboy type, who could be charming, outrageous or beilligerent in turn in order to get his own way. Yet there must be other facets to his personality. There had been no mistaking the respect accorded him in the Savard household. Both of the Savards were his patients. "Paul is an excellent doctor," *madame* had told Karin, adding with a laugh, "You can see how healthy we are."

Karin could not disagree with that. Madame Savard—Sara, as she insisted Karin call her—was a woman who glowed with health and the air of confident pampered well-being that always seemed to hover like an aura around the very rich. Sara was in her late forties, bronze skinned and a little on the skinny side, with a classic facial structure that reminded Karin of the faces in early Byzantine murals. She was a graceful woman with an innate dignity that had awed Karin until she saw the friendly expression in the woman's liquid dark eyes.

Sara had taken to Karin at once, and as she guided her about the house, pointing out the historical features of the architecture and the furnishings that her husband, Marcel, had purchased in France, she rained questions upon Karin about her home in Seattle, her work and her parents. Her inquisition was so thorough it might have been offensive but for the eager interest in her voice and her smiling admission of curiosity about the American way of life. Her favorite niece was going to marry an American, she explained, and would be moving to California with him.

As it happened, that same niece had arrived the

day before on an unexpected visit and was to be
entertained at an Ethiopian-style party that evening.
Which explained, Sara added, the disorganization of
her household, for which she must apologize to Karin
and Paul.

Karin had noticed no disorganization and said so,
whereupon Sara opened a door to a vast brick-walled
kitchen where servants were scurrying around, and
delicious aromas were rising from several large pans
on the stove.

Karin paused in the act of applying gloss to her
lips. Was that when Sara had invited her to the
party? Or did the subject come up later when they
were all gathered in the elegant living room drinking
coffee? Yes. It was after Marcel Savard had joined
them. He stood in front of the imposing fireplace
beneath the magnificent Rembrandt-like portrait of
Madame Savard and suggested quietly, during one of
his wife's rare pauses, that Mademoiselle Hayward
and *cher* Dr. Dufresne might like to attend the evening's festivities.

Sara had seconded the suggestion, insisting that as
the time was now short, Karin and Paul must stay
right here. Toilet facilities would be supplied, she
assured them. They could bathe and refresh themselves and have a short rest before the celebration
began.

Paul had accepted for both of them. Annoyed that
he still thought he could speak for her, Karin demurred, giving the excuse that the Vincents were
expecting her, and also that she was not dressed ap-
propriately.

Her protests were to no avail. Monsieur Savard, it

seemed, had met Charles Vincent through Paul, and nothing would do but that Sara must telephone Madame Lissa and invite her and Charles to the party. Something would be found for Karin to wear, Sara insisted. And Paul would be fine as he was; the party was to be relatively informal.

Knowing how much Lissa would enjoy getting out, Karin had at last surrendered as gracefully as possible.

And so, here she was, applying the final touches to her appearance before going downstairs to join the guests.

In the past few minutes she had heard several cars drawing into the courtyard below, and now she could hear the faint sound of voices joined in conversation.

She stood up, feeling vaguely nervous, looking around the lovely bedroom, feeling more than ever like Cinderella come late to the ball. And the prince, in the form of the domineering Dr. Dufresne, had looked smugly delighted at the turn of events, as though he had arranged the whole thing himself. As well he might, Karin thought angrily, remembering the conspiratorial glance he had exchanged with Marcel Savard the moment before the Frenchman offered the invitation.

Karin's mood softened a little as she thought of her host. Marcel Savard was a slender, rather frail man of about fifty—a little stooped, with a short gray Vandyke beard and kindly blue eyes. In contrast to his wife, he spoke little, but his voice held authority, and Karin had noticed that Sara listened attentively when he did speak. He was a businessman with many interests, she had explained to Karin, of which his favorite was the Savard Art Gallery on rue St. Jean.

The Savards' interest in art was obvious. Karin had already counted three van Goghs, several Cézannes, a Rembrandt, a Daumier and some marvelously surrealistic landscapes that could only be the work of El Greco—not to mention the numerous bronzes and marble statuettes set on tables and niches in the walls.

On their arrival Paul had explained to her that the house was originally a farmhouse. Looking at the exterior of the big house with its high sloping roof and dormer windows, its walls coated with clear ocher mortar and its enormous oak door, Karin had accepted that description. But the interior was like no other farmhouse in the world, unless it was the Petit Trianon at Versailles, where Marie Antoinette had often spent time pretending to be a simple country lady.

And all this evidence of wealth, Karin thought as she unconsciously squared her shoulders and prepared to open the bedroom door, was enough to overwhelm an ordinary librarian from Seattle. How had she let that overbearing man manipulate her into a situation where she felt so inadequate?

A few minutes later she was feeling even more overwhelmed, not only by the number of people in the Savards' huge living room, but by the change in its appearance. During her absence the salon, as Sara called it, had been transformed. Rugs had been rolled up, and most of the paintings had been replaced by silken embroideries and shields made of basketwork and porcupine quills, complete with crossed spears. The high-backed sofas and chairs had been carried out to make room for an array of low chairs set around basket tables that were vivid with abstract designs of rich earthy colors. In the doorways, silver baskets of burning charcoal sent incense wafting into the room, adding to the exotic atmosphere.

As Karin hesitated on the threshold, Sara came toward her, dressed in a gown similar to hers. She laughed as Karin voiced her surprise at the changes. "An Ethiopian party must have an Ethiopian motif, *n'est-ce pas*?" she said, then added approvingly, "You look very lovely, *ma chère*. Come and meet my guests."

Gaily she introduced Karin to couple after couple, following each introduction with a few words in French or English or Amharic, the Ethiopian tongue, depending upon the people involved, changing from one language to another with an ease that impressed Karin. "Sara speaks six languages," Paul informed her when they reached his side. Evidently he had noticed Karin's amazement.

"Pooh, that is no virtue," Sara exclaimed. "Amharic is my mother tongue. I learned Italian as a child during the Occupation; French from my husband; and English, German and Spanish because I wanted to."

With that, she indicated a chair at the basket table in front of Paul and excused herself to supervise the serving of dinner. Obviously Karin was expected to sit with Paul. Surprisingly she didn't feel as annoyed as she might have at the prospect, perhaps because in the room full of strangers she was suddenly shy.

To his credit, Paul did his best to make her feel at ease, introducing her to the French-Canadian couple René and Marie Leclerc, who were to share their table, and drawing her into their conversation about Montreal, which Marie said she loved mostly because of the nightlife and the wonderful sailing in summer. She and Karin discussed sailing for a while. Karin had sailed on Puget Sound with Ray, and Marie invited her to join René and herself and their two teenage sons sometime. Then she turned to Paul again. "You must like Montreal, also," she said. "You seem to spend a lot of time there."

Paul shrugged. "It is an interesting city."

Marie's dark eyes danced with mischief. *"Interesting?* How deliciously vague. Do you have *special* interests there, Paul? Tell me, are they business interests or romantic ones?"

Her husband laughed. "My wife is not inquisitive," he said to Karin. "She just likes to know everything."

"But of course," Marie said. "Gossip is always stimulating. Are you going to answer me, Paul?"

His face was bland. "I've forgotten the question."

Marie pouted. "You are very unresponsive tonight; that is not like you." Her face brightened. "Tell me, is it true that your mother is in Paris again?"

"It is."

"How goes it for her there?" she asked with a small laugh.

"It goes very well," Paul replied.

For some reason this exchange struck the three of them as humorous, and they all laughed. But Paul had very neatly evaded Marie's curiosity about his trips to Montreal, Karin noted.

What kind of woman would the mother of Paul

Dufresne be, she wondered as the conversation flowed around her. She was a widow, Lissa had told her. She was probably the original grande dame type—tall and regal and strong, with blue eyes like her son's. Her eyes would no doubt be haughtily cold, though, as befitted the chatelaine of a château, rather than brilliantly vivid like Paul's.

She became aware that those brilliantly vivid eyes were watching her now. The Leclercs had turned away to exchange a few words with an Ethiopian couple at the next table.

"This is an unexpected pleasure," Paul said as her gaze crossed his.

"Was it really unexpected?"

He affected an injured expression that was belied by the amusement dancing in his blue eyes. "Mademoiselle Karin, you surely do not suspect me of intrigue?"

She refused to let him off so lightly. "You knew there was going to be a party, didn't you?" she accused him.

He spread his hands, palms upward. "I had perhaps heard a rumor to that effect."

"And you arranged for me to be invited?"

He inclined his head. "You make such a charming Ethiopian."

"You're avoiding my question."

"Am I?"

It was no use. When he looked at her with that blatantly false air of innocence, she could not sustain her anger.

As though he sensed her softening, he smiled knowingly and lifted her hand to his lips.

"You are quite incorrigible, Dr. Dufresne," she said, hoping her light tone would distract him from the sudden tremor of her fingers.

But he wasn't fooled. He studied her hand for a moment, then returned it to her lap but kept it clasped firmly in his.

As the Leclercs had finished their conversation, and Marie was now smilingly observing their joined hands, Karin could hardly tug her hand free. Fuming at the way he had trapped her, she was obliged to sit in enforced intimacy with him, trying to respond to remarks from René and Marie. To add to her distress, her treacherous heart began the wild beating his touch always seemed to arouse.

When Charles and Lissa entered the room, she saw her chance to disengage herself. But when she said she wanted to greet them, Paul merely tightened his grip and pointed out that the Vincents were already being seated, and dinner was obviously about to be served. "You persist in trying to escape me," he said softly. "Why do you fight the attraction between us?"

"Because it isn't there," she said through clenched teeth, glaring at him while the Leclercs' attention was elsewhere. But her glare was met by a wicked smile, and her voice faltered as his fingers moved against the back of her hand, detonating tiny explosions throughout her whole body. In another second she would be trembling again. She shrugged in a way she hoped he'd interpret as indifferent, then turned to wave at Lissa, ignoring Paul's murmured, "That's better, *chérie*."

Lissa waved back, looking very cheerful and

pleased with herself. She was dressed in a long cotton caftan of lime green, her favorite color, and seemed delighted to find herself in this enchantingly unusual setting. Charles was smiling, too, and looking at Lissa with admiration. All the buttons of his white shirt seemed to be in the right buttonholes, Karin noticed, and he was wearing smartly creased dark pants and well-polished shoes. His hair had been tamed into neatness, and he looked very handsome and alert, without his usual absentminded expression.

He and Lissa were chatting happily now with the other couple at their table—Sara's pretty young niece, Karin saw, and a young man she remembered being introduced to: Pierre something—another French Canadian. Lissa's hands were gesturing prettily, and her face was animated. She was obviously having a good time.

Karin wished she could relax, too, but how could she as long as Paul's hand continued to press against hers? She had never known, she thought despairingly, that so much sensation could be conveyed from one hand to another. She could almost feel the blood coursing through the veins in her wrist, throbbing into her palm, throbbing against *his* palm.

To her relief, as a prelude to the meal, a bevy of servants brought lovely brass bowls filled with scented water for the guests to wash their hands. Paul was forced to relinquish her hand, which he did with such obvious comical reluctance that Marie Leclerc laughed aloud and made a teasing remark that brought a flush to Karin's face. But at last she was able to relax, especially as the meal was evidently intended to be eaten with the fingers, and Paul could hardly capture her hand again.

Following the ritual hand washing, each table was topped by a round basketwork platter on which were placed layers of what looked like extra-large pancakes. This was *injera*, Paul told her, a kind of bread. More *injera* was draped, folded, around the edge of the platter, and Paul explained that the *doro wat*, or chicken stew, that the servant was ladling onto the *injera* was meant to be scooped up in broken-off pieces of the extra bread and popped into the mouth. "So," he concluded, demonstrating.

At first, Karin had difficulty with the process, but she soon became adept. The chicken was delicious, savory and well spiced. Karin recognized the taste of ginger and pepper and lemon and something almost fiery, which Paul told her was *berberi*—a hot-pepper seasoning used in many Ethiopian dishes. "Allow me to show you one of the niceties of Ethiopian etiquette," he went on gravely. Carefully wrapping a choice morsel from the center of the platter in a small piece of *injera*, he popped it into Karin's mouth before she had a chance to guess his intentions. His fingers lingered on her lips. "A charming custom, *n'est-ce pas*?" he asked.

Karin's body flooded with a heat that had nothing to do with the *berberi* seasoning. Taken by surprise, she swallowed convulsively, forgetting to chew. And choked. At once Paul's hand clapped her on the back, and as she continued to cough, his other hand moved to a spot just below her breasts. "Do you require the Heimlich maneuver?" he asked.

She looked at him blankly, at last managing to control the spasms in her throat.

"The Heimlich maneuver is a well-known medical procedure designed to prevent accidental choking to death," he explained solemnly. "One pushes here, sharply." Suiting action to words, his fingers pressed intimately into the gossamer stuff of her dress.

"I'm in no danger of choking to death," she said stiffly, aware of the Leclercs' fascinated interest. She was becoming very annoyed at Paul's deliberate and public flirtation. He knew perfectly well that she could not protest. She had no desire to create a scene, and he was playing with her, playing on her emotions by touching her unexpectedly, unpredictably.

She chose to ignore the fact that her emotions seemed perfectly willing to be played with, betraying her at every turn.

Fortunately for her peace of mind, the rest of the meal passed without incident. The food was accompanied by a delicious honeyed wine that reminded her of a mead she had sampled at a medieval inn in Vancouver. Fresh strawberries were served as dessert and then strong black coffee, redolent with cloves. Karin clutched her handleless cup gratefully, hoping the hot aromatic liquid would clear senses set swimming by the sweet wine and the heady scent of incense.

After the tables had been cleared, and everyone had had a chance to recover from the feast, a group of musicians entered the room—musicians unlike any Karin had ever seen. Tall and dark, they were dressed in long flowing robes of white cotton identical to Karin's dress. Their instruments were unusual, too. The one like a hide-covered box with a handle was a one-string fiddle, Paul told her, and the horn was a kudu horn. The drums she could recognize for herself, and the flutes, which Paul thought were probably made of sugarcane.

She enjoyed the music, though it seemed intentionally atonal and primitive in rhythm. To her delight, Sara and her niece and the other Ethiopians moved to the center of the floor after a while and performed a fast-moving folk dance, which Sara afterward announced was traditional in the northern Ethiopian province of Tigre. The dance was followed by a program of folk songs from other regions, the final one a beautifully rendered lament, sung by Medhin, that brought the entire company to their feet to applaud. As long as they were on their feet, Sara said with a wide smile, there was no reason why they could not join in the final dance. She clapped her hands, and a servant came in with a pile of wide white scarves decorated with woven multicolored borders. These were called *shammas*, Sara said, and she proceeded to pass them out two by two to the men in the party, including Paul.

Paul promptly tied one of the long scarves around his lean waist and draped the ends over his shoulders. Then he wound the other veil over Karin's head, drawing one end over her face so that only her eyes showed. "Now you are a respectable maiden," he said cheerfully. "Your beauty is modestly hidden from view."

About to pull the veil loose, sure he was teasing her again, Karin saw that the other women were now similarly attired and were forming a circle with their partners in the center of the room. Sara was happily

guiding everyone into place. "I don't know how..."
Karin began.

"Did I not tell you I would be your teacher?"

She was immediately reminded of the incident in
the basement of the Vincent house, as he probably intended her to be.

Feeling suddenly weak—the coffee had not after
all overcome the effects of the wine, she told
herself—she allowed him to take her hand and lead
her into the group.

And then the music began again, and Sara and
Medhin demonstrated the steps.

A trained dancer, Karin had no difficulty following their simple shuffling movements. The rhythm
was precise, ordered, almost dictating the steps they
should take. At first only the feet were involved, but
after a while Medhin showed them they must move
their shoulders, each separately, in a stiffly jerking
backward motion that was difficult to copy. A whole
series of complicated body movements followed, and
some of the guests gave up, including Charles and
Lissa, but Karin, thoroughly engrossed now, managed to mimic Medhin perfectly.

"Bravo, Karin," Sara called, but Karin barely
heard her. All her training had come to the fore now,
and she was lost in the music, her body moving
almost of its own accord, her white dress drifting
around her legs as lightly as thistledown. Paul was
smiling at her in evident approval, his tall lean frame
moving gracefully, easily. Obviously he had performed this dance before.

Facing him as they stepped around each other,
Karin followed his lead, seeming to know instinctive-

ly when to turn, when to jerk her shoulders in time
with his. Under the influence of the music she had
entered fully into the role that was surely intended by
the dance: the willing maiden echoing the seductive
movements of her partner's body. One of her hands
held her full skirt free of her feet, the other held her
veil in place across her face. She caught a glimpse of
herself in a wall mirror and was instantly bemused by
the sight. She looked completely unlike herself, she
thought—almost alien, exotic; only her eyes showed
above the white veil, dark and brilliant. As she
turned, her gaze caught on Paul's face, traveled upward to his eyes and was immediately held there.
How expressive his eyes were! She could see in their
blue depths the instant warning of a change in pace
or rhythm. Vaguely she realized that the beat of the
drums had changed, increased in rapidity. Unconsciously she and Paul had followed the change.
Now their feet were barely moving, taking small,
almost stilted steps. Their upper bodies swayed
toward each other, then jerked apart. She became
aware that the others had stopped dancing, had
formed a circle around the two of them and were
clapping to the ever increasing beat of the drums.

From time to time, during a particularly sensual
movement, one of the musicians made a suggestive
ululating sound in the back of his throat—a sound
that was at once primitive and exciting, an animalis-
tic sound that seemed to penetrate Karin's body and
call up an answering response from her blood.

She felt totally free of self-consciousness, no
longer inadequate. In truth, she was barely aware of
anything but the pounding, throbbing drums that

echoed the beating of her own heart. It was as though she and Paul were alone in the room, enclosed in an emotionally charged magnetic-force field in which they moved as though bewitched. Their bodies moved in unison, meeting as they turned sideways, sliding together, holding, moving reluctantly apart.

Karin could not tear her gaze from his face, from which all trace of humorous teasing had fled. He was serious now, almost frighteningly somber, his blue eyes unsmiling and hooded, dark, his mouth stern.

She wanted suddenly to touch his stern sensual mouth, his half-closed eyelids, wanted to press herself against him, to sink into his embrace and never, never surface. Yet still her feet moved in rhythm with the drums, and her body responded fluidly to the changing beat.

Then the music ended in a wild crescendo of sound. The dance was over. Everyone applauded, laughing and exclaiming over their performance.

Paul took her hand, and they bowed to their audience. Under cover of the general acclaim, he said softly, "You see, Karin. It is as I said. It has begun."

And she, dazed as though she'd just awakened from sleep, answered yes and saw something very like triumph flare in his eyes.

CHAPTER FIVE

As soon as the party began to break up, Paul informed Karin he was going to take her home by taxi. She had expected to drive back with Charles and Lissa, but "You came with me, you leave with me," Paul had said. His voice was quiet, but its even tone left no doubt of his determination.

Still under the spell cast by that strange, erotic dance, she didn't protest. She hadn't wanted to argue with him and perhaps give Sara's guests something more to gossip about, she told herself weakly as she changed into her shirt and vest and blue jeans in the Savards' guest room. She'd already noticed the others watching her curiously. For which she could hardly blame them.

Paul was waiting at the foot of the stairs. "The taxi is here," he said. That somber stern expression had not left his face. In the dim light of the hall his blue eyes seemed shadowed, unreadable.

Karin looked at him nervously, then glanced at the closed salon door. "I'll just tell Charles and Lissa I'm leaving."

"I have already told them."

"Oh, then Sara...."

"You said good-night to Sara before you went upstairs."

"So I did." There didn't seem to be any delaying tactics left.

But she hadn't needed to delay their departure, she told herself as the taxi sped from the courtyard. Paul was merely escorting her to her door. And yet there was no doubt that she had been manipulated again.

"I didn't mean to leave before Charles and Lissa," she said, making no attempt to hide her annoyance. "You have a way of taking things into your own hands that is very annoying."

"Arrogant, would you say?"

"Yes."

"I must try to mend my ways."

She glanced at him suspiciously, but he was sitting back on his side of the dark back seat, only his head turned toward her. She wished she could see his expression.

"Charles and Lissa seemed quite content that I should see you home," he said. Evidently he expected the statement to reassure her. Why did he feel she needed reassurance?

When the taxi drew up at the Vincents' door, he helped her out, paid the driver and escorted her up the steps, not touching her, not speaking.

Suddenly nervous, she fumbled in her handbag for the key Lissa had given her, dropped it with a clatter on the stone porch, barely managed to pick it up. Paul took it from her helpless fingers and opened the door.

The house was quiet. Evidently both Etienne and Madame Durocher had gone to bed.

Karin swallowed. Turning to Paul, she held out her hand. "Good night. Thank you for a lovely evening."

He looked down at her hand, then at her face, his

eyebrows slanting together. He didn't smile. "I'll wait with you for Charles and Lissa," he said matter-of-factly. "Perhaps you would offer me a drink?"

It seemed a reasonable request. "Of course," Karin said. Her own mouth was dry, she realized.

Leading the way into the living room, she switched on every light she could find, then looked around the room helplessly.

"I believe the bar is in the basement," Paul said. His voice was gentle.

"Oh, yes. I. . . ."

"Shall we go down, then?"

Karin gave herself a mental shake and moved purposefully toward the door, then down the stairs to the basement. Paul followed.

The crimson and white room seemed smaller than she remembered—and airless in spite of the air conditioning. Again Karin switched on all the lights. Then she walked over to the bar and looked at the array of bottles. "What—what would you like?" Her voice sounded strangled. Something seemed to have moved into the room with them—something watchful and silent.

No, it was Paul who watched her. What was he thinking? Was that amusement quirking the corner of his mouth or impatience?

As she still hesitated, he moved past her to the bar. Quickly and skillfully he mixed two drinks, handed her one and sat down on one of the crimson couches, one arm along its back, the other hand holding his glass. He looked at her, raising his glass in a silent toast.

Hurriedly she sat down on the edge of the opposite

sofa and sipped her drink. She had no idea what it was, but at least sipping it gave her something to do. She wished she could think of something to say.

For no apparent reason her mind dredged up a memory from her childhood. Often, in the winter, her parents had taken her sledding on Mount Rainier. Bundled in warm clothing, she would clutch the sides of the sled with mittened hands as her father climbed in behind her. He did so very deliberately and solemnly. Both her parents were solemn people. They had not really planned on having a child. But they knew their duty; they made sure she did all the things a child was supposed to do whether they enjoyed them or not. Her mother would carefully hold the sled steady at the top of the snow-covered slope until Karin and her father were safely settled in place. Then she would let go.

Always at the last moment, looking ahead down the steep icy slope, Karin wanted to shout, "No, wait, I've changed my mind. I don't want to go." But she never did speak out.

Why remember that now, she wondered.

Paul was standing up. Was he going to leave? Did she want him to?

He put his glass down on the table between them, came around it and took her drink from her, setting it down beside his. Then he sat beside her, looking at her. His eyes were very blue in the lamplight. "What are you thinking of?" he asked.

She swallowed. "Charles and Lissa will be home soon," she said stupidly.

A ghost of a smile touched his lips. "The last I saw of them, Charles and Lissa were preparing to look at

Sara's collection of photograph albums. If I know Sara, that should take at least two hours."

She stared at him, unable to speak. Somehow his hand had moved to the back of her neck. Now his fingers played with tendrils of hair that had come loose from the style Thérèse had designed for her. "Such wide eyes," he said. "Are you really so afraid of me? You did not seem afraid when we danced together."

She managed a weak smile. "You must understand that I'm a trained dancer. A dancer is also an actress. When I'm dancing, I'm not myself."

"Ah, c'est comme ça?" Amusement creased the skin at the corners of his eyes. Then he was solemn again. "Can you look at me and tell me you were acting during that entire dance?"

She could not meet his direct gaze. "No," she whispered.

His fingers felt cool and gentle against her skin. There was no breath in her. And the room seemed to be fading. The corners of her vision could no longer discern the furnishings, the arched white walls, the framed sketches.

No, she thought, *I don't want to do this.* But there seemed to be a separation between her mind and her body. One of her hands moved slowly up to touch his face—the palm of the other came to rest on the smooth skin at the base of his throat. He tensed, then his mouth came down softly over her own. She felt an ineffable sweetness, a kind of gentle languor, invade her body. It seemed to her that nothing had ever moved her as deeply as the gentle touch of his lips.

His hands were behind her now, gliding across her back, easing her slowly closer to him. His mouth played softly against hers, the tip of his tongue now outlining the shape of her lips, now touching delicately at one corner, seeking entrance.

Hesitantly she opened her mouth to his, feeling safe and warm and protected. This kiss was not at all like the first time he'd kissed her in this very basement. That had been demanding and raw. This was very deliberate, but gentle, unthreatening, and she could allow herself to relax against him, to return his kiss softly. Slowly her hand stole across his thick hair to the back of his neck.

The kiss lasted a long time, but she felt no need to end it. It was Paul who moved. His head lifted, and he looked at her for a long moment. His hands had released their pressure on her spine. To her astonishment, his face had assumed the sardonic expression that always irritated her.

Before she could speak, he laughed shortly. "Is this what you like, Karin, to be treated gently, to be cherished?"

"I don't understand what you mean," she said stiffly.

He made an impatient sound. "We are not children, you and I."

"I know that." Still bewildered, she removed her hand from the back of his neck and looked at him helplessly. "I don't understand," she said again.

His eyes narrowed. "In that case I shall demonstrate," he said. And then his arms gripped her fiercely, and his mouth moved over her face, kissing her eyelids, her cheeks, her mouth—his lips insistent, brutal, demanding.

For a second she was too startled to struggle. And

then it was too late. He was easing her down on the couch, murmuring endearments against her mouth, his body pressing hard against hers. Panic-stricken, she reached for his head to pull it away, but somehow all she succeeded in doing was pulling him closer. When his mouth finally freed hers, she tried to speak, to protest, but her voice had deserted her; she could only stare up at him in speechless wonder.

His hands were doing things to her hair, taking out the pins so that it tumbled across his palms. Without taking his gaze from her mouth, without giving her time to recover from his onslaught, he lifted the dark mass of hair in both hands, winding his fingers into it, bringing her head up so that he could kiss her again, deeply, intrusively, explosively.

To her dismay, something inside her responded to his dark power. She was filled with an exhilaration she had never experienced before—and yet it was familiar. She was hurtling into space, out of control, sliding downward into a bright whiteness of light that waited to envelop her. Her body strained to his, meeting fire with fire.

Not taking his mouth from hers, he eased away from her to kneel beside the couch, his hands moving impatiently first to the snaps of her denim vest, then to the buttons of her shirt. There was the sound of rustling silk moving away from her body, and then her bra was skillfully removed, and she felt the velvet of the couch, soft against her spine.

Sanity returned, bringing panic with it. She wrenched her mouth free. "Stop, Paul, please," she begged, but her voice had no force in it.

He smiled lazily. "It is too late, *chérie*. Admit it, you want me as much as I want you."

"No," she whispered. "Not like this."

"That's not what your body told me when we were dancing. Your body told me it wanted to be taken, possessed."

His face was so close to hers his features seemed blurred. As she stared at him, so horrified by his words that she couldn't speak, he reached out to touch her face. Roughly his thumb traced the line of her jaw. Then his hand traveled downward to cup one bare breast. He stared down at her, his eyes darkening. *"Tu es ravissante,"* he murmured.

Her thoughts worked to untangle his meaning, then dissolved again as his fingers stroked circles around each taut nipple. She started to reach for his hands, to push them away. "Don't move," he commanded. "Please don't move."

And though her mind protested, her body obeyed.

With great delicacy he leaned to her breast and touched one nipple with a gentle tongue.

Falling. She was falling. Paul's hands were fumbling with the waistband of her jeans now, and she seemed helpless to prevent him. Her hands flailed at him but met only the smooth skin of his shoulders. When had he taken off his shirt? He must have pulled it roughly over his head. His dark hair was tousled, curling over his forehead as he leaned over her, lowering his hard virile body onto hers, his hands sliding under her to lift her, his dark head and bare shoulders blocking out the light.

Yet though his face was in shadow, his features no longer seemed blurred. Her vision was clear, acutely clear. She could see the slanting dark brows, the blue shine of his narrowed eyes, the well-defined mouth. His lips were relaxed now, smiling, showing the edges of his even white teeth. He looked triumphant. He was the victorious conqueror, she his helpless victim.

Abruptly her body recovered its strength. Her flailing hands finally found his wrists beneath her, tugged at them. Breath sobbed in her throat. "No," she cried out, but his mouth was on hers again, closing out the sound. Her hands were pinioned beneath her own body, her legs helpless under the weight of his. She felt the warmth of his skin against her breasts as his bare chest moved against hers. The beating of his heart thudded in counterpoint to her own.

Desperately she twisted her head to one side. "No," she cried again. "Please don't. Please don't do this."

For a moment she thought he was going to ignore her protest again. The pressure of his hands increased against the bare skin of her back, drawing her hips tightly against his. His head was bent, his mouth unyielding against the softness of her shoulder.

And then the taut strength of his body relaxed. His head lifted. Startled blue eyes looked into hers. "You really mean it," he said.

She couldn't answer him at once. She could only lie stiffly, staring up at him. "Please let me go," she pleaded at last.

He made a slight sound in his throat, but she didn't know if it was a sound of derision or anger. She lay still, waiting, not looking at him until the pressure of his body eased, and he lifted himself up and away from her.

Hastily she sat up and pulled on her bra and shirt, fingers clumsy on the buttons. Adjusting her jeans, she swung her legs to the floor.

Paul was standing with his back to her. He had picked up his shirt and was pulling it down over his head. She saw muscles move across his lean back. He might be slender, but he was in superb physical condition. He could easily have continued to hold her down, forced her to submit to him.

What was he thinking? What would he say to her? What could she possibly say to him?

Nervously she watched him as he bent to pick up his forgotten drink. His throat worked as he swallowed the contents. With a decided click he set the glass down on the table. Then he fixed his unflinching gaze on her, his head at an arrogant angle, his arms folded, long legs planted in an aggressive stance. "*Mon Dieu,* Karin," he said coldly. "If this is how you treated your friend Ray, it is not surprising that he turned to another woman."

Humiliation flooded her. Whatever she had expected from him it was not sarcasm. She forced herself to meet his direct gaze. "I realize that I encouraged you in the beginning," she said stiffly. "But I didn't expect that you would go so... so far."

He greeted her words with silence, then his mouth twisted. "I am not accustomed to having a woman look at me as though I am a rapist," he said harshly. He took a deep breath. "However, I had no right to insult you. I can only plead that I was... distressed. The male ego is a fragile thing at such times." His posture relaxed a little, and he almost smiled at her. "It is perhaps understandable that I should be distressed, wouldn't you say?"

"I'm the one who was distressed," she said angrily. "I asked you to stop. I tried to push you away. How could you be so callous, so—brutal?"

Her voice trembled, and at once he knelt beside her, lifted her chin with a gentle finger. "Oh, sweet Karin, was it so terrible? Anyone would think you had never been made love to before."

She dropped her gaze, fixed it on her hands, clasped between the knees of her blue jeans. She heard him draw in his breath sharply. "You have been made love to, haven't you? You were engaged to this man Ray. How long did you know him?"

"Four years."

"Four years. He must surely, in all that time. . . ."

She couldn't just sit there. She had to defend herself. Yet why should she feel the need to defend herself? Was she supposed to apologize for her inexperience, apologize for expecting him to be satisfied with a few kisses, a few gentle caresses, as Ray would have been? A quiet man, Ray—comfortable to be with. He had never seemed to want more than she had been prepared to give. He had at least never *insisted* on more. He respected her, he had said often. He would not ask her to love him completely until they were man and wife. Passion was an animal thing, formed in the loins, not in the heart, he had said. Sometimes it had seemed to Karin, though she was certainly not promiscuous herself, that Ray's restraint was unnatural in view of their commitment to each other. But she could hardly tell Paul that or tell him she'd often wished Ray was a little less respectful, a little more demanding, that she'd suspected she had more to offer than he was asking for.

But that didn't mean she was ready to become intimate with a—what was the French word—"roué," like Paul Dufresne. She was not a prude, but she had seen too many examples of the ravages the so-called sexual revolution had caused. Several of her friends at school had declared themselves "free spirits," which evidently meant they felt obliged to go to bed with every man they dated. Many nights she had stayed up trying to comfort those same girls when they cried in bewilderment and pain over yet another man who had moved on in search of new thrills.

No, she had no wish to expose herself to that kind of shameful rejection.

She could feel Paul's gaze still on her, but she couldn't bring herself to look at him. After a while she said stiffly. "I realize I shouldn't have danced the way I did. I didn't think of...."

"The consequences?"

"I didn't mean that. I meant I didn't intend to lead you to think that I would....." Her voice trailed away.

"My dear sweet Karin." There was an odd note in his voice. Was he *laughing* at her? "It seems I have made a grave mistake. I mistook your struggles for answering passion. Your body, you see, belied your words. For a while there I think you were not reluctant. Don't you agree?"

Before she could speak, reply hotly that she certainly *didn't* agree, his fingers touched her lips to silence. "Don't answer, *chérie*. It was not a fair question. Do not upset yourself. I understand everything now."

How could he possibly understand when she did not? For a few minutes she *had* wanted him, wanted him desperately. A man she had known less than two days. How could she have acted so wantonly?

Now she felt only confusion and an obscure shame.

He was still studying her face, his eyes thoughtful, kind. It was more than she could bear that he should be kind now.

She averted her eyes. "I think you'd better go."

"Very well. I can probably get a taxi outside the Château Frontenac." He stood up, hesitated. "I'm afraid I won't be able to escort you tomorrow. I have business to attend to. I'm sorry."

About to brush his apology aside, thinking he was merely seeking a plausible way out of an uncomfortable situation, she suddenly remembered his hurried words to Maggie earlier in the day. He had arranged to meet *her* tomorrow.

Well, perhaps he'll have better luck there, she thought, not pausing to consider why she should feel so bitter. "It isn't necessary for you to escort me at all," she said stiffly. "I told you that before."

There was a silence. She became aware again of the humming of the air conditioner. It seemed suddenly loud in the stillness. Then Paul sighed. With a slight bow he turned on his heel and moved toward the stairs.

Quite suddenly Karin wanted to call him back. But instead she sat helplessly, silently, and watched him leave.

A minute later the front door closed behind him. She felt all the tension drain from her body, leaving her limp with relief—and something else. Was it, could it possibly be—regret?

CHAPTER SIX

KARIN SAT IN THE LITTLE STUDY adjoining her bedroom, gloomily sifting through the papers that were
strewn all over the desk in front of her. She'd
brought them in here from Charles's office, intend-
ing to sort them into chronological order. Charles
had given her a neatly written synopsis of Quebec
City's history, beginning in 1535 when Jacques
Cartier, the French explorer and mariner, left the
shores of his native Saint-Malo and sailed across
the Atlantic to the New World for the second time.
Guided by friendly Micmac Indians, Cartier had
pushed upriver this time to explore the land the Indians called Canada. One discovery was the Indian
village of Stadacona—predecessor of Quebec City—
then a mere collection of huts huddled together
beneath the crest of Cape Diamond on the edge of a
vast forest.

Karin, always fascinated by history, had started
reading enthusiastically, glad she had something to
occupy her thoughts. But somewhere along the way
her mind had become distracted. Paul Dufresne's
lean face kept coming between her and her papers,
his blue eyes narrowed, smile triumphant.

No. She must not think about last night. She
brushed at her forehead as though that would erase

her thoughts, then forced herself to concentrate on her work.

The next stack of papers, she discovered, dealt with the dwellings of the French colonists, especially the Habitation constructed by another French explorer, Samuel de Champlain. Cartier had somehow survived that first winter in Quebec despite the scurvy that raged among his men. He had returned to France, then back to Quebec a third time in 1541. He went back to Saint-Malo the following year. It was left to Champlain to begin colonizing, which he started to do in 1608. His aim was to establish a strong French colony and to convert the natives to Christianity.

Champlain formed a strong friendship with the Indians of Canada and helped them in their constant battles against the Iroquois. He also did all he could to protect his small colony from the deprivations of winter, from warring Indians and eventually from the English, who wanted to drive the French from Quebec. This last was beyond his power, and in 1629, Quebec City was captured, and Champlain was taken as a prisoner to England. Still, Champlain worked unceasingly for his colony, and in 1632 an agreement was reached between France and England. At last, Champlain was able to return to Quebec in 1633 as Governor of New France, only to die two years later of a stroke.

The collection of notes and rough sketches dealing with the second French regime was a large one. The period had lasted more than one hundred years, until at the close of the Seven Years' War, France had ceded the colony to England again. The French regime obviously interested Charles the most. During it, Quebec had been made the administrative capital of New France. Intendant Jean Talon had been responsible for the master plan that established the importance of the port. Governor de Frontenac had arrived after him.

According to Charles's notes, Frontenac began the construction of the ramparts that eventually enclosed the Upper Town and protected it during the almost incessant wars with the Iroquois and the English colonies.

It was during the French regime that the city had acquired its ecclesiastical character. The Jesuits' college had been built then, and the Ursuline Convent and the Hôtel-Dieu Hospital. Many of the streets had been laid out, and elegant dwellings were constructed by French merchants.

Had Paul Dufresne's ancestors been rich merchants, Karin wondered. Lissa had said he came from an old family, a noble family. He owned a château. She hadn't come across a mention of it so far. Where was it, exactly? What was it like? Would she see it?

Would she even see Paul again? She hoped not. How could she have responded to him the way she did? If only she hadn't stayed for the Savards' party, danced to that strange, exotic music. Thank goodness her sanity had returned in time to avert....

Work. That was what she had come to Quebec to do. She picked up another paper. But she couldn't concentrate. She sat back in her chair, disgusted with herself. She had always been able to close out unwelcome thoughts when there was work to be done. Why was her usual discipline failing her now? Why did that insidious warmth keep stealing through her body, reminding her of the previous night and its subsequent embarrassment? She couldn't go on blaming the erotic nature of the dance for the way she had responded to Paul. He had affected her physically from the first moment she saw him. In his company she was not herself. It was as though she were enchanted—in the original meaning of the word. Bewitched. . . .

She laughed shortly at her choice of words. If this was enchantment, it was a dark enchantment that had nothing to do with her own free will or sense of logic.

Sighing, she swung her swivel chair to the window. She stared out at the green turrets and roofs of the Château Frontenac, noting that the sun was shining now. The early mist had dissolved, and it looked like it was going to be another glorious day.

The thought did not improve her spirits.

"How goes it?" Charles asked from the doorway behind her.

Startled, she swung her chair around to face him. "I was just. . . sorting things out in my mind," she said. She couldn't help smiling at Charles's appearance. He evidently had a habit of tugging at his brown hair while he worked. It was standing up on his head like a rooster's comb. And the clothes he wore! This morning he'd pulled on paint-stained trousers and a gray sweat shirt that had seen better days. There was even a tear in one shoulder. He looked so much like an untidy adolescent that she warmed to him all over again.

"I feel guilty about keeping you indoors on such a lovely day," he said earnestly. "It's too bad Paul couldn't make it today, but perhaps Lissa...."

"It's okay. I don't mind at all. I've already made a start." Quickly she showed him what she had done so far, and he gave her an approving smile. "Lissa said you'd get everything organized for me," he said. "God knows, I needed you. I'm amazed you can make head or tail of my mess."

"It's not a mess at all. Your writing is easy to read, and the synopsis helped a lot." She hesitated. "I wondered, though, are you going to use these sketches in the book?"

Charles picked up one of the papers from her desk—a set of drawings of Champlain's Habitation. Admittedly the construction itself had been rather crude—a group of two-storied wooden buildings with galleries around the second stories, a surrounding wooden wall and a moat around that. But these sketches were even cruder than Champlain's own.

Charles frowned. "Not very good, are they? We will be using photographs, of course, but for the old buildings that no longer exist or those that have been altered over the years, we will require drawings. My publisher is trying to find someone to do them."

Karin wondered if the publisher would consider André Moreau. The young man appeared to need money. But perhaps she should wait and ask him if he'd be interested before suggesting his name to Charles.

Charles had drifted toward his own study, looking at the paper he'd picked up. Obviously his mind had returned to his work. He was standing in the doorway now, frowning as though he didn't really see the paper. "There was something...." His frown faded and was replaced by a self-deprecating smile. "I never seem to remember things. I came in here to tell you that Paul telephoned."

Karin kept her face blank. "Yes?"

"He said... let me see now, what did he say? Oh, yes. He forgot to tell you last night that he will pick you up at ten tomorrow morning. He wants to show you the Lower Town."

"I understood he was going to be too busy," Karin said evenly.

"Oh, no. He's made arrangements for a colleague to take over his practice for several days. I'm really grateful to him. He's already given me so much help. I don't know what I'd have done without Paul." He looked at the paper he still held in his hand. "Now what was I going to do with this? Oh, yes." He came back into the room, briskly handed the paper to Karin and went out again, closing the door behind him.

She shook her head, smiling. What a dear he was.

The smile faded, but her face still felt stiff. She should have told Charles she didn't want to go with Paul. What a nerve the man had, calling Charles like that and leaving a message! Obviously he had not given up his pursuit of her. As André had said, he insisted on taking over people's lives. But how could she refuse to go with him when Charles was so grateful to him?

Paul Dufresne was an impossible, annoying, presumptuous man, she thought angrily. She was not going to waste any more time thinking about him.

By the time Lissa peered around the study door, she was deeply involved in her work. Lissa looked astonished to see her. She hadn't been up when Karin began. "I thought I heard someone in here," she exclaimed, coming into the room. "Isn't Paul working with you today?"

"Not until tomorrow." Karin was proud of the evenness of her tone. "Today I'm committed to paperwork."

"Good Lord, you *are* efficient. I don't know how you can work after that terrific party. My head feels as though it's coming apart at the seams. What do you suppose was *in* that wine?"

"Something potent, that's for sure," Karin said dryly. "I take it you had a good time?"

"Fantastic. It was so wonderful to meet all those people. There were some pretty important people there, you know. René Leclerc is a real-estate tycoon, and that fellow at our table—Pierre Fontaine—is one of the shipping Fontaines. I'm sure last night will lead to more invitations." She pirouetted with sudden excitement, her headache evidently forgotten. "I knew Paul would be the key to unlock doors in this city. Isn't he just too, too divine?"

"Indubitably."

The dryness of Karin's tone escaped Lissa. She smiled happily and flopped into a chair on the other side of the desk. "A lot of those people are Paul's patients, you know," she confided. "He has the wealthiest practice in town."

"So you said."

"Well, I suppose wealthy people have a right to

medical care just like the rest of us peasants," Lissa said with a laugh.

"And I'm sure they pay their bills without complaint."

This time her sarcasm penetrated Lissa's bubbling mood. She looked sharply at Karin, her green eyes wide. "Hey, you sound a bit unraveled this morning."

Karin sighed. "I'm sorry. It's just that I think a doctor should be available to all people—not just those who can afford his services."

Lissa shrugged. "Paul's a good doctor. Sara Savard was telling me last night how much he's helped her. She suffered from migraines all her life, she said, but since Paul took over her medical care, she hasn't required any medication at all. He taught her relaxation procedures to get rid of tension, and as long as she practices them, she has no trouble at all." She raised her eyebrows at Karin. "I would think Paul Dufresne could teach anyone to relax, wouldn't you?"

"No doubt."

Lissa ignored her sarcasm. She leaned back in her chair, a slow smile spreading across her pretty face. "We had a marvelous lunch yesterday. It was super to have lunch with a man for a change. Charles always has a sandwich in his office. Even Etienne was bearable, thanks to you. I guess he enjoyed his walk with you." She sat forward abruptly. "What happened to you, by the way? Paul was quite put out when you didn't turn up."

"I just . . . forgot," Karin said carefully.

"How could anyone forget Paul Dufresne? What

about last night? Did *you* have a good time? You were sound asleep by the time we got home, and I was dying to talk to you. You certainly looked as though you were enjoying yourself. Wow—that was quite a dance! Everybody was talking about it.''

Karin sighed. She was not going to admit to Lissa that she had pretended sleep when she heard her footsteps on the stairs, that she had barely slept all night. And she was not, definitely not, going to get drawn into another discussion about Paul Dufresne. She had made a fool of herself, yes, but it wasn't going to happen again. All she wanted to do was to forget last night, forget her own stupidity.

BUT DESPITE ALL HER GOOD INTENTIONS, that proved impossible to do. By the time Paul arrived the next day, she had lost patience with herself. She had not been able to banish him from her thoughts at all. That scene in the basement had repeated and repeated itself in her mind while she worked, while she studied French with Etienne, even while she slept. More than anything, she had dreaded seeing Paul again, sure that he would continue as before, perhaps even make reference to her humiliation.

But to her surprise, though his greeting was pleasant, it was also somewhat distant. "Karin, how nice you look," he said when she entered the living room.

She murmured something unintelligible, trying to ignore the quickening of her pulses. Evidently he liked wearing cotton knit shirts, she thought. He was wearing a blue one today with tight-fitting white chinos. Probably he knew how well the knit fabric molded itself to the hard muscled contours of his lean upper body. Or perhaps he wore such shirts because they were cool, she amended, trying to be fair.

He was looking her over with obvious approval of her lemon-colored shirt and white linen slacks. "I see you are wearing sensible shoes," he said. "Very good. I have planned much walking for us today. I hope you don't object?"

"I like to walk."

"So Etienne has told me."

She hadn't even noticed Etienne was in the room. He was standing next to the windows, smiling shyly at her. "Would you like to come with us?" she asked impulsively.

"Another time perhaps," Paul said before the boy could answer.

Etienne shrugged and looked down at the floor. Then he left the room, his shoulders hunched. Annoyed, Karin looked at Paul. "We could have taken him. He gets bored here. I really don't understand your attitude toward Etienne. Can't you see that he needs help? Lissa told me you said he could eat as much as he wants to. Surely he should be on a diet."

"That is true. If he were an adult, I would prescribe a diet for him. But a child must first be motivated, or he will sneak candy or something similar when no one is watching. Etienne uses food as an escape. Or perhaps he associates it with nurturing." He frowned. "Charles has confessed to me that his first wife believed in feeding Etienne on demand when he was a baby. Which is all right, unless the mother feeds the baby every time he cries whether he is hungry or not. He comes, then, to look upon food as his only source of attention. I understand that

Louise carried this custom beyond infancy. Whenever Etienne was upset, she comforted him with food. So naturally when she died, he knew of no other way to comfort himself.''

He shrugged. "However, that is a simplistic diagnosis. Until I can discover precisely what is troubling him, it will do no good to antagonize him by taking away his food. I see Etienne at my clinic every week. I am attempting to get to the bottom of his troubles. And he is beginning to trust me. I believe he will confide in me soon.''

"Oh," Karin said lamely.

"As for my refusing to allow him to accompany us," he went on, obviously enjoying her discomfiture, "Lissa has told me that she and Etienne are going swimming today. He does not want to go. That is why I was a little sharp. I think it is necessary that he spend time with Lissa, and the Leclercs have invited her to use their swimming pool. Their boys are older than Etienne, but they are nice boys. They will make Etienne feel welcome, I'm sure." He paused. "You remember the Leclercs?"

The indirect reference to Wednesday's party brought a flush of heat to Karin's face, and she turned away to hide it. "Of course, a charming couple." She hesitated. "I'm sorry, I guess I misjudged your attitude toward Etienne."

"I think perhaps you misjudge me quite often," he said with an insufferably superior smile. With difficulty she bit back the retort that had sprung to her lips.

She had to wait a moment outside while he locked his car. He was leaving it parked in front of the Vincent house for the rest of the day. A silver gray Mercedes, she noted. Probably he felt a status car like that was necessary to maintain his image as a successful man.

"That's quite a car," she said as they began walking along the street.

He smiled. "Very distinguée, is it not? It belongs to a friend of mine who is away. I drive it occasionally while she is gone, to keep the battery charged. My own car is more serviceable—a small American Buick."

She, Karin noted. Yet another woman in Paul Dufresne's life? How many did that make?

"My friend is seventy years old," Paul said as though he'd read her mind. "She insists on keeping her large car in spite of the energy shortage. She is too old to change, she says."

So she had misjudged him again. What did it matter?

They were walking past the Château Frontenac now, heading toward the river. Paul told her that Franklin D. Roosevelt and Winston Churchill had met at the hotel with Mackenzie King, the Canadian prime minister, during World War II. "This city has had many connections with war," he said.

"Yes. I read about some of them yesterday," she said, matching his casual tone.

He nodded approval. "Charles told me you occupied yourself well. I am sorry I was unable to be with you."

His voice sounded genuinely regretful. But he was with Maggie, Karin reminded herself.

As though Karin's thought of Maggie had conjured her up, the girl herself hailed them a moment later. They had reached the edge of Dufferin Terrace where the calèches were parked. "Good morning, Dr. Paul, Karin," Maggie said. She was perched on her high seat, smiling at them. Behind her, two middle-aged ladies, obviously tourists, were sitting together under a load of packages, staring at Paul. With a great deal of appreciation, Karin noticed.

"*Bonjour,* Maggie," Paul said easily. "How are you today?"

"Never better."

Behind Maggie's calèche two others waited to be hired. They were also attended by young women. Paul greeted them by name, but they didn't respond. The thin blond girl pretended to be busy polishing the brasses on her horse's harness. The other had glossy black hair that hung to her waist. She pushed it back with her hands and avoided Paul's gaze, looking as though she wished she were somewhere else.

Paul frowned at their lack of response but made no comment. "They didn't look too happy to see you," Karin couldn't resist saying as she and Paul descended a flight of steps.

His glance was quizzical. "Sometimes my charm fails me."

Insufferable man.

At the foot of the steps a very steep road wound down toward the wide shining river. "Côte de la Montagne," Paul said. "But we will take these steps to the side. They are called the Breakneck Steps. An enchanting name, don't you think?"

"Enchanting," Karin echoed flatly.

Again Paul glanced at her, and she thought she

saw his mouth twitch a little at one side. "You are angry with me, Mademoiselle Karin?"

"Of course I'm not angry," she said airily.

"*Vraiment?* Really?" He frowned. "I had thought you were perhaps...upset because of our little contretemps the other night."

"Little contretemps"! Was that all it had meant to him?

"You must not worry," he went on before she had a chance to object to his wording. "I am not one to hold grudges."

Goaded by his effrontery, Karin stopped abruptly on the steep steps—an unwise thing to do. She might have stumbled if his hand hadn't shot out to support her elbow. Immediately shock waves reverberated all the way up her arm to her shoulder. She knew at once that he had felt her reaction, but she didn't pull away. She wouldn't give him that satisfaction. For a moment his eyes held hers, then he smiled lazily. "I have not *forgotten*, however, my Karin." His fingers moved gently over the cotton sleeve of her blouse. "I have not forgotten anything."

"You would do well to forget," she retorted. "It won't happen again."

"No?" He shook his head ruefully. "Ah, yes, you mentioned that you do not believe in fate. But you are wrong. Some things are inevitable."

"Like death and taxes?" she asked sarcastically.

"Like love and war."

"Then we will be at war."

He laughed appreciatively. "I enjoy battling wits with you. You are a worthy combatant." He started down the steps again, still holding her elbow but exerting no pressure on it. "As I said before, this city has seen many wars. Whole armies have attempted to storm the cliffs there." He waved a hand in the general direction of Cape Diamond. "But you know," he went on easily, "no commander expects to win a war with the first skirmish. Sometimes it is necessary to be patient, to lay siege. The British General Wolfe could have told you that. It took him almost three months to win this city from the French General Montcalm at the end of the Seven Years' War."

He accompanied this statement with a disarming smile. Was that supposed to be an analogy, Karin wondered. She certainly wasn't going to ask. But she must remember to be wary. He was a clever man, Paul Dufresne. Too clever.

But then as they strolled the streets of the Lower Town, Paul became the perfect tour guide again. Karin felt herself relaxing as he talked interestingly about the buildings in terms of construction, describing how they had originally been built with hatchets and wood chisels and other simple tools, and held together with wooden pegs. At the end of the nineteenth century, he told her, the district had been disfigured by the construction of tall flat-roofed brick buildings. Around 1960, when fire destroyed several houses, the old walls of the French regime were rediscovered. This led to the restoration and the recreation of Place Royale, which the early colonists had used as a meeting place.

Place Royale itself was a charming square with a bronze bust of Louis XIV on a stone pedestal at its center. On three sides of the square, beautifully restored stone houses huddled together, their steeply sloping roofs shining in the sunlight. Windows sparkled with cleanliness, and fresh paint gleamed on doors and window frames. In several window boxes the blue-and-white fleur-de-lis flag of Quebec fluttered proudly, and bright flowers bloomed. A small stone church made up the fourth side of the square.

"The Lower Town contains the largest concentration of seventeenth- and eighteenth-century buildings in North America," Paul told her. "The first colonists copied the Norman style with which they were familiar. Gradually, though, the style accommodated itself to the climate and new ways of life." He gestured expansively. "Imagine, Karin, Champlain walked on this ground, and Cartier, also. Noble men and women, priests, nuns, fur traders, shipbuilders. Frontenac was here and Montcalm and Monseigneur François de Laval, who founded the Quebec Seminary. And before them all, the Indians."

His voice had softened as he spoke. He was looking inward now, apparently not seeing the sunlit square at all, feeling for words as though he spoke to himself and not to her. "When I was a boy," he said slowly, "I used to love to walk through the city at twilight on a quiet evening in autumn, when leaves were blowing about in the old streets. It seemed to me then that I could feel those people all around me, that great company of the past. What courage they had! So many frontiers to cross, so many dangers to meet and overcome. I would walk past the Séminaire de Québec in the Upper Town, and I would think that if I looked up quickly, without warning, I would see tall old Bishop Laval walking by with a lantern swinging from his hand, or Champlain striding along, rugged and noble in his bearing. When I stood on the Plains of Abraham and narrowed my eyes just so, I saw tall-masted ships from France riding at anchor in the river, their rigging making patterns against the sky. The river was a highway in the old days as it is now, a moving glittering highway along which men could travel in search of adventure. What men they must have been!"

He stopped talking abruptly, slanted a sideways glance at Karin's bemused face and laughed a little sheepishly, she thought. It was an odd experience to see the lordly Paul Dufresne looking sheepish—a refreshing experience. "You must excuse me," he said. "Sometimes I get carried away."

"You really love this city, don't you?"

"Yes," he said. "It is in my bones, I suppose. One of my ancestors came here during Champlain's time." He laughed. "I understand from letters I have read that he was more interested in the variety of wildfowl to be shot on these shores than in Champlain's noble aims, but he grew up in a hurry once he was here. He worked side by side with the peasants, hauling supplies from the ships that came and helping with the building. Eventually he sent for a girl of good character he had known in France, and she came out to be his bride. According to her diaries, she was not impressed by Quebec at first. The house her husband had built had a leaky roof; the wind shook the doors on their rusty hinges; and she was sure the fine linens she had brought with her would mildew. But she stayed for love of him. And my ancestor did eventually make a fortune in the fur trade. He and his wife had five children; most of the Dufresnes were quite prolific. And they all loved Quebec. However, wars and illness and various calamities took their toll on their numbers. I am the last Dufresne. Which is why my mother nags me constantly to marry.''

"Why haven't you married?" she asked curiously.

He shrugged. "Becoming a doctor takes a long time. I have been very busy establishing my practice. And I have other business ventures that require much of my time. Most of the Dufresnes, you see, were singularly unambitious. They were content to live here on their inheritance without increasing it to any degree. My grandfather, for example, was something of a profligate. He preferred the gambling casinos of Monte Carlo to his home. And he wasn't a very *good* gambler. My father tried to restore the family fortunes through investments, but he was not a strong man and was unable to supervise his affairs as he should have done. He was afflicted with chronic asthma.''

His eyebrows quirked in that disconcerting way they had. "You don't happen to have a fortune hidden away in Seattle, do you? My mother feels it would be fortuitous if I were to marry a rich woman.''

"I'm afraid not," Karin said lightly. "And if I had, I doubt I would invest it in a man who has the reputation of breaking female hearts.''

"Ah, you should not listen to gossip. Can I help it if women throw themselves at my feet? It is not my fault, you see. The Dufresnes may have been rogues, but they have always been charming rogues.''

This smug conceit was so humorously presented that she could not prevent herself from laughing. All the same, she thought, he had shown her a different side of himself today, one she could admire and feel comfortable with. She watched him curiously as they continued their tour of the old houses. Without reading any of the signs or literature, he was able to explain the various displays to her, and he talked easily of the early Amerindian culture and the ways in which the city had developed since then.

She was amazed at the extent of his knowledge. What an accomplished man he was! He knew history and architecture and an impressive amount of anthropology. And he was also supposed to be a very good doctor.

None of which, she cautioned herself, made him any more reliable where women were concerned.

SHE COULDN'T BE SURE AFTERWARD exactly when she first saw André. She thought possibly he might have gone past the little grocery store when she and Paul were eating a quick lunch there. But she wasn't sure. The city was full of bearded young men.

The grocery store had a long counter down one side, serving fast food and beverages. Paul apologized for its lack of atmosphere but assured her the sandwiches were very good. Which they were. Now that he had stopped baiting her, it was possible for her to relax. He could be so very charming when he chose. He drew her out to talk about her childhood in Seattle, her parents, her school. She had attended a parochial school as he had. He could imagine her, he said, in a starched white blouse and pleated skirt. "And ankle socks," he added.

"White ankle socks," she admitted.

She found herself telling him more about her childhood that she had ever told anyone except Ray. It had been a lonely childhood, she supposed. Yet she had thought she was happy. She had plenty of books to read always and her ballet lessons. Her parents were good to her, taking her everywhere they went. Her mother was a mathematics teacher, and she played the piano brilliantly. Her father taught science at the local university.

"You were an only child?" Paul asked. "So was I. My father died when I was seventeen. Until then we were good friends, but he and my mother did not encourage me to be with them too much once I was past elementary school. However, I always had many friends to play with. There was ice hockey and skiing and football and bicycling—always much to do. Do you not ski, Karin? I have heard there is good skiing in Washington state."

"My mother was always afraid I would break a leg," she said with a small laugh. But he did not look amused. He regarded her so intently for a while that she felt every thought she had ever thought must be on display. It was a disconcerting feeling, and she was relieved when he suggested they return to their tour.

When they came out into the square again and crossed over to examine the bust of Louis XIV, she looked around, but no one who looked like André was anywhere in sight. A wedding party was emerging from the old church on the other side of the square, stopping to pose for photographs on the stone steps. The sun shone on the obviously happy couple, and the church bells began pealing merrily. Karin felt a pang of regret. If Barbara Travis had not come along, she might have stood so in a long white gown and veil, holding securely to her groom's arm.

"Notre Dame des Victoires," Paul said behind her, and she came to herself with a start. "The church is named 'Our Lady of Victories.' It was built on the original site of Champlain's Habitation. Would you like to see inside it after the wedding party leaves?"

She nodded absently, watching the wedding guests bombard the bride and groom with confetti. The bride was smiling up at her new husband as he held open one of the wedding-car doors for her. The sight saddened Karin. Would she have been happy married to Ray, she wondered. Or would she have ended up like Lissa, discontented with her lot? The thought made her feel vaguely disloyal. She had *loved* Ray. She had been heartbroken when he left her for Barbara.

"Your face is very interesting," Paul said.

She looked at him blankly.

"I have been watching you for several minutes. So many emotions flitting across your face. Not happy thoughts, I think."

"No, not happy thoughts."

"Then you must put them out of your mind. A day like this is meant to enjoy, *n'est-ce pas*?"

He took her hand and held it as the wedding cars drove past. Quite suddenly Karin felt a lifting of her spirits. "Weddings always make me sad," she said lightly as they climbed the steps to the church.

Paul laughed. He had released her hand. "They

make me happy," he said. "I am always grateful that I am not the groom."

"I suppose you would be," Karin said with an edge to her voice. "Marriage would curtail your social life considerably."

"It does not bear thinking about," he said with a mock shudder.

And then they were inside the church. Karin wondered how one small building could contain so much beauty. Such a glory of religious paintings and a blur of candles burning in front of a high altar that was built curiously in the form of a castle with turrets, battlements and windows. From the ceiling of the church hung a large model of a sailing ship, all tall masts and rigging. "Is the ship a votive offering of some kind?" she asked Paul.

"*Oui*. It was donated by the Marquis of Tracy, who was for a time lieutenant-general over all the French dominions in the West. The church has an interesting history. It was originally dedicated to the Infant Jesus, but in 1690 the inhabitants changed it to 'Our Lady of the Victory' to celebrate their survival of a siege. Later, during another attempted attack, a fleet of English ships went aground in a dense fog. So the church became 'Our Lady of Victories.' That did not stop the church from being destroyed in Wolfe's bombardment, but it was restored again to its original glory, which is a kind of victory, also, don't you agree?"

"It's beautiful," Karin said, feeling the word was inadequate. She felt a sense of serenity in the place. Paul, too, seemed to be affected by the calm atmosphere. As he wasn't looking at her now, she took the opportunity to study him. She was becoming very curious about this man. He was standing straight and tall, head thrown back, the fingers of one hand lightly caressing the end piece of a high-backed wooden pew. Noble in his bearing, she thought, remembering his description of Samuel de Champlain. He looked lean and strong and self-confident—invincible. The shadows thrown by the flickering candlelight had softened the features beneath the thick black hair and darkened his eyes. He had drawn into himself again. He was something of an enigma, this man. He was obviously more complex than she had first thought. Had he really held her in his arms and kissed her so violently? Had he really stripped her of her clothing and. . . .

She caught herself up, horrified at the direction of her thoughts. At the same time she saw that Paul had become aware of her scrutiny and was amused by it. His lean body indicated watchfulness, and his mouth was curving in that certain way that meant he was about to say something provocative.

Abruptly she turned on her heel and left the church. The sunlight on the stone buildings blinded her for a moment after the candlelit interior of the church, and she hesitated outside the door.

A bus was parked at the corner now, and a large group of tourists had invaded the square. Europeans by the sound of them. Leaning against the pedestal that supported the bust of Louis XIV was a young man playing a guitar and singing "Sur le pont d'Avignon." He had a very good voice, a tenor voice, rich and true. The tourists were crowded around him, listening and clapping in time to his music. For a second, Karin thought again that she saw André, and she tried to pick him out from the crowd, but she couldn't see him now.

Some of the tourists were aiming cameras at the church, and Karin felt self-conscious as Paul took her arm to escort her down the steps. He waved to the photographers, totally unconcerned. "Smile, *chérie*," he said. "Just think, we will be preserved as a couple in a multitude of otherwise boring slide shows." He inclined his head to look at her face. "What were you staring at just now?"

"I thought I saw André."

"Here? Possibly. This area is one of his favorites for sketching." His voice was casual, but his hand had tightened on her arm. What had caused his tension? "Why don't you like André?" she asked. "He seems a nice boy, though a bit moody. Why are you always so unkind to him?"

His smile was thin. "I am not unkind to André."

"How can you say that? You act as though you own him—ordering him around, speaking to him as though he were a stupid child."

Paul laughed shortly. "Sometimes he is a stupid child," he said, but his tone was vague, as though he had no interest in the conversation.

They had paused at the foot of the steps, and as his voice trailed away, she felt him stiffen again. He was looking between the milling tourists in the direction of the grocery store. A man was half sitting on the low window ledge outside the store. A man in a shabby brown suit. The jacket looked too big for him. He was wearing an equally disreputable cap pulled low down on his forehead. He looked, Karin thought, like one of the derelicts that abounded in Seattle's Pioneer Place. Except that instead of a wine bottle, he was clutching an ice-cream cone and eating it as though he were half-starved—oblivious of the camera-wielding tourists or the pigeons pecking hopefully around his feet.

Paul gripped her arm more tightly and hurried her around the corner. "Do you know that man?" she asked.

"There was a particular man?" His voice sounded vague.

She stared at his profile. His face had closed out all expression. Why was he urging her along as though they were fleeing from something—or someone? He seemed to be deep in thought. She could almost hear his mind working. "Paul?" she said tentatively, but he ignored her.

Suddenly she heard the sound of pounding feet behind her. Paul whirled around even as she did. She half expected to see the man in the shabby brown suit, but it was André who was chasing after them. *"Il est ici,"* he said to Paul. *He is here.*

"I saw him," Paul answered impatiently in French. "I've been watching for him, but I didn't expect him so early. I had to get Karin away first."

It took a second for Karin to realize she was understanding every word. Etienne's lessons were paying off. What she didn't understand was the significance of the exchange between Paul and André. Paul was looking at her now, frowning. "I am afraid I have been most forgetful," he said hastily. "I have an unavoidable appointment." He pointed along the street. "If you go in that shop there, the

Nautilus, you will see the *funiculaire*, the elevator. It will take you back to Dufferin Terrace. No doubt you can find your way home from there.''

''But Paul....'' Karin found she was talking to empty air. Paul and André had already gone. Dumbfounded, she stood still for a second, then hurried back to the corner. Both men were edging around the tourists who were now boarding their bus. The guitar player was still singing. As she watched, Paul and André reached the grocery store and stopped beside the man in the brown suit. They were soon engaged in conversation. After a moment the seedy-looking man laughed.

Afraid they would look up and see her spying on them, she retraced her steps around the corner and headed toward the *funiculaire*. Her mind was seething with curiosity. What business did that odd trio have together? And why had she been dumped around the corner like so much excess baggage? Why had Paul been so secretive, so devious? Had he felt ashamed of his friend's shabby appearance?

She was abruptly furious with him. Which seemed to be a common enough occurrence. He was not only conceited and domineering, he could also be impossibly rude. How dare he desert her so abruptly, just when she'd begun to...admire him?

CHAPTER SEVEN

PAUL DID NOT TELEPHONE or come over that evening, but then Karin hadn't really expected him to after the rude way he'd deserted her. His car still sat in front of the house. After dinner with the Vincents she went upstairs to her room and began reading a book about the history of the St. Lawrence River, one of the dullest books she had ever read. But it served its purpose. It put her to sleep.

Dinner had not been a success. Charles was preoccupied, Lissa jittery, Etienne withdrawn and sullen.

Madame Durocher had tried to jolly them all into a better mood as she served the *omelettes aux fines herbes*, but she'd given up after a while, discouraged by the lack of response. Etienne and Charles were the only ones who finished dinner. Etienne also ate two helpings of dessert with the manners of someone who had been starved for a week. Lissa hadn't commented but watched him with eyes that glittered with unshed tears. She didn't speak until the meal was over, and then she took a deep breath and poured out the story of her day.

Apparently the outing to the Leclercs had been a disaster. Etienne had refused to swim, had refused to even put on his swimsuit. He had locked himself into one of the dressing rooms on the Leclercs' lanai, and all Lissa's pleading and threats had failed to bring him out until it was time to come home. "Can you imagine how embarrassed I was?" Lissa wailed. "The boys tried so hard to be nice to Etienne, and he wouldn't even talk to them. René and Marie will never invite us back—never!"

Charles had murmured sympathy, then took Etienne into the living room for a scolding. Five minutes later Etienne had emerged, his father's hand on his shoulder pushing him to stand in front of his stepmother. Eyelids lowered, mouth set mutinously, he muttered, "I am sorry, *madame*," through clenched teeth, then marched to the doorway, where he turned. "Are you going to leave us soon?" he asked Lissa coldly.

Then he'd taken himself off to bed.

Lissa burst into tears.

Charles patted her shoulder in an abstracted way until she stopped crying. "He'll come out of it, dear," he'd said kindly as he wiped her eyes with his table napkin. Then he went quietly off to his study with the relieved air of one who has performed his duty to his family and is now free to pursue his own interests.

For a few minutes Lissa had sat staring moodily into space, while Karin tried to think of something to say that might help. "Is there anything I can do?" she asked at last.

"I don't want to talk about it," Lissa said in a choked voice, and she stood up and left the room. A moment later Karin had heard her going down to the basement, and a few minutes after that she heard the sound of the television set downstairs. That was when she'd decided to go upstairs to bed.

IN THE MORNING Karin awoke early. Feeling a need to get out of the house, she put on a sweat suit and sneakers and let herself quietly out of the front door.

She saw that the Mercedes was gone. She wasn't sure how she felt about that. Relieved, perhaps.

After a good brisk walk along Dufferin Terrace she felt she could face the day. A shower and fresh clothes added to her sense of well-being, and she went downstairs with a light step.

Charles and Etienne were in the dining room, breakfasting. Charles was reading a newspaper, Etienne eating stolidly. Neither of them looked up. The general atmosphere was glum.

Karin's spirits sank again. But then to her amazement, she heard Lissa chattering brightly to Madame Durocher in the kitchen. Something had evidently improved Lissa's mood overnight. What, Karin wondered as she helped herself to a half a grapefruit and a croissant from the sideboard and sat down.

She wasn't left in doubt for long. After Etienne took himself off, mumbling that he was going to the park, Lissa came in and gave her a brilliant smile. "Paul dropped in last night," she announced.

"I noticed the car was gone," Karin said noncommittally, aware that beyond the kitchen door Madame Durocher was all ears.

Lissa nodded. "I thought I heard something and looked out the basement window, and saw him unlocking the door of the Mercedes—isn't that a fabulous car? It belongs to one of his patients, a friend of his mother, I understand. But can you imagine, he was going to just drive off without even telling us. He was afraid it was too late to disturb us, he said. Naturally I insisted he come in for a drink.''

''What time was that?'' Charles asked, glancing over the top of his newspaper.

Lissa shrugged. ''About midnight, I suppose.''

Charles put the paper down, gave Lissa an aggrieved look. ''You should have called me, dear. I was still up.''

Lissa pouted prettily. ''You always say you don't want to be disturbed when you're working.''

''That doesn't apply to Paul. I would not want to offend him.''

''He didn't seem to mind being alone with me,'' Lissa said. ''He was rather tense when he came in. He'd had a rough evening, he said, but he relaxed after a drink.'' She giggled. ''Well, we had two actually. And we talked for a long time.'' She hesitated. ''Paul is *such* a good listener,'' she added with a small sigh and a sideways glance at Charles.

Karin squirmed uncomfortably in her chair, but Charles didn't seem to notice that Lissa was deliberately baiting him.

Lissa glanced at Karin. ''Paul said to tell you he'd be free again on Monday, but not before. He will call for you at ten o'clock Monday morning. He said he regretted having to run out on you yesterday, but it was unavoidable. What was that all about?''

''He had an appointment he'd forgotten.''

Lissa raised her eyebrows. ''That doesn't sound like Paul. You two didn't have a fight, did you?''

''Why should we have a fight?''

"Well, you do seem a bit prickly when he's around. I'm sure Paul's noticed it. He seemed quite relieved when I told him you'd gone to bed."

Charles was looking at them both with a questioning expression. "Is something wrong?" he asked.

Karin managed a smile that felt stiff on her face. "Nothing at all."

"And guess what, Charles," Lissa exclaimed. "Paul's agreed to teach me the relaxation procedures he taught Sara Savard. I'm to make an appointment at his office the week after next."

"I'd rather you didn't do that," Charles said, and Karin thought, *well, he's finally seen the light.*

But when Lissa demanded to know why not, he answered, "Paul's a friend. He might feel he can't bill us for treatment. It might be awkward."

Karin sighed.

Lissa gave Charles an exasperated look. "He billed us for Etienne's consultations."

Charles's face brightened. "So he did. I suppose it will be all right, then." He patted Lissa's hand. "It will probably do you good, dear. Paul's a good man."

And with that he picked up his newspaper again. Lissa glanced at him with an expression on her pretty face that Karin couldn't quite interpret. It looked almost...pitying. After a moment Lissa sighed but didn't speak. She had a dreamy expression on her face now, her small chin propped on her hands, elbows leaning on the table. Was she thinking about Paul Dufresne? Had she entertained him in the basement? Had he sat beside her on the crimson couch and taken her drink from her hand and looked at her and....

Karin straightened in her chair. "Did Paul happen to mention André?" she asked Lissa.

"Who's André?" Lissa asked in an uninterested voice.

"An artist. I met him a couple of days ago. He's an acquaintance of Paul."

Lissa shook her head. "No, I don't recall the name. Why do you ask?"

"He's the one Paul had the appointment with, I think."

Lissa's smooth forehead puckered a little. "No, I don't remember Paul mentioning him at all." She glanced quickly at Charles as though checking to see if he was listening. "I don't remember *what* we talked about most of the time," she said and giggled.

With another sidelong glance at Charles and a wink at Karin she collected her breakfast dishes and headed into the kitchen. Charles put down his paper, glanced at his watch and stood up. "Time to go to work," he said, still blissfully unaware. He smiled good-naturedly at Karin. "For me, not for you. Why don't you relax today? You look a little tired."

Hardly surprising, Karin thought as she watched him amble out of the room. Meals at the Vincent house were a draining experience.

As she drank her coffee, she picked up the newspaper Charles had left and thumbed through it. It was written in French so didn't offer much distraction. She should go out again, she thought, or go down to the basement and see how the bar rail worked out for ballet exercises. Perhaps that would help her recapture some of the good feeling her earlier walk had given her. Or she could go back to her paperwork. Refolding the newspaper, she set it down and pushed back her chair, then froze, staring at the photograph on the paper's back page. The picture was a little grainy and rather blurred, but the face was that of the man she had seen in Place Royale—the man André and Paul had met with in the square as soon as she had been hustled out of the way. This was a Montreal paper, but the dateline on the feature was Ville de Québec—Quebec City.

She studied the caption under the picture. *Henri Valier.* That was all she could make out apart from a verb or two. The headline didn't mean anything to her, either. What did *drogues* mean? She attempted the first line of the story. *Un criminel*—that must be a criminal. And dear God, *drogues* must be drugs! She had to have someone translate this for her. Lissa's French wasn't much better than hers. Madame Durocher? No. How could she explain why she wanted the story translated? Ditto Charles. That left Etienne.

She found Etienne sitting disconsolately on a bench in the Jardin des Gouverneurs, holding a large red ball on his lap. Poor little lonely boy, she thought. He was obviously still distressed about yesterday. And probably he had refused to swim only because he was afraid he would look ridiculous in a swimsuit.

He didn't seem particularly pleased to see her. "It's time for another French lesson," she told him, handing him the newspaper. He looked at her blankly. "I want you to help me translate the news of the day," she said, then sat as patiently as she could while Etienne laboriously pointed out words on the front page and interpreted them for her. Then she turned the section over and indicated the story that interested her. "*Drogues* means drugs, *n'est-ce pas?*"

"*Oui, mademoiselle.* This is about a criminal who was arrested yesterday. He is a—how do you say it— a dealer in unlawful drugs."

"What kind of drugs?"

He looked back at the story, moved his lips in silence for a moment. "I don't know these words," he said. Then he spelled out "heroin" and "marijuana" and hesitated again. Karin looked over his shoulder at the place where his finger was pointing. "Amphetamines and barbiturates," she said. She hadn't gone that far into the story.

Her brain was racing, trying to understand. Henri Valier was a drug dealer. Amphetamines and barbiturates were obtainable from a doctor. Paul was a doctor. Paul had met with the man yesterday afternoon. And André. André had red-rimmed eyes— she'd thought perhaps he didn't sleep well. But hadn't she read somewhere that marijuana users sometimes had bloodshot eyes?

Etienne was staring at her now. He must be wondering. "That's very interesting," she said lamely. "Does it say anything else?"

"Only that the police had been looking for this man, Henri Valier, for some time. He has been arrested before, but not convicted. He is a go-between, they say. But they do not know where he obtains his supplies, and he has always refused to tell them."

About to ask Etienne if there was much of a drug problem in the city, she hesitated. How would he know? He was only ten years old. And anyway, if a drug pusher had been arrested in the city, there must be a problem. Drug abuse was an international problem nowadays, especially among the young.

She couldn't seem to think coherently. She kept staring at the newspaper photograph as though if she stared at it long enough, the microdots would rearrange themselves into another face, one she had never seen. Her mind kept flashing images of Paul and André hurrying away from her, rushing back to this man Valier. Somewhere in another part of her mind she could hear Maggie saying about Paul, "Know him? I couldn't get along without him."

The statement seemed to have an ominous significance now, as did André's words: "He makes people too...dependent upon him." Dependent in what way?

And what about the envelope Paul had pressed on André the first time she saw them together? What had that envelope contained?

"Thank you," she managed to say at last. *"Merci beaucoup."*

Her use of French brought out Etienne's shy smile, but he was still looking at her in a puzzled way, and she tried to put the newspaper feature out of her mind and concentrate on him.

For a while they played a desultory game of ball, but Karin kept fumbling; her mind wouldn't stay on the game. She was shocked beyond measure, though she kept telling herself that there must be a perfectly logical explanation for Paul's behavior yesterday. And André's. Yet somehow too many things had fallen into place—even the girls who had ignored

Paul's greeting yesterday. They had really acted very strangely, had not wanted to meet his eyes. Why? Did they know something about Paul? Could she ask them? Should she go to the police? But what could she tell them? She had no *proof* that Paul had done anything wrong.

Another thought stopped her hands in midair as she was about to throw the ball to Etienne. "Did the paper say where the man, Valier, was from?" she asked him.

He frowned, thinking. "It said he was from Montreal," he said at last.

And she could hear Marie Leclerc's teasing voice: "Do you have *special* interests there, Paul? Tell me, are they business interests or romantic ones?"

Paul had avoided answering her.

She shook her head. Her imagination was running away with her. And yet why was Paul unable to take her touring this weekend? Supposedly he had arranged for free time. Was he also in trouble with the police?

Etienne was taking the ball from her. "I think you do not really want to play," he said reproachfully.

"I'm sorry, Etienne. I guess I'm not in the mood. Would you like to do something else?"

"It is all right. I will play by myself."

Should she take him for a calèche ride? Perhaps she could find one of those girls and—no, she couldn't do that. If she asked the calèche driver about drugs, Etienne would wonder what on earth she was up to. He might even get the wrong idea about *her*.

And Etienne was looking at her expectantly. She

couldn't desert him now. She glanced at her watch. It was nine-forty-five. "How about the Changing of the Guard?" she said on a sudden inspiration.

He considered. "Very well, *mademoiselle*."

"Why don't you just call me Karin?" she suggested after they dropped the ball and the newspaper off at the house.

He looked shocked. "My mother always told me not to call adults by their Christian names. It is not polite."

"Aunt Karin, then," she suggested, though the title didn't appeal to her. It sounded stodgy.

"Tante Karin?"

"Even better. Tante Karin it shall be."

Together they scrambled up the hillside to the Citadel, arriving a few minutes after the ceremony had begun. There were hundreds of spectators already there, most of them photographing the spectacle for posterity. The guards were smart in their tight red jackets and tall black furry hats. The music was stirring. But Karin couldn't really enjoy the intricate marching or interpret the orders being shouted in French. Her mind kept bouncing thoughts back and forth in time to the beating drums.

But it was pointless to speculate about Paul's involvement with Henri Valier, she decided at last. She would have to wait until she saw him again—demand an explanation.

After the ceremony was over, she and Etienne went to rue du Trésor to collect her painting. André was there. So were a lot of tourists. She had forgotten this was Saturday. André handed her the painting and took her money without comment. She thought he seemed a little distant. But then when Etienne wandered away to look at the next artist's lithographs, André glanced at her in a rather apologetic way. "You were kind to me the other day, *mademoiselle*," he said. "I am afraid I was rude. I apologize."

Karin smiled. "It's okay. I had no right to ask such personal questions. Especially about Céleste. I was just curious because she is so lovely."

He looked tired, she thought. His eyes still seemed unnaturally red. *Did* he use marijuana? She hoped not. But it was possible. She had caught a whiff of marijuana as she entered the alley this time. She'd recognized that sweetish smell, like burning rope, from the rest room at the library. They'd had trouble occasionally with high-school students going in there to smoke.

"She is beautiful, isn't she?" André said gloomily.

"Absolutely gorgeous," she agreed, trying to brighten him up. "*Is* she your girl friend?"

His face darkened, and she could have kicked herself for letting her curiosity show again. But he answered her readily enough. "She was." He hesitated, seemed unsure whether to say more. Then he blurted out, "But she is not now. It is hopeless, completely impossible." He looked so bleak suddenly and so young, so very young and uncertain that Karin wanted to reach out and touch him, to say something comforting. Which would be meaningless, she realized.

A possible customer approached André with a question, and she seemed to be in the way. Yet she didn't want to leave when he had let down his guard a little. "Did you make your appointment on time yesterday?'' she asked as the customer checked his pockets for cash.

"Mademoiselle?" He seemed genuinely puzzled, but before she could go on, she saw the memory flash into his eyes. For a second he seemed at a loss for words, then he shrugged. "Oh, *that* appointment. Yes, I was in time."

"I'm glad. The way you and Paul rushed off, I was afraid—"

He interrupted her with a look so ferocious she automatically took a step backward, away from him. "You must excuse me, *mademoiselle,*" he said stiffly. "I am very busy."

He turned back to his customer, and she knew she would get nothing more from him. But his reaction had confirmed the secretiveness of yesterday's meeting. Not that she was any wiser than she had been. But somehow she would find out what André and Paul were up to, she vowed as she went in search of Etienne. And if they were doing something illegal, she would go to the police.

LISSA APPROVED OF THE PAINTING and offered to find a frame so that Karin could hang it in her bedroom. She looked a little wistful as she examined the painting. "I wish I could paint like this," she said.

"You used to draw very well," Karin reminded her.

Lissa sighed. "I could never manage anything original. All I could do was copy. What's the use of that? A photostat machine or a camera could do that." She sounded defeated.

Karin gave up.

Lissa began to leave the room, then turned back. "Are you feeling all right? You look a little drawn."

"I'm okay," Karin said shortly, then apologized. "I'm not used to the heat, I guess."

Lissa nodded. "It affects me, too. Why don't you take a nap?"

"I'll do that," Karin said, but knew she wouldn't. How could she rest with that awful newspaper feature on her mind? Questions were still swirling around in her head. And the more she thought, the more confused she became. She wished she were seeing Paul today, only to satisfy her curiosity, of course.

Much to her surprise, she *did* see him that evening, but not under circumstances that made it possible for her to question him about the incident in the square. Instead she was left with more questions, which didn't improve her state of mind.

She and Lissa had decided to go to a movie—a mistake, as it turned out. The film, which had been billed as a "crowd pleaser," was one of those epics that relied more on sound effects and peculiar camera angles than story. As far as Karin could tell, there wasn't any story at all.

When they came out of the cinema, it was raining. Luckily Lissa had brought along a large bubble umbrella. She put it up, and they hurried along the rain-slick streets under it, laughing together over some of the more absurd parts of the movie. At least the film had served a couple of purposes, Karin thought. It had taken her mind off Paul Dufresne, and it had revived a feeling of closeness between her and Lissa.

They had always seen the same funny side of things when they were in school.

And then she looked up and saw Paul. Lissa had just steered her toward the front of the Château Frontenac so that they could derive some shelter from the porte cochere. Emerging from under the umbrella, Karin shook back her hair and immediately froze. Paul Dufresne was hurrying out of the front door of the hotel, hand in hand with a petite blond girl. Both of them were resplendent in evening clothes—Paul in a black tuxedo outfit, complete with tucked white shirt and bow tie, the girl in swirling blue green chiffon that matched her eyes. They looked like the models in a television commercial for expensive perfume. The beautiful people. They were both laughing. All life's gaiety and carefree happiness shone in their faces. Paul called out, "Taxi!" without waiting for the uniformed doorman's help, and as a taxi drew up in front of them, he helped the girl in and followed right on her heels. As the taxi swept by, Karin saw the two of them clutching at each other and laughing like children, the girl's long hair startlingly blond against Paul's well-tailored shoulder.

No more than a second could have passed. The incident had happened so quickly that for a moment Karin wondered if she had hallucinated, but a glance at Lissa's face showed her that she had seen Paul, too. She was gazing openmouthed in the direction the cab had gone. And then she said the name that had come unbidden to Karin's mind. "Céleste Lepage."

Karin swallowed, panic and dismay battling for position in her scattered thoughts. She had been right, then. The girl was the one from André's painting. Trying to sound casually interested, she asked, "Who's she?"

Lissa turned toward her, green eyes alight. "Friend Paul is really a rascal, eh? That was Céleste Lepage. Her father's one of the richest men in the province, if not the country. He owns the controlling interest in a couple of hundred businesses—hotels, insurance companies—you name it, he's in it. And Céleste is his only child. The 'Golden Girl,' the newspaper call her. I've seen her photograph in the society pages countless times." She shook her head, made a face. "If Paul's courting the Lepage girl, I don't know how he's going to have time to be my lover," she murmured to herself.

"Lissa!" Karin exclaimed.

Lissa blushed, and her gaze slid away from Karin's. "Oops," she said. "Forget you heard that, will you?" She shook her head again and laughed. "Céleste Lepage can't be a day over nineteen. Paul's really robbing the cradle, isn't he?"

And also robbing André Moreau, Karin thought indignantly as she turned with Lissa to resume their journey home. Not to mention Charles. Was there no limit to this man's treachery? Poor André—and poor Charles. How could either of them hope to compete with a man like Paul Dufresne? No wonder the sight of Paul brought out André's hostility; no wonder he'd accused him of meddling; no wonder he had looked so bleak.

But even though she now knew the reason for André's dislike of Paul, she thought later when she had changed out of her rain-damp clothes, she still had no idea why the two of them had met with Henri Valier. That puzzle was still unsolved.

Later still, as she lay in bed, staring stony eyed at the blue and white canopy above her head, she wondered if Paul would explain it to her if she asked him. Somehow she doubted it. And thinking of Paul, she also wondered despairingly how she could explain to herself the utter desolation that had struck her the moment she saw him with that stunningly lovely girl. Such cold *desperate* desolation. It had increased when Lissa forgot to be discreet. It was with her still.

CHAPTER EIGHT

ON SUNDAY EVENING Charles and Lissa were invited to visit the Leclercs. Evidently Marie and René had not been offended by Etienne's bad behavior after all. Karin had also been invited, but she declined. The past week, she explained to Charles and Lissa, had been so exciting and hectic that she was in need of some rest. She didn't tell them that she was afraid to go to the Leclercs in case Paul was there. He might even have arranged for the invitation. And she didn't want to see him socially as long as so many questions were clamoring in her mind. She would prefer to wait until she could see him alone.

After Etienne went to bed, she felt restless. She and Etienne had retreated earlier to the basement to escape the sound of yet another rock concert on Dufferin Terrace. They had enjoyed a television program about wild animals, but there was nothing else she wanted to watch. The rock concert had come to an end, but she didn't feel like going to bed, either. She felt dispirited, depressed.

It had rained all day. And while she had not been idle, had made a considerable dent in Charles's mountain of paperwork, she had been sitting most of the day at her desk. She needed exercise, she decided. She would try out the rail on the basement bar and see how it worked for ballet exercises.

In her bedroom she changed into a navy blue leotard and tights, pulled on long white knitted leg warmers, pinned her hair into a knot on top of her head and searched out her satin toe shoes and a box of rosin.

The bar rail made quite a satisfactory barre, just the right height. Karin began slowly with a series of pliés—squatting knee bends—and worked up through a series of warm-up exercises to some grands battements, concentrating on keeping each high kick sharp and precise. She was out of shape, she realized. The pull in her thigh muscles was severe, and her back felt stiff. She persevered, remembering the high-pitched voice of her instructor, Madame Elena, quoting the old ballet maxim: "If you miss one day's class, you know it; if you miss two, your teacher knows; and if you miss three, the audience knows." How many days had she missed exercising? Almost a week?

She worked steadily until she felt her muscles easing, becoming supple. And as always, when she was through, she felt like dancing. Why not, she thought. There was no one there to see.

Searching through the Vincents' record collection, she found excerpts from Delibes's *Coppélia* and Tchaikovsky's *Swan Lake*. After a little thought she decided on *Coppélia*—*Swan Lake* was rather pretentious for a solo performance.

She turned the stereo on, pulled off her leg warmers, then folded the bearskin rugs and tossed them in a corner. Then she waited, poised, until she could feel the music entering her bones, imagining the story in her mind. She was the young girl, Swanilda, pretending to be a wooden doll, waiting, unable to move until the toy maker's magical gestures infused her with life. Ah, now she was moving delicately "on point," first with little jerky chassé steps, gradually moving into some piqué turns and arabesques and bourrées, and a series of fouettés that almost, but not quite, made her dizzy. Soon she lost awareness of the room around her, felt the music lifting her until she was dancing effortlessly, floating like an ice skater.

As the music began to wind down, so the doll wound down, the clockwork movements becoming stiffer and stiffer until Karin froze altogether and held the pose, her feet in the fifth position, arms down, wrists bent upward, head to one side.

And breathing much too heavily, she chastised herself as she straightened and went to turn off the stereo. Her heart was pounding as though she'd run five miles, and perspiration was running down her back. All the same, she had enjoyed herself, and considering how long it had been since she actually danced like this, she hadn't done too badly. A little wooden in parts, but then Coppélia was supposed to be made of wood. "Not bad at all," she said aloud.

"I agree, *mademoiselle*," Paul Dufresne said. "Though your fouettés were a little off."

She would not have thought it possible for her heartbeat to increase, but it did. She whirled around awkwardly in a way that would have brought her a sharp reprimand from Madame Elena. "A dancer must always be graceful," Madame had told her hundreds of times. "Even when walking in the street, even when taking a shower, even when making love. Graceful, always graceful."

Paul was sitting halfway down the carpeted steps, watching her through the stair rails. Horrified, wishing the stone floor would open up and swallow her, Karin stared at him, unable to think of anything to say.

In the silence Paul stood up and descended the stairs. "Bravo, that was *magnifique*," he said as he came toward her. He was wearing a cream-colored jacket over the dark shirt and pants he'd worn when she first saw him. His dark good looks, those incredibly blue eyes, his lean lithe frame—the sheer physical *impact* of him—struck her with the same force now as then. She'd read in romantic novels that people's knees turned to water. She hadn't known it was true.

She finally found her voice. "How did you get in? Were you watching me the whole time? Why didn't you say something?"

Smiling, he stopped a couple of feet away from her and held up one hand to stop the flow of questions. "One: Madame Durocher let me in. Two, or was it three: I watched from the beginning of your dance, yes. You were quite obviously engrossed, and I did not want to disturb you, nor did I wish to deprive myself of such delightful entertainment."

Entertainment. That was his sole purpose in coming here—to be entertained. How had he the nerve to do so after the way he'd *disposed* of her down in the Lower Town?

"I'm surprised you didn't go to the Leclercs," she said dryly. "Surely you were expecting to be entertained there."

He looked puzzled for a moment, then his face

cleared, and he grinned wickedly. "Ah, I begin to see. Madame Durocher told me Charles and Lissa had gone to the Leclercs. You did not go because you thought I might be there. Is that correct? But you were wrong, *chère* Karin. I was not invited. So *voilà*! You are unable to escape me after all. As I have told you before, it is your fate, *n'est-ce pas*?"

To cover her discomfiture, Karin bent down and began to untie the ribbons of her satin shoes. Her fingers were awkward, and she was conscious of his gaze on her. Fumbling, trying to hurry, she pulled the wrong ends of ribbon and tightened them into hopeless knots.

"Allow me," Paul said. He guided her to the couch and knelt in front of her, lifted one of her feet to his knee and began working the first knot free. She could feel his fingers against her ankle through the stretched nylon of her tights, moving delicately, skillfully. His head was bent. She could see drops of rain caught in his dark hair. He must have waited outside in the rain a minute or two before Madame Durocher let him in. She could hear the rain now in spite of the pulse that was beating a tattoo in her ears. It was a steady rain, spattering on the sidewalk above, whispering against the basement windows. Paul's dark head was close enough to touch. . . .

He had removed her shoes now, but he held onto her feet for a moment, flexing them slowly, massaging the arches with his thumbs, sending alarming vibrations into her nervous system. She was afraid he intended teasing her by holding onto her feet, but when she attempted to tug them free, he released them and stood up.

She rose at once, conscious of a feeling of reprieve. "May I get you a drink?" she asked in a voice that was not as calm as she'd intended.

He inclined his head, and she mixed a gin and tonic for him without consulting him, then poured plain tonic water over ice for herself. She wasn't taking any chances with alcohol this time. Cool indifference, she told herself. That was the only way to handle this man. She must work up to her questions gradually.

She established herself in one of the white velvet chairs and raised her glass, mocking his gesture of the other night. "To your good health, Dr. Dufresne," she said lightly.

"And to yours, Karin."

He seated himself on the sofa at right angles to her chair and regarded her with interest. "You dance beautifully. Why did you give up ballet as a career?"

She let out a breath she hadn't known she was holding. This was safe enough ground. "Professional ballet dancing is not really a career; it's a way of life," she explained. "Daily classes, constant practice and performances. Dedication. I wanted something else."

"To be a librarian?"

"There's nothing wrong with being a librarian," she said sharply. "I enjoy my work. And besides, I couldn't have gone beyond the corps de ballet. Even for that I was too tall. I'm five-feet-eight, so when I'm on point, I'm over six feet tall. Made me stand out a bit. Also, my instructor told me that while I was technically excellent, I didn't have enough...." She broke off.

"Passion?" His voice lingered on the word. How wicked he looked when he slanted those dark eyebrows in that certain way.

Karin swallowed, but she was determined not to let him provoke her. "Something like that, yes."

He smiled lazily. "It seems your instructor did not know you as I know you."

Cool indifference be damned. She set down her glass and glared at him. "You do not know me at all."

"Don't I? Perhaps you are right. But I *wish* to know you. Already I know that you are beautiful in face and in—body." Again his voice lingered. Then he smiled at her over the rim of his glass. "You are also intelligent and talented, and I think, compassionate. But you have led rather a sheltered life, I think, which has contributed to your one major flaw."

"And that is?"

"You are much too—how shall I put it—too controlled."

She tried to speak evenly, though she was beginning to feel very angry. This conversation was not going in the direction she'd intended at all. "I had always thought self-control was a virtue."

"Not when carried to excess."

"You know all about excess, don't you?" She was suddenly on her feet, unable to sit still. How this man goaded her. "Is it impossible to have an ordinary conversation with you? Do you have to pick on my words and twist them and use them against me all the time?"

He looked up at her. His face was serious now, and

his eyes met hers without mockery. "It is necessary for me to stir you in any way I can," he said quietly. "I do not want to arouse your anger, but if that is the only emotion I can call forth, it is better than nothing."

Now she had an opening. "Is that why you deserted me in Place Royale? To make me angry?"

He frowned and ran a hand through his thick hair, an oddly disturbing gesture. Did it disturb her because she remembered so well how his hair felt to her touch, crisp and clinging and alive—so alive? She pushed the thought aside, waited.

When he spoke, his voice sounded weary. "The situation in Place Royale required that I...." He hesitated.

"That you get rid of me as quickly as possible?"

"Exactly." He looked up at her with a rueful smile.

"What *was* the situation—exactly?"

At once his expression altered, became bland. "That is a very dull story. It was nothing important."

Nothing important. Could she believe him? She wanted to believe him.

"But I want to know—" She broke off, suddenly aware that she had reached a point of no return. If she told him she'd seen him and André with the other man, he would know she'd returned to spy on him. And then what? She would have to tell him she had seen Henri Valier's photograph in the newspaper, that she knew Valier was a drug dealer. She would have to ask him if he and André were *involved* with Valier.

To her despair, she realized that she was afraid of the answer. Looking at him now as he sat on the sofa, looking so damnably sure of himself, so much at ease, so devastatingly attractive, so *clean*, she couldn't believe he could be mixed up in anything as sordid as drug dealing. Why would he be? He was a respected doctor, a member of a respected family, an educated intelligent man. She was rationalizing, she knew. But she also knew, and despised herself for her weakness, that she couldn't go on questioning him, couldn't face *knowing*. It was one thing to suspect—another to know for sure.

To give herself time, she picked up her glass and moved to the bar for more ice, aware that Paul was watching her curiously, waiting for her to finish what she had begun to say.

"I had expected to be working with you this weekend," she said at last. "Wasn't that our understanding?"

She could have sworn he gave a sigh of relief. He covered it up immediately, rising to his feet as she turned from the bar, smiling at her. "I am sorry," he said softly. "It became necessary for me to be elsewhere."

"Really?" She sipped her tonic water, her gaze fixed innocently on his face. "Were you out of town?"

A small frown puckered his forehead as though he were annoyed at her inquisitiveness, but then he shrugged. "I spent most of the weekend at the police station," he said with a disarming smile.

"The police station! Why?" Surely he wouldn't expect her to let that statement pass?

"Business," he said blandly. "Why else would an honest citizen spend time with the guardians of the law?"

"An investigation of criminal activities, perhaps?"

He laughed without amusement. "You have a re-markable imagination." His face had sobered abruptly. "Let us change the subject, shall we? I am afraid it is not possible for me to discuss this affair."

What now, Karin thought desperately. The tone of his voice had ruled out further questions. But if he had spent time at the police station, she realized with relief, then the police must be aware of his connec-tion with Valier. In which case the matter was out of her hands, and she could forget about it.

Paul was looking at her questioningly now as though he wondered what she was thinking. And she was still reluctant for some unknown reason to tell him how much she knew.

She sighed and put her glass down on the bar. "All right, we'll change the subject. If there is something you *don't* mind discussing."

That bit of sarcasm was a mistake. His expression changed at once to one of mischief. "We could return to the discussion we had the last time we were in this room."

Her treacherous heart skipped a beat, but she managed to control her facial expression. "I don't think that would be a good idea," she said briskly. "There must be more palatable topics."

"But none so interesting." He hesitated. "Do you mind if I make myself more comfortable?" Without waiting for her response, he removed his jacket and turned away to fold it neatly across the back of the couch. She watched him nervously, unable to keep herself from admiring the easy grace with which he moved, the economy of his movements, the way the fabric of his dark formfitting shirt hugged the contours of his back and shoulders.

A little sentinel awoke in her brain, telling her to leave this room *now*. But when he turned to face her, she hadn't moved. He took her unresisting hands between both of his and folded them against his chest. "Let us discuss the making of love," he murmured in a mock-theatrical tone.

She forced herself to look at him directly. "Can't you be serious?"

His mouth quirked at the corners. "Not when you are dressed like this, *chérie*." Deliberately he let his gaze move down over her body.

Following the direction of his gaze, she drew in her breath and felt her heart lurch sickeningly. The thin blue nylon of her leotard was so comfortable, so familiar, she had forgotten it fitted her like a second skin. All this time, while she pretended indifference, he had been watching her, able to see every line and curve of her body so boldly revealed. And she, not thinking, not realizing, had stood and moved and gestured as carelessly as though she were covered from head to toe in heavy wool.

"Such a beautiful body, *chérie*," he said huskily. "Watching you dance was an exciting experience. Your instructor was wrong. There is passion in you when you dance. It is only when the music stops that you deny it."

He was studying her face now, his blue eyes appraising her expression. She could feel color rising in her cheeks. She pulled away from him, but he held her hands imprisoned in his. "Don't fight me," he said. "I will not do anything to you that you do not want me to do."

His grip on her hands sent heat flooding through her, awakening all the responses he had awakened before. She wanted, how she wanted, to let herself sway toward him, to lean against him, to feel his arms around her. But she steeled herself against the insidious warmth that was weakening her will. "Was Céleste not available tonight?" she asked coldly.

He released her so suddenly she almost fell. His astonishment was so great it might have been comic if she hadn't felt so sickened. "What are you talking about?" he demanded when he recovered himself.

"Céleste Lepage. Are you going to tell me it is not necessary for me to know about *her*?"

"There isn't anything *to* know." His amazement seemed so genuine she might have believed him if she hadn't seen him with her own eyes. "I saw you," she said grimly. "Lissa and I saw you coming out of the Château Frontenac with her."

"And?"

"And it was obvious that you and she were. . . ."

He was standing very still suddenly, watching her, his head at a courteous angle, a half smile curving his lips. "Yes, Karin? Don't stop now, please."

"It was obvious that you and she were—more than a little fond of each other."

"Ah, now, a librarian should have a more precise vocabulary than that. You mean we looked like lovers, do you not?"

"Yes," she said defiantly.

His smile had faded, to be replaced by a cynically amused expression. "The sight distressed you?"

"Not at all. I brought it up simply because you were about to attempt to—to make love to me, and I have no desire to be one of your many women."

She was handling this badly. His amusement was increasing, and she was beginning to feel very foolish. How he loved to humiliate her. "It doesn't matter to me what you do with Céleste Lepage or with Lissa or Maggie or anyone else," she said bluntly. "Although I don't know how you can be so cruel to André or to Charles. You are obviously without conscience. No wonder André doesn't have a good word to say for you."

There was a silence in which he looked at her, his expression unreasonable, his blue eyes remote. "Céleste, Lissa and Maggie," he repeated slowly.

"I heard you arranging to meet Maggie," she said stiffly.

"Did you?" His eyebrows rose. "And André? What is his connection with all of this?"

"You know very well what his connection is. He showed me his other paintings. One of them was of Céleste. It's obvious that he is in love with her and heartsick because she prefers you."

"Truly? So many things are obvious to you, Mademoiselle Karin. Are you always so sure of everything?"

She took a deep breath. He was mocking her as usual. "It doesn't matter," she said. "I just wanted you to understand that I see you for what you are, and I am not...."

"Not what?" he asked kindly as her voice faltered.

"I am not attracted to you."

"No?" His hand reached out to touch the side of her neck, gently, so gently. Then his fingers slid downward, tracing the edge of the round neckline of her leotard. His eyelids lowered. "No?" he repeated.

She did not need to look down at herself to know that his light touch had aroused an immediate response in her breasts. She could feel them straining against the thin fabric, sense the sharp involuntary tightening of the nipples that must be outlined clearly for him to see. "Paul," she said in protest, but her protest came much too late. His head was bent, his mouth searching out the betraying nipples through the clinging nylon, his lips gently sliding over first one then the other, while his arms moved around her. "Paul," she said again, and her hand reached to his hair, meaning to force his head away from her. His hair was still a little damp—soft and sensuous to her touch. She snatched her hand away, let her arms hang stiffly at her sides. But he paid no attention to her rejection of him. Lazily he moved his head upward and began kissing her mouth gently, his long firm fingers moving down her back, pressing her against his body so forcefully that she could feel the fabric of his clothing through the thin leotard. Her traitorous body responded instinctively to the powerful pressure of his body against hers, growing tight with wanting, so tight that she shook with the strain of fighting against it. But she was determined to fight. She would not give in.

He lifted his head and looked at her, his eyes dark with an emotion that terrified her as it thrilled her. "Don't be afraid," he said softly.

"I'm not afraid," she lied. "I'm just not interested."

"But you are trembling, *chérie*. You must not fight against me so. You must not fight yourself. I will not let you."

His mouth hardened against her throat, sending adrenaline rushing into her bloodstream so that she shuddered all the way down to her toes. "There is no other woman," he murmured, the words vibrating against her skin. "Since I first saw you looking at me with those startled velvet eyes, I have thought of no one but you. Trust me on this. I am telling you the truth. Since I first touched you, I have wanted to go on touching you. Like this, and this." His hands moved to the sides of her body, moved upward until his thumbs were circling her breasts, touching, probing.

And still she held herself rigid, as though she were indeed Coppélia, held herself woodenly, afraid to let down her guard, afraid to lose control. But she would not fight him and expose herself to his mockery. She would wait him out, prove to him that he could not affect her in any way.

When his face moved back into her line of vision, she closed her eyes against the sight of his sensually curving mouth, so close to her own, prepared to resist the terrible power of his kiss.

But he didn't kiss her. "It is a scientific fact," he said slowly, his mouth against hers, his breath mingling with hers, "that a lover's touch causes blood to rush to the parts of the body touched, engorging the tissues of the mouth—here, and earlobes—here and breasts—like so." The touch of his mouth and fingers was light as a whisper of air.

"A lover's touch," he murmured again, "increases pulse rate and blood pressure and raises the temperature of the skin to fever pitch, like this, and this. It is a scientific fact, not to be argued with." His lightly probing fingers had charted the anatomy of her body while he spoke, and she was dissolving into herself, losing the sense of herself as a separate person, so mesmerized by the hypnotic sound of his softly accented voice that it was only with an effort of will that she could keep herself from softening against him.

How had he known that words could excite her even more than touch? How had he known when she had not? Ray had never talked to her when he caressed her, she thought wildly, almost hysterically. And Ray had never, ever, aroused her to this exquisite, almost painful sensitivity, where the slightest movement of hand or mouth could instantly ignite more feeling.

She waited for the familiar twist of pain that always came when she thought of Ray. But it didn't arrive.

Paul's face was moving against her cheek now. It had evidently been some time since he'd shaved, and the faint rasp of his beard against her skin was a pleasurable, sensuous sensation, his mouth a tender yet electrifying force that moved constantly, now to her hair, her eyelids, her ears, her throat, back to her mouth.

It wasn't fair, she thought desperately. It wasn't fair of him to keep trying to seduce her. The little sentinel in her brain was going to sleep or perhaps simply disappearing.

In another moment her body would begin to move against his, and if that happened, she would not be able to stop herself from giving in to him completely.

With a strength born of desperation she pulled herself free of him. *"Mon Dieu,"* she said harshly, deliberately mocking him, "is this how you treat Céleste and Lissa, forcing yourself upon them whether they want you or not?"

He was not annoyed or humiliated as she had been by similar words. He simply looked amused. "I am disappointed in you, *chérie*," he said. "I had thought that if I was more gentle in my approach, you would feel less threatened." His gaze swept the length of her body, and she wished despairingly she was more decently clothed. She might as well be naked to his gaze. He was smiling suggestively now, his gaze lingering on breasts that were still distended, moving to her throat where she could feel her pulse beating rapidly, giving her emotion away. "You must surely admit, dear Karin, that you are not exactly unmoved."

"I'll admit no such thing," she said hotly. "I am angry, yes, but—"

"Angry for no reason," he interrupted. "I have no interest in Céleste, except perhaps as I might feel toward a little sister. She is just a child."

"And Lissa? Is she a child, too?"

"Mon Dieu," he breathed. He ran an impatient hand through his hair and strode abruptly to the sofa where he picked up his jacket and pulled it on. He turned to face her, his blue eyes mocking her. "This was a demonstration only," he said evenly. "I wished you to realize that you are a passionate woman. Obviously I have failed."

He walked toward the stairs, and she felt a tearing inside her as though if he left, some part of her would physically separate from her. At the bottom of the stairs he turned to face her, one foot on the bottom step, one hand gripping the banister. "I am thirty-four years old," he said slowly. "I have known many women. You asked me once why I had not married, and I told you I had financial obligations to meet that kept me busy. There is another reason. I have never found a woman who didn't jump to conclusions based on very little evidence. My own faults are many, but I am honest in my relationships. If I wanted Céleste, I would not pursue you. If I wanted Lissa, I would not pursue you."

She looked at him uncertainly, impressed by the sincerity in his tone. "But Lissa said. . ." she began.

He made a small sound of impatience. "I care nothing for what Lissa said. And I will defend myself no more. You will think what you have chosen to think. That is obvious. It is as well you stopped me again. You would probably have convinced yourself once more that I had taken advantage of you. When you are prepared to admit that you want me as I want you, come to me. I will be waiting. Until then I will attempt not to disturb you again."

CHAPTER NINE

By MORNING the rain had stopped. But in spite of the sunshine she could see from her bedroom window, Karin decided against going for a walk. She didn't feel like walking, didn't feel much like doing anything.

After breakfast with Etienne and Charles, during which Charles entertained her with stories about the evening at the Leclercs and tried unsuccessfully to elicit information about Paul's visit, which Madame Durocher had reported to him, Karin forced herself to settle down in her study and go to work.

Paul was the last person she expected to see that day. But when Madame Durocher summoned her downstairs at ten o'clock, there he was in the Vincents' blue and ivory living room, standing with his back to the empty fireplace, rocking idly back and forth on his heels, looking relaxed and comfortable in a vivid blue short-sleeved turtleneck of ribbed cotton and trim-fitting white Levi's.

He seemed surprised at her obvious amazement. "Did Lissa not tell you I would call for you this morning?" he asked.

She stared at him, astonished by his gall. How could he walk in here like this, acting as though nothing had happened?

"She told me on Saturday, yes," she stammered. "But I thought after last night...."

His eyes were as clear blue as this morning's rain-washed sky. "But our—what shall we call them—our *private* negotiations are separate from our business arrangements, are they not?"

"How can they be?"

"We are adults, *n'est-ce pas*?"

Which very nicely put her on the spot, she thought, exasperated. If she refused to go with him now, she would be made to feel she was acting like a child.

As she deliberated, Charles came into the room and greeted Paul warmly. "Off again?" he asked, looking from Paul to Karin with a gentle, almost avuncular smile.

"As soon as Karin is ready," Paul said.

Karin felt a sinking sensation. How could she refuse to go with him now? She would have to explain to Charles, and she couldn't possibly do that.

"I *am* ready," she said stiffly, indicating her shirt and blue jeans. "It surely isn't necessary for me to change?"

A spark of humor glinted in Paul's eyes as he appraised her gravely. "A dress today, perhaps," he said thoughtfully. "We are going to the Séminaire de Québec and afterward to the Ursuline Convent, so probably...." He let the thought trail away.

Probably, Karin thought, she would be perfectly acceptable as she was. The majority of young people in the city dressed casually. But she wasn't going to start off what might be a very difficult day by making an issue out of her clothing.

As Karin left the room, Lissa drifted in, looking

adorably feminine in pink and white lounging pajamas, her red curls charmingly disheveled. Karin heard her apologize through delicate yawns for her appearance. And heard Paul assure her that she looked delightful, which of course she did.

Without haste Karin changed into a man-tailored olive green shirt and matching linen straight skirt. It was the most unattractive outfit she owned—her mother had bought it. A perfect choice, she thought as she pulled her hair brutally back into its single braid and tied it with a drab piece of ribbon. She applied no makeup at all.

"Most suitable," Paul commented, and she could detect no irony in his tone. Only the merest quirk of one eyebrow betrayed the fact that he knew exactly what she was doing and why.

Everything was glittering when they stepped out onto the front porch and descended the stone steps. Sunlight glinted on streets still slick from last night's rain and struck brilliance into the drops of rain that clung to slate roofs of red and gray and green.

"How fresh the air smells," Karin murmured as they walked along the street.

"A brand new day," Paul said.

She glanced at him quickly. The words were innocent enough, but there had been special emphasis in his tone. As she had expected, he was looking at her sideways, that well-shaped sensual mouth of his curved at one corner. Even as she realized, almost telepathically, that he was going to mention the previous night, he spoke. "Have you given any thought to our relationship?"

She had thought of little else. "I can't," she said and stopped.

"Can't talk about it or still can't admit to wanting me?"

"I can't—*won't* talk about it."

"Very well, we will talk of other things."

Before she could decide how she felt about his abrupt change of manner, he went on to tell her about a pair of birds he had watched feeding in a tree on his property that morning. It was a while before she grasped the point of the story, and she was annoyed all over again when she did. The male bird, Paul said, was colorfully feathered in gray and white with a rosy breast and wing patches, but the female was a rather dull combination of brown and buff. "That is so often the case in the bird and animal kingdom," he concluded. "I wonder why the female is so often the dowdy one."

Dowdy.

"Possibly the male's bright plumage is intended to make up for his insecurity," she suggested in a silky voice. "Perhaps, unlike the female, he has nothing to rely on but his handsome appearance."

Paul laughed. "Ah, yes, Mademoiselle Karin, you are indeed a worthy combatant."

Which unaccountably lifted Karin's spirits. It was an enjoyable challenge, she conceded, to match wits with a man of Paul's intellect. So often she had made a humorous remark that had passed right over Ray's head. Not that Ray was without intelligence, but his sense of humor had not been anywhere near as sharp as this man's.

She must stop comparing the two men, she warned

herself. Ray was out of her life, and Paul Dufresne was much too dangerous to be allowed in. She had decided that somewhere around two o'clock this morning after thinking over everything that had passed between them.

It was impossible to believe in Paul's supposed lack of interest where Céleste was concerned. Compared to the evidence of her own eyes, his statement that he looked upon Céleste as a child did not ring true. As for Lissa, why should she imply that Paul wanted to be her lover unless she'd been encouraged to think so by him? She was especially worried about Lissa. If Lissa became too restless over Charles's long working hours and too irritated by Etienne, she might find it difficult to resist the prospect of happiness an affair with Paul might promise. And then there was Maggie. She'd *heard* him arrange to meet the girl. It was easy enough for a man to assure a woman he thought of no one else—possibly at that moment it had even seemed true to him. But she would be a fool to believe him against all evidence to the contrary.

As for all that talk about her being a passionate woman—all right, she would concede that. He had made his point there, more than once. She was capable of a passion she hadn't guessed at. Which made her even *more* vulnerable where this man was concerned.

In that attack of clear-eyed honesty that had come upon her at two o'clock in the morning, she had realized that her heart had not been as badly damaged by Ray's defection as she had thought, yet she had suffered terribly when he went out of her life. At the same time she had seen very clearly that were she to submit to Paul, as her body kept urging her to do, the letdown afterward, when he lost interest and moved on to somebody new, would be unbearable.

So then, she had told herself at the end of those wakeful hours, she was now armed with honesty. Physically, sexually, she was weak where Paul Dufresne was concerned. She must guard against herself as much as against him. Confident that she could manage that now that she was completely aware of the danger, she had at last allowed herself to go to sleep.

She had certainly not expected that she would be forced to spend another day in his company. The man was a master of manipulation. But here she was, and she must prove equal to the challenge.

"Here we are," Paul said, echoing her thought. He was looking at her curiously; she had been silent a long time. But she owed him no explanation, and she would give him none.

They were greeted beyond the seminary's impressive wrought-iron door by a young priest in a soutane. He appeared to be expecting them. Like the Savards', his manner toward Paul was respectful, perhaps even more so. As he led them around the seventeenth-century buildings, which turned out to cover more ground than seemed likely from the street, he deferred continuously to the man he had greeted as *"mon cher Paul."*

He and Paul conversed in English in deference to Karin, and as they progressed, she found, as she had before, that she was forced to admire Paul not only for his knowledge, but for the fact that he obviously cared a great deal for this city of his birth. He spoke of Monseigneur François de Laval, who had founded the seminary as long ago as 1663, as though he were a loved and respected friend. And when they entered the bishop's funeral chapel and gazed at the recumbent white marble statue of Monseigneur de Laval, he appeared as moved and awed as Karin herself.

The chapel, he told her, had been designed quite recently by an architect named Adrien Dufresne, who was unfortunately not connected to Paul's family at all.

Looking at his solemn face in the amber light filtering through the stained glass of the round window, she thought again what a mistake it had been in the beginning to dismiss him as merely a spoiled playboy. He was quite obviously a man of many parts—parts that added up to an exceptional human being, whether he was flawed in some ways or not.

She was impressed by her tour of the seminary, especially the lovely interior courtyard and the old kitchens, whose walls, Paul told her, were eight feet thick. Gradually she was lulled into forgetting her misgivings about the man beside her until she was reminded of them by a small, but rather curious exchange between the two men.

She was admiring the huge iron-and-stone staircase that climbed up through five stories, supported by a single iron column. This staircase, the young priest told her, had been designed by an architect, but it was left to an illiterate farmer to work out how to put the massive structure together.

As she stood there, looking upward, the priest stepped back and spoke to Paul. "I heard about

Anne-Marie," he said in French. "It is a terrible thing."

"It could have been tragic," Paul replied. "Her roommate wasted time trying to find me instead of taking her to the hospital."

"But she was treated in time?"

"Fortunately, yes."

The name Anne-Marie rang a bell in Karin's memory, but she didn't place it until after they'd left the seminary. Paul had addressed one of the calèche drivers as Anne-Marie. Anne-Marie was the very thin blond girl who had turned away, ignoring his greeting.

"Is Anne-Marie a patient of yours?" she asked as they headed toward the Ursuline Convent.

He glanced at her sideways. "You miss very little. Yes, she is a patient of mine—in a way."

In a way? What did that mean?

"What happened to her?"

She thought for a moment he wouldn't answer, but he did. "An overdose of drugs on Saturday. She took too many barbiturates—sleeping pills. I suspect she attempted suicide, but she insists it was an accident. In any case, she has recovered."

His voice was clipped. He seemed to be suppressing anger, but she wasn't sure if his anger was directed at Anne-Marie or at herself. "You said her roommate couldn't track you down," she ventured. "I thought you had a colleague covering for you."

"I do," he said shortly. "The girl wouldn't tell him why she was looking for me. She was frightened, I suppose, afraid Anne-Marie would get in trouble. She was lucky Anne-Marie didn't die. Fortunately she realized in time that Anne-Marie needed treatment urgently so she took her to the hospital. I was at the police station, as I told you. It is perhaps not surprising that Violette did not look for me there."

Violette. That was the name of the other calèche driver, the one who had looked embarrassed to see Paul. All Karin's earlier qualms about this man returned. A patient of his had attempted suicide, using drugs. *Why* had Violette preferred to track Paul down instead of taking Anne-Marie to the hospital at once? Had she trusted him not to inform on her friend?

"Is something wrong, Karin?"

She glanced at him. Apparently his anger had subsided. He was looking at her questioningly, his blue eyes clear, candid. She was letting her imagination run away with her, she told herself. This man could not possibly be guilty of any wrongdoing.

She forced herself to pay attention to the parts of the Ursuline Convent they were allowed to see, especially the beautiful Louis XIV chapel, but it was difficult to concentrate, and she was also a little unnerved by the grisly sight of General Montcalm's skull, which was preserved in a glass case in the convent museum. She was glad when they came out again into the open air. She lingered in front of a statue in the peaceful garden outside the main entrance, surprised by the sudden feeling of sadness it gave her. It was a grouping of three figures: two little Indian girls and Marie de l'Incarnation, the great mystique of French Canada, first mother superior of the convent.

"You like children, don't you?" Paul asked quiet-

ly. "I have noticed how good you are with Etienne."
He hesitated. "Etienne told me what you said to
him—that he didn't have to be fat. He was most impressed by that. He is going to think about it deeply,
he said."

Karin managed a smile. "I hope it helps. I'm
becoming quite fond of Etienne." She turned back to
the statue. "Yes, I do like children. They are the
main reason I enjoy my work." She paused, then
spoke more to herself than to him. "Actually I
wasn't thinking only of the children, attractive as
they are. There's a feeling of warmth about this
statue, isn't there? The way the mother's hands are
placed so close to the children's heads, not so much
in benediction as in love. And there's love in the
angle of her head, the expression of her face."

"You were thinking of your own mother?"

His insight continually surprised her. "How did
you know that?"

His eyes were kind. "A certain sadness in your face
that I have seen before when you spoke of your
childhood. Is your mother not a loving person?"

Karin tried to be fair, as she always tried to be
when referring to her mother in her thoughts. "She—
I think she didn't intend having a child. She was
not...naturally maternal. Both she and my father
were dedicated to their careers. But they tried. They
have always been very conscientious. But not very...
demonstrative."

"I see," he said gravely. "That is why it is difficult
for you to give freely of your emotions."

"Not at all," Karin said flatly, her somewhat
sentimental mood destroyed. "I give of myself very

easily to anyone who deserves it." She sighed as he glanced at her quizzically, obviously about to make some humorous retort. It had been a mistake to relax her guard. "Please don't start analyzing me again," she said. "I don't enjoy it."

"Then I shall desist." He touched her arm lightly as they turned away from the statue. As usual she felt his touch through her whole body. But when she flinched, he removed his hand at once, though his mouth curved in a knowing smile.

She must stop reacting every time he came within an inch of her flesh, she told herself. She must not let him know how strongly he affected her still.

That, she found, was difficult to do. As they continued their tour, visiting several churches and monuments, she could not shake off her awareness of him. Just walking beside him, matching her stride to his, she could feel the warmth of his body charging the air between them. He was careful, she noticed, to touch her only when politeness directed—as they crossed a street, or when he wished to draw her attention to some key point of architecture: an arched doorway, perhaps, or the intersection of vaults and roof. He had evidently meant it when he said he would attempt not to disturb her again. But still, every time he did touch her, she felt that same tingling of her nerve ends, as though he had first run his hand over some rough surface, gathering up static electricity in his fingertips to transfer to her. It was a phenomenon she had never encountered before.

If Paul recognized her awareness, he gave no further sign of it. He was casual, polite, friendly and informative. By the end of the afternoon Karin had learned a great deal about elevation and perspective and colonnades and galleries. She had also absorbed a large amount of Quebec's history, for as Paul said, history and architecture went hand in hand.

"Every culture has its own forms," he remarked as they left the Anglican Cathedral with its pews and communion rail of solid English oak, and crossed rue Ste. Anne to the wax museum, which was housed in a simple whitewashed building of the eighteenth century. "These forms are determined by religion and ideology or sometimes by practicality, as well as by materials available and the technology of the times. To view the buildings is to view history."

Yes, she thought again—a very intelligent and perceptive man. If only he was like this at all times, she could enjoy his company. But there was always that other Paul.

WHAT MUST ALSO BE TAKEN into account, she reminded herself after Paul had deposited her at the Vincent house and left without mentioning any future meetings, was the inescapable fact that he was a manipulative man who used sly methods to get his own way. This last thought occurred to her after she was called into Lissa's bedroom to find her feverishly sorting through her wardrobe. Pants and tops were scattered on the bed, and Lissa was in the process of pulling more hangers out of the wall-long closet she shared with Charles. They had been invited, she told Karin with great glee, to spend the evening of the next day, which happened to be Dominion Day, on the yacht of no less a personage than Monsieur Claude

Lepage. And the invitation had specified that Karin was to be included.

"There's to be a parade of boats on the St. Lawrence," Lissa added. "And fireworks on the Plains of Abraham, which we'll watch from the yacht. Isn't it exciting? The Leclercs will be there, and the Savards, so it's not as if we won't know anyone. And a lot of really important people are going. The Lepages know absolutely everyone. There's to be a buffet dinner and drinks on board, and it will be great fun. Even Charles is pleased about it. Madame Durocher has promised to take Etienne with her own nephew to see the fireworks from Dufferin Terrace, so we don't have to worry about him missing anything. Isn't it super that we've been invited?"

"Super," Karin echoed. "Do I detect the fine hand of Paul Dufresne at work?"

"But of course," Lissa bubbled. "Madame Lepage told me on the telephone that Paul had said she and Céleste really must meet all of us, and what better time than this?"

"What better time indeed," Karin murmured.

Lissa's face fell. "Please don't say you don't want to go. Madame Lepage particularly asked for you. It's to be very casual, blue jeans and so on, she said, though, of course, with that crowd the jeans will probably be designer made. That's why I'm hunting for something suitable. I know I had a good pair of jeans here somewhere." She turned back to her closet. "Do say you'll go," she begged over her shoulder. "Even if you don't like Paul, you'll enjoy it, I'm sure."

Karin smiled. "Don't worry. I wouldn't dream of

missing it, if only for the pleasure of seeing you so happy.''

Curiosity, she thought privately as she headed for her own room, was a powerful instinct. In spite of her annoyance at his continued manipulation of everyone to suit himself, she could not resist the opportunity to see Paul with Céleste Lepage. It would be interesting to see how his supposedly brotherly attitude held up.

CHAPTER TEN

THE LEPAGE YACHT was docked at a large and very exclusive-looking marina, among a veritable forest of tall masts. It appeared to be the largest one there. It was certainly the biggest privately owned vessel Karin had ever boarded—and the most luxurious. Obviously no money had been spared.

As Lissa had expected, everyone who was anyone had been invited. Even so, there was far too much food. Dinner was served buffet-style in the large, rather ornate saloon, and Karin had a difficult time deciding among all the dishes: veal cordon bleu, coq au vin, ten different kinds of crepes, salads and fresh fruits, pâté and huge wheels of cheese. Not to mention a tableful of mouth-watering *gâteaux*. Other guests kept urging her to try this and sample that until she was sure she could gain ten pounds if she let them have their way.

Everyone was very friendly, especially when Karin produced a few phrases in French. She didn't have to say much; most of the guests talked nonstop. The decibel level in the saloon, she thought, must be very high.

After the meal the yacht moved majestically downriver toward the city—a distance of several miles. Liqueurs and coffee were served on the forward deck.

Karin sat in a canvas chair, one of a circle that included Lissa and Charles, Paul and Céleste, the senior Lepages and the Leclercs. She felt superfluous, the odd one out. Everyone else was paired off.

Céleste had staked her claim to Paul the moment he stepped on board, clinging to his arm when they all went on a tour of the yacht, holding him back, talking to him in whispers that he answered in kind. His voice, when he spoke to the girl, Karin had noticed, was softer than she had ever heard it—almost tender, definitely fond.

To be fair, he had been courteously attentive to Karin, also, making sure dishes were passed to her at dinner, sometimes serving her himself, but he had not attempted to separate himself from Céleste for a moment and had seemed perfectly willing to accept the almost deliberately adoring smiles she favored him with at every opportunity.

Karin couldn't blame her. Paul looked irresistibly attractive in denim—totally masculine. Nor could she blame Paul for being so charmed by Céleste. She was an enchanting girl, sweet and funny and full of life, though not boisterous. There was a frailness to the boyishly slim body that showed in the small bones of her wrists and ankles, and there were faint shadows under the dancing mermaid eyes, as though someone had touched them lightly with a blue-stained thumb.

Like Karin, Céleste was dressed for the heat in slim-fitting blue jeans and a sleeveless shirt, her narrow bare feet thrust into rope-soled sandals. But there all resemblance ended. Comparing herself to Céleste, Karin felt rudely healthy and much too tall.

Céleste was talking now, entertaining their group with a story about her Siamese cat, Mei Ling, who had a habit of climbing window draperies and crouching on the wide valance box at the top. On this particular occasion Mei Ling had suffered a fright when Monsieur Lepage snapped open a newspaper as he sat in the armchair below her. She had launched herself into space, Céleste said, and dived straight through the middle of the outstretched newspaper.

"Tore out the entire financial section," Monsieur Lepage said in his gravelly voice.

"Poof—like that," Céleste added, demonstrating the cat's dive with one slim hand across Paul's shoulder and down to his knee. Head tilted, she laughed merrily. Her laughter was as enchanting as the rest of her—musical and infectious. Everyone laughed with her. Her father even produced a grudging smile, an unusual event so far. The smile didn't seem to fit his rather tough features. A sinister-looking man, Karin thought.

How on earth had the Lepages produced such a delicate and beautiful child, Karin wondered, trying to distract herself from the sight of Céleste's slender fingers resting on Paul's knee.

Claude Lepage was a large, balding, ponderous man who was lolling back in his deck chair, his eyes hooded, his rather fleshy face set in somnolent lines. He was apparently half-asleep, but actually he missed nothing. Whenever a guest's glass was empty, a flick of one of his stubby fingers brought a white-jacketed waiter scurrying. And when he spoke, which he did very brusquely, Karin could feel the company snapping to attention. A man of power, she thought, used to instant obedience. No wonder his wife was so nervous. A fidgety woman, Madame Lepage. Her blue green eyes, the same color as her daughter's but surrounded by a network of wrinkles, were in constant motion, and she had a habit of ducking her head as though she expected to be rebuked at any second. Her hands moved just as often, compulsively rearranging the rings and bracelets that glittered against her rather doughy-looking flesh. The jewelry looked incongruous with her self-consciously casual clothing. A woman the size of Madame Lepage, Karin thought, should never wear pants—especially not purple pants—no matter if they *were* made of the finest raw silk.

Madame was watching her daughter now, glancing from her to Paul, nodding as though with approval. "Do you not find dear Paul a divinely attractive man?" she asked Karin with another little jerk of her head. "So *splendide*, so *charmant*," she went on without waiting for a response. "They make an attractive couple, do they not?"

Karin agreed that they did indeed.

For which Madame Lepage rewarded her with a long detailed account of Céleste's childhood. Céleste, it seemed, had suffered from rheumatic fever before she was ten. The illness had left her with some slight damage to one of the valves of her heart. "She is well enough now," Madame Lepage assured Karin. "But it has often been necessary to restrict her activities. It comforts me that dear Paul has taken such an interest in her."

"Is Paul her doctor?" Karin asked.

Madame's head bobbed sideways. "*Non*. She attends a specialist in Montreal." She hesitated. "It seems Paul's interest is personal. I am pleased. One would feel so safe with a doctor in the family, you understand?"

Karin did not feel able to comment on that. Gradually over the last couple of hours she had been conscious of anger building up inside her. It was not due to jealousy, she told herself firmly. She had no reason to be jealous of Céleste Lepage. No, her fury was because of Paul's attempted deception.

All the same, she couldn't help feeling sorry for the girl. It must be rough having to watch your health all the time. As she thought this, she glanced at Céleste and to her astonishment surprised an expression on the girl's face that could only be described as miserable. The soft rosebud mouth was trembling. And her beautiful eyes looked misty, as though they were holding back tears. Paul was talking to her father now. Was she upset because his attention had left her? No. In retrospect Karin realized that the girl's bright chatter had held an edge of nervousness the whole time, and her animation had seemed forced. Now, in repose, her face showed her true mood, and it was not a happy one.

Puzzled, Karin turned her attention toward Paul and Monsieur Lepage, who seemed absorbed in their conversation. Evidently her host was questioning Paul about his investments; at least, she thought, that was what *investissements* probably meant. Paul's responses, though polite, seemed a little curt. And Monsieur Lepage's pale gray eyes were narrowing coldly as though he resented the fact.

Marie Leclerc was also watching the two men, her

dark eyes bright with interest. But their voices were low, and she apparently could not make out what they were saying. "I hate it when people talk too quietly, don't you?" she murmured when she caught Karin's eye.

Karin managed a smile. "It doesn't make much difference to me. I understand French only if it is spoken quite slowly. And some of the words seem different here, not quite like the textbooks I had in school."

"We have a patois of our own," Marie explained. "I will be your interpreter." She glanced mischievously at Monsieur Lepage, then back at Karin. "Our host is trying, I think, to find out about some business Paul is engaged in. We have all been curious. Recently Paul had indulged in some mysterious activities. Evidently Monsieur Lepage smells opportunity. He is always looking for a chance to add to his huge fortune; some people are never satisfied. But I think Paul is playing—what do you call it—hard to get, which is very wise of him. Claude Lepage is what in America you would call a 'take-charge guy.'" She sighed. "But now I cannot hear them, and I was curious to know the nature of Paul's business myself. I heard Claude mention Montreal, and I was so hoping Paul had some *divertissement* in Montreal, of a female nature, perhaps."

She chuckled softly. "You must excuse me, Karin. We have all played matchmaker for Paul for so long it has become a habit. But I think now it may be unnecessary. There is a rumor that he is engaged to Céleste. Is that true, do you know?"

Her gaze was fixed on Karin's face in humorous

challenge. Probably, Karin thought, she was remembering how Paul had flirted with *her* at the Savards. "I don't know," she managed to say.

Marie shrugged. "I do not think it is wise. Céleste is pretty, yes, and rich and very sweet, but she is not enough woman for our Paul. He would require a strong woman, that one. But all the same, it is an interesting rumor, and he seems fond of the little one." She darted a merry glance at Karin's face, her mobile mouth turning down at the corners. "It is a secret, you understand. Claude has not yet been informed. I think there is no doubt he will approve. He and Suzanne are overprotective of little Céleste, but Paul is eminently eligible, *n'est-ce pas*?"

"Yes, I suppose he is," Karin said.

She was becoming restless, she found. Her anger had increased as Marie Leclerc gossiped on. What a fool Paul Dufresne must have thought her to attempt to deceive her so. A little sister indeed.

Excusing herself abruptly, not caring if she seemed rude, she pushed her chair back out of the circle. Sara Savard and Lissa tried to stop her for conversation, but she managed to indicate a little urgency and headed in the direction of the small lounge that had been set aside for the women of the party. But she didn't go in. She stood at the rail of the boat, wanting only to be left alone.

Paul followed her, of course. No doubt he wanted to check to see if his deceitfulness had aroused her to anger again.

"You didn't need to come after me," Karin said shortly.

He laughed. "Ah, but it was such a fine excuse. I

can only bear with Claude Lepage for a short time, I'm afraid.''

"That must be difficult, considering he's to be your father-in-law. I suppose I should offer you congratulations. It seems you have found your rich wife.''

He whistled softly. "You've heard that rumor, then? Is that why you're upset?''

She lifted her gaze upward, watching weaves of rich crimson slowly washing across the evening sky. The sun had dropped with incredible swiftness. They were approaching Cape Diamond now; she could see the faint looming outlines of the star-shaped Citadel high on its crag. They would anchor below the fort to watch the fireworks, she understood. There were quite a few boats of various sizes anchored there already. The yacht was moving very slowly, the water splashing gently against the hull, stirred by their passage and the still-warm breeze.

"I'm not upset," she said at last.

"You told me that you always tried to be honest," Paul said in a voice of mild reproach.

She faced him. "All right. I *am* upset, but only because you lied to me. I don't understand why you felt it was necessary.''

"I did not lie.''

"How can you say that?''

"Very easily.''

"Yes, very easily," she retorted. She turned away. "I would like to be alone," she said.

"You do not wish to question me about my engagement to Céleste?''

"Not at all.''

"You do not wish even to ask me if I am in love with her?"

"You know nothing of love."

"And you do?"

She refused to answer.

"You were in love with your friend Ray?"

"Stop calling him my friend. He was my fiancé."

"But I think he acted more like a friend, did he not? He did not push you toward intimacy. He did not arouse you as I have aroused you."

All she could do was ignore him, Karin decided.

"You are silent, Mademoiselle Karin," he mocked her. "I think you recognize the truth of what I am saying, but will not admit to it."

When she still remained silent, he changed his tone abruptly. "Are you familiar with Tchaikovsky's *1812 Overture*?"

She stared at him. His expression was challenging. What was he up to now? "I know the piece," she said at last.

"*Bon*. Then you know that at the end of it there is much noise: bells ringing, cannons booming, much excitement and color."

"Yes."

He reached to the rail and took her hand between both of his. His gaze held hers. How blue his eyes were in the reflected twilight. "That is what love is," he said softly. "Much excitement and color and noise—cymbals clashing, trumpets blaring, lightning and thunder and passion. Fire in the blood and pulses pounding."

Her hand was trembling in his. *Damn*. Why was he so impossible to resist? She must resist him. She must settle this once and for all. "That's not true," she said in a voice that shook. "Love is soft and warm. It has to grow steadily and quietly out of friendship. It has to be nurtured with trust, and it grows as trust grows."

He made a small sound of disgust and dropped her hand. "Friendship is a necessary ingredient, yes, I will agree with that. Trust? Yes, that, too, though often we use trust as a weapon. We say, 'I trust you, therefore you must not do anything that would displease me.' But the excitement is most important. If the excitement is not there in the beginning, it will never be there. Surely you must see that?"

He seemed very angry suddenly. "You will not admit to the truth, will you?" he went on. "You are going to fight the attraction that is between us and deny us both the joy of it." He swung away from her and gestured toward the Citadel, now looming closer. "You are like that Citadel there," he said bitterly. "You have built a wall around yourself, and you crouch behind it, afraid to look out, afraid to let me in. You must beware, Karin, patience is not one of my virtues. You have had evidence of that before. I will storm that wall, and I will breach your defenses. Someday soon you will find it impossible to refuse me, to refuse yourself."

Karin was unable to speak. She stared at him in the gathering dusk, astonished by the passion of his voice. He held her gaze, his eyes unblinking, his mouth twisted in a harsh line.

At the same moment they both became aware of increased activity on board. A deckhand ran past them, calling to someone at the stern. There was the sound of anchor chains, and a moment later the engines coughed into silence. And then the rest of the guests were crowding alongside them, leaning on the rail and pointing out various features of the city and the purple line of the Laurentian mountains to the north. In the crush of people she was separated from Paul. Céleste had claimed his attention again.

Until darkness fell completely and the fireworks began, Karin felt as though she moved and talked in a daze or perhaps in a dream. Nothing had been settled, she realized. Nothing at all.

THE FIREWORKS LASTED AN HOUR. One after another, brilliant flashes of light shot upward to explode into glittering fountains or else bloomed outward like enormous chrysanthemums before fading away into a smoky blur. At every burst the people on the yacht applauded, their applause echoed by the crowds watching on the shore. Gradually Karin forced herself to respond to the magnificent show. It was not until the final salvo of fireworks exploded into the night sky that she allowed herself to think of what Paul had said. When she did, her anger returned.

The other guests had begun moving forward to the bow where the white-jacketed bartender was again serving drinks, but she lingered in the dark corner of the stern, her hair blowing slightly in the westerly breeze, her hands gripping the deck rail.

She stared up at the ancient Citadel three hundred and sixty feet above the St. Lawrence River. Now that the rockets and flares were no longer lighting up the sky, the looming walls on top of Cape Diamond were a forbidding sight. She could easily imagine a regiment of soldiers in antiquated uniforms scurrying around behind those sturdy walls, armed with muskets, desperately preparing to repel all invaders.

How dare Paul compare her to the Citadel. How dare he accuse her of building a wall around herself to keep him out. When all the time he was engaged to someone else. Obviously she represented a challenge to him; it was impossible for him to accept defeat. How egotistical he was. *A citadel.* She hated him for that.

Damn! She had bitten down on her lower lip so hard she could taste blood. She forced herself to breathe deeply of the salty air, trying to cleanse herself of anger. Paul Dufresne wasn't worth her anger.

There. She was calm now. Her slight shivering was due only to the fact that the sleeveless shirt she'd worn with her blue jeans was not enough protection now that the breeze had freshened.

She turned her head toward the bow, thinking reluctantly that she should probably follow the others before she was missed. But as she stepped away from the rail, someone moved in the shadows a few feet away—a tall lean man, silhouetted against the fairy lights strung from the mast. Her breath caught in her throat. *Paul.* She'd thought he'd gone forward with the rest of the party. How long had he been standing there?

"Are you cold?" he asked as he approached her. "I thought I saw you shiver a moment ago."

So. He had been watching her, spying on her. Had he returned to torment her again? Apparently not. His voice had held concern and perhaps conciliation, and she could see the ghost of his tentative smile in the gloom. Probably he thought she was ready to forgive and forget as usual. He would soon discover she was not to be taken in by his change of mood this time.

But she would not offer him the weapon of her anger. He had used that against her too many times.

"I am a bit chilled," she said politely. "I left my jacket in the saloon. I'll get it now."

"No. Stay a while. I'll give you mine."

Before she could protest, he had taken off his short denim jacket and draped it around her shoulders. "There," he said, giving her shoulder a brisk pat. "Isn't that better?"

She eyed him warily, distrusting his breezy nonchalance. What was he up to now? There was certainly nothing in his manner she could reasonably object to. Even when he started rubbing her spine through the jacket's rough cloth, his touch was casual, almost absentminded. He wasn't even looking at her. He was watching the hordes of people scrambling down the Citadel's grassy flanks, heading for Dufferin Terrace to watch the parade of boats in which they would soon take part.

She stood very stiffly, aware that Paul's jacket had somehow retained the energy of his body and was clinging suggestively to her bare arms and neck. She wanted to snatch the jacket away, fling it to the deck, but if she did so, he would only laugh at her, humiliate her again. No, her best recourse, her only recourse, lay in immobility. She'd heard a phrase once, associated with Mahatma Gandhi—"passive resistance." Yes, that was the course to follow.

She steeled herself not to move, her eyes fixed on the massive rock face in front of her, her stiff pose exaggerated by the fact that her hair was caught under the jacket's collar, forcing her neck into an unnatural position. Apparently Paul noticed this. His hands moved swiftly, ignoring her immediate attempt to forestall him. Gently setting her hand aside, he carefully freed the heavy dark mass of hair, his fingers accidentally brushing against the skin at the back of her neck. Accidentally? Nothing this man did was accidental.

Head rigid, she held her breath while he smoothed her hair into place outside the jacket. "My beautiful Karin," he said softly, one hand lingering against the nape of her neck. "When are you going to admit you want to be seduced as much as I want to seduce you?"

"As it wouldn't be true, I suppose never," she said, proud of the evenness of her voice.

"You prefer forcing me to say things that make you angry? Is that the only way I can make you respond to me?" His voice lowered to a sensuous murmur, his breath stirring her hair at the side of her face. "I don't want to fight with you."

Then why do you torment me so? The hot words rose to her lips, but she bit them back before they could escape. No. She would not rise to his baiting.

After a moment he sighed. "I see. We are to act like civilized people? Very well." Before she had a chance to reply, he draped his arm loosely around her shoulders, his hand curling around her upper arm.

Warmth spread insidiously from his hand, turning her bones liquid, arousing sensations she had sworn would not be allowed to return. But Paul seemed not to notice her quivering response. He had begun pointing out features of the shoreline as dispassionately as though he were again a guide conducting a tour.

Why did she have such conflicting emotions where this man was concerned, she wondered wearily. Even now she had an urge to lean against him, to surrender to her own mindless senses.

He had fallen silent, she realized. Perhaps he had noticed her inattention. She stole a glance at his face, saw that he was watching her, looked away. But he had obviously caught her quick glance. His hand tightened around her arm, his fingers spreading dangerously close to her breast.

In immediate response, adrenaline shot into her system, speeding up her heartbeat so that she was sure he must feel the blood coursing through her veins. Is this passive resistance, her mind mocked.

She swallowed hard, set her teeth. "The fireworks were marvelous, weren't they?" she managed.

"*Magnifique.*" The usual amused note was back in his voice, telling her he knew perfectly well that his touch was affecting her. His dark head had moved closer, and when she glanced sideways again, she could see a pulse beating in his throat below the strong line of his jaw. Obviously he was not unmoved himself. The thought should have dismayed her. Instead it excited her. Dear God, she was a fool.

Paul was gazing off to their right toward the city now, apparently unaware that his fingers were so close to her breast. But that was nonsense. Of course he was aware. He was always aware. And yet when he spoke, his voice was perfectly level. "It's a beautiful sight, isn't it?"

She followed his gaze to where the lights of the city glittered like jewels against the dark buildings. The Château Frontenac dominated the scene as it did from every angle of view. Floodlighted, the turreted hotel looked more enchanted than ever. *Enchanted.* How empty that word sounded to her now.

"Of course, any city is beautiful at night," Paul continued in the same conversational tone. "But when the terrain is hilly, the pattern of light is even more attractive, don't you agree?"

"It *is* lovely," she said in a strained voice.

"You will enjoy my city in winter, also," he went on. "It is very lively, especially during the Winter Carnival in February. An ice palace is constructed on the hill facing the Parliament Buildings I showed you, and there are marvelous ice sculptures along the sidewalks of Ste. Thérèse Street. Also, we have an exciting boat race through the ice on the St. Lawrence and parades at night. Thousands of people come to join in our celebration."

Would she still be here in February, she wondered. Would Paul be married to Céleste then? Why did the thought of his marriage make her feel so sad?

"Perhaps we should join the party now," she suggested as casually as possible. "The parade will begin soon, surely?"

He moved his head to look at her. In the dimness she could not make out his expression, and when he spoke, his voice gave nothing of his thoughts away. "Several boats have to maneuver into position before we can come about. There is no need to hurry. Everyone is managing very well without us."

She glanced beyond him to the brightly lighted bow. The wheelhouse and saloon and other structures hid them from the Lepages and their guests, but she could hear their voices calling out to people on other boats. Lissa must have noticed by now that they were missing. And so must Céleste.

She managed to speak airily. "I don't want to miss anything."

"Karin," he chided. "I am trying to entertain you in an unthreatening manner, which is not an easy task when I want you so desperately. But in spite of my self-restraint, you still want to run away from me."

She turned her head to glare at him. But even as she began to speak, a part of her mind was noticing the way his light blue polo shirt fitted his lean body, noticing, too, the bulge of muscle under the tight short sleeve, remembering how those hard muscles had felt beneath her hands. "I wasn't going to run away," she said shakily. "I simply meant—" She broke off, let out her breath in an exasperated sigh. She was not going to get involved in another battle of wits with him.

"It is all right, *chérie*," Paul murmured close to her ear. "I will not let you fall overboard."

Puzzled, she glanced at him and saw that he was looking down at her hands. Her hands were gripping the rail as though it were a lifeline and she a drowning woman, her knuckles showing whitely in the dark.

She released the rail at once, flexing her fingers to

restore the circulation. Immediately Paul's free hand moved to clasp both her hands close to his chest. His heart was beating in a staccato rhythm that matched her own.

"Please don't," she whispered.

He touched her forehead with his lips. "I want only to warm you, *chérie*. Your hands are cold."

"No. They are fine. I'm not cold at all," she insisted stupidly.

"But you are trembling. Are you still afraid of me, then?"

"Of course I'm not afraid."

"No?" Before she could guess his intention, his hand, still holding hers, pressed against her pounding heart, giving the lie to her words. His gaze was fixed on her mouth. In another second he would kiss her, and if the rush of heat through her body was any indication, she would not stop him.

With a superhuman effort she wrenched herself free of him. "Don't you dare try to kiss me," she said through her teeth.

They faced each other on the shadowed deck, and she thought for a moment that he was going to reach out for her. But instead he laughed. "*Mon Dieu*, but you are a maddening woman." His slanted eyebrows mocked her. "How can you be so sure I *wanted* to kiss you?"

Infuriated, she turned her back on him and looked down at the water lapping the side of the boat, wishing fiercely that she had the strength and the courage to push him overboard.

In the dark water a few stars were reflected. They disappeared as a wave rippled backward from the shore, and she noticed for the first time that the yacht was moving. She could feel the vibration of the powerful engines in the trembling of the deck beneath her feet. How had she missed the sound of the engines starting?

The breeze was stronger now. It caught her hair and whipped it across her face. Brushing it away with the back of her hand, she staggered slightly as the deck shifted beneath her. The boat was angling across the river, rocking as it moved through the swell of the waves. She reached for the rail and missed as the yacht rocked again. The dark horizon seemed to tilt suddenly, first one way then the other. The lights on shore skidded upward, then dipped down.

She felt abruptly dizzy. An uneasy quivering had begun in the pit of her stomach. She took a deep breath, but the quivering didn't go away. Surely she wasn't going to be seasick?

With his usual prescience Paul sensed that something was wrong. As the yacht vibrated again, his arms came around her, steadying her, and she made no objection, glad to have something solid to hold onto.

"You are unwell?" he asked softly, and as she managed to nod, he looked at her with concern. "Your face is very pale. Come, we will go inside."

Without giving her a chance to object, he pressed her close to his side and steadied her across the deck. She didn't seem to have the strength to protest, anyway, and in any case, she thought he meant to take her to the saloon where they had eaten dinner. The saloon was brightly lighted. She would be safe there—anyone could walk in. She felt no apprehension until he ducked down into the chart room, pulling her along through a companionway and into one of the cabins that she hadn't seen on her earlier tour.

Her heart thudded as the door closed behind them. He released her as soon as she moved away, but he kept his back to the door, effectively blocking her escape. She stood still for a second, trying to regain her equilibrium, looking around the cabin for another exit. There was none that she could see. It was a fairly large cabin that seemed to glow with a golden warmth. She was stunned by its decor. Surely a room like this belonged in a sultan's harem, rather than on board a family yacht? Was she hallucinating now?

The almost wall-to-wall bed, covered with gold satin, looked real enough. So did the piles of satin pillows and the silken draperies that hid the porthole from view. "I can almost see Scheherazade whispering to the sultan through a thousand and one nights," she said nervously.

"Quite a nest, isn't it?" Paul said from behind her. "Suzanne Lepage likes her luxury. Do you know she actually refers to this as 'camping out'?"

Karin opened her mouth to tell him she didn't want to trespass in *madame*'s private quarters, and she certainly didn't want to be alone with him, but as the yacht turned to head downstream, and the entire hull vibrated once more, she thought better of it and sat down abruptly on the thickly padded bed, trying to concentrate on regaining her sense of balance.

She barely noticed that Paul had taken his jacket from her shoulders and was removing her sandals, but when he swung her legs up and began easing her down on the bed, she struggled to remain upright. "What are you doing?" she demanded shakily.

"It's perfectly obvious, *ma chère*," he said patiently as he pulled the covers free from under her body. "I'm trying to get you to lie down. You are evidently suffering from mal de mer, and you will feel better if we can get your head lower than your body. You need to lie still for a few minutes."

Deftly he eased her down again and pulled pillows under her back and feet. She did feel less dizzy almost at once, but she still felt vaguely light-headed. Yes, she needed to rest, just for a minute. Eyes closed, she let herself relax into the soft mattress. Satin sheets. Madame Lepage certainly did enjoy her luxury. What a strange woman she was. Such a contrast to her daughter, Céleste. What would Céleste say if she saw Karin lying down on her mother's bed with Paul in the room? That was for Paul to worry about, not her. As soon as her head cleared, she would insist on returning to the bow.

The boat was rocking gently now like a cradle, rocking her almost to sleep. Drifting, she was startled to hear Paul rummaging around in a cupboard. He was certainly making himself at home. She forced open her heavy eyelids and saw him pouring something green from a bottle into a crystal glass. As he came toward her, she heard the clink of ice cubes. "I was sure *madame* would have a well-stocked liquor cabinet," he said as he held the glass out to her. "This is iced crème de menthe. Sometimes it helps to settle the stomach."

She had never cared for crème de menthe, but she

dutifully raised herself on one elbow and took the glass from his hand. He was a doctor after all; he must know what was best for her.

To her surprise, the cool green liquid did seem to help, and she sipped it appreciatively. "Thank you," she said when she was done. "I'm feeling much better now."

Paul smiled. "*Bon*. I was quite concerned. But you must lie still for a while longer until we are sure you have recovered."

Gently he eased her down again, placed another pillow under her head, then covered her to the waist with a fleecy blanket, tucking it tightly under her so that her legs were effectively imprisoned. Before she could loosen the blanket, he sat down on the edge of the bed and leaned over her, one arm lightly resting across her limp body.

Weakly she closed her eyes against the image of his face, so close to hers. "That was very stupid of me," she said nervously.

"Not stupid at all. It happens to many people. Especially when the water is a little choppy, and the vision is forced to accommodate a fluctuating horizon. We are not sure of the exact cause of mal de mer, but we do know it is related to stimulation of the eye."

She felt his fingers, feather light, brush against one of her closed eyelids and was appalled at the immediate fiery response that they evoked. Every nerve end she possessed was following his fingertips as they traced a searing path across her cheekbone to her ear. She forced herself to lie motionless, hoping desperately that he wouldn't sense her response.

"The ears are also affected," he continued calmly. "The ear is an organ of balance, you see, as well as one of hearing—a very delicate balancing structure affected by unusual motion."

On the surface his words were merely textbook language, intended to explain her dizziness to her, but as he spoke, his breath was warm against her face, and his fingers were delicately caressing her ear, barely touching, gently rubbing the lobe between fingers and thumb before moving down to her neck.

He made a sound that was somewhere between a laugh and a groan. "Oh, Karin, my good intentions are all destroyed. I just can't resist you. And look here, your pulse is very rapid. It beats in your throat like a prisoner begging to be free. Shall we set it free?"

Her eyes shot open as he began unfastening the upper buttons of her shirt. His blue eyes were fixed in apparent candor on her face. "In cases of stress it is very important to loosen the clothing," he explained solemnly.

She remembered at once that because of the earlier heat she had decided against the restraint of a bra, confident that her cotton shirt was opaque enough to conceal everything. She struggled against his confining arm, pushing at it with ineffectual hands, but without pausing in his self-imposed task, he moved his other hand to grip both of her wrists, pinning them down against her waist. Arching her back, she tried desperately to break his grip, but his fingers were like steel. Kicking was impossible, her legs were useless in the tightly wrapped blanket. Panting, she glared at him. "Do you take advantage of all your female patients, Dr. Dufresne?" she demanded furiously.

He shook his head absently, ignoring her struggles. His gaze was concentrated now on the soft valley between her breasts as he slowly, methodically, undid the last button. "You are not my patient, Karin. You have not registered at my clinic; there are no records of your medical history on file. We are not doctor and patient, *chérie*—only man and woman."

His expression softened as he stroked the fabric aside from her breasts, but he still paid no attention to her futile attempts to pull away from him. "See how your heart beats," he said softly. "How can you keep insisting you do not want me?"

Belatedly she remembered her earlier resolution. If she continued to fight him, he would only become more persistent. *Passive resistance*, she repeated silently.

With an effort she stopped struggling, forced her voice to be even, cool. "Very well, Paul, I won't fight you. But if you continue, I will scream. You will be surprised how loudly I can scream. Perhaps that will put an end to your game."

His mouth was suddenly stern. "Scream if you wish. No doubt you will be heard. Then what? My reputation would hang in shreds. This incident could possibly mean the end of my career as a doctor. Is that what you want?" He took a deep breath, and the corners of his mouth tightened again. "Has it occurred to you that I would not risk so much just for a game? Has it occurred to you that if I want only a playmate, I have a whole town to choose from? No, Karin, lovely Karin, I assure you, this is not a game."

She stared at him, astonished. The intensity in his voice told her that he meant what he said.

And now she could feel a tingling sensation as her traitorous breasts distended, the nipples hardening under his gaze. "You are not fighting me, anyway, *chérie*," Paul added softly. "You are fighting yourself. You know that you want me. Tell me so. Let yourself be a woman, my woman."

Moving deliberately, he released her hands, shifted his weight and placed an index finger on each of her erect nipples, not pressing, just touching lightly, producing an electrifying response of such force that she gasped involuntarily.

And then he did finally raise his gaze to meet hers. The light from the shaded lamps shadowed his eyes, darkening them so that she shivered under their challenging intensity. And then she saw that his mouth was no longer stern, was in fact curved upward, his lips slightly parted. He was going to kiss her—now. And she wanted his kiss, his touch, wanted *him*. Her own lips parted. A million miles away she heard his voice murmur, "Yes, Karin, yes."

The room was disappearing around her, dissolving into its own shadow, its golden light fading into a distant glow. Her hands lifted to pull his face fiercely down.

His lips were cold from the night air, instantly demanding on her own. Her hands tangled in the thick softness of his dark hair and held as his hands moved intimately over her body, lifting her hips, pressing her against his entire length. They had become a single unit—one heart beating, throbbing to the rhythm of their rapid breathing. She felt a kind of aching sweetness invade her body, coupled with an overwhelming relief that the fighting was over, relief because there was such a rightness to this feeling of unity, such a rightness to this act.

There was a moment's coolness as he freed her legs from the tangled blankets, then heat again as his hands fumbled at her waistband. Without hesitation she reached to help him, and then his mouth left hers and moved with exquisite torturing slowness down her throat to her breast, his lips opening finally to enclose the rigid nipple.

She had one instant of startling clarity, remembering that she was on a boat crowded with people—Céleste's boat. Céleste was expecting to marry Paul. This whole episode was absolute madness, utter insanity. But then her thoughts disintegrated as Paul's hand moved across her bare abdomen and touched lightly, with great delicacy, between her legs. A tremor ran through his body, his strong male body, and she clutched him tighter, filled suddenly with a sense of her own power. Her mouth groped for Paul's as his head came up to hers once more. Finding his mouth, her tongue searched out his hunger, answered it with her own. Her hands slid under his shirt, moved across his back against firm skin that felt so different from her own. She was beyond thought, carried away on an irresistible tide of desire. She didn't want to think, not about Céleste, not about consequences. She wanted only to feel, to stay here forever with Paul, the two of them locked together in an endless embrace, spinning deeper and deeper into the flickering shadows of the night.

She felt the tension in him a second before he moved. Abruptly he pulled away from her, adjusted the zipper of her jeans, buttoned her shirt across her aching breasts and dragged the blanket up to cover her to the chin.

She felt bereft, deserted, disoriented. "Wh-what?" she stammered.

He put his fingers to her lips. "Someone's coming," he said huskily. And now she, too, could hear light footsteps in the companionway beyond the cabin. As Paul hastily smoothed his hair and adjusted his own clothing, the footsteps hesitated outside the door. Someone tapped lightly.

"Céleste?" Karin breathed.

Paul shrugged. "It does not matter, *chérie*," he said softly. "As I tried to tell you earlier, I am not engaged to Céleste." As the knock was repeated, he picked up her hand and called, *"Entrez!"*

By the time the door opened, and not Céleste, but Lissa, stuck her head around the door, he was sitting upright on the edge of the bed, holding Karin's wrist loosely, his gaze fixed on the watch on his left wrist.

"Seventy-eight," he announced. "Much better, but still not normal. You must rest a few minutes more." Over his shoulder he added casually to Lissa, "Poor Karin has had an attack of mal de mer, Lissa. She has been quite distraught."

"What a shame," Lissa replied. She was trying to look sympathetic, but there was a note of utter disbelief in her voice.

Shame flooded Karin's entire body. This was sordid—so very sordid. She glanced at Paul. He was still holding her wrist, looking completely unperturbed, in control of the situation and himself.

Her own acting ability was not so refined. She had no idea what to say, or how to meet Lissa's suspicious gaze. So she did the only thing left to do. She groaned slightly and closed her eyes. The groan at least, she thought, had sounded convincing. It had come directly from her soul.

After a moment she sensed that Lissa had moved forward toward the bed. She opened her eyes.

"You do look awfully flushed," Lissa said uncertainly.

"I feel a bit hot," Karin admitted. "And very foolish." Which was the truth.

"Do you think you are well enough to get up now? We're heading back to the marina. I don't think anyone actually missed you, but Céleste was asking about Paul. I could go and explain...."

"No, that isn't necessary," Karin said. "I can make it."

Paul stood up, looking down at her solicitously—the concerned doctor. How easily playing a role came to him, she thought. She sat up, swung her legs over the side of the bed opposite Lissa, glanced quickly down at her clothing. Yes, she looked all right. "Thank you for helping me, Paul," she said carefully, playing a role herself.

"My pleasure, Karin." There was a hint of laughter in his voice now, but Lissa didn't seem to notice.

No one except Céleste appeared to have noticed their absence. They managed to mingle with the others just as the yacht slid into the dock. Céleste slipped her hand under Paul's arm. "Can we go now?" she asked in French.

She had spoken quietly, but Karin heard her. Puzzled, she glanced at Paul. He looked extremely uncomfortable. His gaze shifted to Karin then back to Céleste. *"Je ne sais pas,"* he said slowly.

The girl's face was luminous with pleading. "You promised," she said plaintively.

Paul sighed. Whatever Céleste was asking him to do, he was weakening, Karin saw. Something cold and hard and cynical was growing inside her. She could see the indecision on his face. Surely he wasn't going to—yes, he was. He smiled a little ruefully at the girl and patted her hand where it still clung to his arm. "All right," he said.

At once Céleste smiled beatifically and reached up to kiss him on the cheek. Then she turned to her mother. "Paul is going to take me for a drive, *maman*," she said happily.

Madame Lepage seemed a little unsure. "It is very windy now," she said slowly. She looked doubtfully from Céleste to Paul, then back again. While she was debating with herself, Paul spoke softly to Karin, who was still standing there in stunned silence.

"I am sorry. I did promise. I will explain."

Karin swallowed, suppressing the angry retort she wanted to make. "Whatever happened to 'You came with me, you leave with me'?" she asked coldly. Then she shrugged. "I can drive home with Lissa and Charles. It makes no difference to me."

"But I want to tell you why...."

"It is not necessary," she said in that same clipped voice, afraid if she didn't get away from him immediately, she would burst into tears. How could he? After that heated—that *ardent*—scene in the cabin, after denying he was engaged to the girl, how could he go off with her into the night?

"Chérie," he said softly. He raised one hand as though he were going to touch her, but at that moment Madame Lepage decided to give her permission, and Céleste turned back, beaming, to take Paul's arm, looking up at him with absolute adoration, her smile blinding.

The gangplank had been lowered. The guests began streaming down it, laughing and calling, *"Merci, merci beaucoup,"* to the Lepages, their voices gay. Paul and Céleste went with them arm in arm, the girl hurrying him along eagerly. He looked back once at Karin, made a helpless gesture with one hand. "I'll see you tomorrow," he called.

Not if I can help it, Karin thought, but she didn't say it aloud. What was the use? He wouldn't have heard her anyway; she could hardly scream it out. And even if he had heard her, he'd have ignored her. No doubt he would turn up tomorrow, acting as though everything was normal.

She took a deep breath and held it against the cold fury that was threatening to choke her. This might be normal behavior for Paul Dufresne, she thought angrily, but it wasn't for her. When he came around tomorrow, she wouldn't be there.

CHAPTER ELEVEN

THERE WAS A THUNDERSTORM during the night. Karin lay listening to it, watching lightning fork across the inky sky outside her bedroom window, trying not to remember Paul's reference to the *1812* Overture. *Lightning and thunder, fire in the blood and pulses pounding.*

She had always enjoyed thunderstorms, found them exciting, exhilarating, especially when she was cozily tucked into bed, out of danger, safe from nature's dramatic demonstration of her powers. She was not in a mood to find this storm exhilarating, but it did seem fitting—it certainly reflected her feelings.

In the morning the storm had receded into the distance, but it had not stopped. She could hear an occasional muffled crackle of thunder as she dressed, and a glance out the window showed a threatening sky, boiling with angry clouds. It was raining, not hard, but with a persistence that seemed to indicate the sun would not appear all day.

All the same, she dressed in her red and navy sweat suit; she had walked in the rain before.

No one else was around, she found when she descended the stairs. She was not surprised. Etienne and Madame Durocher had returned only a little while before them the previous night. Charles and Lissa had stayed awake even later. She'd heard them arguing in their bedroom. Evidently Sara Savard had invited them all to go on somewhere, and Charles had refused. He had to get back to work early the next morning, he'd insisted. He had taken too many holidays lately. To please Lissa, he had sacrificed precious hours of his time. He could not go on doing so.

Karin sympathized with his attitude. He'd set himself a monumental task; he had to get it done in the time he had allotted to it. But she also understood why Lissa was upset. She'd had a taste of Quebec society, she wanted more.

Their argument had lasted a long time. Karin had buried her head in the pillow, trying not to listen, wondering if Etienne was also awake. At last the thunderstorm had drowned out the voices in the next room. And eventually she had slept.

Someone had been up before her, she saw when she entered the kitchen. The remains of a lonely breakfast had been left on the white table. Coffee and toast. Lissa preferred tea in the mornings, and Etienne usually drank milk. Charles must have risen early and gone to work. She should probably join him, but she didn't feel up to concentrating.

After drinking a glass of water, she wrote a note for Lissa on the pad beside the telephone. She would get breakfast out after her walk, she said, and then do some exploring on her own.

The rain increased when she was halfway along the deserted Promenade des Gouverneurs, and she took shelter in one of the green and white kiosks that looked out over the river. She sat there for a long time, staring at the choppy gray water, trying not to think about anything. Which of course was impossible.

What she needed, she decided at last, was some final

concrete thing that would put an end to the hold Paul Dufresne seemed to have on her. Something that would turn her off him altogether, something that would convince her body, as well as her mind.

The idea that came to her seemed to have been lying in wait in her mind for a long time.

Breakfast first, she decided. Perhaps food would soothe the gnawing ache inside her, help her decide on the best course.

She went into the first café she saw in town and ordered an omelet. She was the only customer. The rush period had just ended, the waiter told her. The offices and stores were open now, and all the clerks had gone to work. Probably, he said, the majority of tourists would not venture out this morning. He sighed. "We have a saying, *mademoiselle*. 'In Quebec we have two seasons: July and winter.' And here it is July, and we have rain."

"It was beautiful yesterday," Karin reminded him.

He smiled engagingly. He was very young. "We should have sunshine every day to match your smile, *mademoiselle*."

Typical French gallantry, Karin thought, rather bitterly. Flowery compliments came as naturally to Frenchmen, even Canadian Frenchmen, as breathing. They must feel an obligation to live up to their mother country's reputation for romance.

She felt better physically once she had eaten, but her spirits hadn't risen at all. The skies were still gray. She found herself making up objections to the things she'd decided to do. She would look foolish trying to hire a calèche today. Who would want to go sight-seeing in weather like this?.

When she reached the Place d'Armes, only two calèches were in sight, and neither of them was attended by Violette. It had been a silly idea, anyway, she told herself as she turned away. And then she saw another calèche just turning into the square. *Violette.* There was no mistaking that long glossy black hair. Without allowing herself time for reflection, Karin waved the girl to a halt and climbed up into the back seat. "I'd like to see the city," she said. "One hour, perhaps?"

"Certainly, *mademoiselle*," the girl replied. "My name is Violette, and I speak English pretty good. It will be twenty dollars." She laughed. "Perhaps I should charge less today. I cannot supply the sun."

She seemed very cheerful. And healthy. Wholesome like Maggie. Karin could not imagine either of them using any kind of drugs. And how she was going to introduce the subject, she had no idea.

As the horse clopped steadily along, patiently ignoring the water splashing around his feet, and Violette pointed out sights she had already seen with Paul, Karin racked her brain for an opening but couldn't come up with one. Violette's cheerful voice prattled on about the weather, yesterday's fireworks, the buildings they were passing—a group of small hotels. "Château this, Château that," Violette laughed at one point. "Nearly all the hotels are called a château of some kind, whether they have six rooms or sixty."

"I know someone who owns a château," Karin offered, seizing her chance. "I don't know if it's a real one, either. Perhaps you know my friend? His name is Paul Dufresne."

"Dr. Paul?" Violette turned around to smile at Karin. "I thought I had seen you before. You were with Dr. Paul, weren't you? Last week sometime."

Karin hesitated. "I think I remember you, too. I didn't realize you knew Paul." She gave a small false-sounding laugh. "As I remember it, you looked as though you didn't want to know him."

Violette laughed without inhibition. "Oh, that was because I was embarrassed. I had been avoiding him, you see. I was afraid he would be angry with me."

"Why should he be angry with you?" How difficult it was to keep her voice casual.

Violette did not seem to notice her strain. She merely shrugged and looked forward again. They were negotiating a rather steep turn now, and she gave all her attention to the task for a while. Then she said lightly, "He has a murderous temper, Dr. Paul, when any of us misbehave. His anger will freeze one's blood. You should have seen how angry he was with Anne—" She broke off suddenly.

"Yes?" Karin encouraged.

But Violette had evidently decided she had said too much. "We are coming to the St. John's Gate now, *mademoiselle*," she said. "Would you like to go through it, or shall we turn around?"

"Turn around, please. I'm mostly interested in the old city." She took a deep breath. "Does Paul really have a temper?" she asked. "I've never seen it."

"Then, perhaps you haven't crossed him yet," Violette said ambiguously, then launched into a description of the view that could be seen from the top of the stone gate, insisting that Karin should go up there sometime when the weather was better.

From then on she kept up a rapid commentary that left no room for questions. Karin tried once more after they had returned to Place d'Armes, as she was pulling her billfold out of her sweat-shirt pocket to pay Violette. "Do you know André Moreau?" she asked. "I think he is a friend of Dr. Paul's, too."

Violette frowned prettily, then shook her head. "I don't know him."

"He's a young man with a beard. An artist," Karin persisted.

"No, I don't think I know him. Does he use drugs?"

Karin's breath caught in her throat. "I don't know," she said in a strained voice.

Violette hesitated, then laughed. "He probably does if he knows Dr. Paul."

Before Karin could respond to that, Violette clicked her tongue, and the horse dutifully pulled away. *"Au revoir, mademoiselle,"* Violette called to Karin. "Come and see me again, okay?"

"Okay," Karin said automatically. She was stunned. Somehow she had taken it for granted that her twenty dollars would be wasted. She had not expected Violette to volunteer such shattering information.

How had she let herself be lulled into thinking Paul must be innocent because the police had not detained him? That fact didn't prove a thing. For all she knew, they could have let him go for lack of proof. He might even be out on bail. No—they'd never let him practice medicine. But he *wasn't* working just now. Dear God, what was she supposed to believe?

She shook her head abruptly. She couldn't stand here thinking about it. She had to *do* something. The rain was intensifying again. She couldn't keep walking around the city in the rain. And why should she now? If Paul Dufresne turned up at the Vincent house, she would demand a full explanation. She should have done that earlier.

BY THE TIME she reached rue des Fleurs, the rain was pelting down, and ominous rolls of thunder were heralding another storm front. She hurried along the street, head down, barely looking where she was going. She didn't see Paul until she almost bumped into him. He had evidently been sitting in the car that was drawn up to the curb. It was a bright red Buick. The passenger door was open. As she recovered her balance and stared up at him, he indicated the passenger seat. "Get in," he said, taking her arm.

"No," she said just as tersely. She pulled her arm free.

He sighed audibly. Then his eyes narrowed, and he spoke very slowly and distinctly as though he were speaking to a child. "You will get in the car, or I will lift you up and put you in it." There was so much menace in his voice that she was sitting in the car before she quite realized she had moved. Paul walked around the front and folded himself in beside her.

"Where are you taking me?" she demanded as he started the engine.

"You will see." The car was moving along the street, gaining speed.

"But I don't want to go anywhere with you," Karin protested. "I do want to talk to you, but we can talk in the house. Anyway, I'm wet. I need to change."

He darted an exasperated glance sideways. "This won't take long—a few minutes only. There is someone I wish you to talk to, or rather to listen to."

Karin digested this in silence for a while before asking, "Who?"

He sighed. "I wish you to appreciate, Karin, that I am a proud man. I do not like to defend my actions, especially when my actions have been misinterpreted. But it seems that I have met a woman as proud as I. So we will rely on another to straighten out this most recent contretemps."

He was driving down the steep Côte de la Montagne now, and before Karin could ask any more questions, he drove around a corner, stopped the car and pressed the horn. "Sit still," he ordered when she reached for the door handle. Then he got out of the car and pulled his seat forward. To Karin's surprise, André Moreau came out of a nearby house and climbed into the shallow back seat, murmuring a greeting to her.

"What is going on?" she demanded as Paul climbed back in and closed the door. Without answering, he drove along the street and around the corner into a little lane. The car coasted to a stop. Paul switched off the ignition and looked at André in the rearview mirror. "Tell her, André," he said.

"You are sure she will not tell anybody?"

"Tell her."

Karin had turned in her seat to stare at André. He smiled at her weakly. "I don't know where to begin," he said.

Paul made an exasperated sound. "Tell her you love Céleste."

André nodded. *"Oui."* He looked a little sheepishly at Karin. "I am in love wth Céleste," he said.

"Oh," Karin said. She had hoped André was going to explain about Valier. That whole business with

Céleste didn't seem so important now. But she supposed she'd have to hear André out. "I guessed that you loved her," she said.

"And Céleste is in love with me."

She glanced at Paul. "I don't understand."

"Just listen," Paul said implacably.

"Céleste and I met at the university," André explained. "We wanted, we felt. . . ." He inhaled deeply. "We fell in love. But her parents took one look at me and said *non*." He grinned wryly at Karin. "Her father has a way of saying no, *mademoiselle*, that makes one feel one's head is not too safe on one's shoulders."

"I can imagine," Karin said. A faint understanding was beginning to dawn. "Did he forbid you to see each other?"

"*Oui*. He and Madame Lepage both. And Céleste is a dutiful daughter. She would not defy her parents, you understand, at least not openly." He paused. "But there are ways around things. It was Céleste's idea to use Paul—I mean, to ask Paul. . . ."

"To use me," Paul put in emphatically. "That little minx has been able to twist me around her finger since she was three years old."

"She is very devious," André said with pride. "She concocted the idea of persuading Paul to seem interested in her. He would invite her to go out with him, but in reality he would bring her to meet me."

"That is where we were going when you saw us leave the Château Frontenac," Paul put in, looking at Karin. "We were attending a formal dinner in honor of a friend of Claude, who was also a friend of my father. Once the meal was over, Céleste decided the amenities had been satisfied, and no one would mind if we disappeared. I realize my deceit of her parents must seem inexcusable, but I'm afraid I've rather enjoyed deceiving Claude and Suzanne. They are such terrible snobs." He shrugged. "To go on. As you saw yesterday, Céleste can be very persuasive. It was important to her to see André last night. She was most unhappy because the last time they were together, they quarreled."

"I had told her we could not go on meeting in secret," André said, taking up the story. "I do not like this sneaking around corners. I do enough of that in other ways."

He accompanied this last statement with a glance at Paul. Paul frowned but made no comment, and as André went on talking, Karin filed the odd remark away in her mind to be examined later.

"The problem is, *mademoiselle*," André continued gloomily, "if Monsieur and Madame Lepage knew that Céleste and I were still meeting, they would send her to their other home in Montreal. I could follow her, of course, but my father is there, and he would pressure me again to keep on with my studies." He smiled sadly at Karin. "Last semester I dropped out of too many classes, and the university wrote to my father, informing him of this. So he stopped my allowance. I have only what I can make myself. And that is not enough to suit Céleste's parents. The only way I can get into their good graces is to apply myself in school and proceed to the making of shoes. Which I do not want to do."

He sat back in the seat. "Céleste does not want me to do this, either," he added loyally. "She encourages me to go on with my painting. She is content, she says, to meet me whenever Paul can arrange it, at least until something else can be arranged."

"If you would follow my suggestion—" Paul began, but André cut him off.

"You have done enough. I will work this thing out for myself and Céleste. Someday my work will speak for itself."

"Not if no one sees it, you idiot!" Paul exclaimed.

André ignored him. He looked at Karin again. "I understand that you have. . .misconstrued Paul's attentions to Céleste, and it is important to him that you understand. Have I explained well enough?"

"Yes," Karin said impatiently, "but there is something else. . . ."

Paul groaned. "Lord help us, André." He chuckled softly, then looked at Karin with a challenging smile. "Surely you are satisfied that I am not engaged to Céleste?"

She was annoyed at his mocking tone. "Yes, but there is still. . . ."

Paul's black eyebrows had slanted upward. "I am surprised you could not see I was acting as Cupid," he said with mock solemnity. "Surely I look the part." He glanced at her questioningly when she didn't smile. "What is this something else?"

She looked away, trying to collect her thoughts. She still didn't want to ask about Valier—that was the trouble. She was suddenly feeling very warm in spite of her damp clothing. The car felt airless. The windows were tightly closed, and their breath had steamed up the windows. She wished Paul had chosen a better place for this discussion. Why could he not have taken her to meet André in a restaurant, or perhaps to his home?

It didn't matter. She could no longer delay. But still she couldn't just come out flatly with an accusation. She turned to look at André. "Am I to understand, then, that the reason you spoke of Paul so negatively was because you resented his help?"

He looked a little shamefaced again. "Paul does too much for me." He glanced at Paul. "I *am* grateful, Paul. But you see, I was right. This silliness might have jeopardized—"

"André," Paul said warningly, and again Karin wondered.

"But you sounded as though you hated him," Karin persisted.

"This is not the only area in my life in which Paul interferes," André said stiffly. "A man has his pride, *mademoiselle*."

"Even Michelangelo accepted help," Paul said sternly. "It would all be so easy if you would just—"

"No, Paul," André said. He sounded weary. This was evidently an argument they'd had before. Karin couldn't follow all of it, but it seemed to have no bearing on the questions that were most pressing.

She swallowed against a sudden dryness in her throat, then forced herself to look directly at Paul. "None of this explains what you and André were doing with Henri Valier," she said.

For a second there was a thunderstruck silence. Then she heard André draw in his breath sharply. *"Nom de Dieu,"* he breathed.

Paul stared at her as though she had suddenly grown two heads. "What are you talking about?" he asked. His voice was harsh.

"I saw you," Karin said. "I watched you and

André go back to Place Royale and meet with Valier.
The next day I saw Valier's photograph in the newspaper.''

Paul's face was darkening dangerously. "And you
concluded—"

"I concluded that you and André were somehow
mixed up with his disgusting business. What else
could I think? What *is* your connection with Valier?"

Paul didn't answer. He had turned away. He was
inserting the key in the ignition. Karin glanced at André. He was staring at her, his bearded face pale with
shock. "You'd better let me out here," he said suddenly to Paul. "It is best if we are not seen together
right now."

Paul nodded shortly. "Don't worry, André," he
said as he opened his door to let André climb out of the
car. "I will deal with Karin. I will make her see. . . ."

See what, Karin wondered and was suddenly
afraid. There was an expression on Paul's face she
had never seen before. She had seen him angry, yes,
no matter what she had said to Violette. But this was
a grim anger that did, as Violette had jokingly suggested, freeze her blood.

Without consciously deciding to do so, she opened
her door and got out. "Where are you going?" Paul
asked as she slammed the door behind her. But Karin
was already halfway across the street, running, wanting only to get away from the man who had so suddenly looked like a stranger—a dangerous stranger.

He called her name twice, and then she heard him
say something in French that sounded profane, but
she didn't slow down.

He caught up with her halfway up the Côte de la

Montagne. She heard his shoes on the wet sidewalk and tried to increase her speed. But she kept stumbling on the steep hill.

He grabbed her arm and swung her around to face him. He wasn't even out of breath, she noticed. She stared up at him, trying to recover her own breath. His mouth twisted as he looked at her. His eyes were very blue. "*Mon Dieu*, Karin," he said. "I am sorry. I didn't mean to frighten you. I was taken by surprise. Please, *chérie*, don't look at me like this."

"How else can I look at you?" she asked. "I should have believed Violette when she told me what a temper you had. I should have—"

His expression of astonishment stopped the words on her lips. "You know Violette? How did you— what are you talking about?"

"I rode with Violette this morning," she said flatly. "I asked her about you and André, and she told me—"

Again he interrupted her. "You mentioned André and me at the same time?"

"Of course. Why not? Is your relationship a secret? Surely anyone could have seen you two together the same way I did."

He was holding her as though he wanted to shake her, his grip tightening on her arm. Then he frowned, not in anger, more as though he were trying to remember something. "I took a chance that day, and again when I came looking for you. But that was before. . . ." His voice trailed away. He seemed to be thinking hard. "You actually told Violette that André and I were friends?"

Karin made an effort to keep her voice low. People

were passing them on either side, glancing at them curiously. "I'm not sure," she said. "Yes, I think so. Why? What does it matter?"

"It may not." He seemed to be talking more to himself than to her. Then his gaze sharpened, focusing on her face. "You may have put André in the gravest danger. Tell me everything you said to Violette. Everything. I have to know if you mentioned Valier to her."

"I'm not going to tell you anything as long as you hold onto me like this," Karin said hotly, trying to pull her arm free.

And then he did shake her. "This is no time to be stubborn. Tell me."

"I will not," she said. And then everything seemed to happen very fast so that afterward she wasn't sure if Paul had shaken her again, or if she had tugged herself free. Whichever it was, he released her suddenly, and she backed away hastily. Too hastily. She crashed into an old man who was toiling up the hill at the edge of the sidewalk, tried to support him as he seemed in danger of falling, then fell herself, stumbling over her own feet in an effort to regain her balance.

She landed on her right side, half on the sidewalk, half in the street. Her rib cage hit the high curbing with a thud that she felt down to her toes. Pain shot like a sword thrust through her side, and all the breath left her lungs.

CHAPTER TWELVE

SEVERAL PEOPLE CROWDED AROUND KARIN to offer help. One man wanted to assist her to her feet, but Paul curtly told him to leave her alone until he'd had a chance to check her over. He knelt beside her in the rain-wet street, his voice reassuring her as his hands gently moved over her. She managed to gasp out answers when he questioned her about the location and severity of the pain, but most of her concentration was involved in trying to breathe. Each breath seemed more painful than the last.

Paul had taken off his jacket and put it around her, but it wasn't much protection. They were both getting soaked to the skin. "I'm okay," she managed to say. Her voice sounded strangled.

His eyes flashed her a concerned glance, and he muttered something in French that included the word *stupide*. She wondered weakly which one of them he was referring to. Herself probably.

After a few minutes he lifted her carefully to her feet and supported her into a shop doorway out of the rain. He had sent someone to bring his car, he told her.

In a short time they were at the Hôtel-Dieu Hospital, and he turned her over to a young doctor in the Emergency Room.

The next hour was a blur of pain. The X rays were the worst part of it. She had to stand and press herself against the machine—front, side, back. The machine was cold, and she recoiled from it, the movement sending waves of pain through her body again. But she was able to breathe more easily now.

"No lung damage," the young doctor informed her at last. "Only a couple of fractured ribs."

"Is that all?" Karin managed. "What happens now?"

She was sitting on the end of an examining table, wearing a skimpy white hospital gown that tied at the back. Someone had helped her off with her damp clothing, toweled her wet hair. She remembered a red-haired nurse who had smiled sympathetically and had been very gentle. She must look a fright, she thought, and didn't much care.

The doctor smiled at her. He was blond, very young and clean looking, and almost callously cheerful. He sounded American. "Not much happens now, I'm afraid," he told her. "We don't believe in strapping ribs anymore. The strapping restricts breathing, and there's a danger of pneumonia. I'll give you some pain pills, which will help." He grinned. "They will also make you as woozy as a happy drunk. The rest is up to your body. With proper care it will heal itself in two or three weeks."

"Two or three weeks!" Karin exclaimed, then grimaced as pain shot through her again. Gingerly she clasped her right hand to her side, feeling a need to hold herself together.

"Maybe longer," the doctor added cheerfully. "You've also got dislocation of the chondrocostal junction—the place on the ribs where the cartilage and the bony parts come together. That'll probably take longer than the ribs to heal." He had her take a couple of pills with water from a paper cup, gave her a prescription for more pills and then told her to call him if anything felt worse. "Don't sneeze under any circumstances," he concluded. He left the room, whistling, leaving Karin alone with an immediately tickling nose.

A few minutes later the red-headed nurse turned up with a hospital robe for Karin to wear home. Paul arrived as the nurse was helping her into it. He looked a little drier, but not much. His black hair was clinging damply to his forehead. His eyes looked concerned, but his mouth was grim. "What are you so angry about?" the nurse asked in a teasing voice.

"I'm angry with myself for being so stupid," he said shortly. He looked at Karin, his eyes darkening. "Karin, I don't know what to say to you."

She managed a smile. "My own fault. I tend to overreact."

She was aware that the nurse was watching them both with obvious curiosity. "May I go home now?" she asked.

Paul nodded and helped her carefully off the table while the nurse went off to find a wheelchair and a bag for her wet clothes. Karin was glad of Paul's enfolding arm. The pain had intensified as soon as she moved. She let herself lean against him, still holding onto her side. "This is getting to be a habit," she said breathlessly through the pain. "If it's not exhaustion or seasickness, it's broken ribs. This is some vacation you're having."

He didn't smile. Which wasn't very friendly of him, Karin thought, considering how much effort had gone into trying to make the joke. "Not very friendly," she said aloud, feeling suddenly light-headed. Her voice sounded slurred, and she realized the pills had begun to take effect. She looked up at Paul. "I don't think I'm going to...." she began, and then her knees started buckling under her.

Immediately he lifted her up into his arms, moving carefully to avoid giving her pain. She held onto her side and settled her head against his shoulder. His shirt was still damp. Someone told him so—some disembodied voice that seemed to come from inside her own head and yet was a long way away.

"Don't worry about it," he said, and his voice was tender. She could feel his breath warm on her cheek. She looked at his face, so close to hers. He was gazing at her with concern. So worried. So solemn. Such a nice face. She really did like his face. Had she spoken aloud again? She wasn't sure. But he was smiling now.

"That's better," she said and closed her eyes. She felt herself beginning to drift away, but she heard the nurse return with the wheelchair. Paul refused it. He didn't want her to move more than was necessary, he said; he would carry her. Then they were traveling through the hospital corridors, Paul walking slowly so she wouldn't be jarred. She heard people greeting him from every side. They would know him, of course. They sounded pleased to see him, curious about his burden, which was hardly surprising, but affectionate and respectful. If they knew what she knew.... The thought trailed away. She couldn't remember what it was she knew.

A moment later she felt a change of air. They were going outside, she supposed. Someone must have opened the door for them. Her eyelids felt too heavy to open. A sort of warm darkness seemed to be gathering around her, numbing the pain. She heard Paul say, "*Merci*, Martine." Who was Martine? Oh, yes, that was the red-haired nurse.

"*Merci*, Martine," she murmured and heard the girl laugh. She was still with them then. Yes. She was opening the car door, and Paul was thanking her again. She was telling him in French that he was welcome, and then she added something else. Something about *jeudi*. She said it two or three times in among a lot of other words. And Paul said he was glad she would be free. *Jeudi*. *Jeudi* meant Thursday. Karin realized she was laughing weakly but had no idea why the fact that *jeudi* meant Thursday should be so funny. And then the warm darkness rushed up around her, and she stopped laughing and sank into it gracefully and disappeared.

FOR A COUPLE OF DAYS she drifted along on a drug-induced high. The pain was always there, but it was dull and didn't seem to matter. She slept, woke, ate and drank, swallowed pills, slept some more. She was unable to lie down. Charles had moved a reclining chair into her bedroom. She had difficulty getting out of it, and Etienne and Lissa and Madame Durocher took turns manipulating the chair for her. Lissa helped her in and out of the bathroom and washed her like a baby. Paul was there often. Charles drifted in and out.

All these things she was conscious of with some part of her mind, but none of it was very clear.

On the third day she refused the pills. As long as she stayed put in the recliner, the pain was bearable, she told Lissa. She'd rather put up with it and have a clear head.

Lissa worried and argued, but when Paul arrived again, he gave approval, though he suggested she take the pills at night for a while. Reluctantly she agreed. "I don't like pills," she told him. "I'd rather not rely on drugs of any kind."

She watched him carefully when she said that. But he merely shrugged. "They have their place," he said.

She noticed that he was holding a small package wrapped in bright paper. Something for her? He had brought her flowers the day before. Dark purple pansies. No one had ever given her pansies before. How had he known they were her favorites?

"They reminded me of you," he said as she glanced at the delicate porcelain basket Lisa had arranged the flowers in. "They are dark velvet like your eyes. I hope you like them. We call them *les pensées*. The same word means 'thoughts.'"

His voice sounded stilted. She was conscious of constraint between them. She looked at him helplessly. "Paul," she began, but he had turned away to look out her bedroom window.

"I am very sorry, Karin," he said softly. "I feel I am to blame for your injury."

She sat forward, wished she hadn't, carefully

leaned back. "That's nonsense," she said weakly. "It was an accident. If I hadn't pulled away, if that old man hadn't been there—"

"If I hadn't frightened you," he interrupted.

There was silence. Then he sighed and turned back to her. "I want to tell you. . . ."

She waited, breath held, but all he said was, "There is no problem with Violette. I have talked to her. No harm has been done."

"No harm," she echoed. "How can you say that?"

He looked at her blankly. Anger ripped through her like a red flare. "This whole business is inconceivable to me," she said heatedly. "You are a respected doctor, a man people look up to. You are intelligent and well educated and...attractive." She hesitated as she saw the hated sardonic expression come into his face and settle there. Then she plunged on. "You could be a leader in the community, an example of all that is good and clean and decent." She paused again in the face of his piercing blue gaze. Her side was aching unbearably, her heart beating too fast. But she was committed now, and there could be no turning back this time. "There is no possible reason for you to be mixed up in narcotics traffic. It is disgusting, despicable. You of all people—a doctor—should know how it degrades, destroys—"

She stopped, not because she'd said all she wanted to say, but because he had moved abruptly. He put the small package down on the table next to her, placed his hands on the arm of her chair. He was looking down at her with an expression she couldn't fathom, frightening her with his chill intensity.

"Have you finished?" he demanded. "Or do you have more adjectives to hurl at me?"

Karin swallowed. "I'm not finished by a long shot. You must certainly be aware—"

"I am aware of a great deal." He straightened, but his cold gaze did not release her. "I have this to say to you. I am not and have not ever been engaged in anything illegal."

Relief flooded through her with such force she had to close her eyes. And with the relief came something else—the knowledge that she had suppressed because of her doubts and stupid suspicions, knowledge she had been afraid to face.

She loved this man. She loved him as she had never loved Ray Covington, loved him as she could not in a million years have loved Ray Covington.

The flash of joy that followed this self-admission warmed her body to a radiant heat. *Fire in the blood and pulses pounding,* she thought.

And then she opened her eyes, and her happiness died as though it had never been born.

Paul was still glaring down at her. "It is inconceivable to me that you should have so little respect for my privacy that you would stoop to spying on me. Your research project was supposed to deal with the architecture of Quebec City. It was not supposed to include research into my private concerns. I do not want you to say anything more on this subject, not to me, not to anyone. You have stumbled onto dangerous information, and you must put it completely out of your mind. Do you understand?"

"How can I do that? You haven't explained anything. Do you really expect me just to wipe my mind free—"

"That is exactly what I want you to do. You can pretend to yourself that you did not see me with that man. I want you to promise me you will do that." His gaze held hers mercilessly. "Will you promise?"

"Yes," she said, afraid to say anything else. All the doubts he had laid to rest had resurrected themselves as he spoke.

He continued to look at her coldly for another second, then he walked away from her, turning his back on her to look out the window again. His hands were thrust in his trouser pockets, his back ramrod straight. She could almost feel the tension in his body, the tension in the air, almost hear all those angry words still reverberating between the walls.

The tension in her own body was causing the pain in her ribs to increase. She made a conscious effort to relax.

She sensed his movement when he turned, but she couldn't bring herself to look at him. She could feel his gaze studying her face. After a long moment he spoke again. His voice was without emotion. "You have overtired yourself. I will go and leave you to rest."

She looked up at him, but she didn't answer, couldn't answer.

He sighed. "I will not be able to see much of you for a while, Karin. I must return to my duties now." His voice was clipped.

"You don't need to see me at all," she said slowly. "If I have any problems, I can go back to the hospital."

"That is your privilege. But I will call daily to assure myself of your comfort. I feel responsible for your condition, and I cannot neglect that responsibility."

He paused as though waiting for her to say something. But she couldn't find the strength to reply. He was looking at her as though she were a stranger. It was impossible at that moment, even knowing that she loved him, to believe there had ever been any warmth between them.

At last he indicated the package at her elbow. "I brought this for you," he said. "I saw it in Marcel Savard's gallery and thought immediately of you. It is a small thing. I hope you will accept it, even though—" He broke off. "It is not something that would be suitable for anyone else," he concluded. A note of bitterness had come into his voice. He looked at her face once more, looked away and shrugged. Then he left the room, closing the door quietly behind him.

Karin clutched the arms of her chair, feeling as though all her strength was draining out through her hands. For a long time she sat there, her gaze fixed on the closed door, not moving, not thinking.

At last she stirred and reached one-hand for the brightly wrapped package. Dully, without real interest, she pulled the wrappings free to disclose a rectangular box. Inside, in a nest of tissue paper, was a silver ballerina about four inches high, a beautifully made figure of consummate grace in a romantic-style *tutu*. She held the statuette in the palm of one hand, studying the marvelous workmanship. The little dancer was poised on one point, the other foot arched to one side, her arms curved in the croisé position, her head tilted at a graceful angle. There was a perfect line of balance from head to toe, and a feeling of life in the swirling lines of the layered skirt that made the little figure appear to be frozen in a perfect moment of her dance. Yet not frozen. At any moment that small foot might lift into an arabesque, body bending at the hips, arms gracefully reaching forward.

Abruptly Karin put the little figure back in its tissue-paper nest and closed the box. Tears were prickling behind her eyelids, and as she eased back in her chair and closed her eyes those tears squeezed out between her eyelashes and rolled unchecked down her cheeks.

She could hear Paul's voice echoing in her mind: "I am not and have not ever been engaged in anything illegal." She knew what he'd been waiting for there at the end. He'd wanted her to say she believed him, that everything was all right now. And for a minute or two she *had* believed him *totally*.

But how could she be *sure* he was telling the truth? He'd hardly be likely to admit he was guilty. Especially if he'd convinced the police of his innocence.

Nothing "illegal," he had said. But what about "unethical," or "immoral"? Surely if he was not involved with Valier, there would be no reason to hold back, no reason to forbid further discussion. A truthful person would explain *everything*. There had already been too much secrecy, too much evasion.

She felt empty. And very, very sad. As though a cherished friend had died. She would not be able to wipe the memory out of her mind, she knew. But she would not speak of Valier to Paul again. And she would look no further for proof of his guilt, for if she found it, she would not be able to bear it. But she could not trust him. He had given her no foundation for trust.

When Etienne came in with her lunch tray, she was still sitting there with her eyes closed, but her tears had dried. In a voice that seemed to echo hollowly in her ears, she asked Etienne to put the box in her dresser, which he did without apparent curiosity.

When Paul came to visit her the next day, she thanked him awkwardly for the gift but suggested that under the circumstances he might wish to take it back.

He refused curtly and she didn't argue. But she felt curiously reluctant to look at the ballerina again after he'd gone or at any time in the days that followed.

THE DAYS SEEMED ABNORMALLY LONG and empty, though everyone tried to make them more interesting for her. Lissa waited on her hand and foot and sat with her often, talking of the times they'd spent together in school.

Karin was glad of her company and enjoyed their talks. She felt she and Lissa were becoming close again. And it was less painful to worry about Lissa's restlessness, her complaints about Charles's neglect of her, her annoyance with Etienne's constant rudeness, than it was to worry about her own emotions.

"I have to admire Etienne's stamina," Lissa said one day with a rueful smile. "Charles and I have been married nineteen months now, and Etienne is as determined not to accept me as he was the day we met."

In spite of Lissa's light tone, Karin could tell that her friend was really upset. Lissa had tried hard to get close to Etienne, but he met every effort with a stubborn lack of response. And when Lissa tried to talk to him, to communicate with him, he invariably made some comment about her going away. His implacable behavior was enough to frustrate a saint, Karin thought, and Lissa was only human. Any day now her patience was going to end.

Etienne had formed the habit of bringing his own lunch upstairs when he brought Karin's. They ate together every day, and he spoke to her in French, pointing things out in the room and insisting she repeat the words over and over until she pronounced them correctly.

"The window—*la fenêtre*; the door—*la porte*; the bed—*le lit*; the chair—*la chaise*," she repeated obediently.

She learned to count up to one hundred. She learned that *rouge* meant red, *vert* was green and *jaune* was yellow. "As in jaundice, Tante Karin," Etienne said.

Which was how she felt, Karin thought—jaundiced, sour, morose.

But the pain was lessening. After a few more days she could walk around her room a little, though she wasn't ready to venture downstairs.

She benefited from her sessions with Etienne, and her French improved daily. It was a week, though, before she noticed something odd about Etienne. When she did notice, she wondered how she could have missed it before. When he ate with her, his manners were impeccable. He chewed his food slowly, used his knife and fork and spoon properly, sipped his milk or tea with care.

"You have excellent table manners, Etienne," she told him.

He looked pleased. "My mother insisted everyone should know how to behave in public," he said. "She told me people judge us by our habits, and I should take care to make a good impression."

Karin took a chance. "Then why do you deliberately use bad manners in front of Lissa?"

A dull flush spread over his cheekbones. His eyelids lowered, but not before she saw the flash of resentment in his gray eyes. She thought he wasn't going to answer, but he did. "It doesn't matter what Madame Lissa thinks of me," he said. "She will be leaving us soon."

"Is that what you want?"

His eyes wouldn't meet hers. "It makes no difference what I want, Tante Karin. If Madame Lissa decides to leave, she will leave."

"You do realize that your behavior might hurry her away?"

"Oui." He gathered his dishes and hers and left the room. She was afraid she'd gone too far and had only succeeded in offending him, but he came back later and offered to play a card game with her. She recognized that he was trying to make amends for his rudeness. Neither of them referred to their earlier discussion.

It was difficult, though, for her to concentrate on the card game or on the French lessons they resumed the next day. She felt depressed every time she thought about Lissa and Etienne, Lissa and Charles. She could not let herself think about Paul.

To HER SURPRISE, about a week after her accident, Céleste came to visit her. She entered the bedroom like a breath of spring, her arms full of roses, which she said she had picked from her parents' garden, incurring the wrath of the gardener. "He said I disturbed the symmetry of the flower beds," she told Karin without a sign of remorse. "Can you imagine such a thing? As though roses were not meant to be enjoyed."

Etienne went off to find a vase big enough to contain the mass of flowers, and Karin moved the pile of papers she'd been studying to the table so that she could take the blooms from Céleste and sniff their full fragrance.

"You were working?" Céleste asked with an apologetic glance at the papers.

"Not very hard," Karin admitted. "I'm trying to do a little each day. I feel so useless sitting around."

Céleste made a face. "I know how that is. I am constantly being made to rest. My mother is afraid I will fall into little pieces if I do not take a nap every day."

She smiled at Etienne as he came back with a large pottery bowl. "But what an efficient young man you are," she exclaimed.

As Etienne solemnly helped her arrange the roses, she chatted blithely to him in French. It was soon clear from the entranced expression on Etienne's face that he was captivated. How sad it was that he couldn't seem to feel any of that warmth for Lissa,

Karin thought. He was such an attractive little boy when he let himself relax.

She certainly couldn't blame him for being so charmed by Céleste. The girl was delightful company. As she moved around the room, making no attempt to conceal her curiosity about Karin's possessions, fingering ornaments on the dresser, studying the pictures on the walls, exclaiming when she saw the painting Karin had purchased from André, she was a study in light and airy grace, now tossing her blond curls to emphasize a point, now pirouetting with sudden excitement, her pretty print dress flaring. She was telling Karin how she had met André.

She'd been hurrying down the school hall to one of her classes, she explained, late as usual, and she had crashed, literally *crashed*, into the young man as he leaned against a wall in a shadowed corner. "He was staying away from a class," she said. "Even then he was always bored by his classes. Anyway, I banged into him, and we hung on to each other to get our balance, and he all at once had my face between his two hands like this, you see, and said very solemnly in a deep, deep voice, 'I must paint you.'"

She sighed and let herself drift down onto the bed. She sat on the edge, looking at Karin, mermaid eyes wistful. *"Très romantique, n'est-ce pas?"*

"Very romantic," Karin agreed, smiling.

She felt better in spirits than she had since the day of the yacht party, pleased that this alluring young woman had come to visit her. She didn't even mind when she found out there was an ulterior motive behind Céleste's kindness. Forty-five minutes after the girl arrived, Madame Durocher ponderously ascended the stairs and announced with a twinkle in her eyes that a young man had come to call. And of course, the young man was André.

Briefly Karin wished he had arrived first so that she could question him, but looking at the bright expectancy on his bearded face as he came into her room, she suspected she wouldn't have wanted to bring up the subject of drugs or of their last meeting even if she had been willing to disregard Paul's orders. She wasn't going to think about that, she told herself for the hundredth time. She was going to pretend nothing had happened to upset her. She was going to enjoy her visitors. She needed to enjoy *something*.

André had taken pains with his appearance. His beard had been trimmed and so had his hair. He was even wearing new jeans and a white T-shirt whose neck band was not frayed.

"You look nice, André," Karin said, making her voice cheerful. "How kind of you to go to so much trouble for me."

He looked very sheepish, especially when Céleste giggled. But then he realized Karin was teasing and laughed with her. He looked different when he laughed—young and carefree. Yet when his face sobered, Karin saw that his eyes were still bloodshot.

Céleste had evidently noticed his eyes, too. She made a sympathetic comment in French, and André shrugged. "I do not have time to sleep. I must work. Everything is in my head, wanting to go down on canvas. And there is not much time."

"You have a lifetime ahead," Karin demurred, even as she wondered if the redness of his eyes was really due to lack of sleep. Obviously Céleste suspected nothing else.

He looked at her sadly. "No, *mademoiselle*, I have little time. I have told my father on the telephone today that I will return to school in the fall—in October."

Céleste exclaimed and he turned to her. "I have made up my mind, *chérie*. It is the only way to impress your father."

"I'll run away," she said at once. "We will be together. I can get a job until you begin to sell your paintings."

André shook his head. "I cannot let you do that. How long would it be before you missed your big house, your maid, your pretty dresses, your forty-five pairs of shoes?"

Céleste pouted. "I don't care about those things."

"You say that now, but it would not be long before you hated me for forcing you to live in poverty. And you must frequently have medical care. I could not afford it. Also, you love your mother. You could not go against her that way."

This last was obviously a telling argument. Karin could see Céleste's enthusiasm flicker and fade as though a light had gone out inside her. It was a crime, Karin thought, for anyone to let that brightness be dimmed.

André had moved to sit beside Céleste on the bed. He took her hand and gazed into her eyes. "We will manage," he said softly. "I will go to school and become a good businessman. You will finish your education. Perhaps then your parents will let you marry me. In the meantime I will paint when I can, as much as I can.''

"You have enough for a show now," Céleste said. "Paul says—"

"Paul says too much," André said, silencing her. "This is not a matter for Paul. This concerns only you and me."

They had forgotten she was in the room, Karin saw. They were gazing at each other helplessly, hopelessly. This was the first time she had seen them together. If she had been given the chance earlier, she thought, she could never have thought Céleste in love with Paul. The expression on the girl's face was almost despairing, but there was no mistaking the love that showed in her eyes for André. He was quite obviously her whole world.

As for André, he was willing to compromise with the thing that meant life itself to him—his art. He would become a part-time painter in order to placate her family and his own. It wasn't right.

André had turned to look at her with a suddenly embarrassed expression. Evidently he'd just remembered she was in the room. As he turned, her mind recalled the shock on his face when he sat in the back of Paul's car, and she revealed her knowledge of Henri Valier. She felt abruptly depressed again. André might seem to be the noble young lover at this moment, but he, like Paul, had some connection with Valier.

That was a fact, no matter how hard she tried to put it out of her mind. She was glad Céleste didn't know. How could anyone as innocent, as unsophisticated, as Céleste, handle something like that?

The young couple stayed an hour, and then André left, promising to come often to see Karin until she was well. "And even afterward," Céleste added with an irrepressible giggle.

"I have a feeling I'm being used," Karin said lightly.

The girl grew solemn. "We would not do this if we did not like to be with you," she assured Karin earnestly. "We can trust only two people, you and Paul. Please say you do not mind if we come here to meet."

Karin smiled. "Of course I don't mind. I enjoy seeing you, too."

Céleste leaned over and hugged her, creating all kinds of havoc with Karin's ribs. Then she, too, was gone, leaving behind a trace of light floral perfume and the memory of her bright trusting smile.

Karin felt sorry for her. What use was an hour in someone else's room? If only Céleste's parents would accept André. If only André's father would see his son for the genius he was.

But there was still the matter of her suspicions, she reminded herself. She could not sympathize with André completely until she knew for sure why he was involved with Valier.

In any case, she had troubles of her own. She and Paul were growing daily more distant. There was no way she could do anything about that, and he didn't try. She wished he would stop coming around so that she could forget him, try to pick up the pieces of her life.

Lissa, however, was always delighted to see Paul. She made a big fuss over him, brought him coffee or a drink, insisted on seeing him to the front door when he left. She had already gone for a session at his clinic, come back full of enthusiasm, but rather secretive. She had nothing to say about the relaxation methods he was supposedly teaching her. She would be going every week to see him, she told Karin. She was quite sure she was going to feel better about everything soon.

"Fantastic," Karin said dourly.

"Grouchy," Lissa said with a grin.

"Grouchy," Karin acknowledged. She took a deep breath to prevent herself from saying something revealing to Lissa. At least she could breathe deeply now without everything exploding inside her. And she was able to sit up a little straighter, which made it easier for her to work. Lissa had found her a lapboard that fitted over the arms of the big chair. She sorted through the papers on it now, determined not to waste any more time worrying about André and Céleste, or Lissa and Paul, or anyone else.

"Could you bring me another pile of these?" she asked Lissa. "There's a stack on my desk marked 'churches.' I'm ready to work on them now."

Lissa went off cheerfully to get the papers, returned to put them in front of Karin. She sat on the arm of the chair and looked over Karin's shoulder.

"Don't you find all this old stuff terribly dull?" she asked after a while.

"Not at all. It's fascinating."

Lissa didn't seem convinced. "I should think it would be utterly boring," she insisted. "Just look at all these dates and lists of things. Who cares what kind of stone was used to construct this or that, or why the roofs were built one way and not another.''

"A lot of people care," Karin murmured, abstracted, wishing Lissa would leave her to her work.

She turned over a page, looked at the sketches under it, drawings of the Anglican Cathedral. She wrinkled her nose. The drawings were very poor. A child could do better. And she'd forgotten to mention the subject to André. Maybe she could bring it up tomorrow.

Lissa's hand came over her shoulder and lifted the sketches. "Gosh, these are awful," she said.

"I agree."

"He's got the perspective all wrong. Look at this side projection. This wall looks as if it's two feet tall. Nobody would be able to stand up straight inside. Even I could do better than that."

Karin turned her head to look up at Lissa, drawn by the note of interest in her voice. "That's right," she said slowly. "You *could* do it better. I remember the scale drawings you did of the old Olympic Hotel in Seattle. A draftsman couldn't have improved on them."

"Sure—a draftsman," Lissa said dolefully, letting the drawings drift back into Karin's lap. "This kind of stuff has nothing to do with art."

"Of course it has," Karin said, speaking more emphatically as an idea took hold. "Don't you see, your kind of skill is just what Charles needs. You could do the drawings he needs for his book."

"Oh, come on now." Lissa's laugh was brittle. She stood up and stretched, but her gaze was still fixed on the sketches, Karin noticed.

"You could do it, Lissa," she said.

Lissa picked up the drawings again, studying them, her eyes thoughtful. "I could, you know," she said slowly. "It's been a while but...." She looked sheepishly at Karin. "I've got a couple of books of sketches I've done since school, just to keep my hand in."

"Has Charles seen them?"

"No, of course not. He's such a perfectionist. He wouldn't like them."

"How do you know? Show them to him. I'm willing to bet he'll want you to do the illustrations. Think, Lissa, you'd be working *with* him instead of getting bored all the time."

She broke off as a mischievous expression darted into Lissa's eyes, then continued, "You *do* think it's a good idea, don't you?"

"It has possibilities," Lissa said dreamily. "I've just realized something," she added softly. "If I work on the sketches, I'll have to go look at the buildings that have been altered, won't I?"

"You'd enjoy it, really you would," Karin urged. "It's not at all boring."

"Mmm." Lissa looked back at the papers in her hand, smiled over them at Karin, her red gold eyebrows raised. "Do you suppose Paul would explain the buildings to me the way he did to you?" she asked, then nodded, apparently not seeing the dumbfounded expression Karin felt sure must be showing on her face.

"Yes," she added slowly. "I'm sure he wouldn't object. What could be more natural, after all? Think of all the time I could spend with him, just as you did." She giggled again, and before Karin could come up with anything to say, she danced toward the doorway, pausing there to wave the drawings at Karin. "A terrific idea," she bubbled. "Thank you, Karin."

With that she was gone, leaving Karin sitting in stunned solitude. Without even thinking of the consequences, she had made it possible for Lissa and Paul to see more of each other. Charles would never suspect a thing. He'd be delighted to have Lissa's help.

And whatever happened now, she thought despairingly, would be her fault.

CHAPTER THIRTEEN

IT WAS ALMOST A MONTH after her accident before Karin was able to work again in her study. In spite of her discomfort, she had made quite a lot of progress with her sorting, but it was a lot easier with the desk and drafting table to work on. On her first day back, a Saturday, she was dealing with the notes on the Kent house, which had actually been built during the French regime but was most famous as the three-year residence of the Duke of Kent, Queen Victoria's father, toward the end of the eighteenth century. Originally constructed in 1636, the house had frequently been improved and enlarged. There were no sketches of the original, she noticed. Something for Lissa to work on. Lissa had already produced two fine pen-and-ink drawings that Charles had submitted to his publisher. He expected to hear soon if her work was acceptable.

Karin smiled to herself, remembering how astonished Charles had been by that first drawing of Lissa's. "A bit of an insult that he should be so taken aback," Lissa had joked.

Karin reached for a notebook to jot down instructions for Lissa, wincing as a sharp jab in her side reminded her she wasn't completely healed.

It was then that she realized Charles was talking to

someone in the next room. It was possible he was talking to himself, of course; he frequently did. But she had a feeling she'd heard someone coming upstairs earlier. Perhaps Lissa was home from her outing with Paul. They'd gone to look at the Notre-Dame Basilica. Paul's idea. No, that wasn't a female voice answering Charles. It was Paul's.

Determinedly Karin turned her attention back to her work, careful not to make any sound that might attract Paul's attention. But she might as well have saved herself the trouble. After a few minutes she heard Charles say, "She's in there," and the door opened and Paul walked in.

As always the sight of him made her heartbeat skitter erratically. There was something about this blatantly virile man that hit her with fresh impact every time she saw him. He had dressed very smartly for this morning's expedition—sharply pressed gray slacks, a white corded madras shirt and a dark tie. She couldn't remember him wearing a tie for her. His right hand was trailing a navy blue blazer over his shoulder. Very *Esquire*-macho, she thought nastily and realized at once that she was overcompensating for her own intense response to the sight of him.

He stood in the doorway, eyeing her cautiously, something he'd been doing lately as though he wanted to be sure of her mood before coming too close. She could hardly blame him for his wariness. She'd been showing her irritation too openly in the past week or so. He thought she was irritated by him, of course, but she was mostly irritated with herself. How could she possibly love a man she couldn't trust, she asked herself constantly. Yet she did love him. She had tried desperately not to let her confused emotions show, but so far her nervous system hadn't cooperated.

"Come in, Paul," she said carefully. "Did you and Lissa have a. . . successful outing?"

"Oui." After closing the door, he sat down in the chair opposite her and smiled. "Lissa is enjoying herself. It is nice for Charles that you pushed her into uncovering her talents."

"Isn't it?" She was careful to keep any suggestion of sarcasm out of her voice. But perhaps not careful enough. His lips twitched momentarily, then he regarded her with a clinical expression. "I am glad to see you up and about. You are feeling better?"

"Much, thank you."

"No pain at all?"

"Only when I laugh."

"I do not see you laughing much lately."

"No." This was getting too personal. She indicated the papers on her desk. "I'm making more progress since I stopped taking pain pills at night. My head is much clearer."

"Bon. Then there is no need for further delay."

It was her turn to look wary. He had a peculiar expression on his face. She had an idea he was about to say something she didn't want to hear. "I really am very busy," she said briskly.

"So I understand. Charles tells me you have not been outside since your accident."

"It's still difficult for me to walk any distance."

"But you are able to enter a car?"

Karin swallowed. "I suppose I could, but. . . ."

"I have my car below. It is a good day for you to come to my house. Charles wants you to look at the

papers I have. We will stop at my office on the way
and pick up a small copy machine. We can take
copies of those you will need, all right?''

"Yes, but I don't think...."

That sardonic twist was back in his smile. "You
need not worry, Karin. We will not be alone. I have a
couple of household servants in residence, and also,
my mother has returned from Paris. I think you will
enjoy meeting her.''

Remembering her imagined picture of an autocratic
grande dame, Karin somehow doubted that. But she
was certainly curious about Madame Dufresne. And it
would be nice to have a change of scene. And to be
with Paul, a traitorous voice whispered in her mind.

He sensed her weakening and stood up. "Shall we
go?''

"I guess so.''

Karin looked down at herself. She had worn a
dress this morning, as she had every day since she was
able to manage more than a robe. It was still hard for
her to wriggle into slacks. This particular dress had
become a favorite because it buttoned up the front
and so was easy to get in and out of. It was fairly cool
too, made of a softly striped shirting in gray and
white. And this morning Madame Durocher had
helped her wash and blow dry her hair, still a tricky
procedure. Yes, she would do.

"Very nice," Paul said softly, startling her by
reading her mind.

It felt marvelous to be outdoors even for the brief
moment before she got into Paul's car. The sun was
high overhead, turning the street into a silver glare
that had her reaching in her purse for sunglasses as

soon as she was seated. Paul was putting on dark glasses, too, the first time she'd seen him wear them. If anything, they added to his appearance, even though they hid his blue eyes. He smiled at her as he started the engine. It was the first time she'd known his smile to lack confidence. "Shall we declare a truce for today?" he asked.

"Why not?" she said, ignoring the tiny thrill of alarm the suggestion generated. Just for today, she thought, it would be a relief to forget suspicion and past intimacies, to enjoy being a young woman out with an attractive man. Just for today.

They left the old city by the St. Louis Gate and drove along the broad and breezy Grande-Allée and west to Ste. Foy. On the way Paul told her he had attended a medical meeting that morning before picking up Lissa. Which explained his smart appearance, of course. Karin was relieved she hadn't made any caustic comments about him dressing up for Lissa.

The drive didn't take long. Paul brought the car to a stop beside a complex of high-rise offices, and Karin looked up in wonder. "I'd forgotten there was a twentieth century," she said.

Paul laughed. "I recognize the feeling. It affects me every time I leave the city." He hesitated. "Would you like to come up with me? There is an elevator, of course. And it will be cooler than waiting in the car." He seemed to have marshaled his arguments carefully.

Karin nodded. "I'll admit to some curiosity," she said. She looked upward after Paul assisted her out of the car. "Wow! This is the twentieth century with a vengeance. So much glass!"

Their footsteps echoed on the tiled floor of the

foyer. Few people were around. She began to feel a little nervous in the elevator. This was the first time they'd been quite so alone since their half hour in Madame Lepage's satin-lined cabin. Not a good thing to think of.

"I wonder why everyone automatically watches the floor indicator in an elevator," Paul said. His voice sounded strained, and she realized he was nervous, too. Funny, she wouldn't have imagined he would ever *be* nervous.

Just to be on the safe side, she declined Paul's invitation to come into his office with him. She remained in the waiting room of the clinic, wandering over to the floor-to-ceiling windows. The panoramic view was tremendous, but it gave her a touch of vertigo, and she backed away and looked around.

It was a large room, beautifully furnished with upholstered chairs grouped in conversation areas. *The carpet must be two inches thick,* she thought. She liked the color scheme—earthy tones of russet and orange and beige. The lamps were nice—ginger jars topped with pleated silk shades. Real plants abounded. And the magazines, mostly French, were up-to-date. A large green-lighted aquarium took up almost all of the lower half of one wall. A far cry from her own doctor's plastic chairs and artificial bamboo tree, she thought.

"Would you mind feeding the fish?" Paul called from one of the back rooms.

She wandered over to the tank. At her approach, angelfish and neon tetras swarmed toward the glass, and she caught a glimpse of a pair of kissing gouramis in among the eelgrass. No plain old guppies for Dr. Dufresne.

She found the fish food in a small cabinet to one side of the aquarium, sprinkled some lightly on the surface of the water, delighted by the fishes' immediate zooming response.

Not so delightful was the irritation the smell of the fish food produced in her nose. Surely she wasn't going to sneeze? She must not sneeze. Both Paul and the young doctor at the hospital had warned her not to. In vain she pressed her finger against her upper lip. There was no way to hold the impulse back. The first sneeze was loud, violent, explosive, and it was followed by two more. At the last moment she clapped her hand to her right side, but it didn't help. She felt a tearing sensation that was almost audible, and then pain ripped through her.

"Did you see the kissing gouramis?" Paul asked from behind her. She tried to answer, to tell him, but she hurt too much to speak. She saw his reflection in the fish tank. He was carrying what must be the copying machine. "Karin?" he said, sounding puzzled.

"I sneezed," she gasped out.

"Mon Dieu!" Hurriedly he set the machine down on a table and came to her. She felt his fingers lightly probing her rib area. "Can you straighten up?" he asked.

She shook her head. "Hurts."

His arm was around her shoulder, helping her to walk toward the treatment rooms. All she could manage was a slow shuffle, but at last they reached a room, and he helped her onto the examining table. "Stupid," she said.

"You or me?"

"Me."

He was doing something at the side of the room,

getting out a rather large hypodermic syringe and a vial of liquid, washing his hands. "What...?" she asked.

"This is the quickest way to relieve your pain," he explained. "It will only last for a couple of hours, but it will enable you to straighten up and breathe properly. It is a local anesthetic, much as you would get from a dentist. Sometimes the relief lasts even after the effects have worn off because of the relaxation of the muscles."

She nodded. "It won't knock me out?"

"No."

He had moved in front of her and was looking at her with a speculative expression. "It will be necessary to remove your dress."

"For a shot?"

"It is a local anesthetic. It does not go into your arm. I must make the injections directly under your ribs." He made a small sound of impatience as she hesitated. "This is no time for false modesty, Karin. Normally I would call in a nurse as chaperon, but as you see, there is no nurse present. If you insist, I will take you to the hospital, but I would prefer to relieve your pain as quickly as possible."

She nodded. He was right, of course. But still it was very difficult for her to remain unmoved as his fingers skillfully unfastened the buttons of her dress and eased it off her shoulders and arms. It was a painful procedure, but even through the pain she was relieved she'd taken the trouble to put on a bra this morning, even though she'd had to have Lissa fasten it for her. Not that it would have made any difference to Paul, apparently. He was obviously unstirred by the sight of her. He was concentrating on drawing the contents of the vial into the syringe. It really was an awfully *big* syringe.

He must have caught the fearful flash of her eyes as he moved behind her. He grinned. "Do not worry. The needle is very fine, but I have to give you at least four injections in order to bracket the whole area. It will not hurt at all." His fingers stroked along the outlines of her ribs, and then she felt the tiny prick of the needle followed by a sense of pressure. He repeated the procedure three times, then straightened. "It will take a few minutes. Just breathe shallowly until the anesthetic takes effect."

She nodded, trying to ignore the light touch of his hand on her bare shoulder. It had been such a long time since he touched her, and even though his touch, his whole attitude, was as properly objective, as sexless, as a doctor's touch was supposed to be, she could feel heat rushing to the spot where his fingers met her skin. She glanced at his face. He had taken off his sunglasses. The expression in his blue eyes was purely clinical.

"Better?" he asked, and she realized the pain had gone.

Tentatively she straightened her upper body. No pain at all. She managed a smile. "It's a miracle."

"Bon." In that same dispassionate manner he helped her on with her dress. She was able to fasten it herself and managed to get down from the table without help.

Paul smiled. "What do you think? Would you prefer to go home and rest, or shall we still go on to the château?"

She took a deep breath, testing. Still no pain. "The château," she said.

Within a few minutes they were retracing their route to the highway. "My house overlooks the Plains of Abraham," Paul explained. "It is not far."

Karin had formed a tentative picture of the Château Dufresne in her mind, mostly based on pictures she had seen of châteaux in France. She was expecting a tall castlelike building with fenestrated towers and turrets, something like the Château Frontenac, perhaps. The reality was far different, but not disappointing. They entered the grounds by a wide gate at the end of an avenue bordered with lofty elms. The house was set in the midst of formal gardens of luxuriant growth—squares and circles radiant with flowers, dissected by narrow paths. It was a long tall house, built of large weathered stone blocks, topped by the steeply sloping roof common to the area. The roof was gabled and pointed in the style of the seventeenth century.

Sunlight reflected from the silvery tile of the roof, but the mullioned windows were in shadow. The total effect was restful, charming, gracious, more like a country manor than a château. It had obviously been constructed as a comfortably luxurious place to live, rather than as a showplace. As Karin climbed out of the car, she heard dozens of little birds chirping in the hedges that surrounded the parking area. She could hear nothing else, she realized, even though the city was not far away.

"It's beautiful," she murmured as they walked between the hedges and on to one of the footpaths that led to the house.

"I'm glad you like it." The response sounded

automatic. He was looking toward the side of the house, where someone was bent over, working among a patch of rosebushes. Karin could see only the top of a wide-brimmed straw hat until the figure straightened and looked toward them, and she saw it was a woman—a very shapely petite woman in a bikini. She waved at them with a gloved hand and called out an enthusiastic greeting in French.

"Your gardener?" Karin asked dryly.

Paul laughed. "My mother."

Astonished, Karin stared at the woman who was now approaching them. She had the figure of a sixteen-year-old. But as she came closer, she pulled off her hat, and Karin saw that her tousled dark hair was streaked with gray. Her face was youthful, though—only a slight softening of the jawline, and a few faint lines radiating from the corners of her blue eyes revealed that she was much older than Karin's first estimation. Possibly early fifties, Karin thought, though she didn't look it. She must have been very young when Paul was born. Her skin was beautiful, like the proverbial peaches and cream. She was smiling in a very friendly manner, her gaze on Karin. As Paul introduced them, she wrinkled her nose charmingly. "You must excuse my appearance," she said. "This was my first opportunity to expose my body to the sun's rays this summer." She pulled off her gardening glove and took Karin's hand. "*Bienvenue à Château Dufresne.* You are most welcome. Paul has told me much of you. I am sure we will be great friends. My Christian name is Jeanine, and I hope you will call me by it. I do not care for formality."

Karin smiled, feeling an instant liking for this attractive soft-spoken woman. "Paul didn't tell me *anything* about you. I imagined someone quite different."

Jeanine's laugh was low and charming like her voice. "Paul likes to surprise people with me. Because of his height, they always expect someone *très grande*—big and tall, no? They forget he was not so big when I gave birth to him." She sent Paul an affectionate teasing smile, then turned back to Karin. "You must come inside and have tea with me. I will put on some clothes so that I can be a most proper mother."

"We came to work, *maman*," Paul said with a smile. "We can't delay. Karin is under the influence of an anesthetic, and I'm not sure how long it will last."

Then, of course, the incident in Paul's clinic had to be explained. Jeanine was at once full of sympathy for Karin and insistent that under the circumstances she could not possibly work. "Besides," she concluded with a delightful smile, "Karin and I have to become acquainted." She slanted a mischievous glance at Karin. "It is necessary to be very firm with my son. He is inclined to want his own way at all times, and it is up to us to show him he cannot always get it."

With that she swept them into the house, calling to some invisible person to bring tea, before going up to her room to dress.

Paul and Karin waited for her in the salon, which overlooked a brick patio. Steps led from the patio to front gardens that were laid out as formally as the back and as brilliant with color. Beyond the gardens was the green sweep of the Plains of Abraham, then the blue glint of the St. Lawrence. The town of Lévis showed hazily in the background.

The room itself was fairly large, formally paneled in rectangular oak panels with raised moldings. The muted gold of the walls was repeated in the thick carpeting and the silken draperies at the tall windows. As Karin had expected, the furnishings were antique, representing several periods. She recognized the classical style of Louis XVI, as well as the less restrained Régence and Directoire.

She also recognized two well-known paintings on the walls—she had them in her bedroom at home, except that hers were prints, and these were originals.

Paul allowed her to look around in silence, though he was obviously enjoying her pleasure. She felt at ease with him for once and certainly at ease in this lovely room, as though she belonged here. She had never felt quite so much at home, she admitted to herself, not even in her own home. Her parents' house was comfortable, but it lacked the warmth that was apparent here, the caring that had gone into the selection of the pieces and their placement. The sofas and armchairs were large-scale, suitable to the room's dimensions, and all the colors in the room were muted, giving an impression of quiet comfort, setting off the polished splendor of the antique tables and side chairs.

The antiques were very fine. Karin was particularly drawn to a lovely little ebony cabinet with a marble top and to the twin étagères that flanked the wood-framed fireplace, displaying delicate porcelains and someone's collection of miniature glass bottles. "My mother's," Paul said as she stopped to look at them.

"They are mostly perfume bottles dating from the seventeenth century on." He paused. "You like my house, don't you, Karin?"

She smiled at him. "That's something of an understatement," she said. "This is the most beautiful room I've ever seen."

"That bodes well," Jeanine Dufresne said as she came into the room. Karin wasn't sure what to make of the remark, or of the knowing glance Jeanine gave Paul at the same time, but she decided to let both pass.

Jeanine had changed into a slim off-white dress of soft linen. Her short straight hair was brushed into a precisely angled style that must surely have been designed by Vidal Sassoon. She looked extremely well-groomed, the epitome of chic, and still far too young to be Paul's mother.

Behind her came a very distinguished elderly man in a dark suit, evidently a servant. He carried a silver tray with tea things on it. "Jules, this is Karin Hayward, Paul's young lady," Jeanine said.

Karin was a little taken aback by the description, but Jules didn't seem surprised. He gave her a warm smile and a slight bow of his head. He had beautiful silver gray hair, brushed smoothly back from a face that was lined and gentle. "I am most happy to meet you, *mademoiselle*," he said.

"Jules has been with us for twenty-five years," Jeanine said after he'd left the room. "When he came to us, he intended to retire after five years, but he is still here. He won't tell us his age, but we think he must be close to eighty." She busied herself with the tea things, then glanced up at Karin. "Jules evidently approves of you. It is very rare for him to smile. He feels smiling is beneath his dignity, you see." She laughed merrily, then looked at Paul. "I thought you had work to do, *chéri*."

Paul's dark eyebrows slanted upward. "Are you trying to tell me my presence is superfluous?"

"I'm trying to tell you to get lost," Jeanine replied, her voice honeyed. She beamed at Karin. "I love Americanisms like that. They are so much to the point." To Paul she added, "Karin and I are going to indulge in girl talk, *chéri*, so perhaps. . . ."

"I'm leaving," Paul said. "I'll bring in the copy machine," he told Karin. "If you still feel comfortable later on, we can work on the papers."

Karin smiled uncertainly, not at all sure she wanted to be left alone with the unpredictable Jeanine. She had a feeling Jeanine meant to quiz her about her relationship with Paul, a feeling that proved to be true. As soon as Jeanine had poured tea for both of them and made sure Karin was settled in a chair that offered enough support for her back, she came straight to the point. "How do you feel about my son?"

Karin swallowed. "I really don't know him too well, *madame*."

"Jeanine."

"Jeanine, then. I. . . admire him, of course. He's a very knowledgeable man. And very charming."

"Hmm." The amused expression in Jeanine Dufresne's blue eyes was almost identical to her son's. "You *admire* him. I had hoped for more than that. May I be frank?"

Karin nodded. She was pretty sure Jeanine would be frank whether she gave her permission or not.

Jeanine held up her left hand on which a large diamond solitaire shone like a miniature sun. "I am going to be married soon," she said. "My fiancé is Michel Armand. He is a banker in Paris. A very annoying unpredictable man." She chuckled at Karin's obvious surprise. "One would not want to marry a man who is ordinary and dull and predictable. It would be too easy to become bored."

Karin thought of Ray but refrained from comment.

Jeanine nodded emphatically. "Believe me, I know what I am saying. My Michel is *très dominateur*—domineering—so I have to fight for my rights. Which is very stimulating to me. He is also very sexy, and I adore him." She shrugged delicately. "I have been alone for seventeen years, Karin. It is past time for me to make a new life. But my home will be in Paris, and it worries me that my son will be alone here. It is time for him to marry, also. That is why I hoped you had more than a passing interest in him."

Karin stared at her, astounded. "Are you asking me my intentions?" she asked in a voice that showed a tendency to crack.

"You are not offended?" Jeanine asked seriously.

"Offended? No. But I am—" Karin broke off and laughed as Jeanine's smile became mischievous. "I don't know what I am. Astonished, I guess."

Jeanine nodded. "I suppose you would be. It is an unusual approach, *n'est-ce pas*? Mothers of sons are not supposed to want to marry them off. But you see, my son is very dear to me. He is a fine man. But in affairs of the heart he shows no sense. In the past he has filled his time with—what is the expression—'bits of fluff.' He has said many times that he has no wish to marry. But I have noticed that when he speaks of you, there is a difference in his voice, in his face, and I hoped...."

Karin felt a sudden twist of pain that must have shown on her face. Jeanine leaned forward, setting down her teacup. "Your ribs are bothering you?" she asked.

"No. I'm fine," Karin said weakly. She could hardly tell Paul's mother that the pain was in her heart and didn't stem from any physical injury.

"So." Jeanine's blue eyes could be as intense in their regard as Paul's. She was studying Karin's face now, her own expression sobering. "I see that my son has not handled things well," she said matter-of-factly.

"Please, *madame*—Jeanine—could we talk about something else? I do like Paul, yes, and I know he likes me, but no more than he likes any other woman. I'm afraid you are mistaken."

"Jeanine Dufresne is often mistaken," she said, "but not in matters of the heart." She smiled sympathetically. "But I see I have embarrassed you, so we will change the subject."

To Karin's relief, she then began to talk of the work that needed to be done on the château. "It is very old," she explained. "The roof must be replaced soon, and the foundations need repairs, and there is much interior work to be done. We have had to close off some of the rooms because the ceilings are not completely safe. But Paul has many plans. He wishes eventually to move his clinic here. Such work takes much money, and so it goes slowly. Now, though, it will move more rapidly. Paul's investments in Montreal have proved sound.''

"Investments?" Karin murmured.

"Oui." Jeanine spread her hands, palms upward in the feminine version of the Gallic shrug. "I do not quite understand what he is doing. I have not much of a business head, so I do not ask.''

So much for curiosity, Karin thought.

Jeanine chuckled. "It is a good thing I am marrying a banker. I will learn at last to balance my checkbook, perhaps. But my son is a good businessman. Much more so than his father. Did he tell you of his father's illness?''

"That he had asthma, yes. It must have been very difficult for you.''

"For me, yes, and for Paul. It is not good for a child to grow up in the atmosphere of a sickroom. Though in a way he gained much from it. He and François were close, and Paul took an active interest in his father's treatment from the time he was small.'' She laughed. "He used to drive the doctors crazy. He was always unpacking their satchels, you know—the little black bags—and asking questions about everything in there. And he would repeat the words over to himself in bed like a litany: 'stethoscope, clinical thermometer, hypodermic syringe.' Such a solemn little boy. I think he knew before he was five that he would be a doctor.''

Karin was conscious of growing dismay. The images that Jeanine was offering her of Paul as a child were not lessening her pain. She had the insane urge to cry out that Jeanine did not need to convince her of Paul's attractiveness; she already loved him.

She wondered what Jeanine's reaction would be to that. And how she would react if Karin told of her suspicions about those mysterious investments in Montreal. What if she were to be as frank as Jeanine? What if she were to say, "Yes, I love Paul, but I'm still afraid he may be involved in drug dealing so I am fighting against loving him. And as for his feelings for me? Short-term only. He would like very much to get me into his bed. At least he did want to at one time. Now I'm not so sure he wants me at all."

That would be quite a revelation to make to a man's mother. And of course, Karin had no intention of making it.

She sipped her tea and tried to keep a smile on her face as Jeanine talked on about Paul's education and the way he had studied night after night until she feared for his health. "He works much too hard," she was saying now. "I had to consult his own doctor, his colleague, Dr. Caron. Have you met Jean? No? He and I had to enter a conspiracy to make Paul take a vacation. Paul has never learned, you see, to be objective about his work. He analyzes everything, *feels* everything. *Mon Dieu*, I remember when the Lucien baby died of sudden infant death syndrome, I heard him pacing the floor of his bedroom every night for a week. I was afraid he would have a breakdown. I think perhaps he was afraid of this, too. At least he let us talk him into a vacation. And I was so pleased when I heard you had come to the city, and Paul was taking an interest in you. Without you he would not have stayed away from his work for so long."

"You mean he was already on vacation when I met him?"

"*Mais oui.* Did he not tell you?"

Karin shook her head. And she had thought him callous to desert his patients so suddenly.

"Oh, that Paul is a devil," Jeanine said. "He makes secrets when there are no secrets. He is always afraid people will see how soft he is inside."

"Is this what you call girl talk, *maman*?" Paul asked from the doorway. He was leaning against the doorjamb, looking sternly at his mother. How long he had been there, Karin had no idea.

Jeanine was not the least put out. "What would girls talk of if not men?" she asked with a smile.

Paul laughed. "You are irrepressible, *maman*." He smiled at Karin. "I'd like to take you on a tour of the house if you feel well enough."

"I'm fine," Karin said, "but I'm not sure I should take up more of your time. Perhaps we should look at the papers and—"

"Work, work, work," Jeanine exclaimed. "You are as bad as my son, Karin. This is a very nice house, and it will offend me if you do not make a tour of it. Now go, you two, and take your time. I am going to telephone my Michel."

"It's the middle of the night in Paris," Paul reminded her.

"So? Michel is a night person like me. Off with you."

In the face of her good-natured bullying, Karin had little choice. And she had to admit that she was dying to see the rest of the château.

They started in the kitchen where Jules was presiding over some food preparation at a huge butcher block in the center of the big room. He introduced her with great formality to the cook, Madame Blain, and to a young, very shy girl called Rose-Anna, whose blond hair was tied back in the fattest braids Karin had ever seen.

The kitchen was an inviting room with rough exposed ceiling beams and an open fireplace. Displays of pewter and glass decorated the wall space between windows and the mantel above the fireplace. All the most modern appliances were there, but cunningly placed and colored so that they blended in with the warm chestnut paneling of the walls. Just off the kitchen was a small breakfast nook with a view of the back gardens. "My mother and I often eat here," Paul told her. "Formality has its place, but not in everyday living."

Karin agreed with him, especially when she saw the baroque grandeur of the formal dining room. Next, Paul showed her what he called his gymnasium. There was a bench press in the middle of it—an incredible number of weights on the steel bar. No wonder his lean body was so strong.

Beyond the gymnasium, a marvelous curving staircase led to the upper story. Its balustrades were hand carved, Paul told her, and no two were exactly alike. They were still held together by their original wooden pegs.

Karin lost count of the bedrooms. Some of them, like some of the rooms on the ground floor, were uninhabitable, but Paul had plans for their restoration. His mother's rooms—bedroom, dressing room and bath—reflected her personality. They were light and airy, decorated in a charming blue toile de Jouy. The bedroom contained several cabinets filled with what Paul told her were ivories from Paris, enamel work from Limoges and ceramics from Rouen.

And then they came, as Karin had known they would, to Paul's section of the house—a suite of three rooms with its own bathroom. The furnishings were scaled to his height, and any decorations were strictly functional. Books lined one wall of the bedroom and another in his study. The paintings were more abstract than those in the rest of the house—originals, but contemporary rather than old masters. His bed, as Karin might have expected, was a massive four-poster with tapestry hangings in brown and gold that matched those drawn across the windows against the afternoon sun. "Very masculine," Karin commented from the doorway.

Paul stood in the center of the room, his face shadowed. He hadn't switched on any of the large lamps. In the dim light of the filtered sunshine it seemed to Karin that his expression was the one his face had worn when they danced together at the Savard house. "Are you afraid to come in?" he asked.

"Of course not." Defiantly she took one step into the room, then stopped. There was tension here. A crackling feeling in the air. She put her hand to her side. "I think I'd better go back downstairs," she said. "I'm getting some feeling back. I should sit down."

"What kind of feeling?"

She tried to laugh lightly, but all she managed was a breathless frightened sound that disturbed her even more. "Just a little discomfort," she said.

"You can sit down here," he said firmly. He came toward her, took her hand and led her into the room. "Come, you must not run away. I have looked forward to seeing you in my rooms. See how well the colors become you. This room might well have been decorated for you."

Nervously she freed her hand from his. He made no attempt to stop her. She walked over to the windows, stopped to examine a world globe that stood on a table there. She turned it gently, stopped when it squeaked. The sound seemed very loud in the quiet room. She was holding her breath, she realized.

"There is something here I want you to see," Paul said.

She turned to find him indicating a framed cheval glass on a burnished wooden stand. The mirror was slightly cloudy, as though it had been stored at some time in a damp climate. "There is a rumor in my family that this mirror belonged to Marie Antoinette," Paul told her.

The room was dim, her mirrored reflection indistinct. Framed by her long dark hair, her face looked pale, her eyes enormous, the pupils dilated. Pale, too, was her gray and white dress, almost ghostly in the shadows.

Paul came up behind her, put his hands on her shoulders lightly. She could have moved away easily. But she had no desire to do so. The blue of his eyes seemed even more vivid than usual in the warped glass—a trick of the light, perhaps. His gaze held hers. "I'm not sure I believe the story about Marie Antoinette," he said, "but it is an interesting thought. Do you suppose a mirror contains the reflection of everyone who has stood in front of it? If we gaze at it for a while, perhaps we will see all the people who have gazed here before us.''

Karin swallowed. ''Marie Antoinette lost her head,'' she reminded him.

He laughed softly, then turned her around to face him. ''So practical, my Karin,'' he murmured. His hands had slid around her waist. Her own hands reached to his arms to stop him from pulling her closer. Yet she didn't push him away. She didn't want to push him away. And he knew it. She could see the knowledge in the narrowing of his eyes, the curve of his mouth. ''Sweet Karin,'' he said. ''I have missed you so much. Let us not fight anymore.''

''I don't want to fight you,'' she said. ''It's just that I—''

He stopped her words with a kiss. And as soon as his mouth met hers, she knew she had been waiting for him to kiss her ever since the awful day she fell in the street. She loved him. She wanted him. Her traitorous mind was telling her suddenly that it didn't matter if theirs was only a short-term affair. She would at least have something to replace the emptiness of the past month. Neither she nor Paul was tied to anyone else. There was no one to get hurt by their intimacy.

Surrendering to this conveniently presented logic, she moved her hands farther up his arms. His mouth closed on hers, his arms tightening around her.

At once, even as her body strove to melt against his, her ribs sent out an agonizing message of pain, and she gasped involuntarily.

''*Mon Dieu*, I forgot,'' Paul exclaimed, relaxing

his grip immediately. He looked into her face and gave a mock groan. "Not only is my mother downstairs, quite probably listening hopefully—which, I must admit, inhibits me—you are not physically capable, either." There was wry amusement in his voice.

She could only laugh with him. Once he had released her, the pain had dulled, but it was there. As Paul had said, she was physically incapable. "I'm sorry," she said.

"Me, too, *chérie*. It seems we are fated to be frustrated. At the clinic you were in too much pain, also, and in any case, you were my patient there. I do have a certain amount of ethics, you see." His eyes challenged her. "You are ready to admit the truth? You do want to make love with me?"

She looked away. "It appears so," she whispered. "I can't seem to resist you."

He lifted her chin and made her meet his gaze. To her surprise, his expression showed disappointment. After a moment he spoke. "I don't really believe I am saying this, but I do not want you only because you cannot resist. I don't expect you to understand this. I hardly understand it myself. I had always thought it was only necessary to sweep a woman off her feet, and nature would take care of the rest. But I find that if you cannot come to me gladly, of your own free will, sure that you want me as your lover, then I do not want you. I do not wish to take advantage of a temporary weakness. I want you to have no reservations. There can be no holding back." He guided her over to the massive bed, helped her sit down and sat beside her, holding her hands in his, looking into her face. "Can you possibly understand?"

She forced herself to look at him directly. "I think so, but I can't come to you wholeheartedly unless—"

"Unless what? *Dieu*, I don't know why I keep returning for more punishment. Why do I put up with all the frustrations you put me through? I don't understand myself." He was half amused, half serious, she saw. "Go on," he urged. "What argument do you have for me now?"

"You have forbidden me to speak of it," she began.

"Karin! That business has nothing to do with you. Nothing to do with what is between you and me." He had risen to his feet in one swift lithe movement and was looking down at her coldly, all amusement gone. "No more accusations," he said firmly. He made an impatient sound. "Sometimes I think it would be better for the human race if they didn't talk at all," he said with bitter humor. "Come, I will take you back down to my mother where you will be safe."

"I am not a child," she protested.

"No, you are not," he agreed, and there was weariness in his voice now. "Probably I am the one who is the child. I want from you what is evidently too much to ask. I ask you to have faith in the person I am."

"Blind faith? When I have told you I value honesty above all things?"

His mouth twisted. "It is a great deal to ask, isn't it?" He shrugged. "Perhaps neither one of us is ready for a mature relationship. And as the circumstances and your physical condition preclude any attempt to overcome our joint idiocy, perhaps we had better delay further discussion. Probably you were right in the first place. We should act like civilized people and be more distant with each other."

"I don't know if that's possible now," she said quietly.

He laughed. "You are probably right again. It is very strong chemistry, *n'est-ce pas*? So we will go downstairs to do our paperwork. If you are able?"

She moved tentatively. "I guess I'm okay as long as I don't stretch or move too fast."

"*Bon*. Afterward we will have dinner, and my mother will be very entertaining as always, and then I will take you home." He paused, then continued in a dismissing tone. "Tomorrow I go to Montreal for a few days. Perhaps when I return, you will have recovered from this latest mishap, and we can decide what the future holds."

Karin was conscious of disappointment and relief at the same time. And mixed with her confusion was a wretched rebirth of suspicion. Why was he going to Montreal? How could he expect her to trust him when he always refused to explain anything to her?

"It's the timing," he said suddenly. "It's all wrong." Again he had seemed to read her mind. But surely she wasn't supposed to be content with such an ambiguous statement?

He had helped her to her feet and was now guiding her toward the door, his hand at her elbow. Yes, it seemed she was supposed to be content with that.

CHAPTER FOURTEEN

THE NEXT FEW DAYS were busy ones for Karin. Purposely she made them so. The effects of her sneezing fit had not been as serious as she'd feared, and within a couple of days she was able to return to work full-time, though she still had some pain.

What she wanted was to bury herself in her work so that she wouldn't have time to think about Paul, wouldn't have to contend with the pull of her emotions in one direction, the pull of her common sense and instincts for self-preservation in the other. Unfortunately the work she was doing now didn't interest her very much. She had moved beyond the second French regime to the British takeover, right through the unsuccessful siege of Quebec City by the Americans shortly before the American War of Independence. Now she was dealing with the era of expansion promoted by the development of the wooden shipbuilding industry. This had evidently been a time of prosperity, and there had been enormous activity in the port and quite a lot of building by the numerous immigrants, but the period did not appeal to her as much as the earlier years.

Lissa was working hard, too. Her drawings had proved acceptable to Charles's publisher, and she was steadily producing more. Sometimes she worked in Charles's office; occasionally she sat on the high chair in front of the drafting table in Karin's study. And of course, being Lissa, she found it impossible to work long in silence, which proved distracting to Karin. Especially as Lissa's subject was often Paul.

Charles had decided that a drawing of Château Dufresne should be included in his book, so Lissa was working on that now. She had taken a camera to Paul's house a couple of days after he left for Montreal, using up two rolls of film. She was really taking her work seriously. She had also met Jeanine Dufresne for the first time.

"I really like Jeanine," she said to Karin the next morning when they were both working in Karin's study. "She's so natural and so much fun."

"Mmm," Karin murmured, hoping Lissa wasn't going to be in one of her talkative moods. It was a vain hope. After a minute or two of silence Lissa put down her pen and swung around on her stool. "Jeanine told me Paul will be home tomorrow," she said.

Karin's stomach lurched. When Paul was out of sight, she was able to convince herself of the foolishness of getting involved with him. When she was in his presence, or even when someone mentioned his name, the sensible parts of her mind ceased to function.

"I have an appointment with Paul on Friday," Lissa went on. "I must remember to tell Charles." There was an emphasis in her voice that puzzled Karin, and she glanced at Lissa's suddenly mischievous face.

"What are you up to?" she asked.

Lissa laughed merrily. "What makes you think I'm up to something just because I'm anxious to see my utterly devastating doctor?" she asked.

Karin bit back the exasperated retort she wanted to make. Lissa had glanced at the closed door of Charles's office, but she'd made no attempt to lower her voice. "It's really getting to be a problem," Lissa continued in the same audible pitch. "If Paul's not up to his eyes in work, he's off in Montreal. I know he wants to spend more time with me on this project. I suppose we'll have to work over the weekend. Paul said he would arrange his schedule so we can spend as much time together as possible. I'm really looking forward to it."

She was idly swinging back and forth on her high swivel chair as she talked, her gaze fixed on Charles's door now. When Karin didn't reply, she darted a frowning glance at her. "Hey, Karin, is anything wrong? Are you hurting again?"

"No," Karin managed. "I'm fine."

"Well, you don't *look* fine. You looked really odd there for a second." She shrugged, returned to her swinging. "Anyway, Paul's going to take me down to the little church in the Lower Town on Saturday. I must say all these places seem much more interesting when I'm with him."

Karin bent her head over her work, gripping her pencil so hard her fingers hurt. Her ribs were hurting, too. She welcomed the discomfort. She didn't want to think about Paul taking Lissa to see Our Lady of the Victories. That was a special place in her mind.

"Something *is* wrong, isn't it?" Lissa had slid from her chair, come to stand beside Karin.

"No, nothing," Karin said carefully, and then to her dismay, she suddenly found herself throwing down her pencil and glaring up at Lissa. "I just wish for God's sake you wouldn't keep talking about Paul Dufresne," she blurted out.

Lissa's green eyes widened. "What on earth is the matter?" she began, and then as she stared at Karin, her expression went through an abrupt change. "Good Lord," she said. "You're in love with him, aren't you?" She had finally lowered her voice.

Karin nodded miserably. Obviously she'd given herself away; there was no point in making a denial.

Lissa was still staring at her, the expression in her green eyes changing from shock to consternation to compassion. "Dear God," she breathed at last. "What have I done?"

Karin averted her eyes. She looked down at the papers on her desk, seeing them through a blur. "Forget it, Lissa," she said wearily. "Let's just get back to work, okay?"

"We'll do nothing of the sort. Come on, let's go into your bedroom and talk."

"There's nothing to talk about."

"Oh, yes, there is. Come on. I don't want Charles hearing us."

Karin allowed Lissa to persuade her into the bedroom. They sat in the easy chairs that bracketed the window. Lissa stared at the ceiling for a few minutes, then she leaned forward and looked at Karin in a disarmingly appealing way. "I've been an absolute fool," she said.

Karin attempted a smile. "Don't feel lonely; you're not the only one."

"You don't understand. I don't mean I've been a fool over Paul. I mean I've been a fool to think I could play games and not hurt anyone. I've hurt you, haven't I?"

"Well, it hasn't been easy to think of Paul and you...."

"I bet it hasn't. Especially with all my talk about Paul becoming my lover. Good God, when I think of what I must have put you through. I thought you didn't *like* him. You always seemed irritated by him."

She ran both hands through her mass of red curls as though she wanted to tug the hair out by the roots. "I'm so disgusted with myself for being so blind," she exclaimed. "I should have recognized your irritation for what it was. I acted exactly the same way when I fell in love with Charles."

She sighed explosively, then after a pause, raised her eyebrows. "Have you any idea how impossible it was to get Charles to notice I was alive? He made me so mad, I could have killed him. I had to practically throw myself under his feet before he even saw me. When I finally managed to get him to propose, I felt as though I'd gone through a whole war to get him." She shook her head and grimaced. "I also thought the war was over. But when we came here, and Charles settled into his book, he seemed to forget again that I was alive." She laughed shortly. "Just before you came, I walked into his office one day stark naked and told him I was going shopping. And he looked at me with that glazed expression he gets when he's working and asked me kindly if I needed any money. He didn't even *notice* I had no clothes on!"

She sat back in her chair and clasped her hands in her lap and looked at Karin in a helpless way. "I feel an awful fool. All that nonsense about Paul was such a childish game to play, but I really felt desperate." Her mouth tightened. "It didn't do any good, anyway. Charles hasn't even noticed me flirting with Paul. And even if he had, he's so damnably sweet and honorable himself, it would never occur to him that his wife and his friend could do anything dishonorable."

She looked sadly at Karin. "Can you ever forgive me? If I'd known how you felt about Paul, I would never have implied all that stuff about him. I certainly won't do it anymore."

Karin couldn't prevent herself from smiling. Lissa looked so woebegone, so penitent. "Am I to understand that there was nothing between you and Paul after all?" she asked.

Lissa nodded, looking like a child who'd been caught with her hand in the cookie jar just before dinner. "I just wanted to make Charles jealous," she admitted. "I love him so much, and I was getting so damned frustrated." She sighed. "I still can't believe how much I love Charles," she said softly. "When I first met him, that was it. I knew instantly. And he was so different from any man I'd known before. Perhaps that was why. He kept me on edge, uncertain. Always before, I'd known exactly how to handle my boyfriends. But Charles was, well, he was just Charles."

She was silent for a minute or two, then she laughed. "Paul knew what I was up to, I think, though I startled even him a couple of times." She took a deep breath, let it out. "Paul's a good friend. He let me talk out all my frustration over Charles's work and Etienne's rudeness, and he tried to help by making sure Charles went along with any invitations he arranged for us." She looked hopefully at Karin. "*Will* you forgive me? I want to be sure everything's all right now."

"Of course I forgive you," Karin said. "And I can sympathize with your reasons." She sighed. "But I'm afraid I can't tell you that everything is all right. There are other reasons why I can't—why nothing can work out between Paul and me."

"What reasons?"

Karin shook her head. "I don't want to—*can't* talk about them." She made an effort, smiled at Lissa. "What are you going to do now? I really don't think your campaign has worked on Charles. I've noticed myself that he doesn't seem to see what's going on around him."

Lissa laughed shortly. "I know. It's been a complete waste of time and energy. Having something to do has helped a lot, though." She sighed. "I'll just have to hope that when the book is done, Charles will surface again." She hesitated, looking at Karin. "I won't pry, but in case there's any lingering doubt in your mind, I want to tell you that Paul has never once made an approach to me in any way. As for this weekend...." She looked down sheepishly. "I asked him in front of Charles if he'd take me to see the church, and he said he'd try to fit it in, but he wasn't sure if he could manage it. And of course, Charles didn't even notice that I'd asked him."

"Asked who what?" Charles said from the doorway.

Lissa and Karin both jumped. Charles was smiling benignly at both of them. Evidently he'd heard only Lissa's last words.

"What are you doing away from your desk in the middle of the morning?" Lissa asked. She was looking at him with an expression of fond exasperation. Karin couldn't blame her for the exasperation. As usual Charles's hair was standing on end, and he was wearing his ragged sweat shirt again, this time with a pair of brown dress pants. Evidently he put on whatever came first to hand in the mornings.

He was pulling at one ear, frowning, as though he were trying to remember *why* he'd left his desk. "I don't really know," he said at last. "I just felt in need of company. My office suddenly seemed empty. I suppose I've become used to you being in there with me."

"Well, well," Lissa murmured. "I do believe we are witnessing a miracle." A radiant glow appeared on her pretty face, and her eyes blazed like emeralds.

Charles looked at her, obviously puzzled. "A miracle?"

Lissa stood up and walked toward him, smiling. "Never mind, dear. Let's get back to work." She reached up to kiss him on the cheek, and he beamed at her. As they left the doorway, Lissa turned and winked at Karin. Charles was still beaming. His arm was around Lissa's waist.

Perhaps, after all, Karin thought, Charles and Lissa would be able to work out their problems. Evidently they did love each other; that was the most important thing.

How stupid she had been not to realize that Lissa's pitying glances at Charles had indicated her own frustration, not her guilt. Looking back now, she could see so clearly that all Lissa's flirtations with Paul had taken place in front of Charles. And most of her provocative statements had been aimed at Charles. She had *raised* her voice, not lowered it as she would have if she'd been trying to deceive him.

Yes, now that Lissa and Charles were working together, they might very well solve their difficulties. Karin was pleased that she was partly responsible for that. But all the same, the prospect of Lissa's renewed happiness didn't make her feel any happier about her own situation. She felt ashamed that she'd accused Paul of dallying with another man's wife. She'd made the same mistake where Céleste was concerned. But dammit, there was still the question of Henri Valier. And there was still the fact that Paul couldn't seem to resist other women. Witness his dates with Maggie and the nurse, Martine, made right under her nose.

She'd better get back to work, too, she decided at last. Thinking didn't seem to solve anything, so it was probably wiser not to think.

PAUL DIDN'T APPEAR at the Vincent house the next day, though Karin had half expected that he would. But then, she reminded herself as night fell, and there was no sign of him, Paul never had done anything she'd expected him to.

The following day she went to see Céleste. Céleste had been pressing her to visit for some time, but she hadn't felt up to driving until now, and the Lepage house was some distance out of the city. However, that morning Céleste telephoned and begged her to come. Lissa had gone to Paul's clinic for her appointment, but she'd taken a taxi. Charles insisted he wasn't going to use the Renault, so Karin couldn't think of any excuse. She had enjoyed seeing Céleste, had encouraged the girl and André to visit her when she was unable to get out herself, but she wasn't sure how she felt about seeing either Claude or Suzanne Lepage if she didn't have to. They didn't come under her heading of favorite people.

The Lepage house astonished her. If Paul's office building had reminded her this was the twentieth century, the Lepage house transported her to the twenty-first. It was built entirely of concrete and glass, and its roofs, if they could be called roofs, soared off in ten different directions. The whole thing reminded her of diagrams she had attempted in her high-school geometry class. The landscaping consisted of terraced expanses of beauty bark surrounding stiff ranks of roses and precisely centered trees.

She was relieved to find that Monsieur Lepage was not at home. But *madame* was, and she ushered Karin into what she called her "little boudoir" the minute she arrived. "I came to see Céleste," Karin exclaimed.

Madame Lepage ducked her head and gave a jerky smile. "*Oui.* I know that. But I thought we should have a little chat before you go up to her room."

Karin frowned, feeling puzzled. Why wasn't Céleste able to join them? "Céleste isn't sick, is she?" she asked.

"Oh, no, she is quite well." *Madame* seemed as

uncomfortable as Karin. She kept fiddling with the array of gold chains and necklaces around her neck. She was wearing a blue dress of some floaty material that might have looked pretty on Céleste but was too frilly, too fussy, for a woman of her mother's size and age. The whole room was too frilly for Karin's taste. She had never cared for flounced cretonne upholstery and ruffled lamp shades and organdy curtains. This decor had come as a shock compared to the rooms Karin had glimpsed on the way in. *They* had reminded her of avant-garde museums—huge pictures and strangely shaped sculptures and furniture you could see through. The frills certainly didn't suit the stark lines of the ultramodern house, which *madame* had hastened to inform her was designed by an architect chosen by her husband. Probably, Karin thought with sudden sympathy, this room was Madame Lepage's revolt against her husband's austere taste.

"You are recovered now?" *madame* asked.

"Thank you, yes. There is still some discomfort, but nothing too bad."

"That was a long convalescence."

Karin felt puzzled again. The woman's voice had sounded faintly hostile. "I guess I don't heal rapidly," she said lightly.

"Céleste was most concerned." Again a note of—what? Not exactly hostility, more like suspicion.

"She was certainly very kind to me," Karin said.

"Indeed?"

"Well, I mean, the way she came to see me so often. She really cheered me up. She's such a sweet girl."

For some unknown reason Madame Lepage was looking extremely relieved. "I hope you didn't mind her coming almost every day?"

"Not at all. I enjoyed seeing her."

The relief was even more apparent now. Understanding finally dawned on Karin. Madame Lepage was checking up on her daughter. Her own idea or Papa Claude's?

"I'm so glad you are feeling better," *madame* said kindly.

Evidently Karin's answers had satisfied her. She was almost purring now. Encouraged by the lightening of the atmosphere, Karin offered a smile. "I hope you don't mind me coming to see Céleste?" she asked, adding when *madame* nodded graciously, "This is only my second time out of the house. I did go to the Château Dufresne with Paul, but—"

She broke off. At the mention of Paul's name, *madame* had looked as though she'd just swallowed something that had an incredibly bad taste. What had happened to change her mind about "dear Paul"? For a moment Karin had the horribly guilty feeling that perhaps *madame* had seen her leaving her cabin with Paul, but she didn't see how that could be.

Her question was answered a few minutes later, after *madame* finally released her. A servant conducted her along a strangely angled hall with a pointed ceiling and up a free-floating starkly modern staircase to Céleste's room. The girl greeted her with a restrained hug in deference to her ribs, then burst into tears against her shoulder. "My mother knows Paul has been taking me to see André," she explained between sobs. "She is very angry. My mother told everyone I was to marry Paul, and she had convinced herself I would, so now we are both in disgrace, and I'm not allowed out alone. I can't even use the telephone unless *maman* listens in.''

Karin patted the girl's shoulder ineffectually, then guided her over to the bed to sit down. She was relieved to see that Céleste's room was a compromise between *madame*'s frilly trappings and Claude's arid tastes—an odd-shaped but pretty room, sunnily decorated in yellow and white. ''How did your mother find out?'' she asked when Céleste's tears stopped.

''I had to go to the bank with *maman* yesterday—Thursday,'' Céleste said in a dreary voice. ''It was my own idea, too. I wanted to buy a girl friend a birthday present, and I'm not allowed to draw out money without *maman* or *papa*'s signature. When we came out of the bank, who should we bump into but Paul, and he was walking along with a woman on his arm.''

''Oh,'' Karin said flatly.

Céleste sniffed delicately. ''*Maman* was too astonished to say anything then, but as we drove home, she became more and more angry that he should be seeing someone else. She recognized the woman, you see, as one of the nurses at the hospital, and well, my mother is a little bit of a snob, and she felt I had been insulted. She wanted to go to see Paul and demand an explanation, and of course, I couldn't let her do that.''

''So you confessed that the only reason you'd been seeing him was because he was helping you to see André.''

"Oui." The admission brought on a fresh bout of crying. *"Maman* is furious with Paul, and it wasn't his fault."

"He does seem to come in for his share of blame, doesn't he?" Karin said dryly.

"He has been so good to me always," Céleste said. "And now he will be annoyed that I have made trouble between him and my mother."

"I don't think he'll worry too much about that," Karin said, remembering Paul's attitude toward the Lepages.

"You really don't?" Céleste was looking at her hopefully. "I've been so worried that he would be angry with me. Though I did make *maman* promise she would not tell my father, which is all right because she never tells my father *anything*, and anyway, he is away at present on the yacht. Paul was most insistent when he agreed to help André and me that my father must not know. He does not want him even to know that he is acquainted with André."

"Why not?"

"I do not know." Céleste's face was crumpling again. "What am I to do? *Maman* won't let me see André. I can't arrange to see him at your house. I see now that it is wrong to involve other people. But I *must* see André, to tell him what has happened—and I must explain to Paul."

"Well, I can explain to both of them for you." Karin looked at Céleste sympathetically. "I don't know what you can do. Perhaps you'd better wait a while before doing anything. Let things simmer down. If André does go back to school, your parents might accept him."

"But he will be so unhappy. After a while he would blame me, I know. How could he not?"

"I don't really know. But I do know that if two people really love each other, things have a way of working out." The wise counselor, she thought, mouthing platitudes that didn't do anybody any good.

But Céleste was suddenly smiling through her tears. The smile was tentative, but at least it was there.

For a while they talked of other things, while all the time Karin was longing to ask Céleste about the nurse she had seen with Paul. And at last she did. "Was the woman with Paul a redhead?" she asked, thinking of Martine.

"No, a blonde." Céleste made a face. "A not very attractive blonde. Stringy hair. Much makeup. That was what incensed my mother. She kept saying, 'What a cheap-looking woman.' To make matters worse, the woman was smoking. My mother hates to see anyone smoke. She worries constantly that I will take up the habit." She wrinkled her nose. "I know my mother loves me, and she is a kind woman, truly she is, but it drives me crazy that she is so anxious about everything. She makes me swear at least once a week that I am still a virgin. She is sure my generation is headed for disaster in every way. When school is in session, she is always examining the pupils of my eyes to make sure I haven't been talked into trying marijuana or L.S.D."

"Have you?" Karin asked after a pause in which she decided Céleste had nothing more to say about the nurse.

Céleste shook her head. "Some of my friends smoke pot, but I haven't wanted to."

"Drug abuse *is* a problem nowadays," Karin said carefully.

"I know. I remember when I first met André, he told me about—what are they called—'uppers' and 'downers'? I hadn't even heard of them then, but since then I've discovered that some of my friends take them, too."

"André uses drugs?"

"No, no," Céleste protested. "It was just silliness. He was going to school full-time to please his father and then painting most of the night. To keep himself awake he began taking amphetamines, and then he couldn't sleep at all and had to take sleeping pills. But he stopped as soon as he realized how stupid it was."

"He doesn't smoke marijuana?" Again she made an effort to sound casual.

"No. He says that while marijuana may not be addictive, it still distorts the mind, and he does not want to take chances on losing his creativity."

Privately Karin wondered how true that was, but she didn't comment. "How did André meet Paul?" she asked.

Céleste frowned and played with a strand of her blond hair. "I'm not sure. Paul pays André to do odd jobs for him, but I don't know how that began."

"What kind of odd jobs?"

Céleste shrugged. How expressive the French shrug could be, Karin thought, and how uninformative.

"Paul tries to help André in many ways," Céleste went on. "Sometimes I get very angry with André

because he seems to resent Paul's help." She glanced
at Karin. "André is very proud," she said with more
than a touch of pride herself.

"But you don't know what he does for Paul?"
Karin persisted.

"No."

She was as much in the dark as ever, Karin thought
ruefully when she left Céleste some time later. Céleste
was apparently not the inquisitive type. She was content to accept André without question. How she
wished she could do likewise with Paul. But she
couldn't. She knew herself well enough to know that.
Even though for a little while she'd contemplated
having an affair with him, she now knew that would
be a mistake, too. She'd recognized that when
Céleste talked about the woman she'd seen with
Paul. She'd felt an automatic revulsion as Céleste
described the nurse—not for this particular woman,
though she hadn't sounded too savory, but for the
fact that Paul kept switching from one woman to
another. *Thursday must be his day off,* she thought
wryly. It was obviously his day to play.

ON THE WAY HOME she stopped by rue du Trésor to
deliver Céleste's message to André. He received the
news of Madame Lepage's discovery with a grim expression that made him look much older than his
years. "Does Monsieur Lepage know?" he asked.
Karin shook her head, and he seemed relieved, but
still gloomy. "It is as well I am going back to
school," he said under his breath. "It may make a
difference."

"There doesn't seem to be much choice, does

there?'' Karin sympathized. ''I wish I could think of a way to help. Perhaps I could talk to Madame Lepage....''

André stopped her impulsive offer with a sarcastic glance. ''No one can talk to Madame Lepage,'' he said. ''In any case, the problem is mine, not yours. I have enough trouble keeping Paul's nose out of my business. I don't need to have you interfering, also.''

With that he folded his arms and glared at her as though she was his worst enemy.

Karin felt like the fabled messenger who had brought the bad news to the king, in imminent danger of losing her head. And that reminded her of her remark about Marie Antoinette when she was at the château. Which reminded her of Paul. She felt very tired suddenly, and her right side was aching. The left side didn't feel too good, either, especially the area around her heart.

Maybe what she should do, she thought after smiling rather weakly at André and hurrying away, was to get on a plane and head back to Seattle. Somehow the problems there that had seemed so overwhelming before, in retrospect, in comparison, seemed rather tame.

SHE REACHED PAUL by telephone that evening. He sounded tired, but pleased to hear her voice. Briefly she told him what had happened to Céleste, trying not to put any special emphasis in her voice when she mentioned the woman he'd been seen with. When she finished, he was silent for a while. Then he asked, ''Does Claude know?''

''No,'' she answered. ''Céleste says her mother

never tells him anything, and she has promised not to speak of this to him.''

"Thank God for that," he muttered.

Why all this concern for Claude Lepage, Karin wondered. Was he really such an ogre?

"Thank you for letting me know," Paul said after a pause.

"You're welcome."

There was another pause. Karin wondered if he had anything more to say. "Paul?" she said tentatively.

"Yes, Karin, I...look, I'll have to go now. I'm not sure—" He broke off, then muttered as though he were speaking to himself. "It can only be a matter of days now."

"Paul?" she said again.

"Sorry. I'll talk to you later."

He had hung up. He hadn't even asked if she was feeling okay. Thoughtfully Karin replaced the receiver, stared at it for a moment or two, then turned away, feeling more confused than ever. Too many unanswered questions, she thought wearily.

CHAPTER FIFTEEN

ON SATURDAY the temperature soared to the mid-nineties, unusual for Quebec City. The Vincents' air conditioner fought back valiantly but couldn't quite overcome the humid heat.

In her study Karin pushed damp hair back from her forehead and tried to concentrate. She was wearing only a yellow cotton playsuit with a halter neck, a brief garment that would have been comfortable except that her legs and bare back kept sticking to the vinyl-covered chair. Her discomfort was worsened by the fact that she'd decided the evening before to attempt a modified exercise program, and her leg muscles, unused for so long, were stiff and sore with a tendency to cramp.

Around the middle of the morning she decided to go down to the kitchen for some lemonade. She put on the abbreviated jacket that matched the playsuit and descended the stairs, pleasantly anticipating the icy refreshment.

Paul was in the kitchen with Lissa and Etienne. He stood up, smiling, when she entered, and her heart did its usual pirouette. He was wearing tennis whites, cuffed shorts and shirt, an outfit that did a great deal to emphasize the virile strength of his lean

body and brought an involuntary response from
Karin that was purely physical.

"I was just coming up to get you," Lissa said.
"Paul wants to take you out. I'm going to drag
Charles over to the Leclercs' swimming pool if I have
to call the Fire Department to carry him from the
house." She laughed merrily. Lissa had been
laughing a lot more often in the past few days. But it
had been a mistake to let Lissa know how she felt
about Paul, Karin thought. Lissa was looking from
Karin to Paul in a knowing, almost coy way, and
Etienne was watching with an alert puzzled expression that deepened when Lissa suggested he needed a
clean shirt. "My shirt is all right," he said abruptly.

His stepmother flashed him a significant glance no
ten-year-old could be expected to interpret. "Come
along, Etienne," she insisted. "You can help me talk
your father into going swimming with me."

The boy allowed himself to be hustled out of the
kitchen, but he was obviously reluctant to leave.
From the doorway Lissa favored Paul and Karin with
another arch glance. "Have a good time," she called
gaily.

Karin suppressed a shudder. Lissa had sounded
almost maternal. She glanced at Paul. He was still
standing, looking at her. He wasn't smiling, but the
rather cynical amusement that was never far from the
surface showed in the slope of his dark eyebrows.

"How are you, Paul?" Karin asked evenly.

"Well, thank you. And you? Are your ribs giving
you any trouble?"

"A little." She feigned a smile. "I'm suffering
more from the heat. I came down for lemonade.
Would you like some?"

He indicated a full glass on the table in front of him. She hadn't noticed that Lissa had already served him. Her embarrassment deepened, and she turned away to the refrigerator to hide it. Behind her, Paul sat down. "I have to go to Ste. Anne de Beaupré to see an elderly patient of mine, Monsieur Fortin," he said. "It's about a twenty-mile drive. A very pretty drive. I thought you might enjoy going with me." He grinned at her as she turned around. "See how nicely I can ask?"

She sipped her lemonade to cover up the fact that her pulses had quickened at the idea of going off alone with him. "I don't think so," she said at last. "I have a lot of work to do and...."

"On such a hot day I'm sure Charles would excuse you. Ste. Anne de Beaupré is a place of pilgrimage. It is supposedly a place where miracles have taken place. There is a fine church there, not the original, unfortunately, but well worth a visit. And on the way back to the city we can visit Montmorency Falls, a pretty sight, higher even than Niagara, though not nearly as wide."

"I don't think so, Paul. Really, I've missed so much time at work already." A rather sly thought occurred to her, and she acted upon it. "Perhaps we could go somewhere during the week. Thursday? Isn't that your day off?"

"I have other things to do on Thursdays," he said blandly. His eyes narrowed. "Why are you retreating again? Did something happen while I was away?"

Karin swallowed. She certainly wasn't going to tell him how she felt about his outing with the nurse. "No, of course not, I just don't particularly want to go out today."

"That's too bad. Etienne will be disappointed."

She stared at him. "Etienne?"

He shrugged. "I have invited him to go with us. But if you do not wish to go, I will have to disappoint him."

"You could still take him."

"I think not."

His eyes met hers levelly. Blackmail, she thought. If she didn't go, Etienne could not go. He would probably have to accompany Charles and Lissa to the Leclercs, and again he wouldn't want to put on a swimsuit, so he would hide, and Lissa's day would be ruined, as well as his. It seemed she had no choice. To her self-disgust, she found the fact did not bring her annoyance, but pleasure.

THE DRIVE WAS A PLEASANT ONE. Paul's car was air-conditioned, and Karin felt very comfortable, especially as Etienne was bouncing around in the shallow back seat, asking questions, pointing out things to see, so that there was no chance for awkwardness to develop.

The road passed through several villages that had retained characteristic features of French-Canadian hamlets of older days. Old stone houses lined the road, and Paul stopped often to point out old-style vegetable beds and root cellars carved into the rock, as well as bake ovens, some of which were in use.

Paul's patient lived in one of a cluster of picturesque cottages. The church was not far away, Paul said, as they left the car. They would go sight-seeing in a little while. He had brought along a picnic, he added. "Do you like picnics?" he asked Etienne.

Etienne nodded enthusiastically, then made a face. "But you must make sure I do not eat too much. I am trying to stay on the diet you gave me."

This was news to Karin. She glanced at Paul questioningly. He smiled. "Etienne asked me for a diet program. We have worked one out that is not too severe. Progress will be slow but steady." He gave Etienne a mock frown. "But you must not expect me to restrict your food, *mon brave*. I will not play the dictator in this. Remember, your weight is one part of you that only you can control. It is your responsibility. You are in charge of yourself."

"I understand," Etienne said solemnly. "But I hope you have not brought along any cake. I am not yet strong when faced with cake."

"No cake," Paul assured him gravely, and he smiled with evident satisfaction.

"Congratulations," Karin whispered to Paul as he held open the garden gate at the entrance to a pretty little cottage that had roses climbing over its doorway.

"It is mostly your doing," he said quietly. "Etienne has decided you are right. He does not *have* to be fat."

The door of the cottage opened directly into a tiny living room. Paul and Karin and Etienne were greeted by a frail bent old man, who leaned heavily on a cane, and a young woman with a very sweet smile he introduced as his widowed granddaughter, Tina, who lived with him and kept house. Tina was a sturdy round-faced friendly girl with wide hips, a generous bosom and strong-looking legs.

When Paul and Monsieur Fortin disappeared into

a bedroom so that Paul could examine the old man, Tina bustled between kitchen and living room, pressing iced tea and cookies on Karin and Etienne. Etienne staunchly refused the cookies, explaining that he was on a diet. Tina slapped one of her thighs. "I should do the same, *n'est-ce pas*?" she suggested with a laugh. "Since my baby was born, I have gained much weight."

"You have a baby?" Etienne asked. He seemed taken with this easygoing country girl, probably because she was French-Canadian like his mother, Karin thought. Whatever the reason, Etienne seemed more at ease than she had ever seen him. He had already expressed delight with the room that was so stuffed with furniture it was difficult to move around. Tina had brought her furniture here when her husband died, she explained, and *grandpère* could not be expected to dispose of any of his, so they had piled it all in together.

And somehow the crowded assortment seemed to suit the little cottage, as did the model ships that covered every table and the mantelpiece over the empty fireplace. *Grandpère*'s work, Tina told them. He had been a fisherman when he was young, and he was still crazy about boats.

Although the room was cluttered, it was painstakingly clean—every surface free of dust. The whole effect was warm and lived in and friendly.

"My husband was killed on a motorcycle before my son was born," Tina told Karin as they drank their tea. "He was always going too fast, you understand. And it killed him."

There was sadness in her voice, but acceptance,

also. Whatever emotion she had suffered at her husband's death had been put under control. She was giving facts, not asking for sympathy. Karin was impressed by her quiet dignity.

After a while they heard a small voice calling from a back room for "*maman*." Tina excused herself and returned carrying a dark-haired little boy who wore only a diaper. He appeared to be about fourteen months old—a very handsome little boy, healthy and sturdy like his mother. When Tina set him down, he toddled over to Karin and patted her knee, looking up at her solemnly. Then he headed unsteadily, but rapidly, around the furniture toward Etienne. "Jacques has not been walking long," his mother said with a proud smile. "He thinks he can run instead of walk."

Even as she spoke, the baby wobbled and sat down hard on the wooden floor. He didn't cry. He looked up at Etienne and gurgled happily, smiling to show eight small white teeth. Etienne reached a hand down to the baby. Jacques grabbed one finger and pulled himself up, laughing again. A look of wonder lit up Etienne's face. "Such a strong grip," he murmured in French.

Tina laughed. "I think he has decided you are his friend."

"Really?" Etienne's look of wonder changed to one of pride as the baby tried to haul himself up onto his lap. He lifted the little boy carefully and set him on his knees. Jacques leaned against him, smiling around the thumb he had popped into his mouth. The smile looked sleepy around the edges.

"It is so hot," Tina said. "I think he has not slept

long enough.'' The baby's eyelids closed as though on cue, and he snuggled his head comfortably against Etienne's ample chest and sighed.

Karin laughed softly. "I think he's adopted you, Etienne."

Etienne's smile was one of pure joy. His arms awkwardly cradled the little boy, and he gazed down at him with a tenderness that moved Karin. How had she ever thought the boy sullen and uncouth, she wondered. If only Lissa could find a way to tap that reserve of love, the Vincents' family problems would be solved.

When Paul and Monsieur Fortin came back into the room, Etienne was still sitting there, holding the baby. He politely refused the old gentleman's invitation to come out and see the garden. "I don't want to wake Jacques," he whispered.

Paul and Karin exchanged amused glances, and she was suddenly very glad she'd agreed to accompany him. She felt more comfortable with him today, she thought, as they followed Monsieur Fortin out to the garden. So far Paul had been very friendly and charming, without any of the challenging statements or glances that she'd come to expect.

Together they admired the old gentleman's broccoli and beets and tomatoes, and the riotous flowers that bloomed all around. Old-fashioned pink roses climbed over the low wall that surrounded the garden, the same roses that clung to the trellis over the cottage's front door.

"Before you leave, I will cut some roses for you," Monsieur Fortin told Karin in softly accented English. "So beautiful a young lady should always be surrounded by roses."

Karin smiled at him, liking him. "It seems Frenchmen are born knowing the way to a woman's heart," she said.

The old man bowed gallantly, supporting himself on his cane. As he straightened, he winced a little. "I may be as healthy as you say, *mon cher* Paul," he said with a wry smile, "but my rheumatism is still *formidable*. I think I must rest for a while."

Paul nodded. "We must go now, anyway. We have planned a picnic. We can return after we see the church so that Karin can get her flowers." He smiled at Karin. "Why don't you go ahead to the car? I'll bring Etienne."

The car interior felt like one of the bake ovens they had passed on the road. Karin perched on the edge of the seat, leaving the door open for Etienne. She was looking forward to the picnic, she found. This had turned out to be a very relaxing day.

Her relaxation fled when Paul returned without Etienne. He had climbed into his seat before she realized the boy wasn't with him. "A slight change of plan," he explained, looking at her with a bland expression. "The baby has awakened again, and Etienne wants to play with him. Tina says she will give him lunch."

Karin stared at him suspiciously. "Are you sure that was Etienne's idea?"

"But of course." How innocent he could look— yet devilish at the same time.

"We could have our picnic here," she suggested.

"Ah, I see. You are still afraid to be alone with me. Do you not trust me? Or do you not trust yourself?"

How thoroughly he understood her. "I thought we

were going to do some sight-seeing," she said evasively.

He shrugged. "There is no problem. We will first visit the church, then drive back to Beauport to view the falls and have our picnic. Then we can return here for Etienne and your flowers. The distances are not great."

"We could postpone the sight-seeing," Karin said contrarily.

"No, we cannot. I do not intend to neglect your education in any way."

Which was a loaded remark if she ever heard one, Karin thought. And once again she had been manipulated into going somewhere with him whether she wanted to or not. She would just have to make sure they didn't stray from populated spots.

At first that seemed easy to do. There were hundreds of visitors examining the ornate church and also the tiny chapel alongside that was a facsimile of one built by shipwrecked Breton sailors. Because of the crowds they decided not to go inside either structure. As they stood looking at the church's exterior, Karin was surprised to find that she could recognize some details in the construction of the basilica. "It looks as though there was some Roman influence in the design," she offered hesitantly. "And also Gothic. It looks like a cathedral of the Middle Ages."

Paul's glance was approving. "Very good."

She felt absurdly pleased by his praise. He went on to explain that the church was a relatively recent one built to replace one that had burned down in 1926. Monseigneur Laval had visited the original, he told her, and it was soon afterward that three voyageurs were shipwrecked not far away. They attributed their miraculous rescue to Ste. Anne, and from then on the site was credited with many miracles. "Even Mother Marie de l'Incarnation spoke of the Ste. Anne Church as a place where miracles occurred," Paul said.

Karin was bemused by the familiarity of the names associated with the place. She had become so steeped in the history of Quebec over the past few weeks that it seemed almost her own heritage.

The Montmorency Falls were impressive in a different way. A roadside park offered them a magnificent view of the superb cataract that plunged from the Montmorency River into the waters of the St. Lawrence. The water sparkled under the sun, and white vapors rose high into the air like a cloud. There was a story behind those vapors, Paul told her, the story of *"La Dame Blanche"*—the White Lady.

"As usual it began with a battle," he said. "One day a young girl went searching for her fiancé, who had gone off to fight and had not returned. She found his body lying beside the falls. Grieving, she wandered for a while in the area, then disappeared, never again to be seen alive. But since then she appears from time to time above the falls—a woman in a long white dress."

He glanced at her sideways. "I wonder why tragic stories become legends more often than happy ones."

"Perhaps because happy endings are the exception in life."

He turned to look at her. His face was solemn, but

amusement lurked in the gleam of his blue eyes. "I don't agree. But then, I am an optimist. I always prefer a happy ending. I am a romantic, you see. Are you not a romantic?"

"I'm a realist," she said firmly.

The dark eyebrows rose, but all he said was, "We shall see."

Karin had been relieved to notice that the picnic area near the falls was quite crowded. Whole families were enjoying lunches spread invitingly on blankets on the ground or on the several picnic tables. But Paul had other ideas. Over her protests he insisted they carry the large hamper he'd brought along to a spot by the river that was far removed from the other tourists. Under the shade of an ancient and very gnarled tree, whose weighted branches had drooped over the years, he spread a white tablecloth and insisted on serving the meal himself. The food had been prepared especially for her by Jules, he told her; the champagne was his own idea.

"Champagne in the middle of the afternoon!" Karin exclaimed. "What are we celebrating?"

Paul's smile was deliberately diabolical. "I'll think of something," he said, and Karin felt alarm stirring inside her.

The food was plentiful: tiny sandwiches and crisp raw vegetables; fresh fruit; and a selection of cheeses. The champagne, nestled in a container of crushed ice, tasted deliciously cool. In the hot dappled gloom beneath the old tree Karin was lulled by the food and wine into a lazy somnolence. Sunlight poured down onto the river, turning it into a molten glare. It was peaceful here, the silence broken only by the occasional soft slap of water against the riverbank and the distant thunder of the falls.

Paul had little to say. When he did speak, his voice was hushed as though he didn't want to break the spell the heat and peace and absence of sound were casting over them.

As always Karin was totally aware of the tall dark man sprawling on the grass so near to her. From the corner of her eye she could see one long leg stretched out across the grass. It looked lean and strong and eminently touchable. If her heart would stop pounding in her ears, she thought, she might be able to come up with some safe topic to talk about. But the quick thudding pulse only increased the closer they came to finishing the meal. She couldn't look at Paul, but she could feel his gaze on her frequently. She wished she hadn't let him talk her out of changing her clothes. The thin cotton of her yellow playsuit wasn't much protection against that enigmatic blue gaze, especially as she had removed the jacket because of the heat.

"Why don't you stretch out, relax?" Paul suggested after they had packed the remains of the food in the hamper.

She glanced at him. He was burrowing in the bottom of the hamper, evidently looking for something. Had the suggestion really been as casual as it had sounded? No, of course not. He was never casual, this man.

But the cool grass was inviting, and she did feel sleepy. Carefully she lay down on her stomach, propping herself on her elbows. Let him try to find something seductive in that pose!

"Voilà!" he said behind her, and she turned her head to find him flourishing a flat plastic bottle with the smug air of a magician who has just produced a rabbit out of a hat.

"Suntan lotion," he announced. "Even in the shade you must be careful. The river reflects the sunlight, you understand."

"I never burn," Karin said.

"Ah, but without a sunscreen the effect can be disastrous just the same. Too much sun will age the skin faster than the years will do it."

He had dropped to his knees beside her, and before she realized what he was up to, he had poured lotion into the palm of one hand and begun spreading it on her back. Her whole body tightened up in response to his touch, and she gasped involuntarily as the strained muscles in her legs protested.

Paul's hand stopped moving at once. "You still have some pain?"

"Not really. At least not in my ribs. It's just that I exercised too enthusiastically yesterday, and my leg muscles are sore."

"Here?" Immediately his hand had moved to one of her calves, his fingers delicately, expertly probing for tenderness.

"Yes," Karin managed.

She felt the touch of cool lotion, then his hand, alternately stroking and kneading the sore places, gently massaging the pain away. All her defenses were crumbling again, she realized. No matter how many times she decided in his absence that she wasn't going to let him touch her again, she could never seem to remember her arguments when he was near.

Her body was relaxing into the cool grass, her arms unfolding from beneath her to cradle her head.

"Better?" Paul murmured.

"Mmm," she replied sleepily.

His hand had returned to her back. How gentle he was. His fingers sought out every sensitive spot on her back and stroked it so delicately, yet so surely. The movements seemed more like caresses than those of a masseur. They *were* caresses, she realized abruptly. His hands were slyly taking wider and wider strokes, moving closer and closer to her breasts. And every cell in her body was responding. "Paul," she said nervously.

"Don't worry, *chérie*." He sat back on his heels and grinned at her. "My turn," he said.

She looked at him, not at first comprehending. Mischief was lighting his eyes. As she moved awkwardly upright, still not sure what he had in mind, he pulled his shirt over his head, handed her the bottle of lotion and stretched out, face downward. Obviously he expected her to rub lotion on his back now.

She caught herself smiling. He was such an out-and-out rogue sometimes. Carefully she spread lotion on his shoulders and began rubbing it into his skin, sensuously aware of the long hard muscles in his back. If she didn't come up with something to talk about soon, she knew, she would be bending down to trace those ridges of muscles with her lips.

"You didn't ask me if I enjoyed myself in Montreal," Paul said, his voice muffled against his crossed arms.

She breathed a sigh of relief. As long as he kept

talking, she would be safe. "You haven't exactly encouraged questions," she pointed out dryly.

"I don't mind questions, *chérie*, only accusations."

"I asked you a question about Valier the first time—in the car."

"That question I do mind." He was silent for a moment, then he said, "I had a most successful trip to Montreal. Dufresne Industries is now an established fact."

"Dufresne Industries?" Startled, Karin stopped massaging lotion into his back.

He rolled over and looked at her, his eyes reflecting the endless blue of the sky. He was smiling. "Do you not see me as a captain of industry? I assure you that I am. I have been working for a long time to establish my own company. Now at last it is done."

"What kind of company?"

"Electronics, primarily medical instrumentation. We will sell and lease such things as patient-monitoring devices and cardiovascular recording systems, X-ray machines—that sort of thing. Medicine has entered the technological age, Karin. There is a great demand for such machinery. Why do you look so surprised?"

"It didn't occur to me that you were involved in a business like that. I thought—" She broke off, her mind racing. She didn't want to confess she'd thought his trips to Montreal might be connected with Henri Valier. "You were so secretive about it," she said instead.

His mouth twisted in a wry smile. "It was necessary to be so. Claude Lepage was sniffing around me, trying to get in on the ground floor. He is not the type of person I want as an associate. I wanted everything to be signed and sealed before making any announcements. It will be a good business. It will be helpful to people and will also make enough money to restore my house."

"I'd have thought your income from all your wealthy patients would have been sufficient."

He looked surprised. "Not all my patients are wealthy. You have met Monsieur Fortin. Did he seem wealthy to you? And Lissa and Etienne? In any case, it makes no difference how wealthy my patients are. I charge set fees, which are no different from any other doctor's. And the province of Quebec has excellent medical insurance."

His eyes narrowed as he continued to look up at her. "Ah, Karin, I understand. You have seen my so beautiful office building, and you have decided I am a dilettante doctor, making a fortune from the hypochondriac rich."

This was so close to what Karin *had* thought that she had no defense to offer. But Paul didn't seem to be offended. He reached up with one hand to touch her cheek. "I realize how it looked to you," he said softly. "I knew you had such thoughts. And I was too proud to deny them. I thought you should see how wonderful I am without anyone telling you."

Karin laughed a little nervously. "I should have guessed by your modesty," she said.

He smiled. "Oh, you are quick, my Karin." His face sobered. "My office and clinic space belong to my associate, Jean Caron. I am sharing with him until I can make the alterations in the château. And the reason I have so many wealthy patients is that they are mostly friends of my parents, old families in Quebec, and they came to me as soon as I set up in practice. They came out of friendship. I could hardly turn them away.''

"No, I suppose not," Karin said softly, aware once again of how often she had misjudged this man. "I'm sorry, Paul," she said.

His hand was still touching her face, and now his thumb moved to touch her lips lightly. The expression on his face had changed yet again, and he was looking at her very directly. "Do I deserve a kiss to soothe my wounded feelings?" he asked.

Afterward, Karin wasn't sure what happened then. She had meant to laugh lightly and give him a quick kiss, and then suggest it was time to pick up Etienne. But instead of that she found herself lying beside him, clasped tightly in his arms while he kissed her very thoroughly. So much for strength of will, she thought fleetingly, and then she gave herself up to his kisses without reserve.

Mindlessly she gave to him with her mouth, offering kiss for bruising kiss, her mouth returning his own breath back to him. She wanted to stay pressed against him like this for time out of mind, to prolong the sensations that had once seemed so frightening. Before Paul came into her life, never had her whole being focused so single-mindedly on her own body, the shape of it, the feel of her breasts under Paul's roving hands, the vibrations her skin produced as his lips trailed slowly over her face and throat and returned again and again to her mouth. All her senses were alive. She could taste the perspiration on Paul's upper lip, smell the cleanliness of his breath and the citrusy odor of the suntan lotion. She savored the smoothness of his skin against the palms of her hands as she clasped him to her, her fingers spreading across the hard long muscles of his back as though they wanted to hold as much of him as possible. He was murmuring to her now, words with no meaning, but words that seemed to be asking a question.

"Yes," she said softly against his mouth. "Yes, I do want you, Paul."

Heat was rising in her body, welling up from some deep dark place inside her, spreading into concentric rings that rippled and widened into vast circles. She responded to it, moving slowly against Paul, her movements reflecting the rhythm of his. And now she was hovering on the brink of some yet undiscovered place, waiting in unbearable tension, knowing that if she did not stop moving against him at once, the hot darkness inside her would explode into a million fragments, and she would be lost forever. She was not going to stop, could not possibly stop.

But she *must* stop. This was a public place. At any moment a wandering tourist could come by and disturb their solitude. For a second she fought the return of reality, but even as she lessened the pressure of her mouth against his, she felt his own body still. His hands still moved against her back, but gently, as though to calm her and perhaps himself. "This is not the right place," he murmured against her hair.

"No." Her breathing was slowly returning to its normal rate. She leaned her head back and looked at the lean face inches from her own. "Perhaps it is fate after all," she suggested not altogether jokingly. "Perhaps we aren't meant to do this."

"Nonsense," he said. "It is a question of poor management only. We must correct this. Our first time together must be perfect." He smiled and moved away a little, his gaze still fixed on her face. "My mother has returned to Paris," he said softly.

"So soon?"

"It seems Michel cannot manage without her. And she wants to buy a trousseau. They will be married at the château in a month's time." He paused, his eyebrows slanting significantly. Then he brushed his lips across her collarbone. "She will be gone for ten days."

"Oh?"

He chuckled. "Such a nervous little voice. Will you come to my house tomorrow, Karin? Jules and Madame Blain usually go to bed early, and Rose-Anna goes home for the night. If you were to come for dinner, at eight, perhaps, we could be together without interruption. Will you come?"

Karin hesitated for one second more, knowing that nothing had really changed, that she could still not trust this man to want her again after she'd submitted to him, could still not believe in his innocence where Valier was concerned.

For an instant there was a silence so acute it seemed that neither of them breathed. Then she sighed. "Yes," she said. "I will come."

CHAPTER SIXTEEN

ETIENNE WAS FULL OF HIGH SPIRITS on the drive home. He had never been around babies before, he said. He had enjoyed playing with Jacques more than anything. And he liked Madame Tina. She had been very kind to him. She had told him she loved her grandfather's house very much, and she was never going to leave it. "They are a nice family, *n'est-ce pas*?" he said when he finally ran down.

"Very nice," Karin agreed wholeheartedly, her arms full of Monsieur Fortin's roses.

"Monsieur Fortin says he will teach me how to make the model ships sometime. He says it will be quite simple for an intelligent boy like me."

"It would be an interesting hobby for you," Paul said.

"*Oui*. I think so, too."

"I guess the Fortins made quite an impression on you," Karin said.

"*Oui*." He was silent for a while. "I wish I could take Jacques to the puppet show," he said.

"What puppet show?" Paul queried.

"It is one of the events in the summer festival. Tante Karin has promised to take me to see it in the Jardin des Gouverneurs tomorrow evening. I do wish we could take Jacques, but I suppose he is too young to really enjoy it.''

"I think so," Karin said. "But perhaps we can think of another place to take Jacques some other time.''

"I will think of somewhere," Etienne said and sat back, frowning importantly.

Karin was delighted to see Etienne so interested in something. She would suggest to Lissa, she thought, that she arrange something with Tina so that Etienne would have the chance to see the little boy from time to time.

"This puppet show is tomorrow?" Paul said.

She glanced at him. He was frowning. "It will be over by seven," she said softly, and his face cleared. "I was afraid you were working on another excuse for me," he murmured.

She let the statement pass, though she was already having second thoughts about their agreement. Paul had still not made a real commitment to her, and that bothered her tremendously. She supposed she must be old-fashioned. Some of her friends had teased her that she must stop confusing sex with love; that it was not necessary to have the latter in order to have the first. But she had always believed that two people should be committed to each other, in love, before becoming intimate, and it was difficult to give up the principles of a lifetime. She was even becoming unsure of her own feelings. After all, she had thought herself in love with Ray Covington, something she found difficult to believe now. She had also thought herself heartbroken when he deserted her, yet she had almost immediately fallen in love with someone else.

Perhaps she wasn't capable of deep feelings. Perhaps Paul was right, and her parents' lack of emotional warmth had deprived her of the ability to really love anyone. On the other hand, she did feel strongly that she loved Paul. Yet if her feelings had been so transient before, how could she trust them now?

"You are very quiet," Paul said.

She glanced at the back seat. Etienne had fallen asleep. "I was thinking about Etienne," she lied.

"I hoped you were thinking of me."

She made no comment, and after a while he laughed. "I'm sorry. I keep having this suspicion that something will once more prevent us from being together. I suppose that is why I am looking for reassurance."

"I should have thought you had enough *self*-assurance."

He gave her a rather strange look. He looked puzzled, she thought. "Usually I do," he said slowly. "I do not understand why I am so doubtful of myself where you are concerned."

About to make some teasing response, Karin hesitated. He looked very solemn suddenly. He was looking ahead at the road now, apparently concentrating on the traffic, which was fairly heavy, but she had the feeling his thoughts were turned inward again. "I am wondering if perhaps it is—" He broke off, then nodded once as though he were making some kind of interior decision.

Puzzled, she stared at him, but he kept his profile turned to her. "Paul?" she said tentatively.

He glanced at her, still solemn, and then held her

gaze with an intensity that startled her. She had a sudden return of breathlessness. The musky smell of the roses on her lap seemed overwhelming for a second, but then a car horn blared behind them, and Paul turned his attention back to his driving. The moment had passed before she could interpret its significance. Yet it *had* been significant, she felt.

A moment later Paul brought himself out of his reverie and began talking about André. It was a while before she realized what he was saying. Her own thoughts were still tangled in uncertainty over his sudden gravity.

And then he mentioned Monsieur Savard, and she forced herself to pay attention. "Monsieur Savard is going to give André a one-man show?" she asked in surprise.

"*Oui*. It will be a very good thing for André. The Savard gallery is one of the utmost prestige. Marcel has invited art critics from the leading newspapers and magazines."

"You arranged it, didn't you?" she said with sudden conviction.

He hesitated, then smiled. "*Oui*. Over André's objections."

"Why should he object? It's a chance of a lifetime."

"It is a matter of ego, *chérie*. It is difficult for some men, and probably women, also, to accept the help of others. André feels my action is one of charity. I have told him over and over of the many great artists who could not achieve recognition until they were helped by a patron, but he would not let himself be convinced. This was no charity on my part. I recognized André's genius the first time I saw what he calls his real work, and it was apparent to me that it was a crime to keep such work hidden. André, I think, is not as sure of his talent as he would like to be. I think he has been afraid to test himself in front of a knowledgeable audience. But at last he has agreed." He laughed, "Though not without a great deal of pressure from Céleste and me."

"That's what he meant about you taking over his life," Karin said slowly.

"Is that what he said? Yes. It seemed I was doing favors for him at every turn, and he became resentful at times. I understand that. I am a proud man myself."

"I've noticed," Karin murmured, and he grinned but let the remark pass. "I am pleased that André has agreed to show his paintings," he went on. "I've been trying to talk him into this for a long time. It has been frustrating to me. Marcel Savard agreed on my recommendation to see André's work, but I could not persuade André to go to see Marcel. Finally I convinced him that such an attitude is childish." He glanced at Karin, smiling in a somewhat wry way. "Do you remember the first time you saw me, *chérie*?"

Karin frowned, then nodded. "You were arguing with André, making him take something from you—an envelope or something." She stared at him as he continued to smile. "Oh," she said.

His smile broadened. "*Oui*. Being 'brutally unkind,' as you called it, was to persuade André to accept a letter of introduction to Marcel, and I was very angry with myself because I could not find a way to convince him to show his work to Marcel."

Karin winced. "Why didn't you tell me?" She shook her head, furious with herself. "No, don't answer that. Why should you tell me? I should never have accused you without knowing the facts."

He chuckled softly. "We are making progress. That is exactly what I have been trying to tell you all along."

Valier, she thought. Had she done the same thing with Valier? Had she misjudged Paul there? But how else could she interpret the incident in Place Royale? She could still see Valier laughing as Paul spoke to him, laughing as though he were a friend. And she had *questioned* Paul, had been willing to give him the benefit of the doubt. And he would not discuss the matter at all. She pushed Valier out of her mind, unwilling to spoil the pleasure of the day. "When is the show to be?" she asked.

"On Wednesday evening. I would like to escort you to it. May I?"

"Of course," she said promptly while wondering at the same time if he'd still want to see her after tomorrow, after she went to the château, and they.... Again she changed the direction of her thoughts.

"It will be most elegant," Paul was saying. "You must wear your prettiest gown but perhaps not look too beautiful. We would not want *les journalistes* to pay more attention to you than to André's paintings."

Karin accepted the implied compliment without comment. "I'll be looking forward to the show," she said. "I'm an admirer of André's work myself."

"So he told me. He was most impressed by your

response. He sensed your sincerity, he said." He glanced at her sideways. "We make a good team. Together we have encouraged Etienne *and* André. I am hopeful that Céleste's mother will also be impressed by André's work. She is a patron of the arts herself, and sincerely so. She has a good eye and an instinct for good work. This show may make a difference in her attitude toward our young friend. André's father has also agreed, very reluctantly, to attend."

"What about Céleste's father?"

The pleasure went out of Paul's face as abruptly as though a light had been switched off. His mouth was suddenly grim. "Monsieur Lepage may not be in a position to be influenced," he said obscurely.

Karin frowned. About to question him, she realized they had turned into rue des Fleurs. "You did say Wednesday?" she asked.

"*Oui*. The show will begin at 8:00 P.M. I am also inviting Charles and Lissa." He laughed shortly. "After all my arrangements I discovered Marcel had intended to hold the opening on Thursday, but I managed to persuade him to change it to Wednesday so I can be present."

Now all Karin's pleasure dimmed abruptly. *Thursday*. She'd almost forgotten about Paul's Thursdays, about the other women in his life. But at least, she told herself wryly, she rated a different day. Did that make her superior to the others? Or was she not important enough to be included in the Thursday ritual? So far Paul had spent every Thursday that she knew of with a different woman. Would someone else take *her* place after tomorrow?

She pushed the thought firmly out of her mind.

She wasn't going to think about tomorrow. If she thought about it too much, she wouldn't go. She turned around in the car as Paul pulled up to the Vincent house and began calling to Etienne to wake up.

Etienne awoke in a rather grouchy mood, possibly because his nap had not been long enough to help him recover from the heat and excitement of the day. Paul left right away, refusing Lissa's invitation to dinner. He had to make hospital calls, he explained.

Lissa greeted Etienne with a barrage of questions about the trip. Evidently she hadn't noticed his grouchiness in time. He retreated at once into his usual sullenness. Unfortunately Lissa persisted. At dinner she asked him if he had liked Monsieur Fortin, what the house had been like, if he had seen anything interesting on the drive. She was trying, Karin knew, to show an interest in the boy, trying to elicit some kind of response. Evidently she'd had a very good day herself, had even acquired a light golden tan, a difficult thing for a redhead with sensitive skin to do. But Etienne was totally unresponsive. He did manage to eat with better manners, and he didn't overeat, but Karin sensed his determined withdrawal as Lissa probed. Finally he pushed his chair away from the table and glared at his stepmother defiantly. "The Fortins are *my* friends," he muttered.

Lissa kept her bright smile pinned to her face. "I know that, Etienne. I am just interested and curious. Perhaps you can take me to meet them some time."

"You will not be here long enough," he said rudely.

Lissa's patience ended abruptly. "Can't you even *try* to be friendly?" she demanded.

Etienne's face set in its usual sullen mask. "No," he said.

"Etienne," Charles said with a warning in his voice.

Etienne switched his glare to his father. "Why don't you send her away now, instead of waiting for her to leave?" he said.

Karin frowned. There was almost a note of pleading in the boy's voice.

"You are forgetting yourself again," Charles said sternly. "You had better go to your room until you remember how to behave."

For a second, Karin thought Etienne would protest his father's order. As perhaps he should, she thought. It surely did no good to keep ordering the boy out of sight the moment he talked back. But it was not for her to interfere. And Etienne didn't protest after all. His head drooped, his shoulders hunched, and he slouched out of the room without another word, looking so miserable that Karin wished fervently she could think of something to say that would restore the look of happiness his face had worn earlier in the day. So much for her hopes that the Vincents' family problems might be solved, she thought wearily.

Lissa was staring at the empty doorway through which Etienne had gone. There was a wistful expression on her face, and something more. A slight frown was puckering her forehead as though she were puzzling over something. "I wonder," she said slowly, then shook her head. "Did *you* have a good day?" she asked, turning to Karin with a bright smile.

As Karin hesitated, her smile turned down at the corners. "Now don't you go getting mysterious on me, too. Somebody must have had fun."

Karin smiled. "We all did," she said lightly. "Etienne really did enjoy himself. He's just tired, I'm sure."

Lissa gave a sigh of exasperation. "Don't avoid the question. How did you and Paul get on?"

The arch sound was back in her voice. Karin sighed. But she could hardly deprive Lissa totally of conversation, so she gave her an expurgated account of the tour of the church and the waterfall, brushing lightly over the details of the picnic she and Paul shared.

Lissa was not easily discouraged from probing. She kept asking questions as though searching for something that was missing from Karin's account. As there was, of course. Karin was relieved when the meal ended, and she could escape to her room to think.

NOT THAT THOUGHT SEEMED TO HELP. Even by the following morning she had still not decided if it was a good idea for her to go to Paul's house or not.

By the end of the afternoon she had changed her mind a dozen times. No, she definitely wouldn't go, she decided at last, then laughed at herself as she realized she was going through her wardrobe looking for something attractive to wear. She laid out her choice on the bed and studied it, trying to decide if it was too formal, while she again went through her arguments for and against the visit to the château. Unfortunately the pros were as convincing as the cons. Staring at the cream-colored silk dress on the bed didn't help at all. Perhaps she should just stop thinking and see where instinct led her, she decided.

Accordingly she showered and washed and dried her hair. Then she put on her jeans and a cool shirt and went in search of Etienne. It was almost time to go to the puppet show.

She had wandered in and out of several rooms before she realized Etienne wasn't in the house. She stood in the hall for a moment, trying to remember when she'd last seen him. About an hour ago, she thought. He had spent the morning at the park while Karin worked. He'd appeared for lunch. She'd tried to talk to him while they ate, but he'd been withdrawn, monosyllabic in his answers, though not rude. After lunch he'd announced his intention of watching television. Lissa had protested that it was too nice a day to spend indoors, but he had ignored her and clumped on down to the basement recreation room. An hour ago, when Karin had gone into the kitchen to get a glass of iced coffee, just before she'd begun drying her hair, she'd seen him leaving the house by the front door. She'd thought he was probably headed for the park again, though he hadn't been carrying his ball. Had he forgotten the puppet show, she wondered.

She hurried out of the house to the park. The park was empty except for a group of young people setting up the puppet stage. No, they told her politely, they hadn't seen a ten-year-old boy in jeans and a T-shirt, a boy who was somewhat fat.

Karin retraced her steps to the house. She wasn't worried yet. She thought there was a chance she'd missed him in the street or perhaps overlooked a room he might be in.

But there was no trace of the boy in the house. Madame Durocher hadn't seen him since lunch; neither had Lissa nor Charles. Lissa had gone alone to the Savards' house that afternoon. She'd invited Etienne to go along, but he'd refused. "He was watching television then," she said uneasily. "Where do you suppose he's gone?"

By now the four of them had gathered in the vestibule, having searched the house without success once more. "Perhaps he went down to Dufferin Terrace," Karin suggested. "I didn't go that far."

It was decided they would all go in different directions to look for Etienne. Except for Madame Durocher—she would stay in the house in case the boy returned.

An hour later, Karin raced back across the Governors' Garden after checking out the boardwalk and the promenade above. The puppet show was almost over, she saw. She hesitated on the fringes of a crowd of laughing children, searching for tousled brown hair. Etienne was not in the audience.

Nor had he returned to the house. Charles had driven down to the Lower Town. Lissa had searched the nearby streets, asking everyone she saw if they had noticed the boy. She had even climbed the bank to the Citadel. No Etienne in sight. She looked a little pale and very worried. Even Charles had begun to look concerned, though at first he'd dismissed the women's worries. Etienne was not an infant, he'd reminded them. He often wandered about the city alone. "But not without telling us where he's going," Lissa protested, and with that he had to agree.

Lissa ran up to Etienne's bedroom to check his closet. She came down seconds later, looking even more worried than before. "His school satchel is gone," she announced, "and I think a couple of changes of clothes." She looked up at Charles, her pretty face drawn. "I think he has run away," she said.

There was a silence. Then Charles nodded. "I wonder if I should call the police," he said.

He seemed undecided, and Karin felt a twinge of exasperation. But before she could give voice to it, an idea occurred to her. The more she thought about it, the more likely it seemed. "Etienne was very taken with the Fortin family," she said.

Charles frowned. "You think he might have gone to their house?"

"But that's twenty miles away," Lissa said. There was a note of hysteria in her voice. "It's all my fault," she said suddenly. "I just haven't tried hard enough to get close to Etienne. He's rejected me all along, and instead of trying harder, I've let myself get angry with him. Now he's rejected me altogether."

"Take it easy," Karin said softly. Her mind was racing as she tried to decide what was best to do. "I'll call Paul," she said. "He can give us the Fortins' telephone number, and we can alert them to watch for Etienne." She was already heading for the phone.

Charles moved to put his arm around Lisa. "Don't worry, dear," he said. "He's bound to be all right. He's a very self-reliant boy."

"But he's only ten years old," Lissa wailed. "We've let ourselves forget that too often."

Karin felt her exasperation return. They didn't need to establish guilt right now; they needed action. "If someone will give me Paul's telephone number, maybe we can get some action around here." She forced a smile as Charles looked startled. "I'm sorry, Charles," she said in a softer tone. "I've only called Paul once, and I don't remember the number."

Charles supplied the number, and she dialed hurriedly, relieved when Paul answered the telephone himself. *"Chérie,"* he said cheerfully, recognizing her voice immediately. "Don't tell me you've called with an excuse. I warn you, I will not accept it."

Karen hesitated. In the excitement over Etienne's disappearance she had forgotten all about the time. She should have been on her way to Paul's house by now. "We have a problem," she blurted out. "Etienne's disappeared. We think it's possible he's trying to get to the Fortins' house."

To her relief, Paul grasped the situation at once, told her to hang up, and he'd call her back in a few minutes.

The phone rang before she'd even had time to get anxious. "I've tried the Fortins," Paul told her. "There's no reply."

"Oh, Paul," Karin said. "If he *has* gone there, what will he do if he finds the house empty?" Behind her she heard Lissa gasp.

"I will come at once," Paul said. "I will drive you and Lissa to Ste. Anne de Beaupré. I think Charles should get in touch with the police." He hesitated. "Do not worry, *chérie*, we will find him."

Karin wished she felt as confident as he sounded.

By the time Paul arrived, Charles had talked to the police. He would take the Renault, he said, and drive all around the town. The policeman he had talked to had agreed to alert all patrols to watch for the boy.

Karin folded herself into the back seat of Paul's little car. Lissa climbed in the front, and they were soon on their way out of the city, driving slowly, all watching the sides of the road. Luckily the sun was still fairly high, but traffic was heavy. Paul had to keep pulling off at the side of the road to let impatient drivers pass.

There was no sign of life around the cottage; no answer at the door. "Monsieur Fortin has many friends," Paul said. "It's possible that Tina has taken him and Jacques to visit one of them for the evening."

"But where can Etienne be?" Lissa wailed.

"We may have missed him along the road," Paul said. "Or he might have gone in another direction altogether."

Lissa paled. "You don't suppose he'd try to get to Montreal?"

Paul put his hands on her shoulders. "Anything is possible. But we must stay calm. Can you think of anyone else Etienne might have wished to see?"

Lissa shook her head. "He isn't really close to anyone except Charles," she said slowly.

"I still think he might have intended to come here," Karin said. "He might have wandered off the road and—"

"Or he might have hitched a ride," Lissa put in,

her green eyes enormous with fright. "You don't suppose someone picked him up?"

"We will try another route," Paul said suddenly. "I took it for granted if he came this way, he would travel the road we came yesterday, but it's possible he took the road bordering the river."

"The river!" Lissa exclaimed.

Karin put her arm around her troubled friend's shoulders and guided her back to the car. "Don't worry," she said uselessly as Paul started the car. "I'm sure we'll find him soon and...." She hesitated, staring along the road. A familiar figure had just appeared around the corner of the lane, head down, trudging along, carrying a satchel over one shoulder.

"There he is!" she shouted at the same instant Paul braked the car to a stop. Lissa was already out and running. By the time Karin and Paul caught up with her, she was holding onto Etienne, half laughing, half crying, words tumbling out of her mouth. "We searched everywhere and couldn't find you, and I was so frightened. If Tante Karin hadn't thought of this place, we might have searched for you all night. How on earth did you get here? How did we miss you?"

"Some teenagers gave me a ride. They were going to St. Joachim," Etienne explained. He looked a little dazed by Lissa's excitement. "I didn't think anyone would miss me, and I wanted to see Jacques again."

"Not miss you!" Lissa exclaimed. "How could you think that? You know we love you, your father and I."

Etienne had just noticed Paul. "What are you doing here?" he asked in a puzzled voice.

"More to the point, *mon brave*, what are you doing accepting rides from people you don't know?"

"But I did know them," Etienne said. "One of them came to my school to give us some help with soccer. He plays for a high school in Ste. Foy." He glanced at Lissa. "He wanted to take me home, but I told him my father was here." He looked down at his feet. "I suppose I shouldn't have lied to him, but I was afraid he wouldn't bring me. He finally said he would, but first we had to pick up a friend of one of his passengers. A girl." He sighed. "I had walked a long way before their car stopped for me. I am a little tired. Can we go in to see the Fortins now?"

"They aren't home," Lissa said. "That's why I was so frightened. Oh, Etienne, why did you do such a thing?"

He wouldn't look at her.

"Perhaps we'd better find a telephone," Paul suggested. "We must call Madame Durocher so that when Charles checks with her, she can tell him we have found Etienne."

"My father is looking for me, too?" Etienne asked. He looked pleased.

"And the police," Paul said sternly. "This was a thoughtless thing to do, Etienne. Madame Lissa has been distraught. See how pale she is."

Etienne looked at Lissa thoughtfully. "You were really worried, Madame Lissa? I am sorry that I worried you."

"I don't want you to be sorry. I want you to promise not to do such a thing again. I couldn't bear it if anything happened to you."

The boy looked puzzled, as though he wasn't sure whether to believe her. Then he shrugged. "Can we not wait to see Monsieur Fortin?" he asked.

"We don't know how long he will be away," Lissa pointed out. She still had her arm around the boy's shoulder. She had stopped shaking, Karin was pleased to see, but her voice still had a tendency to tremble. She was brushing the hair back from Etienne's forehead with her free hand, looking into his face earnestly. "I'll bring you to see them another day, I promise," she said. "Perhaps later on, when your father is through with his book, we will all come to visit. Perhaps we could find one of these cottages to rent and have a vacation before we go back to Montreal. It will be spring then. Would you like that?"

There was a pleading note in her voice that made Karin hold her breath. *Please, Etienne*, she prayed silently, *don't turn her down; she's trying her best*.

Etienne was staring at Lissa as though she'd said something astonishing. "You will not be here in the spring," he said.

Lissa straightened up as though he'd hit her in the stomach. For a second, Karin thought she was going to make some angry rejoinder as usual, but instead she stared at Etienne thoughtfully for a long moment. "I wonder," she murmured. Then she put her hand on the boy's shoulder and looked into his eyes. "Etienne," she said softly. "I have an idea. Tell me, please, if I am wrong." She took a deep breath. Karin glanced at Paul. He was looking as puzzled as she felt. "Are you afraid I'll leave your father?" Lissa asked.

Etienne nodded miserably and looked down at his shoes again. Lissa gently raised his chin until he was forced to meet her gaze. "Why?" she asked.

The boy shrugged. "Everyone else did," he said defiantly.

"Mon Dieu," Paul breathed.

Lissa nodded. "That's what I thought," she said in that same soft voice. "Your mother left you. Then the housekeepers. You thought I would do the same."

"You did not seem happy, Madame Lissa," the boy said.

"And you were afraid if you let yourself care for me, it would hurt when I went away, as it did when your mother died."

He nodded. "Sometimes I wanted to be nice," he admitted.

Lissa looked at him sadly. "I'm so sorry I didn't understand sooner. It was not easy for me, you see. I am not used to children. Also, I was afraid.... I didn't stop to think out *why* you were treating me the way you did." She took another deep breath. "I am not going to leave you," she said firmly. "Your mother would not have left you if she had had any choice. You know that, don't you?"

He nodded uncertainly.

"Well, then, I want you to know that I love your father and I love you, and I'm going to stay with you both forever." She grinned suddenly. "I have to stay, anyway," she said. She glanced up at Paul who smiled and nodded, then looked back at Etienne.

"This is a secret because I haven't told your father yet, and I want to be the one to tell him." She took a deep breath and let it out. "I am going to have a baby," she said softly.

Etienne's expression was a joy to behold. "Like Jacques?" he asked.

"A little younger to start with," Lissa said with a laugh, "and perhaps it will be a girl."

"I don't mind girls," Etienne said magnanimously. "I will look after her and play with her—" he glanced shyly at Lissa "—if you will let me."

"Of course I will let you. I will need your help."

Etienne's smile was spreading across his whole face. "I am glad you are going to stay," he said slowly.

Lissa hugged him.

At that moment a small old car chugged into the lane, and Karin looked up to see Monsieur Fortin peering through the windshield, smiling his sweet smile.

And then, of course, they had to troop into the Fortins' cottage and embark on explanations while Paul telephoned the Vincent house and the police in the city. Jacques was wide awake and playful, and Etienne was in seventh heaven. "Soon I will tell you something," Karin heard him whisper to the little boy. "Right now it is a secret, but when my father knows, I will tell you." The baby laughed happily and grabbed a handful of Etienne's hair.

Lissa looked radiant. "Relaxation procedures indeed," Karin whispered to her when they were finally allowed to leave the Fortins' house. Lissa laughed but had the grace to look a little shamefaced. "I didn't want to say anything until I was sure," she said. "The first time I went to see Paul, it was too soon for him to make the diagnosis. I was too eager, I suppose. I should have waited. But now we are sure. I intended telling Charles tonight. And I will."

She glanced at Karin. "I know there's still a long road ahead. Etienne will probably still be a problem from time to time, and Charles is not going to change overnight and become totally attentive. But I think I've learned at last that I can't make other people totally responsible for my happiness. Now I'm working with Charles, it's a lot better." She hugged Karin's arm as they approached the car. "That's your doing," she said. "You're a good friend."

Paul overheard her. "Some of us are not so sure of that," he said with mock severity.

For a moment Karin was puzzled, but after Lissa and Etienne had fitted themselves into the back seat of the car, and they had all waved goodbye to Tina and her grandfather and a now sleepy Jacques, she realized what Paul was talking about. It was already past ten o'clock. By the time they got back to the city, it would be awfully late for Karin to suddenly announce she was going to the château. She could hardly walk out on Charles and Lissa right away even though it seemed they might have a lot to talk about. In any case, after this evening's excitement she wasn't sure she had any strength left. Reaction to all the worry had set in, and she was feeling quite exhausted.

"Paul," she said quietly as Lissa and Etienne talked together in the back of the car. "I don't think...."

"I know," he said with a groan. "The circumstances are still not in our favor. It is better, I think, that we delay our—confrontation."

He had spoken very softly so that the others would not overhear. She spoke just as quietly. "I'm sorry, Paul."

Was she really sorry, she wondered, trying to be honest with herself. Was she not feeling just a bit relieved? Perhaps her joking remark yesterday had not been so far off, after all. Perhaps fate *was* against them. But she didn't believe in fate, she reminded herself.

"I guess I won't see you until André's opening," she said after a silence.

"It seems not," Paul said ruefully. "I have several patients in the hospital just now, and I cannot do rounds until after my clinic hours." He glanced at her and smiled. "Do not look so worried. I will see you on Wednesday, and we will make other arrangements then. My mother will be gone during next weekend, also."

Karin swallowed. Next weekend. She had a breathing space she hadn't expected. Sometime before next weekend she had to definitely make up her mind what to do. And this time she would not vacillate. She would make up her mind and stick to her decision whichever way it went.

CHAPTER SEVENTEEN

THE BUILDING that housed the Savard Art Gallery had once been the residence of one of Quebec City's early millionaires, a man who had amassed a fortune requisitioning wheat during the Seven Years' War. Like so many of the French-Norman houses in the city, the lovely old building had been enlarged and improved over the decades. To turn it into a gallery, walls had been removed, ceilings raised and floors resurfaced, without sacrificing any of the original charm. The lighting was superb.

On the night of André Moreau's opening, the gallery thronged with beautifully dressed people whose mood was obviously positive. Some of them sat on benches, gazing at a single painting. Others wandered from room to room, exclaiming, smiling, nodding, admiring.

Karin was amazed by the number of works on display. She'd had no idea André was so prolific. She was amazed, too, by the scope of his talent. His paintings ranged from delicate watercolors to passionate and abstract oils to small frisky pictures of children and animals that had an intriguing twist of line and pattern, and even included a couple of scenes of twisted trees against flashing skies that might have come from an admiration of van Gogh, yet were totally original.

Marcel Savard was smiling happily, his small pointed beard jutting at a jaunty angle, his mild blue eyes showing his pleasure in the success of the show. "Such a major talent is given to very few," he said to Karin as she paused, dazed, beside him and added her congratulations to the rest. He signaled one of the waiters who were circulating with champagne and commandeered a glass for Karin and himself. "The boy sees in a new light," he continued. "The viewer of his work feels he is seeing truth, even though he has never thought of it that way before." He sipped a little champagne. "With proper teaching, André Moreau could rival the greatest artists of any age. I am recommending he attend the School of Fine Arts at the Sorbonne in Paris."

"Do you think his father will allow that?" Karin asked.

Marcel gestured with his champagne glass to where André and his father stood with Céleste Lepage, surrounded by a group of admirers. "I think the senior Monsieur Moreau is basking in the acclaim," he said dryly. "Perhaps that will help him to reach the right decision. It is criminal that he has discouraged the boy. Shoe making of all things—pah!"

Karin smiled at the disgust in the Frenchman's voice, then wandered away as someone else claimed his attention. She joined the group around André, smiling inwardly at the expression of bewilderment on André's face. The young man seemed stunned by all the compliments he was receiving. If it weren't for Céleste, who was clinging to one of his arms, looking heartbreakingly lovely in a pale apricot gown sprigged with flowers, her expressive face flushed with pleasure, Karin had the feeling André would have turned tail and run away.

His father, a tall thin man with graying brown hair and a dour, rather bony face, had his arm around André's shoulders and was accepting the kudos as though he alone were responsible for the exhibition. "André was born to draw," Karin heard him say to a stout lady in a long black dress. "He began sketching before he learned to walk. His mother and I knew from the start that he was not like other children, that we had a genius on our hands."

Karin caught André's eye and raised her eyebrows. He responded with a shrug and a half smile. He looked terribly uncomfortable, she thought. Not only was he wearing a tuxedo and stiff white shirt—an outfit that looked totally out of place on him—but he quite obviously didn't know how to respond to the flattery that was being lavished on him tonight. Karin had the feeling he'd have felt much happier if this exhibition had been held in the rue du Trésor among his artist friends, with himself in T-shirt and jeans and sneakers.

"One of the prices of fame," Paul murmured behind her. Evidently he had also been studying André and had reached the same conclusion as Karin. How odd it was, she thought as she smiled at him, that their minds so often seemed to work in unison.

Paul looked devastatingly attractive tonight. Unlike André, he was completely at home in evening clothes. He could have posed for an advertisement for how the well-dressed man-about-town should look. She felt the usual tug at her heart as he smiled at her, and a sadness that troubled her because she wasn't sure of its cause. She still hadn't reached any decisions where Paul was concerned. Her logical mind was still quarreling with her emotional urges. Why, then, did she so suddenly feel sad? Had she subconsciously reached a decision, after all? Had some part of her mind decided that she would not go to the château this weekend, that she would protect herself from future misery by denying herself the short-lived happiness an affair with Paul would bring?

"Is something wrong?" Paul asked, frowning. Another habit of his—to always sense her mood and any changes in it.

She forced a smile. "Nothing," she said. "I'm delighted for André. You must feel very satisfied to have brought this off."

He laughed shortly. "It would have happened sooner or later, anyway, but I must admit I was afraid the shoe factory would get him before anyone had a chance to evaluate his work."

"Monsieur Savard thinks he should go to the Sorbonne."

Paul nodded. "He's offered to introduce André to a professor he knows there. Monsieur Moreau will agree, I think. Madame Lepage has promised to help persuade him."

He smiled at Karin's surprise and drew her to one side to point out Suzanne Lepage, who was apparently holding court in the next room. Gowned in a far too youthful chiffon dress of vivid turquoise and glittering with diamonds, *madame* was animatedly gesturing at some of André's canvases as though she were explaining them to the small crowd of onlookers who surrounded her. Her round pudgy face was shining with pleasure. "It seems everyone is taking the credit for André's talent," Karin murmured.

"The way of the world," Paul said dryly. "*Madame* is totally converted to the idea of André as a son-in-law. She is even calling him 'dear André.' There is already talk that Céleste will accompany him to Paris as his wife."

"What does Monsieur Lepage think of all this?" Karin asked. "I don't see him here tonight."

An odd expression shadowed Paul's face for a second but was gone before Karin could identify it. "Claude has more important things to do than look at paintings," he said smoothly, but there was a note in his voice that aroused Karin's curiosity. Why was he looking so uneasy suddenly? Why did she have the feeling he was hiding something from her again?

"You look especially lovely tonight," he said before she could come up with any answers. His gaze traveled the clinging lines of her cream-colored silk gown in an intimate way that brought heat to her face. And then his gaze met hers with a challenge that asked a question, a question she still wasn't prepared to answer.

"Has Claude returned from his boat trip?" she asked, ignoring the compliment and his attempt to change the subject.

Again she thought that his bland expression was covering up something else, and his answer seemed purposely vague. "I haven't heard that he is back," he said.

Karin frowned, but in the next moment they were

joined by Céleste and Lissa and Charles, and she had no opportunity to question Paul further.

Céleste was bubbling with joy and pride and gratitude toward Paul. She hung on his arm for a while, chattering away in rapid French, so radiantly happy that everyone around her was soon smiling. Lissa and Charles were both impressed by André's work, they told her. Etienne had gone off on another circuit of the gallery with one of the Leclercs' boys. "He is now torn between building model ships and learning to paint," Charles said to Karin with a smile. "Suddenly he has more interests than he knows what to do with."

"I'm going to help him get started in drawing," Lissa said eagerly. "He seems to have a good eye. Who knows, he may even have some talent in that direction." She smiled prettily up at Charles. "When our book is finished, we must take him to some galleries in Montreal. He will enjoy that, don't you think?"

Our book, Karin noted. She felt suddenly depressed. Everyone's problems seemed to be working out except her own. Paul was talking to Marcel and Sara Savard now, laughing at something Sara had said. And everything in her was urging her toward him as though she couldn't bear to be even a few yards distant from him anymore. As Charles and Céleste talked together, Karin sensed that Lissa was looking at her, noting the direction of her gaze. But she couldn't look away from Paul, so stunningly attractive in his black and white clothing. There was something so alive, so virile about him that compelled her attention to the exclusion of anything else. She knew that Lissa was wondering about her relationship with Paul, though so far she'd refrained from asking questions. She also knew that Lissa's curiosity was growing by the minute as Karin now continued to watch Paul, but for once Karin felt unable to dissemble, unable to pretend an interest in anything or anybody else in the room.

Yes, she thought at last, as Paul's gaze caught hers and held, enveloping her with an intensity that took all the breath from her body. Yes, it would be worth any amount of future pain to have a few magic hours in Paul Dufresne's arms. Yes, she loved him. She would go to him this weekend, and she would hold back nothing.

AFTERWARD SHE WONDERED if it was at that moment of momentous decision that fate, the same fate she had denied belief in, had suddenly decided to pay attention to Karin Hayward and her constant vacillation. Certainly it seemed to her later that not a second passed before a waiter tapped her on the arm and asked softly if she would please point out Paul Dufresne to him. At the same time she became aware of a stir of movement in the gallery's foyer, and a female voice, raised in apparent argument, not loud enough to stand out above the general voice level in the showrooms, but enough to turn the heads of those nearest the entrance. She indicated Paul to the waiter, saw him speak to him in a low voice. Paul's frown was immediately covered up by a smile of regret as he evidently excused himself from the Savards. Then he moved through the crowd in the waiter's wake, smiling still, edging around various groups without haste as though he didn't wish to draw attention to himself.

Surely he wasn't going to leave? Her curiosity alerted, Karin backed as casually as possible from her own small circle and headed for the foyer, too, reaching the door just as it closed behind Paul and the waiter. With a glance behind her to make sure she wasn't being observed, Karin slipped out of the room.

She was greeted by a scene that dismayed her. A gaunt young woman was struggling between two of Monsieur Savard's employees, who were trying vainly to ease her toward the outside doors. The girl's blond hair was wildly untidy, and her face looked as though she'd smeared makeup on it with unsteady hands. It was a moment before Karin recognized her as one of the calèche drivers Paul had spoken to the day he took her to Place Royale. Anne-Marie, the girl who had attempted suicide. She had evidently just caught sight of Paul. She stopped struggling with the two men as Paul approached her, then as he spoke to her, she wrenched herself free and flung herself down on the tiled floor and wrapped her arms around his legs, her grotesquely made-up face turned up to him with a frantic expression. "I've got to have my pills, Paul," she cried out. "I've used up my last goofball, and I can't come down."

She had spoken in French except for the word goofball. Irrelevantly Karin supposed there wasn't a French equivalent.

Paul was easing her to her feet, none too gently. His expression was grim. But the girl didn't seem to notice how angry he was at her intrusion. She kept babbling disconnected phrases about her pills, and how much she needed them, and she didn't have any money, and someone called Bo, or Beau, wouldn't let her have any "stuff" without money. "I've been climbing the walls all day," she wailed. "I'll do anything you want, just ask me, anything."

Karin stood staring, backed against the door. The desperation in the girl's voice was bringing a sick feeling to her stomach. She couldn't tear her gaze from Paul's face. She'd almost forgotten how grim he could look when he was really angry.

Was this the real Paul, this grim-faced man? Was the intelligent caring man, the passionate lover, the amusing companion, someone she'd made up, like a fantasy?

Anne-Marie was evidently telling him what she had taken so far today. Karin heard "bennies" and "dexies" and some French words she couldn't interpret, and then the girl's voice started rising again, and she began clawing at Paul's shirtfront as though she'd tear it from him.

The other men moved forward to his assistance, but Paul waved them back and said something to Anne-Marie that Karin couldn't hear.

At once Anne-Marie calmed down and stopped screeching, though she still clung to him, her whole body shaking from head to toe. He looked down at her head on his shoulder, and the grim expression left his face to be replaced by one Karin couldn't read. Sorrow? Or self-disgust? He was murmuring softly to the girl now, his hands pressing her head close to his shoulder, rocking her gently back and forth. "It's all right, Anne-Marie," he said more audibly. "I'll take care of you."

Until then he hadn't noticed Karin's presence in

the foyer, but he suddenly seemed to sense that she was there and glanced up. He looked appalled to see her. He swallowed visibly. "I'll have to ask you to have Charles take you home," he said over the girl's head. He was so distraught he didn't seem to realize he had spoken in French.

Karin nodded automatically, still sickened by Anne-Marie's abject behavior. "I'll manage," she said stiffly.

At the sound of her voice Anne-Marie turned her head and looked at Karin with frightened eyes whose pupils were totally dilated. "You can't take him," she said in English with a return of hysteria. "He's going to get me my pills. He promised." She flung her arms around Paul's neck. "You promised, Paul. I love you. You've got to do it for me."

"We're going now, Anne-Marie," Paul said gently. "Everything's all right now."

With a last quick glance at Karin he half carried the now sobbing girl between the double doors to the street. Monsieur Savard's employees breathed a collective sigh of relief, glanced at Karin with a mixture of curiosity and pity and returned to their duties, leaving her alone in the foyer, unable to fully comprehend what she had just seen.

Somehow she managed to force herself to return to the showrooms. Paul had been called out on an emergency, she explained to André and Céleste when they questioned her about Paul's disappearance.

"Did a policeman come for him?" André asked quietly, drawing her to one side. He looked very worried.

Karin stared at him. "Why would a policeman come for him?"

His mouth tightened, and a veiled expression came into his eyes. "I thought perhaps...I wondered if.... It's nothing important...." His voice trailed away, and he turned away from her abruptly. After that he avoided her, deliberately, she felt.

Somehow Karin managed to keep a smile fixed on her face for the remainder of the evening, but the smile felt stiff and unnatural. The incident in the foyer and André's mumbled words had awakened all the doubts about Paul that she'd been trying to suppress. "I'll take care of you," Paul had said to Anne-Marie. In what way, Karin wondered.

She had been fooling herself ever since the day she saw Paul with Valier, she realized. It had been the height of lunacy for her to ignore all those unanswered questions.

Like an automaton she made herself smile and talk and sip champagne while wondering all the time if the evening would ever end.

And during that terribly difficult time the conviction grew in her that she would never be able to trust Paul. If she was ever to be happy again, she would have to leave Quebec City.

And somehow, she thought desperately when at last she lay in her bed, she would also have to find a cure for the aching void inside her—a void she suspected only one man could ever fill.

CHAPTER EIGHTEEN

PAUL ARRIVED at the Vincent house at eight-thirty the next morning. Having spent half the night tossing and turning, unable to sleep, Karin wasn't even out of bed when Charles came up to tell her Paul wanted to see her urgently. She hurriedly pulled on linen slacks and a white cotton shirt that knotted at the waist. Then she washed her face, brushed her hair and went downstairs to the living room, quaking inside, but determined to confront him.

He came toward her as soon as she entered the room, his hands outstretched. "*Chérie*, I'd almost given you up. I have very little time, but I wanted to...." Something in the expression on her face stopped him halfway across the room. "What is it, Karin?" he asked.

She looked at him, unable to find words to express the emotions that were churning inside her. Paul looked tired, she noticed, bone tired, as though he hadn't slept, either. But he was as immaculate as always, casually dressed in white chinos and a dark polo shirt.

As she continued to stand there without saying anything, his eyebrows slanted upward, his blue eyes questioning. "You are upset because of last night's incident?" he asked. "That is why I am here—to apologize. I realize how distressing that was for you. I am sorry you had to witness it.'' He took a step forward, hands reaching for her hands, but she turned away. If he touched her, she was lost.

She walked over to the windows, looked out without seeing anything. ''I've decided to leave Quebec,'' she said quietly, willing her voice not to quiver.

''Because of Anne-Marie?'' There was disbelief in his voice.

''Not only that. The thing last night was just an...indication.''

''I do not understand.''

She turned to face him. ''Neither do I. I only know that I cannot accept that part of your life—the drugs and...the women.''

''What women?'' His puzzled frown looked quite genuine. How easily he dissembled.

She let out her breath in a long sigh, feeling suddenly exhausted. ''Every Thursday a different woman,'' she said slowly. ''I know of two of them; Céleste told me of a third.''

''You are still listening to gossip?''

''I *heard* you arranging to meet Maggie and Martine.''

''And concluded I was a—what is the word Lissa used—a 'lady killer'?''

''What else could I conclude? You never explain—''

She broke off. Paul had made an impatient exclamation, drawn himself to his full height and folded his arms across his chest. ''I do not remember that you asked for an explanation about my many women," he said. "You accused, yes, but when did you ask for an explanation?"

His face was stern, but amusement was lurking in his blue eyes, and there had been a playful note in his voice. Karin averted her eyes. She couldn't bear to be teased now. In any case, the women were not the main issue.

"I'm asking for an explanation now, Paul," she said carefully. "I especially want to know about your connection with Valier. You have so far refused to explain that to me, and I find I cannot go on... *caring* for you unless you can tell me the truth—a truth I can accept." Her voice gave out on her abruptly.

With a quick movement he was in front of her, his hands on her shoulders. "That is something we can dispose of," he said with a smile. "It is a long and complicated story, but I am able to tell you about it now." He broke off, glanced at his wristwatch and shook his head. "As usual, circumstances are against us. I cannot take time for a lengthy discussion now. I can only ask you to wait until tonight for me to explain." His fingers lifted her chin, forcing her to look at him. In the reflected light of the windows, his eyes were a deeper blue than she had ever seen them, tender and compelling. His face was suddenly free of the weariness that had marked it earlier. "*Do* you care for me?" he asked softly, then immediately placed his fingers over her mouth to stop any reply she might give. "Forgive me," he said lightly. "It is not fair for me to ask without first telling you about my own feelings." His hands moved to the sides of her face, cupping it gently. His gaze held hers. "It took me some time to realize why it was so important to me to have your trust, and it has taken more time for me to sacrifice that stubborn pride of mine." He paused, then suddenly kissed her fiercely, his mouth hard against hers. "I love you, Karin," he said urgently. "I love you as I never thought I'd love anyone."

For an endless second she stared into his face, too taken aback to speak. If he had taken her in his arms then, if he had held her and kissed her again, she would have set aside all her doubts, all her fears about his honesty. She would have told him without reservation that she loved him, too. Already her body was relaxing its stiff posture, her hands lifting to touch him.

But then he glanced at his watch again and groaned. "I am already late. Forgive me, I have to go." He was heading for the door.

In the doorway he turned back. "This evening," he said with a confident nod. "It will be quite late, I'm afraid, but I will come as soon as I can. All right?" He glanced at his watch once more, made an apologetic gesture with both hands and left the room.

Karin was stunned by his abrupt departure. How could he leave her now after such a declaration? How could he leave when it was so important for him to stay, to explain. . . .

She kept staring at the doorway as though he would materialize again. Some part of her mind recorded the ticking of the ormolu clock on the mantelpiece, the clop-clop of a horse pulling a rattling calèche along the street outside. She felt frozen in place, as though she would never move again. And following those stunned seconds of disbelief she realized that today was Thursday.

Thursday. Paul's day to play. Paul's day for other women.

Once again she had almost allowed herself to be lulled into letting him off without explanations. Once again his physical presence had made everything else—honor, morality, decency—seem unimportant.

How stupid she was. Already she knew that tonight would be a repeat. He would take her in his arms, make up some simple explanation to disarm her, and she would go on as before.

She must leave. She had decided that last night. And she had been right. What she hadn't realized was that she must leave at once before Paul had a chance to convince her otherwise.

She still felt frozen, empty, as though all emotion had fled. And yet somewhere deep inside her, pain was gathering. If she waited to act, the pain would make its presence known. It would overwhelm her, and she wouldn't be able to act. So it followed that she must act now.

BY THE TIME Lissa and Etienne woke up, she had already achieved a great deal. She had found out that a plane was leaving the city that afternoon, and she could make a connection for Seattle in Montreal. She had made the necessary reservations and had packed one suitcase, was in the process of packing another when Lissa wandered into her room.

"Wow, I'm sleepy," Lissa complained through a yawn. "I enjoyed the show, though, didn't you? It looks as though your friend André is off and running, doesn't it? I was ever so impressed by—" She stopped talking and stared at the suitcase on the bed. "What are you doing?" she demanded.

Karin didn't look up. She kept on carefully folding a plaid cotton blouse, tucking the sleeves just so, smoothing the front, setting the collar into place. "I'm sorry, Lissa," she said slowly. "I've decided I have to leave."

Lissa showed instant understanding. "Because of Paul?"

"Because of Paul."

"I noticed he left in a hurry last night, but I didn't— You're sure it's hopeless?"

"Yes."

If Lissa showed any sympathy at all, Karin thought, she would fall apart then and there. Her control was tenuous at best. The emptiness that had sustained her so far was beginning to fray around the edges. Feeling was creeping in. And she could not afford to feel. Not today.

"Can I help with anything?" Lissa asked in a brisk voice.

Karin sighed with relief. She even managed to smile at her friend. "Thanks for understanding," she said. "I hate to leave you so abruptly, but I think everything's going to go well for you now. And you can help Charles in my place, I'm sure." She hesitated. "Could you explain to Charles for me? And Etienne? I don't think I could face—" She broke off as her voice threatened to betray her.

Lissa nodded. "Let's just say you've been called away. I'll think of something to tell them later."

"Thank you." Karin returned to her packing.

Lissa waited for a moment, then turned away. "I'll fix you some breakfast," she said. "I take it you've booked a flight?"

Karin nodded, not trusting herself to speak. She was relieved when Lissa left the room.

And then, a moment later, she opened the drawer where she kept her hair dryer and makeup. On one side was the small rectangular box that contained the silver ballerina Paul had given her. Abruptly her composure was shattered.

For a few seconds she stared at the box, telling herself she was trying to decide if she should just leave it there or give it to Lissa to return to Paul. And then she found herself picking it up, opening it with shaking fingers.

The little ballerina was as perfect as she remembered. Poised, graceful, beautifully formed. She sank down onto the dresser stool, holding the small figure in the palm of her hand, hearing Paul's voice saying, "I saw it in Marcel Savard's gallery and thought immediately of you."

She had suspected that when her numbness wore off, the pain would be severe. She had not known it would be unbearable. Her hands closed tightly on the little figure, her knuckles whitening under the strain. She couldn't cry, mustn't cry. She had to hold herself together long enough to get ready, to get on one plane and then another. She had to hang on to her self-control until she was home.

What then, she wondered. Her mind projected a picture of herself arriving in Seattle, meeting her parents, going home. She would be safe there, insulated against pain, insulated against feeling, insulated against joy. Safe. Empty. Alone.

She didn't realize she was crying until the little silver ballerina blurred in front of her eyes. *There's nothing to cry about,* she told herself in the mirror. Going home was sensible, logical, the right thing to do.

The right thing? Other pictures were forming in her mind now—images of Paul: Paul looking down at her in that teasing way of his, those irrepressible eyebrows slanting upward; Paul, solemn and unsmiling, watching her face as they danced; Paul gazing at her in the sun-dappled shadows of an ancient tree, his blue eyes inexpressibly tender. Her tears increased, running silently down her cheeks, welling up from her eyes as though they would never stop. Tears of sorrow, tears of loss. How could she possibly leave him? How could she bear the emptiness of her life?

Quite suddenly Paul's voice sounded in her ears: "I love you, Karin. I love you as I never thought I'd love anyone."

She could see his face as he said that, feel the sudden hard brush of his mouth against hers. Impossible not to believe him. He *did* love her.

Tears drying on her cheeks, she stared with astonishment at herself in the mirror. He had said he loved her, and she hadn't even answered him! She had allowed herself to become so suffocated by doubts about him that she hadn't responded to his declaration of love. But he *did* love her. He had *said* so.

What had she said to Céleste? "If two people really love each other, things have a way of working out." Could she believe her own words? Could she?

She looked at the silver ballerina, still clutched in her hands. Yes. Paul did love her. And she loved him. He had offered at last to explain his past actions. Even if she couldn't think of any explanation about Valier that would satisfy her, didn't she at least owe him the *opportunity* to explain? If she didn't, she might wonder about what might have been for the rest of her life.

Caution warned her to slow down her tumbling thoughts. Was she rationalizing again? Possibly. But there was no way to deny the sudden leap of joy that came when she thought that perhaps she did not have to leave—not yet, not until she had given Paul one more chance.

Carefully she set the little ballerina on top of the dresser and stared at it until her vision cleared, and she could function again. Then she stood up. For once she would forget caution, logic, good sense. For once she would follow her heart. She would go downstairs, call the airport and cancel her flight.

But first she'd better do something about her face, she thought, even as her feet were taking her toward the door. Impulse was one thing, but she'd never been one of those fortunate people who could cry prettily, and she didn't want to appear in front of the others with swollen eyes.

She was applying careful makeup when she heard a light knock on her door. She looked at her reflection. Still a little pink around the eyes, but Lissa would understand. "Come in," she called.

To her surprise, Etienne came into the room. He looked very gloomy. "Are you really going away?" he asked.

Karin swallowed. "I'm not sure. I may be able to stay a little longer."

His face brightened at once. "Oh, I hope so, Tante Karin." He was standing beside her now, looking at her in the mirror with a questioning expression on his face.

Karin busied herself with repacking her makeup pouch so she wouldn't have to meet his eyes. "Are you sad, Tante Karin?" Etienne asked.

"A little, yes. I can't seem to decide what I should do."

"Were you leaving because of Uncle Paul?"

The sound of Paul's name threatened Karin's new-found composure, but she forced herself to meet the boy's shy gaze directly, surprised by his insight. She didn't know what to say.

"It's very complicated," she said at last.

"Do you love him?"

Karin stared at him, but he didn't wait for an answer. "I think loving someone makes people unhappy a lot of the time," he said hesitantly. "I think when I grow up, I won't try to love anybody."

Karin put her arm around him. He was beginning to lose weight, she noticed. The waistband of his gray flannel trousers seemed a little loose on him. "Loving someone can be wonderful," she assured him. "It's just that sometimes other things interfere."

He looked at her gravely, his gray eyes solemn. "Like when I wanted to love Madame Lissa, but I was afraid she wouldn't love me enough to stay?"

"Something like that, yes."

"Does Uncle Paul know that you love him?"

"I think so," she said slowly. "I haven't told him so, but I think he knows."

"Madame Lissa," he said slowly, then hesitated. *"Maman,"* he corrected firmly. *"Maman* said she had no idea I loved her until I told her so. Perhaps it is this way with everyone—only the words make it true for them."

Karin hugged him. "I think you are very wise, Etienne."

"Really?" He looked immensely pleased. Then he frowned importantly. "Yes, I think you should tell him."

"So do I." She smiled wryly. "Unfortunately I have to wait. I don't even know where he is right now."

Etienne's frown deepened. "It is Thursday today, *n'est-ce pas?*" She nodded. "Then he must be at his special clinic. He is there every Thursday."

Karin stared at him. "What special clinic?"

He chewed his lower lip for a moment, then sighed. "I'm not supposed to say, Tante Karin. It is a secret Uncle Paul told me. He said he trusted me. He does not want his regular patients to know about the clinic because some of them might decide they did not want to go to a doctor who was involved with such people."

"Etienne, you have to tell me. Please. I have seen already that Paul knows some rather, well, shady people. I need to know why."

The boy pondered a moment more, his brow furrowed. Then he looked at her earnestly. "You will not tell anyone?"

"No one," Karin promised.

And then to Karin's horror over the extent of her ignorance, Etienne explained that on Thursdays Paul held a special clinic for people who were on drugs and had medical problems, or who had used drugs and wanted to stop. "Uncle Paul's clinic is run in con—conjunct...." Etienne stumbled over the word.

"Conjunction?" Karin offered and he nodded. "In conjunction with another clinic," he went on. "The other clinic has a psychologist and some other people. Sometimes people who used to be addicted to drugs come and talk to the others. When school is in session, they go to the schools and talk. Uncle Paul says it is very important to educate young people about drugs so they know how bad they can be. And he says it is also important to help them when they are sick. Both clinics are free. Uncle Paul pays for the building and for the supplies and things. The nurses from the hospital help when they can. Everybody gives his time, Uncle Paul says, and the clinics are open for fourteen hours every Thursday."

The *nurses*, Karin's mind echoed. Martine had been offering to help at the clinic. The nurse Céleste had seen with Paul must have done the same thing. Why hadn't he told her? With a sinking feeling she remembered he'd already given her the answer to that. Because she hadn't asked. She had accused, always accused. She had jumped to conclusions instead of having faith in him.

Maggie? Obviously Maggie had also offered to help. Perhaps she had some nurse's training, or perhaps she was one of those who had beaten an addiction and was willing to help others do the same.

And the girl last night had probably come looking for medical help, not for a supplier.

Karin was conscious of deep shame. How quick she had been to judge on circumstantial evidence when all the time Paul had been *helping* the young people. Of course he hadn't wanted his other patients to know. If they had deserted him, where would he have found the income to support the clinics? No wonder he was happy about the success of his investments in the Montreal business.

She squirmed when she remembered the lecture she'd given him: "You could be a leader in the community, an example of all that is good and clean and decent."

Dear God, how holier-than-thou she had been. So shocked, so superior. Yet she had never done anything personally to help fight the insidious increase of drug abuse among the young. She had only condemned. While Paul did something constructive about it. Probably his involvement with Valier had just as commendable an explanation. "Does André help at the clinic, too?" she asked Etienne and felt ashamed again when he nodded.

"I went there once with Uncle Paul," he said. "That was where I met André."

Karin stood up and put her hands on Etienne's shoulders. "I've done something pretty awful," she admitted. "I thought. . . ." She paused. Etienne was only ten years old; she could not expect him to understand the stupidities or false perceptions with which adults could clutter up their lives. "Will you tell me where the clinic is?" she asked.

He hesitated for only a second, then he nodded

again and gave her an address. "It is next to the old hospital, the Hôtel-Dieu," he explained. "You go down Palace Hill and—"

"I know where the hospital is," Karin said. She leaned down and hugged the boy again. "Thank you for telling me."

He returned the hug eagerly. "You are going to stay now?"

Karin straightened. "I am going to stay," she said. "But I do not know for how long," she cautioned when Etienne's round face broke into a big smile. "First I must talk to Paul, and then...then we will see." She went on speaking, almost to herself. "I should probably wait until Paul comes this evening, but I don't think I can do that. It may make him angry if I turn up at the clinic, but I have to tell him, admit I was wrong.... I'll cancel that flight now," Karen said, but as she left her bedroom, she was conscious of a strange reluctance to make the call.

Surely she couldn't have any lingering doubts? Surely she didn't need the security of knowing she had an escape ready just in case? There had to be an explanation of Valier. There had to be.

CHAPTER NINETEEN

AS SHE HURRIED down the steep streets toward the hospital, Karin found that her mind was automatically sifting through the history of the place. How odd, she thought, that her brain could offer up such information when there were so many other things for it to worry about. Perhaps it was a way for her mind to protect itself; as long as she concentrated on historical data, she didn't have to admit to herself that she had consistently misread the facts where Paul was concerned.

Whatever the reason, she found herself silently reciting from Charles's notes. The Hôtel-Dieu de Québec, now a highly acclaimed medical center, dating from the early seventeenth century, was the oldest hospital north of Mexico. Fire had ravaged the building several times, but it always recovered and was added to through the years. Recently excavations had uncovered old subterranean vaults, that were used as shelters by the community and its patients during the wars of the eighteenth century. There was also a museum that she had not yet visited. She must do that soon—if she stayed.

It took an effort of will to ward off the wave of loneliness the thought of not staying brought her. It would not only be almost impossible to leave Paul, it

would be unbearably difficult to leave the city.
had become very attached to this romantic old c
with its ancient buildings and steep winding street.
She felt at home here, as though she belonged.

Waiting to cross the busy street to the hospital, she
remembered she'd experienced a similar feeling when
she first met Paul. The thought had crossed her mind
that she had waited a long time for this man to come
into her life. She had dismissed Paul's assertions that
some things were inevitable, but now she wondered.

She looked up at the tall buildings across the street.
They weren't particularly attractive; ancient and
modern stood side by side without blending. An am-
bulance was emerging from beyond a stone wall;
another was braking to a halt, its siren fading in a last
off-key wail. People were going in and out of doorways, hurrying, giving the place an air of bustling activity common to all hospitals. The business of life
and death, she thought as a break in traffic finally
allowed her to cross. Paul was engaged in that
business. In a few minutes she would find out exactly
how he was engaged.

She stopped suddenly on the narrow strip of sidewalk, realizing fully for the first time what her accusations must have meant to him. He was a doctor,
dedicated to the preservation of life, and she had accused him of dealing on the side of death. How could
he possibly forgive her? How could he possibly love
her?

With a feeling of futility she proceeded along the
sidewalk toward the low building Etienne had
described to her. She would go in; she would talk to
Paul if she could; but she suddenly had little hope

he could really care for her in any lasting way
ter the dreadful things she had believed of him.

The first person she saw inside the clinic was André. He was sitting behind a desk in a rather bare-
looking room, sorting through file cards while he
talked on the telephone. He frowned when he saw
her, then waved her to a seat on the other side of the
desk and went on talking.

Karin looked around. In one corner a group of
young people were watching television. A few others
were slumped on folding chairs here and there
around the walls, looking at magazines or talking
quietly together. An effort had been made to
brighten the room with large posters on the walls,
posters possibly donated by travel agencies, she
thought, recognizing the Eiffel Tower, England's
Houses of Parliament and the Imperial Palace in
Tokyo. Someone had arranged flowers in three large
vases, and there was a square of bright carpeting in
the middle of the floor, but nothing could disguise
the institutional nature of the room.

"Depressing, isn't it?" André said quietly as he
replaced the telephone receiver. "It is all we can
manage for now. When Paul is able to do his
remodeling, we will meet at the château, but for now
it suffices."

He was looking unusually relaxed today, Karin
noticed. For once he looked totally rested and at
ease. The red was gone from his eyes. No doubt her
suspicions there had been unfounded, also. Probably
André had merely been short of sleep, as he'd explained.

He was looking at her curiously now, a half smile

showing between his beard and mustache. "Was Paul expecting you?" he asked.

Karin shook her head. "I came on the spur of the moment. If it's inconvenient, I can wait. But I *would* like to see him."

André nodded. "He should be back soon. He is at the hospital with Anne-Marie. You know about Anne-Marie?"

Karin couldn't quite meet his eyes. "I was there last night when she came to the gallery," she admitted. She hesitated. "Paul brought her to the hospital for treatment then?"

"Right away. I understand she was really flying. He's got her on antidepressants now. She'll be okay until next time." He sighed explosively. "We keep thinking she's learned her lesson, but she slips again and again."

"Paul seemed very angry," Karin said hesitantly.

André grinned. "Paul is the original avenging angel when one of his patients slips. But he's not angry with *them*. He's angry with the circumstances that cause them to turn to drugs in the first place, and with the people who make them available. A one-man crusader, that's our Paul."

Karin managed to meet his eyes at last. "I wish you'd told me all this earlier," she said softly.

André shrugged. "We have needed to maintain secrecy until now. This is the first time I've worked openly at the clinic. Before this I came in with the others as though I were a patient. We kept the records in a back room."

"Why was it so necessary to maintain secrecy? Was it just so Paul's patients wouldn't find out?"

André hesitated. "Until now Paul has needed their fees to keep this place going," he said slowly. "It's not much of a place, but it is expensive like everything else nowadays. But the real reason was that we were working on—" he broke off, glanced quickly at Karin and then continued smoothly "—another project. It was best if no one connected the two of us. And neither Paul nor I could afford to lose the kids' trust. If they had guessed we were reporting—" Again he broke off. "You'd better ask Paul about this."

"Does this project you mentioned have something to do with Valier?"

André's expression changed to one of concern. He glanced around the room. None of the young people was paying any attention to them. "Do not mention that name in here," he cautioned in a barely audible voice.

Karin stared at him for a moment, then nodded agreement, mentally reserving the question for Paul. "You keep saying 'until now,'" she said slowly. "Has something changed?"

The young face opposite her was suddenly grim. His eyes were gold. "Something has changed," he admitted. "During the night the police caught the man who was supplying that...other person—the man you asked about."

"They caught him with your help?" Karin asked on a sudden hunch.

He nodded. "Mine and Paul's."

Karin closed her eyes. How she had misjudged Paul Dufresne. He had told her that she had perhaps put André in the gravest danger. She had "stumbled

onto dangerous information," he had warned. It
not occurred to her that the danger was also his.
had spent the weekend of Valier's arrest with tr
police. He and André must have been helping the
police all the time. She shivered. She had questioned
Violette, linked Paul and André together. If Violette
had talked, Paul and André would have suffered for
her carelessness. She had read enough newspapers,
seen enough television reports to know that people
who engaged in narcotics traffic did not play games.
The stakes were high in the drug-trafficking under-
world. And when stakes were high, life and death
went hand in hand.

She was aware of a feeling that went much deeper
than shame. What a fool she had been.

"Are you all right?" André asked.

She opened her eyes, swallowed, somehow managed to smile. "I'm just facing a few home truths,"
she said. "I've been so very stupid."

He smiled warmly at her. "You could not know
what we were doing. But we could not explain, you
see, because we were afraid word would get out in the
street and frighten away our big fish." He chuckled
quietly. "There is a mixed metaphor for you." He
looked at her kindly. "We all behave stupidly
sometimes. It is part of the human condition, *n'est-ce
pas*? I have been pretty stupid myself lately, resentful
of Paul's help. Without him I would be nowhere."
He leaned forward, "Céleste told me she spoke to
you of my own difficulties with drugs."

"I was probing," Karin admitted.

He shrugged. "It is no secret. There was a time I
found myself taking amphetamines to stay awake

barbiturates to go to sleep. One can only keep at up for a limited time without becoming at least psychologically dependent. Luckily I heard about this clinic and had the sense to come here. Paul got me through the nightmare. It *was* a nightmare. I was becoming deeply depressed. I couldn't paint, yet I couldn't stop taking more pills. I was nervous all the time, not eating, barely sleeping. Paul helped me put my life together. And then went on to make my life worth living." He sighed. "I cannot excuse myself, but for a while it seemed as though I could do nothing without Paul's help. I lost faith in my own abilities. And blamed him for it. But luckily he did not lose patience with me. He saw me through it all. He even insisted on paying me for the work I do here, though everyone else volunteers his time. Now, of course, I can pay him back, but he didn't know that when he was so generous." He looked at her directly. "Paul Dufresne is a good man. I am sorry that I implied anything else. My male ego was suffering." His face brightened. "Did you hear that I am to go to the Sorbonne?"

Karin nodded. "And, also, that you are to marry Céleste. I'm really happy for you." She hesitated. "Has Monsieur Lepage given his permission?"

His face was suddenly bleak. "Monsieur Lepage—" he began, then broke off. With a look of relief he said, "Here is Paul now." He was looking beyond Karin to the door.

Karin was almost afraid to turn around. She wasn't sure she had the courage to face Paul in the light of all that she had learned. He had every right to be furious with her for her suspicions of him.

But she must face him. She must at least apol
to him for her lack of faith, hope that he wc
understand.

When she did manage to stand up and turn
around, she saw Paul standing just inside the doorway, talking to a young man dressed in hospital
whites. Paul himself was wearing a doctor's jacket of
white starched cotton over his polo shirt and chinos.
A stethoscope hung around his neck. He looked
different—professional, businesslike. He had seen
her, she thought—she'd caught the quick sideways
flick of his glance. But for now his attention was all
on the young man beside him. He seemed to be giving
instructions of some kind.

The big waiting room had come alive with Paul's
entrance. The young people were sitting up
straighter, watching him. When the young man
walked away and disappeared into a side room, one
of the girls called, *"Bonjour,* Dr. Paul," and then
there was a whole chorus of *"bonjours,"* which Paul
acknowledged with a half salute of one hand and a
smile.

The smile faded as he approached her. "Did you
come to say goodbye?" he asked. He had spoken
easily, but his eyes were guarded.

She stared at him, appalled by the bleakness in his
face. "How did you know I planned to leave?"

"I called my answering service a few minutes ago.
I was told Madame Vincent had left a message that
you were planning to leave the city today."

"I've. . .changed my mind."

His dark eyebrows quirked upward, but there was
none of his usual humor in the gesture, merely cool

osity. His glance went beyond her to André.
omeone has been talking?'' he asked evenly.

"I've told Karin some of it,'' André said. ''But not
all. I haven't told her about—''

Paul interrupted him with a curt nod. ''This is not
the place to talk,'' he said. He looked at Karin, again
without warmth. ''You'd better come into my office.''

"I don't want to take up your time if you're really
busy,'' she said awkwardly. ''I can go home and wait
until this evening, if you prefer.''

For the first time his blue eyes showed a glint of
humor. ''And risk something or someone changing
your mind about leaving? I wouldn't think of allowing you to go now that you've found your way here.''
He glanced at André. ''Who is here today? Martine?
Ask her if she'd mind bringing us some coffee, will
you, please? I need at least a short break.''

"Anne-Marie?'' André asked.

"She's comfortable for the moment. But she had a
rough night.'' He ran a hand through his hair. He
looked exhausted, Karin thought. Obviously Anne-
Marie wasn't the only one who'd had a rough night.

"Did you have any luck with the drug-abuse center
in Montreal?'' André asked.

Paul nodded. ''They had a long waiting list, but I
pulled a few strings. She'll be on her way there in an
hour or so. She'll sleep a lot at first. After that we'll
have to see. They have a good program with a high
rate of success.''

He glanced at Karin. ''I had to be at the hospital at
nine this morning to make the arrangements for
Anne-Marie. That's why I couldn't stay.''

"Oh, Paul," Karin said, feeling more mc
than ever.

Paul interrupted her before she could go
"Come along," he said. He moved one hand .
though he intended taking her arm but then evidently
changed his mind and gestured instead toward a door
behind André's desk.

Karin preceded him into a small room with green
walls, and he closed the door behind him. With his
usual courtesy he held a chair for her, then seated
himself behind the desk. He was keeping a distance
between them, Karin realized, and the glint of humor
that had shown briefly in his eyes was gone. She
wanted to say something that would erase the distant
cold expression that showed in his eyes now, but she
didn't know what to say.

While she was still groping in her mind for words,
Paul unhooked the stethoscope from around his neck
and placed it on the desk. "Did you change your
mind about leaving because of what André told
you?" he asked.

"No. I . . . Etienne told me about the clinic, and I
saw that I had misjudged you."

"But before that. You weren't going to wait for
my explanation?"

That was the reason for his coldness, of course. As
Karin searched for a reply, Martine, the redheaded
nurse who had helped Karin at the hospital, came in
with coffee for them. She smiled at Karin, then at
Paul. "The natives are getting restless," she said.

Paul gave her a weary smile. "I'll be out in a few
minutes. Has Dr. Lansing started his lecture?"

Martine nodded and left.

r. Lansing is a psychologist," Paul told Karin as ...assed cream for her coffee, "We have another ...ic besides the medical one. It deals more with ...unseling and education. We must educate the young especially. There has been a tremendous increase in drug taking among teenagers in the last ten years. These young people are not criminals, but they need to have direction, to develop a positive image of themselves. Many are from broken homes. Anne-Marie is such a one. She was blessed with four stepfathers, all of whom abused her in some way. She finds it almost impossible to cope with life." He sighed. "Dr. Lansing is from New York. He is spending a few days here giving us the benefit of his expertise. At the moment he is explaining some of the latest findings about marijuana to some of our local students." He shook his head. "Not good findings, I'm afraid. There seem to be more dangers in marijuana than any of us suspected; it can impair judgment and induce a feeling of well-being in the face of real danger."

Karin concentrated her gaze on the cup of coffee in her hands. "I feel so ashamed. I should have known you couldn't be involved in drug dealing. I should have guessed you were working against it. I was just so confused."

He sighed again. "I can understand that. I could hardly expect you to have faith in me when I gave you no real reason for it." His voice was tired. "It is a difficult task we have set ourselves. Sometimes we make a little headway. Maggie is one of our success stories, so is Violette, and André, of course. But often we fail. We can only keep trying." He paused. "What exactly did André tell you?"

"Not a lot. But I gathered you and he were work-ing with the police. Was that what the incident with Valier was about?"

He nodded. "We'd heard a rumor in the street that he was going to be in Place Royale to meet anyone who wanted to buy. I used you, I'm afraid, as camouflage. But I hadn't expected him there so early in the day. André was keeping an eye on him. As soon as you told me André was there, I realized Valier must be somewhere around, and then I saw him. I could not jeopardize your safety, so I had to get you away." He picked up a pen on the desk, stared at it as though he didn't want to meet her eyes.

"But he laughed," Karin said slowly. "Valier laughed, so I thought you must be friends."

Paul smiled wryly. "Valier was not worried at first. His laughter was intended as mockery. He ex-pected that we had no proof. He didn't know that André had arranged for someone to buy from him, someone who was willing to give evidence to the fact. When he realized we had trapped him, he 'went quietly' as they say in police films. We persuaded him to give himself up, but he would not name the sup-plier. You must understand, Karin, that I could not risk telling you all this at the time. I will admit that my pride was also involved. I could not accept that anyone could think me capable of such a terrible crime."

He paused. "In any case, there was another con-sideration. I could not risk word getting out on the street that André and I were responsible for Valier's arrest. Not only would my young patients have lost ust in me, but the supplier would have known of my interference.''

''André said the police caught the supplier.''

''This morning, yes. Around 3:00 A.M. They were waiting for him downriver when his boat docked.''

Puzzled, Karin looked at him. There had been a note of significance in his voice. And suddenly she knew. ''Claude Lepage?'' she asked incredulously.

Paul smiled rather grimly. ''Claude Lepage,'' he echoed. ''There is no need for secrecy now. The news will appear on television this evening.'' He sighed. ''André and I had suspected him for some time. So had the police. Some weeks ago I treated one of Claude's deckhands for a sprained ankle. He told me he was leaving Monsieur Lepage. He'd had enough of the long hours, the night sailings, the danger. As you can probably imagine, Claude was not an easy man to work for at the best of times. And drug running does not qualify as the best of times. He was bringing the stuff in from South America, the deckhand told me, running it along the St. Lawrence to various delivery sites. I began watching Claude carefully. That is why I agreed to Céleste's little game. It enabled me to stay near Claude without arousing suspicion. When the crewman left Claude's employ, with police assistance, the police managed to get one of their men on board. They caught Claude with a cargo of cannabis and heroin—enough to have a street value of six million dollars.''

''Poor Céleste,'' Karin breathed. ''And Madame Lepage.... What a terrible thing for them.''

Some of the coldness left Paul's eyes. ''I have

always appreciated your compassion, Ka
gaze held hers, and she could not look away.

There was a silence. Then Paul broke the s
tension between them. "So," he said lightly,
you satisfied that I am not, after all, the villain of
piece?"

"Of course." She hesitated. "What will happen to
Céleste and her mother?"

"It is hard for them, of course. I spoke to Suzanne
early this morning and offered any help she needs.
She will be all right, I think. She is quite a strong
woman. She seemed somewhat relieved. I think she
has suspected that Claude was not the upright citizen
he pretended to be. But she was too afraid of him to
inquire too closely into his operations. Financially
she will have no problems. She is a wealthy woman in
her own right. As for Céleste—she has André."

Silence grew between them again. Fear was like a
cold hard stone in Karin's heart, blocking the valves
so that her blood couldn't flow, couldn't warm her.
Paul was still so terribly distant. She had pushed him
too far with her lack of trust. God, she had even
thought of this interview as giving him one more
chance. How terribly noble. How insufferable.

She put down her coffee cup, forced herself to
meet his eyes. "I feel so ashamed," she repeated. "I
jumped to conclusions that were far from the truth. I
don't blame you for being angry. And I realize that
you can't possibly forgive me for thinking such
dreadful things about you."

"Aren't you jumping to conclusions again?" Paul
asked softly.

As she stared at him, not comprehending, he

...rward across the desk to touch one of her ...overing it with his own. "Can you not allow ...decide for myself if I can forgive you?"

...onfused, she continued to stare at him. "But it's ...vious that when I decided to leave without waiting ...or your explanation, you lost patience with me," she said miserably.

"So I did," he agreed. There was a stern note in his voice again, but his hand still covered hers warmly. "If Etienne had not told you about the clinic, you would have gone away, would you not?"

"That's not exactly true," she said slowly. With a sudden feeling of hope she placed her other hand on top of his and looked at him earnestly. "I had decided *before* Etienne told me about the clinic that I would wait," she said. "And I canceled my flight before I knew anything about Valier." On top of her thankfulness that she'd had the courage to cancel the flight was the sudden fear that he might not believe her.

She looked away from his intense gaze. "I was packing, you see," she said carefully, "and I came across the little ballerina you gave me. I...looked at her for a long time, and I knew I couldn't run away. Because I love you. I think I've always loved you. But I didn't know for sure until after my accident when you told me you hadn't done anything illegal. I felt such relief then, and I realized that I cared... that I loved you."

"Fire in the blood?" he asked softly.

"And lightning and thunder," she admitted.

His hand tightened over hers. "So then I spoiled that fine moment by insisting you must keep secret something you did not understand."

She nodded. "I don't blame you for that,
now. I hadn't exactly shown myself to be the s
discretion. I realize now the danger you were in.'

He didn't speak for a moment, and at last
looked up. He was smiling ruefully. "We have bo
had our moments of stupidity, have we not?"

She could only nod.

And then Paul pulled his hand from between hers.
He stood up and came around the desk, and she saw
that the last trace of coldness was gone from his face.
Somehow, without knowing she had moved, she was
standing up, holding onto him while his arms went
around her, pulling her so close she could feel his
heartbeat against her breast. He was murmuring in
French into her ear, something about wasted time
and stupid pride and poor timing. She didn't feel a
need to speak herself. She wanted only to hold and to
be held.

When Paul's face moved against hers, she met his
mouth with her own, fiercely, hungrily, feeling once
again that sense of rightness flowing through her
body, melting her bones, warming her. Everything
seemed suddenly very simple.

"I love you, Paul," she whispered against his
mouth.

"And I love you," he said softly. He leaned his
head back and gazed at her. His blue eyes were bright
with amusement, but it was a loving amusement. His
mouth curved in a smile. "Once again, *chérie*, we are
in the wrong place at the wrong time. My patients are
waiting for me. I cannot let them down." His
eyebrows slanted upward. "A doctor's life is full of
hurried exits," he said wryly. "My disappearance

...ne art gallery last night was an example. More ...nore of my time will be devoted to young people ...1 drug problems now that I am financially sol-...nt, though I will retain any of my regular patients ...ho want to stay with me. So you must understand, my lovely Karin, that I must often leave you abruptly, even perhaps in the middle of the night.''

Again there was a certain significance in his voice. As Karin grasped his meaning, she felt a surge of joy unlike any she had experienced before. But she couldn't resist teasing him for a change. ''You are taking it for granted that I will be with you at night?'' she asked.

The smugly confident smile that had so often annoyed her thrilled her immeasurably now. ''Where else would my wife be?'' he asked. For a second, uncertainty clouded his face. ''You will marry me, won't you, *chérie*?''

''Of course I will,'' she replied instantly.

For a moment more she let herself lean against him, then she straightened reluctantly.

''Your patients, doctor,'' she reminded him.

''My patients,'' he echoed with a rueful smile. But his arms didn't release her, and his face was suddenly solemn again. ''First we must make a decision. My mother is to be married at the château in a month's time. It would please her, I think, if we were to make it a double wedding.''

''Whatever you say, Paul,'' Karin said in a meek voice.

He laughed. ''This does not sound like my independent Karin.''

''There are times when independence doesn't seem

too important," Karin said softly. "But I must warn you, I will not always do everything you say." She smiled at him, letting all her love for him show. "For example, I have no intention of letting you leave me right now. There must be something I can do here to help."

He regarded her gravely. "I will admit that André is not the best record keeper, and also, he is planning on exploring new worlds of his own, so perhaps...." He let the sentence trail away.

Karin eased herself out of his arms. "We must get to work."

His hands reached for her immediately. "We will," he murmured as his arms tightened around her again, "but I think my patients will not mind waiting one minute more." His eyebrows met in a ferocious frown. "First, I am going to kiss you more thoroughly than you have ever been kissed before."

"Domineering," Karin accused, but as his mouth closed over hers, she knew that this kind of domineering was something she could become accustomed to. After all, she would have the rest of her life to get used to it.

SUPERROMANCE

Complete and mail this coupon today!

- -

Worldwide Reader Service

In the U.S.A.
1440 South Priest Drive
Tempe, AZ 85281

In Canada
649 Ontario Street
Stratford, Ontario N5A 6W2

Please send me the following SUPERROMANCES. I am enclosing n
check or money order for $2.50 for each copy ordered, plus 75¢ t
cover postage and handling.

☐ 10 HEART'S FURY   Lucy Lee
☐ 11 LOVE WILD AND FREE   Jocelyn Haley
☐ 12 A TASTE OF EDEN   Abra Taylor
☐ 13 CAPTIVE OF DESIRE   Alexandra Sellers
☐ 14 TREASURE OF THE HEART   Pat Louis
☐ 15 CHERISHED DESTINY   Jo Manning

Number of copies checked @ $2.50 each = $_____
N.Y. and Ariz. residents add appropriate sales tax $_____
Postage and handling $_____.7

TOTAL $_____

I enclose_____.
(Please send check or money order. We cannot be responsible for cas
sent through the mail.).
Prices subject to change without notice.

NAME_____
(Please Print)

ADDRESS_____

CITY_____

STATE/PROV._____

ZIP/POSTAL CODE_____

Offer expires June 30, 1982   11256722